Believe In Me

Susan Lewis is the bestselling author of thirty-eight novels. She is also the author of *Just One More Day* and *One Day at a Time*, the moving memoirs of her childhood in Bristol. She lives in Gloucestershire.

To find out more about Susan Lewis, visit her website www.susanlewis.com, or join in on www.facebook.com/SusanLewisBooks.

Susan is a supporter of the breast cancer charity Breast Cancer Care: www.breastcancercare.org.uk and of the childhood bereavement charity Winston's Wish: www.winstonswish.org.uk

Praise for Susan Lewis

'A master storyteller' Diane Chamberlain

'A gripping story of love, uncertainty and betrayal . . . a guaranteed tear-jerker that will keep you at the edge of your seat' *OK!*

'Spellbinding! You just keep turning the pages, with the atmosphere growing more and more intense as the story leads to its dramatic climax' *Daily Mail*

'Utterly compelling' *Sun*

'One of the best around' *Independent on Sunday*

'A multi-faceted tear-jerker' *Heat*

Also by Susan Lewis

Fiction

Susan Lewis

Believe In Me

arrow books

1 3 5 7 9 10 8 6 4 2

Arrow Books
20 Vauxhall Bridge Road
London SW1V 2SA

Arrow Books is part of the Penguin Random House group of companies
whose addresses can be found at global.penguinrandomhouse.com.

Penguin
Random House
UK

First published in Great Britain by Century in 2018
First published in paperback by Arrow Books in 2018

www.penguin.co.uk

A CIP catalogue record for this book is available from the British Library.

ISBN 9781784755614

Typeset in 11.83/15 pt Palatino LT Std by Jouve (UK), Milton Keynes
Printed and bound in Great Britain by Clays Ltd, St Ives Plc

MIX
Paper from
responsible sources
FSC
www.fsc.org   FSC® C018179

Penguin Random House is committed to a
sustainable future for our business, our readers
and our planet. This book is made from Forest
Stewardship Council® certified paper.

Believe In Me

Daniel Marks was standing in the corner of the room watching and listening. He didn't understand what was happening, why people were shouting and being rough with his dad. They shouldn't be here. It was his birthday. He was ten today and he was having a party. All his friends were coming, Nicholas and Jeremy and Thomas and Carl. He'd invited some girls too, Peggy, Jolene and Pearl. His dad had bought special things for them to eat, and there was a cake on the table with candles ready to blow out.

They were still shouting. Everyone was so big. They were filling up the room and no one seemed to know he was there.

'Patrick Marks, I am arresting you . . .'

'You're making a mistake,' his dad cried out, looking more afraid than Daniel had ever seen him.

Daniel wanted to scream, bang his fists against them and make them go away, but he just stood where he was, too scared to move.

There were some handcuffs now, and they were trying to put them on his dad, but his dad pushed them away. 'I need to speak to my son,' he growled. 'Can't I just do that?'

Someone put out a hand to stop him, but someone else pushed the hand away.

His dad came to crouch to his level and held his shoulders, his fingers digging into Daniel's fragile bones. There was a pale, thin line around his mouth; his dark eyes were still frightened. 'It'll be all right, son,' he whispered, seeming to choke on the words. 'They've got the wrong person. Do you hear me?'

Daniel nodded.

His dad took a breath, and then another. His eyes were moist and desperate. 'I want you to remember,' he said, 'that no matter what they do to me, or say about me, I've never done anything wrong, or to be ashamed of. OK?'

Daniel nodded again, and sobbed as his dad's strong arms pulled him close and held him tight. He could smell the caramel and woody scent of him; feel his tears in his hair.

'You need to be brave,' Marks whispered roughly. 'Can you be brave?'

Daniel knew he couldn't, but if he said no it was going to upset his dad more so he made himself whisper a yes.

'I love you, son,' Marks gasped, still holding him tightly. 'Never forget that. I want you to do your best in every way you can, OK? And don't ever believe what they tell you, because I swear on your mother's grave, they've got the wrong man.'

Chapter One.

Today, forty years after the Emmett family – two brothers married to two sisters – had made the neglected sprawl of Ash Morley Farm into a home, it remained as quaintly rustic as ever, albeit in a less reproductive, and definitely more inviting way. It still comprised four honey stone properties of varying sizes – a rambling old farmhouse, a grand barn with dovecotes and arrow slits, some stables and a bakery. The small enclave shared an uneven cobbled courtyard where hay carts, cattle, sheep and tractors used to rumble about their days. Now, in this similar setting, stood a milkmaid fountain at the centre of things, with a giant weeping willow beside it, and two cherry trees and a number of year-round flower beds spread randomly about.

Leanne had loved growing up here, mainly because her friends had been so keen to visit – often their parents came too. Life was always fun at Ash Morley. Wilkie and Glory – Leanne's mother and aunt – were legendary entertainers, and had encouraged all sorts of adventures for the young ones, while providing such scrummy picnics for everyone that Leanne's father and uncle used to playfully grumble that the sisters were stealing business from their thriving seafront restaurant in town.

By the time Leanne reached eighteen she'd been more than ready to break out and start living life to the full. She'd won a place at the London College of Contemporary Arts and was so excited to be off that she hadn't given her parents' distress at losing her a second thought.

Now, twenty-four years later, she was back, an older, and not necessarily wiser woman doing her best to start a new life. Though Wilkie, her mother, still lived in the farmhouse, her father had died five years ago, and her Aunt Glory had succumbed to cancer recently enough for the grief still to be raw. Glory, who'd never had any children, had willed the barn and her share of the rest of Ash Morley to Leanne.

Leanne still missed her father and aunt terribly, almost as much as she missed her elder daughter Kate.

Kate. What a mix of emotions flooded her just to picture Kate's beautiful face, or to think of where she might be and what she was doing now.

And then there was Abby, her youngest . . .

'You didn't answer my question,' Wilkie chided, going to put on the kettle, as at home in the barn as she was in the farmhouse.

'Sorry, I missed what you said,' Leanne replied, shrugging off her coat.

'I asked if you'd treated yourself to something lovely,' Wilkie repeated.

4

Leanne glanced at the bags she'd brought in from the car: Next, Top Shop, Zara. What was in them, for heaven's sake? 'Not really,' she said vaguely, 'it's mostly for Abby.'

Wilkie sighed and planted her hands on her plump little hips. Nature couldn't have made mother and daughter less alike if it had tried, for Wilkie with her lusciously curvy figure and bright orange hair stood no higher than five feet two in heels. Leanne, on the other hand, was tall, like her father, with long slender legs, boyish hips and an abundance of honey-coloured curls.

'There's nothing wrong with indulging yourself once in a while,' Wilkie reminded her.

Leanne didn't argue, because she agreed. However, these days she was quite happy in jeans and a sweater, or occasionally a dress from Glory Days, the vintage shop in town that she'd also inherited from her aunt.

There was a time when her wardrobe had overflowed with silks and satins, glittering tops and impossible shoes. She'd had real diamonds for her fingers and ears; her hair had been styled and highlighted to perfection, and her skin had always shone with as much happiness as health. Today, when she looked in the mirror, she saw a kind of bad watercolour of herself, blurred about the edges, no longer defined as a confident, capable woman, more like someone who'd been left out in the rain. More often than not she wore her glorious hair scraped back from her pale, heart-shaped face, and she no longer accentuated the lengthy lashes around her blue, almond-shaped eyes, or added colour to her lips or cheeks. According to her mother this ghostly image made her look young and vulnerable, and rather like the heroine of a nineteenth-century novel. Since Leanne was forty-three, and felt about as romantic as a pair of baggy tights, she could only conclude that she wasn't presenting an accurate picture of her true self to the world.

In fact, she knew she wasn't, but why should anyone else have to deal with the cauldron of conflicting emotions fermenting away inside her? Talking about Jack, even thinking about him, would be like poking a hornets' nest, and once all those dreadful feelings were unleashed how was she ever going to get them back under control? They'd die away of their own accord given time, she was in no doubt of that. She already felt infinitely better than she had a year ago, when the world as she'd known it had been thrown off its axis in a way she should have seen coming, but hadn't.

Wilkie, in her perennially childlike and mischievous way, had dipped into one of the bags and was trying on a pink beret. 'What do you think?' she asked, admiring her reflection in a sunburst mirror hanging from a hook on Glory's old oak dresser. She tweaked her fluffy hair and pouted her sixty-something lips like a sixty-something model.

'You look gorgeous,' Leanne smiled.

Wilkie's eyes shone, showing she knew Leanne wasn't serious. 'Glory always looked good in pink,' she sighed, taking the hat off, 'but Glory could wear anything and still look like a film star.' Her sunny blue eyes misted for a moment. 'You and Kate are the same,' she declared cheerfully, 'and hopefully Abby will be too when she's older, although she's not as tall as you were at fourteen.'

'There's still plenty of time,' Leanne replied, 'and being tall isn't everything. I mean, look at you, you're an absolute dazzler, and not having your feet reach the floor when you sit down has never been a problem for you.'

Wilkie's laugh was as deliciously infectious as it had always been, and rippled through Leanne's heart in a way that made her feel a little like a child again. 'Dad used to say he could put me in his pocket if it rained,' Wilkie recalled wistfully.

Though Leanne had heard it many times before, she still went to hug her mother. Having Leanne and Abby at Ash Morley went some way to making up for the loss of her sister and husband, but not all the way.

'OK, let's not get sentimental,' Wilkie scolded herself, 'I was making tea. Oh, is that mine or yours?'

'Yours,' Leanne replied, passing over the iPhone that Wilkie was as addicted to as any teenager.

While her mother chatted away with one of her many friends from Kesterly's Welcome Centre, or maybe it was a fellow activist from the town's Better Community Group – with Wilkie it could be anyone from any number of organisations – Leanne reached two mugs down from the dresser and continued with the tea. The Aga was, as usual, making the large oak-beamed kitchen space at this end of the barn feel as cosy as a nest, while the earthy yet citrusy smell that had always tanged the air here, no matter what the season, could so easily carry her back to her childhood.

She took a sip of Earl Grey and turned her gaze to the high vaulted ceilings that ran from the kitchen along the length of the barn. On the far wall was a double-fronted wood-burning stove in the enormous oak and stone fireplace. In between was Glory's flamboyantly eclectic collection of sofas, chaises longues, footstools, oriental rugs and art deco lampstands. There was also a magnificent refectory table between the kitchen and sitting room large enough to seat twelve or fourteen with a quirky collection of spindle-back chairs, not one of which matched another.

The entire east-facing wall consisted of three sets of double French doors that, when open, made the veranda outside with its red tiled roof and wooden pillars seem almost as much a part of the barn's interior as it was a part of the garden. The view was of Ash Morley's gardens with their rugged lawns and vegetable beds, a couple of whirling washing lines, a netted trampoline, a see-saw swing, and a spring-flower meadow beyond that rambled and flowed into a swathe of green fields all the way out to Kesterly golf course in the far distance, and the lower slopes of Exmoor National Park to the sunnier south.

'Everything sorted?' Leanne asked as her mother rang off.

'I think so, but I'll have to be going soon. We've got a meeting at the tourist office at four to start sorting out the summer brochures.'

'It's still only January,' Leanne laughed.

'We like to keep on top of things. Now tell me, what are we going to do about Abby?'

Leanne inwardly groaned. It was a question she was constantly asking herself, and she never seemed to come any closer to an answer. 'Counselling obviously hasn't done the trick,' she stated dismally, 'or not where I'm concerned. She's fine with everyone else, especially you. Apparently I'm public enemy number one, because nothing I do is right.'

Wilkie looked thoughtful and perplexed. 'Maybe we rushed into the counselling,' she said. 'The poor girl barely had time to breathe after it all happened, and suddenly there she was being straightened out before we even knew what the kinks really were.'

'You're right,' Leanne responded, 'it probably was too soon. The trouble is, I don't think I'll have much luck getting her to see someone again. She's adamant that she's fine, and the counsellor's conclusion was that she was adjusting well.'

Wilkie frowned sceptically. 'There are good counsellors and not so good counsellors,' she murmured darkly.

Wasn't that the truth? 'Frankly, I don't think there's anyone better than you,' Leanne declared, meaning it. Her mother had a truly compassionate nature, making her, as far as Leanne was concerned, the easiest person in the world to talk to.

'Well, we know I've tried, more than once, and I'm going to say it again, for all her hostility towards you and love for me, it's you she really wants to reach out to her.'

'And every time I hold out a hand I feel like one of us ends up going over a cliff.' Leanne sighed wearily. 'So what do we do?'

Wilkie shook her head. 'Round and round in circles,' she murmured, glancing at her watch. 'I have to go, I'm afraid, but I'll be back in time for dinner. I've left the slow cooker on. Klaudia and the children are coming,' she added, referring to the rest of the Ash Morley 'family', who'd lived in the converted stables for the past six years. 'If you need me I'll have my phone with me.'

As the back door closed behind her a waft of wintry air thrust itself in from outside and hung about the kitchen like a shivering ghost. Leanne quickly went to make sure the outer porch door had held fast, since it had lately formed a habit of throwing itself wide to feisty winds.

Satisfied it was secure, she returned to the kitchen and tried to collect her thoughts. Since it was half-day closing at the shop she should spend the next hour or so checking Internet orders and customer service requests, so setting up her laptop on the table, she went to the dresser to collect the mail she'd brought in just now. As she flicked through it she found her eyes drawn to her aunt's photo as though it were demanding her attention, and as she gazed down at it she felt submerged by a wave of love and longing. Glory's eyes had always sparkled, almost to the last, and nature had shaped her lips in a smile so that she'd never looked sad, even when she'd felt it, and she must have at times. Losing her husband when still in her thirties had hit her hard. Leanne had few memories of him, having been so young when he'd died in a boating accident, but she knew he was the reason Glory had remained single and childless right up to the age of fifty, when she'd decided to start fostering. What a blessing that had turned into for both her and Wilkie, especially after the coronary that had taken Leanne's father. A constant flow of young people coming in and out of Ash Morley, with all their problems, attitude and love, had made the sisters' world feel worthwhile again.

'We miss you,' Leanne whispered to her aunt's photo. 'You kept us all grounded in your own crazy way and now I'm not very sure where we are.'

'Oh now,' she could hear Glory saying, 'you will live and love again, my angel. You're not broken, only bruised.'

It was true, she wasn't broken. What had happened to Jack had shaken her badly, had ended up changing her life, but it hadn't torn her apart in the way many – Jack's mother for instance – felt it should have. And therein lay the cause of Leanne's conflicted emotions. How guilty should she be feeling about his death? Where exactly did her responsibility begin or end? Could she have prevented it? Would she have tried if she'd known what he was going to do? Yes, of course she would, except the fact that she was asking herself the question . . .

She'd never forget the moment she'd opened the door to his study and come face to face with the gruesome sight of him staring back at her, eyes protruding from their sockets, tongue jutting from purple mouth. For one bewildering moment it had almost seemed like a prank. She hadn't laughed, but she might have screamed. She remembered registering the smell of urine and worse, before staggering out of the room and quickly locking the door before Abby could see her father that way. It was an image no child should ever have to live with.

The police had found the note, but hadn't shown it to Leanne until later in the day. 'You can make up your mind whether you want your daughter to see it,' the female officer had said gently. 'It's addressed to you.'

Leanne had taken it up to her room and sat with it for a long time before feeling able to read it. She'd known, even before her eyes took in the words and they began to gouge their cruelty into her heart, that Jack would be blaming her for his actions. But even then, traumatised as she'd felt by the shock of it, she'd already made up her mind that she wouldn't allow him to have the final word, much less that sort of devastating power over her. The decision to do this terrible thing had been his, and his alone.

My dear wife,

The sarcasm in those three words had made her wince.

This is what happens when you don't love someone enough or respect how difficult life has become for them. I've felt your coldness since everything changed for me, I've heard the bitterness in your voice and seen the scorn in your eyes. You have turned my own daughter against me and now, with the pitiless rejection I have suffered at the hands of so-called friends, I feel I have nothing left to live for.

Jack

Though the terrible sadness of someone dying with so much anger in his heart had racked her own, Leanne's conscience had held firm. She knew how hard she'd tried to reach him, how she'd sacrificed her own happiness in the hope of restoring his, and how hard she'd fought to protect Abby from the worst of him. She'd never have said that she was glad he was dead, but there was no stopping the relief of knowing that the fight was over. It wasn't until later, much later, that she'd fully registered the fact that he'd left nothing for Abby, no attempt at an apology, no plea for understanding, nor a single word of love.

'I don't want anything,' Abby had told her vehemently, her young teenage face white and pinched with shock and anger. 'He's gone and nothing's going to change that.'

With Aunt Glory being so sick at the time and needing Wilkie, it was Kate who'd come to help Leanne and Abby through the worst of it. Kate, her beautiful, capable older daughter, had flown back from the States to be with her mother and half-sister, understanding far more than they had how much they'd needed her. Such young shoulders – she was still only twenty – yet she'd coped in a way that had made her seem so much older. It was she who'd held Leanne's hand when the lawyer had broken the worst of it. The house was mortgaged for more than its value, the cars were on a no-return lease with two years of monthly payments still to be met, even the joint investments and Abby's university fund had gone. Things had been far worse for Jack than he'd ever let on. The vicious circle of drinking to escape the reality of his sinking career, and the addiction making him incapable of work, impossible to cast, had pushed him to even greater depths of anger and depression. In the end it had sucked him into a vortex of inescapable despair.

Maybe she hadn't done enough, she remembered thinking at the time. They'd been together for fifteen years, they had Abby, so why hadn't she found a way to turn him back into the man she'd once loved?

'Because that wasn't what he wanted,' Kate had told her gently. 'He never tried to help himself, not once. I even used to think that there was a part of him, actually almost all of him by the end, that enjoyed wallowing in booze and self-pity and all that rage he had towards the world. He couldn't see anyone else, couldn't even think about anyone but himself. I'm sorry, Mum, I know you probably don't want to hear it right now, but in your heart you know it's the truth.'

Leanne had known it, and for a long time, but her battle with his drinking, her tireless efforts to make him seek help, had only inflamed him to even harsher degrees of fury and blame. Until in the end she'd stopped, accepting that he had become a stranger, only connected to the man she'd once known by the familiar, though now swollen and ravaged, features, and his name.

She'd met him when Kate was five years old. He'd literally swept her off her feet with his charm, his looks, and she had to admit to being impressed by his fame. The acclaimed actor whose powerful performances on stage and screen had made him one of the

14

nation's favourites was madly in love with *her*, the lowly assistant manager of a second-rate art gallery in Knightsbridge. He'd been great with Kate then, in fact he'd loved the whole world, and why not when the whole world seemed to love him? It was true he'd drunk a lot, had been known as a generous host, the life and soul of any party, and many were the times when she'd had to leave him on the stairs, unable to get him up to their room. He'd always laugh it off in the morning, as though she'd fallen for some elaborate prank, and because he'd still seemed able to handle his professional life she had tried to believe that he had it all under control. To suggest otherwise never ended well.

Then Abby had come along, and though he had been a loving and attentive father for the first few years – to Abby much more than to Kate – everything had started to change when his work began drying up. His problem had reached a level where he could no longer be relied on to turn up on time, much less to remember his lines. No one wanted to cast him, or not in roles he considered suitable for an actor of his standing. To make matters worse, it was around the same time that Kate's father's career in financial planning had seemed to take off.

Jack had always felt threatened by Martin. He hated the fact that Leanne had remained on good terms with a man she'd divorced; he'd never felt it was natural. Over time Leanne had come to realise that if her break-up with Martin had been acrimonious, preferably to the point of murderous, Jack would probably have handled things better. But it hadn't been like that. She and Martin had been very young when they'd met, still only eighteen, and by the time they were twenty they were married with Kate on the way. After she was born it had been idyllic for a while, but they'd soon realised that in spite of how much they loved her, and one another, they wanted different things from life. Martin, being American, was eager to return to the States while Leanne didn't want to leave London. It was far enough from her parents and Glory; she just couldn't bring herself to go any further.

In the end they'd agreed to set one another free with an arrangement for Kate to spend part of her summer holidays with her father each year, and alternate Christmases, so that he wouldn't miss out on her altogether.

It was when Jack had learned of Martin's success that his attitude towards Kate became borderline abusive. Not that he ever hit her – in spite of everything he'd never raised a hand to any of them – but his sneering bitterness towards Kate's father had been so ugly that when Kate, at the age of fifteen, had said she wanted to go and live with Martin and his family in Carmel, Indiana, Leanne hadn't tried to stop her. Of course she was devastated by the decision, wretched beyond bearing, but loving her daughter as much as she did, why would she want her to go on suffering the way she was when she didn't have to?

Sighing at the unpleasant memories that had swamped her for a while, Leanne put down the mail and went to pour herself some more tea. She really wasn't making a great success of her life, was she? A failed marriage by the time she was twenty-three; a second husband who'd turned into a drunk and ended up killing himself; a daughter who'd left home to live with her father and another who could hardly stand the sight of her.

'Hey! What gives?'

Startled as much by the fact that she hadn't heard Abby come in as the surprise of being spoken to in what could possibly be considered a friendly way, Leanne raised her mug. 'Fancy one?' she asked.

Abby's head was down, her long dark hair partly masking the phone she was holding. In spite of the freezing temperature outside, her padded coat was open, her scarf was awry and her hands looked bitten red by cold.

'I said, do you want some tea?' Leanne asked again.

She might as well have saved her breath. Abby was stuck into whatever she was doing on the phone, which was presumably some sort of interactive game since Leanne had belatedly spotted the earbuds.

Putting down her mug, Leanne decided to abandon her paperwork for now and reached for Glory's treasured acacia-wood chopping board. Leanne had given it to her for Christmas about ten years ago, and every month since then Glory had lovingly oiled and conditioned it, preserving its beauty and integrity, showing it the same tender respect she had for just about everything anyone had ever given her, especially her darling niece. There were still books of pressed flowers in the attic, including the first bunch Leanne had ever picked for her, aged four. Every card Uncle Keith had given her was in a black velvet box tied with blue ribbon, and every other card she'd received over the years was in another, bigger box that Leanne herself had closed after adding the many condolences that had poured in at the time of her aunt's funeral.

What was Leanne going to do with it all? There was so much of her aunt in this place, from the books, to the sofa throws, the wall hangings and display cabinets full of quaint and mysterious artefacts from down the years, that Leanne would never find the heart to part with it all. And of course there were Glory's treasured clothes in the wardrobe upstairs, including the exquisite 1920s wedding gown, an original that she'd asked Leanne and Wilkie to take to her at the hospice just before she'd died. They'd wondered afterwards whether they should have cremated her in it, but since she hadn't requested it they'd chosen a favoured silver silk flapper dress with matching headband instead.

Everything in this glorious homage to the early twentieth century felt so special that Leanne had more or less accepted that her own cherished possessions were destined to stay in store for quite some time to come.

'What's that?' Abby demanded. She was scowling at the bags from Leanne's shopping spree. Despite the irritable challenge in her eyes and pursed crossness of her lips, the ripe blossoming of her prettiness was hard to miss. She looked far more like Jack than she did Leanne, and by the time the braces came off and spots retreated she would quite possibly be more like him than ever.

'It's a few things for you,' Leanne told her. 'If you don't like them or they don't fit we can always take them back.'

Abby stared sourly at the bags, apparently torn between indulging her curiosity or offending her mother and ignoring them. In the end she said, 'I don't want anything thanks,' and went back to her phone.

Stifling a sigh, Leanne ran the hot tap in order to give the acacia board a good clean before its restorative massage. 'Can you fetch the linseed oil from the pantry?' she asked Abby.

Abby either chose not to hear, or didn't.

'*Abby!*'

Tearing out her earbuds Abby shouted, 'What?'

'Did you have a good day at school?'

'That's not what you said.'

'But it's what I'm asking now. How was school?'

'What do you care?'

Unable to understand why Abby would even ask the question, Leanne said, 'I'm asking *because* I care.'

'No. You're asking because you think you have to. Well you don't.'

Stifling a sigh, Leanne said, 'Abby, we can't go on like this . . .'

'It's not me. It's you!'

'OK, then tell me what I'm doing wrong.'

'If you don't know then why should I tell you?'

'So I can put it right?'

'Yeah, yeah, yeah, yeah. Heard it all before,' and she stuffed her earbuds back in.

Deciding to give up for the moment, Leanne let a

few minutes pass and then said, 'When did you last speak to Kate?'

'*What?*' Abby shouted irritably. Then, yanking out an earbud, 'I don't know. Why?'

'Was it this week, last week . . .'

'I said I don't know, all right?'

Guessing it would have to be, Leanne carried on soaping the board.

'I don't know why I bother talking to you,' Abby muttered.

That could almost have been funny.

'Do you want the truth?' Abby growled. 'I'm totally sick of this place. I can't stand it here. I want to go back to London and if you don't want to come with me . . .'

'You know we don't have a choice,' Leanne cut in sharply. Love her daughter as she did, there were times when Abby's attitude could drive a saint to distraction. 'Where's Tanya?' she asked. 'I thought she was coming home with you today?'

Abby shrugged, walked over to the rarely used front door and plonked herself down on the stairs that led up to Leanne's master suite and a small guest room.

Since she apparently wasn't ready to walk out on her mother yet, Leanne continued what she was doing, waiting for whatever else Abby might have to say.

This resentment, the seemingly constant antagonism between them, could be exhausting, but Leanne never let herself forget that Abby had been through an extremely difficult time, losing her father the way she had, and having to move away from her school and friends. She used to be popular, lively and involved in just about everything. Since Jack's death and coming here it was as though a light had gone out inside her. She no longer seemed particularly interested in making friends – Tanya was a sweet enough girl, but very serious and studious, not Abby's type at all. There were no after-school clubs any more, or girlie trips into town, and there was absolutely zero interest in doing anything with her mother.

In some ways it was as if Abby had stopped moving forward, was even, given how childish she could be at times, starting to regress.

'We're having dinner at Grandma's this evening,' Leanne told her.

'What?' Abby snapped, snatching the buds from her ears again. 'What did you say this time?'

'Don't speak to me that way,' Leanne snapped back. 'If you're in a bad mood about something, which you appear to be, let's discuss it. Just don't come home taking it out on me.'

'Tell you what, I won't bother to come home at all,' Abby raged. 'Would that suit you? I bet it would.'

'Abby . . .'

'It's all right, I can take a hint. I know where I'm not wanted,' and hiking her heavy schoolbag back on to her shoulder she stormed along the hall that led to her room.

When it was time to go next door to find out if Wilkie needed any help, after calling out several times, Leanne found herself banging on Abby's door in an attempt to turf her out.

Apparently it wasn't going to happen without another fight.

Sucking in her breath, as though taking Glory's calm from the air, Leanne turned the handle, pushed hard and to her surprise the door opened so easily that she almost stumbled in.

Expecting an onslaught of 'get out of my space and leave me alone' she took a moment to register that no one was there. Experiencing an uneasy jolt she called, 'Abby?' and glanced along the hall to the bathroom.

No reply.

She looked into Abby's room again and this time spotted the note on the bed.

Decided best if I go. You might be happy then and I know I will be. Bye. See you sometime ... Abigail Delaney.

Chapter Two

Rosy-cheeked from a quick dash outside to take in a delivery, Wilkie set the parcel down for opening later and took out a bottle of supermarket Chablis from the cream-coloured American-style fridge. Plonking it on the antiquated table at the centre of the farmhouse kitchen with its violet-blue vinyl covering and bamboo mats, she said, 'So she's at Tanya's?'

Leanne unscrewed the bottle top as her mother fetched glasses. 'Not according to her,' she replied, still feeling irritable with her daughter, in spite of the relief of finding her so easily. 'I haven't heard from her, but Tanya's mother assures me she's there.' Since Tanya's parents lived in one of the larger houses on the private estate bordering Ash Morley it would only have taken Abby minutes to get there – and back again, when she decided to come.

Wilkie's eyebrows rose. *'To see a world in a grain of sand, And a heaven in a wild flower, Hold infinity in the palm of your hand, And eternity in an hour,'* she murmured, reaching for a cheese and onion crisp and crunching it loudly.

'What?' Leanne asked. 'No, don't bother. It's Blake, isn't it? But exactly what does it have to do with anything?'

'It just came to me,' Wilkie replied, her eyes drifting to the window as the wind chimes outside rattled like a tambourine in the force of a gale. 'It was one of Glory's favourites.'

Giving a moment to her aunt's love of poetry, and her mother's loss, Leanne sipped her wine and longed for easier times. 'We were talking about Abby,' she finally reminded her mother.

Wilkie quickly rallied. 'Indeed we were, and she hasn't run away, which is marvellous. Of course she wouldn't, we know that . . .'

'No we don't, Mum. She's fourteen. Girls of her age do some very stupid things, and considering her history . . .'

'But where would she go, apart from to Tanya's?'

'I've no idea, that's what frightens me.'

'Which is precisely why she does it – to frighten you.'

'Of course, but it's cruel. She knows how I feel about the way Kate left. OK, Kate didn't run away, but it kind of felt like it, and Abby plays on it to torment me. When did you last speak to Kate, by the way?'

Wilkie drank her wine as she thought. 'I think it was the day before yesterday. She rang to ask if you were here, but you were . . . Where were you? Oh yes, you were helping Klaudia to move Jolly Albert's bedroom from upstairs to down. It's very sad that he doesn't have a family to help him. Did he manage a smile at all?'

'What do you think?' Leanne countered. Jolly Albert

24

never smiled, or said thank you, or even spoke if he could help it. He was one of the most curmudgeonly old people Leanne had ever met, but his grumbling, grunting insistence that he wanted to be left alone had never succeeded in keeping Klaudia the self-appointed care angel away. It was one of her missions in life to look out for those no one else bothered with, and she had no competition where Jolly Albert was concerned.

Wilkie looked up at a knock on the door, and before she could call 'come in' two small children in thick winter coats skipped into the room.

'Ah, my little sweethearts,' Wilkie crooned, holding out her arms. 'We were just talking about your mummy. And here's Antoni,' she added, as a large, muscular man with more hair around his stubbly chin than on his shiny head came in after them. He'd been living at the stables with Klaudia for the past several months, and had gone out of his way to be helpful around Ash Morley. However, Leanne still couldn't say that she and her mother really knew him for he didn't speak much, at least not to them.

Closing the door quickly to keep out the cold, he said, 'I hope you don't mind me bringing them early.'

'No, of course not,' Wilkie assured him, hugging ten-year-old Mia and six-year-old Adam to her grand-motherly chest.

'Is Abby here?' Mia asked softly as she came to embrace Leanne. Her silvery-blonde hair curled in feathery wisps around her elfin face; the expression in her large brown eyes was both shy and eager.

Leanne caressed the little girl's cheek. 'I'm afraid she might not be coming this evening,' she replied. 'She has a lot of homework so she's gone to a friend's to do it.'

Mia nodded, but there was no mistaking her disappointment. Abby was her idol.

'Will you have a drink, Antoni?' Wilkie offered, getting up to fetch another glass, or a beer.

'No, no, I must be going,' he replied, moving restlessly. 'Klaudia will be home soon and I want to speak to her before I – I leave for work.'

After ruffling Adam's head with a chapped hand, then placing it gently on Mia's, he gazed down at them for a moment as they looked up at him, clearly not sure what to expect.

With an awkward glance about the room, he gave them a wave and left.

Leanne's eyes met her mother's, but neither of them was going to comment on Antoni's oddness with the children right there.

Wilkie soon had hot chocolate and cookies under way, and within a few minutes Mia and Adam were being bustled through to the sitting room where the gas fire was already lit and the TV was tuned to their favourite channel. 'Our tea is still a little way off,' she told them chattily as she settled them down, 'so you won't spoil your appetites. But you mustn't grass me up, OK? This is our little secret.'

'It's secret,' Adam echoed, with a breathy gulp that almost swallowed the words.

Smiling at how good her mother was with the

children, who were as at home here as Abby was, Leanne started to set the table, adding an extra place for Abby just in case she graced them with an appearance.

'They're happy in there,' Wilkie announced, leaving the door ajar so she could hear what was happening. 'It's lovely and warm, and they don't want to sit around listening to us. Goodness, have we finished that bottle already?'

'It was only half full,' Leanne reminded her.

Going to fetch another, Wilkie said, 'So, was it just me, or did Antoni seem . . . out of sorts to you?'

'He wasn't himself,' Leanne agreed.

Wilkie sighed. 'I just hope everything's all right. We wouldn't want to see a return of any of that nasty business. The way people have turned since the referendum . . . He dealt with it very well the last time, but that's not to say he will again.'

Knowing what her mother was referring to, and agreeing that they really wouldn't want to see Antoni get into a fight with some neo-Nazi types again, Leanne refilled their glasses and returned to the subject of her elder daughter. 'So, you've spoken to Kate,' she said, her eyebrows arching as the wind ghost-whistled down the chimney. 'How was she?'

'She sounded very cheery, as she always does, not that I understood half of what she was saying about all her studies and things, but it's lovely to hear her.'

It always is, Leanne was thinking, feeling sad at how little time Kate had spent with them over Christmas. Just four days, before she'd flown back to the States to go skiing with her boyfriend. She'd returned to IU now – Indiana University – where she was in her third year of a four-year degree course and apparently loving every minute of it. 'We keep missing one another and leaving messages,' she said. 'It was much easier when she was at Martin's, I could always get hold of her then.'

'Yes, well, I remember it was the same when you went off to uni, I never knew where you were from one day to the next. I just had to wait for you to call, and of course you always did in the end. Now, we really must watch the news to find out what's going on in the world, frightening though it is these days.'

As Wilkie turned on the TV the door suddenly swung open, and Abby gusted in with a small riot of leaves in her wake.

'I see you were worried,' she snapped at her mother, glaring meaningfully at the wine.

'I knew where you were,' Leanne told her, choosing to ignore the unspoken accusation that she was going the same way as Jack.

'You're a minx,' Wilkie scolded as Abby went to embrace her. 'I don't understand why you have to torment your poor mother so much. She does her best, you know.'

'You should try being me,' Abby retorted.

Shooting her a look, Leanne said, 'Mia and Adam are in the sitting room. I'll bring you through a hot chocolate if you want one.'

Abby shrugged. 'Where's Klaudia? I thought she was coming too.'

'She'll be here soon,' Wilkie replied, glancing at her retro wall clock with its crooked pendulum and rotating cherubs.

Getting up to make more chocolate Leanne found herself thinking about Antoni again, and Klaudia and those sweet little children in the next room . . .

'Leanne,' Wilkie said darkly.

Leanne looked up, concerned by the tone. Then, following her mother's eyes to the TV, she stopped what she was doing and watched.

Klaudia Marek was the kind of person who could almost always find something to be happy about. She wore a smile like a jewel: sometimes it was carefree and joyful, other times discreet and respectful, or just as often it would be quiet and unassuming. Only when she was alone did she let the façade slip for a moment, but only a moment. It didn't do any good to brood on the difficulties life often threw at her; it wouldn't make them any easier to cope with, nor would it make them go away.

Best to remember that she'd get through them, and that no matter what, there was always someone worse off than herself, or someone who felt just as vulnerable and anxious as she did about what the future might hold.

She loved this country, and had ever since she'd arrived just before Mia was born. Things hadn't always gone well. She and her then husband Igor had never had much money, he'd found it difficult to hold down a job and after Adam was born he'd suddenly decided that marriage and fatherhood wasn't for him. That had been a very dark time, but people had been so kind, especially Glory and Wilkie Emmett who'd taken Klaudia and her children into their hearts and given her the stables of Ash Morley as her home. They had been there for her again when her mother had fallen ill and eventually died, taking her to the airport, caring for her children while she was gone; Glory had even flown to Poland with her to support her through the time of the funeral.

Just like the Emmett sisters, now sadly only Wilkie, Klaudia was well known around Kesterly for the voluntary work she did – in her case mostly with the elderly, caring for a few above and beyond what they deserved, according to some. In her mind everyone was deserving, and her mother had been the same.

On top of all her charity and community work Klaudia also helped Leanne to run Glory Days, and to give her income a hefty boost she put her excellent bookkeeping skills to use for small companies and well-heeled individuals.

She was on her way back from one of her regular clients now, driving a little too fast in her muddy Fiat Uno, wanting to get home before Antoni, her partner of less than a year, left to start his night shift as a security guard. Not that he'd leave the children on their own, he'd never do that, but she didn't want to make him late for work, nor did she want to take Wilkie and Leanne's kindness for granted.

Braking hard to stop herself running a red light, she glanced apologetically in the mirror and waved to the driver behind, who was honking angrily at being made to stop. She wasn't about to let him rattle her, his issues were his own. Uppermost in her mind was the horrible thing that had happened today. She hadn't shown how hurt and humiliated she'd felt, nor would she. She wasn't even sure about confiding in Antoni. It would only make him angry and vengeful, and what purpose would that serve? He'd already got into trouble simply for being Polish and managed to come off the worst. She didn't want anything like it happening again.

It wasn't until she was pulling up next to his car outside the stables that she remembered Wilkie had invited her and the children for supper this evening. She melted at the mere thought of it. Sitting around Wilkie's table, or Glory's (now Leanne's), drinking wine and tucking into their scrumptious winter stews and casseroles was nothing short of heaven, especially at the end of a difficult day. Being with her surrogate family helped her to forget whatever pettiness or stupidity she'd run up against, and that was all that had happened really; something very stupid and petty had been said that simply needed to be forgotten.

Making the short dash through an icy wind to the stables' stone porch, she kicked off her boots and pushed open the front door. She was surprised not to be greeted by one, if not both of her children. They were usually waiting on the bottom stairs when she was a little behind the promised time, almost as though fearing she wouldn't come back. Sweet little Mia, she was so sparkly and happy with lots of friends and a healthy confidence, and yet she could be shy and unsure of herself in ways that sometimes concerned Klaudia, in spite of knowing that most kids were the same. As for Adam, Klaudia felt so powerfully protective of her son that sometimes it was hard to let him leave the house, never mind go to school. His learning difficulties were so upsetting, and yet he seemed not to know he was different. If other children laughed at him he laughed too, and if they teased or bullied him he seemed not to understand and tried to find out what he'd done wrong. In spite of many and various tests no one had yet been able to give a reason for his problems, although she'd been assured he would probably grow out of them soon enough. Thank goodness for the teaching assistant, Victoria Gibbs, who'd been assigned to take care of him in class. She was wonderful and vigilant and helped him so much with his confidence that Klaudia was hopeful he might soon make a friend or two.

Scooping the mail from the floor she shouted, 'Halloooo! Is anyone at home?' and carrying on down the darkened hallway she pushed open the kitchen door to find Antoni speaking to someone on the phone.

'Where are the children?' she asked, glancing through the envelopes and handing over those that were his.

'Aren't you going to Wilkie's this evening?' he asked, ending his call. 'I took them there about ten minutes ago.'

Her head came up, her soft brown eyes lighting with the suggestion of what this might mean. He'd taken the children so they could have a little time to themselves?

When he turned away a frown creased her brow. He seemed ... Upset? Angry? 'What's the matter?' she asked, worriedly.

He dashed a large hand over his closely shaved head, took a breath and turned to look at her. His ruggedly handsome face was taut, pale; it seemed closed in a way that was increasing her unease.

'What's happened?' she pressed.

He stared down at her so hard that she almost took a step back. His powerful six-foot frame had always seemed too big for this small kitchen, too big even for her own tiny self, but it had never unnerved her before.

'I'm sorry,' he said, breaking into their native tongue, 'but I – I'm leaving.'

Klaudia blinked. Leaving as in ... ? Going to work? 'But it's not time,' she protested, 'and there's obviously something on your mind, so ...'

'I mean I'm leaving you.'

Klaudia continued to stare at him, knowing she was hearing correctly, but not wanting it to go any further.

She swallowed drily and tried to think what to say. He'd threatened it before, several times, but this time it was feeling different. There was a steeliness, a determination about him that she wasn't going to penetrate. A smile with some cajoling wouldn't do it, she knew that instinctively. Nevertheless she tried. 'Whatever's happened,' she said, 'we can work it out. We always have before ...'

'No, Klaudia, we're papering over things, pretending the way some people feel isn't happening, but it is. I don't want to stay somewhere . . .'

Knowing what he was going to say, she came in quickly. 'But we're . . . We've become a family. This is our home . . .'

'If you want to call this home, you can,' he interrupted, 'but I don't want to be here . . .'

'Stop, just stop.' She needed to think, to sort out what was really happening, but she was finding it hard, things were moving too fast. 'Have you said anything to the children?' she asked.

'No, of course not.'

Did he care what it would mean to them to see him go? In truth she wasn't sure how they would view it, since their relationship with him had never been close. He was kind to them, was always generous and ready to take them anywhere, but when it came to engaging with them as a father might . . .

She raised a hand, as though to touch him, but pulled it back again. 'What happened?' she asked shakily. Something must have for him to be landing this on her now, like this?

He shook his head. 'I've had enough,' he growled. 'It's not working for me any more. I've already quit my job . . .'

Her heart somersaulted. He'd given up his job without saying anything to her?

'I'm sorry,' he said gruffly. 'I know I should have given you more notice, but an opportunity's come up . . .'

'What sort of opportunity?' Her words seemed to echo out of a dream that she needed to wake up from.

He swallowed hard.

'Are you talking about a job?' she pressed.

He nodded. 'Yes, a job. In Germany.'

She looked about the room as if something there could tell her what to do next. He'd mentioned Germany before. His brother was there, and his cousin . . . A while ago he'd asked her to go with him, but he didn't seem to be asking that now. 'When we got together,' she said hoarsely, 'you told me you wanted to be a father. Was it a lie?'

He couldn't meet her eyes. 'It's more complicated than that,' he muttered.

'How is it? I need you to tell me.'

He pushed a fist to his head. 'Don't force me to say things,' he growled.

'What things? What aren't you telling me?'

His eyes flashed as he rounded on her. 'He's not right, that boy of yours, and you know it. There's something wrong with him, and I can't deal with it. You can, because you're you, and you're his mother. I'm sorry, but I can't make it my problem.'

Klaudia stared at him aghast. It was true Antoni hadn't been finding it easy to cope with Adam, but she hadn't tried to make him. She'd done everything she could to help Adam herself, to make sure he wasn't a nuisance for anyone else. So was this her fault? Had she driven a wedge between Adam and Antoni without realising it?

Or was Antoni just using this as an excuse to leave?

The fact that she was even asking the questions, feeling the doubt, put steel into her heart and words into her mouth. 'You need to go,' she said quietly. 'You need to leave right now. You can come back for your things . . .'

'They're already in the car,' he told her.

She flinched.

'Klaudia, I'm sorry,' he cried. 'You're a good person, you deserve someone who can give you . . .'

'Just go,' she cut in tightly, and turning her back she kept her head down until she heard the front door close behind him and the sound of his car driving away.

Her vision was so blurred by tears, her heart so racked with the awfulness of what was happening that she felt unsteady on her feet. She must breathe, she told herself. *Take breaths. In and out. It'll be all right.*

Her hands went forward and she realised she was still holding the mail. She let it drop on the counter top and made herself turn around.

'It's for the best,' she whispered through a hopeless, tremulous smile. She could cope without him. She had before, and now she knew how he felt about Adam . . . Her heart contracted painfully. Her precious, innocent little boy was finding things hard enough without having a father figure who didn't want to help him. How could Antoni have said what he did? It was cruel and unfeeling, and for someone who'd suffered scorn and ostracism himself, albeit on a different level and for a different reason, it was utterly shameful.

Her hands were shaking as she opened her bag.

Having no idea what she was looking for she went into the hall, still not sure what she was doing. Seeing Adam's little bike propped against the wall she let out a howl of anguish and slumped to her knees as she started to sob.

'That poor family,' Wilkie was murmuring, as the news report she and Leanne were watching drew to an end. 'And that dreadful man still won't say what he's done with their little girl's body. I can't imagine how terrible they must feel, but at least that monster has got what he deserved. He won't be able to hurt anyone else's child now.'

'You have to wonder how he had the nerve to plead not guilty when there was so much evidence against him,' Leanne commented. 'If that person hadn't come forward . . . Who was it again?'

'His boss at the hot air balloon company,' Wilkie reminded her, 'and what I can't help asking myself is how long he had his suspicions before he went to the police. It's all a very peculiar and deeply tragic business, if you ask me.'

As the screen changed and a new story began about the failings in the NHS, Leanne continued to think about little Kylie Booth's family. She acknowledged that their tragedy was greater than her own – what could be worse than losing a child? – but she had a sense of how that family might feel right now, because in her own small way she'd been there. Jack Delaney had hanged himself. It was reported one day, investigated the next and all but forgotten by the next – until the funeral had taken place and for a moment they were front-page news again.

It was far worse for this family, of course. They still had no idea what Patrick Marks had done to their child, or with her, so they had to live with the nightmares their cruel imaginations would conjure. Was there any comfort for them in knowing that Marks's punishment would be more fully taken care of in prison? But who cared about him? What was going to happen to those poor parents now?

Things like that bothered Leanne, they always had, and they certainly bothered her mother. It wouldn't surprise Leanne if Wilkie sat down to write to the parents tomorrow, expressing how deeply she felt for their loss and offering to help in any way she could. It was the kind of thing Wilkie did, reach out to those who were suffering, even if she didn't know them. In fact, it wasn't only victims she wrote to, it was law enforcement, councillors and MPs, anyone she felt needed encouragement to make sure the right thing was done.

'Now look at this,' Wilkie cried angrily as the screen showed a frantic rescue operation off the coast of Italy. 'It's a disgrace the way these people are led to believe that the navy is going to be there for them. Of course it's true, but so many of them die . . .'

Used to how involved her mother became in random, though nonetheless vital issues, Leanne turned as the door opened and Klaudia came in, seeming to trip or spin or at least not to have quite the right balance. 'Ah, Klaudia, here you are, sweetie,' Wilkie declared, her expression softening as she went to greet her unofficially adopted daughter. 'I was wondering whether or not to start worrying. Is everything all right?'

Klaudia's small, round face with its chocolate eyes, Slavic flared nostrils and tiny mouth looked wind-ravaged and taut. Not just the result of having dashed across the courtyard to get here, Leanne thought, turning off the TV.

Although insisting everything was fine, Klaudia didn't look or sound herself as she whirled off her scarf and unbuttoned her coat. 'Mm, dinner smells good,' she smiled too brightly as the delicious aroma of rosemary and garlic filled the air. She twinkled at Leanne. 'I sold a set of fans this morning,' she told her, 'the ones that Glory decorated with feathers and made so glamorous. The girl who took them was over the moon. Apparently she wants to put them in her bedroom as a kind of ornament. Are the children in the sitting room?'

'They are,' Leanne confirmed, noticing how eagerly Klaudia grasped the glass of wine Wilkie was handing her.

'My granddaughter ran away a couple of hours ago,' Wilkie told her, 'but she's back again now. She likes to keep us on our toes. Time to fetch them in so we can eat. *Children!*'

For one curious moment Klaudia looked as though she was going to object, but then she was all smiles again as Mia and Adam rushed at her with open arms.

As she fussed and kissed them, whooped at their news and praised their accomplishments, Leanne checked to see if her mother was picking up any strange vibes. It would be unlike Wilkie not to, but she was also very good at keeping things hidden until it was the right moment to reveal them.

Abby came to stand in the doorway and glared at her mother. 'We were watching *Frozen*,' she declared sourly.

'So freeze it,' Leanne replied wittily.

'You are so not funny. Can't we eat in there?'

'No, you're eating here. Now ask Mia and Adam what they'd like to drink, and if you're a very good girl we might let you have half a glass of wine.'

Abby snorted. 'Like as if I'd want your wine.'

'The offer's there,' and taking the ladle from Wilkie, whose little wobble made it clear she'd already had enough, she began serving up.

The meal passed reasonably well, Leanne decided, provided she was prepared to overlook the fact that Abby was ignoring her, her mother was tipsy and Klaudia didn't appear to be following much of the conversation at all.

Just before eight, because it was a school night, Leanne walked round the table and started to whisper in Abby's ear.

'Don't do that,' Abby growled, pushing her away.

'Oh for heaven's sake,' Leanne cried, throwing out her hands. 'Come with me,' and grabbing Abby by the arm she marched her into the sitting room and closed the door.

'I need you, as a special favour,' she said, 'to offer to go and put the young ones to bed.'

Abby regarded her as if she'd gone mad. 'And I would do that because?'

'Because something's not right with Klaudia. She's upset and she can't talk with the children there, so if you were to give them a special treat, by offering to . . .'

'You are *so* manipulative. Just where do you get off thinking I'm one of your pawns?'

Leanne blinked. 'I thought you liked the children.'

'Of course I do, I love them, but . . .'

'Oh sorry, I forgot, it's just me you don't like. Please try to put aside the fact that it's me asking, and think about Mia and Adam – and Klaudia . . .'

'Did it ever cross your mind that Klaudia might not want to talk about whatever's bothering her? You can't solve everyone's problems, you know.'

Leanne frowned. It hadn't actually occurred to her that Klaudia might not want to pour out her troubles. They'd become close since Leanne had moved here. They ran the business together, worried about their children together, their advancing ages, the state of the world since 2016, and even how or where they might like to end their days (preferably together, ha ha ha). In fact, as far as Leanne was aware they never held back on anything – certainly she hadn't over Jack. So in spite of what Abby said, she couldn't imagine that Klaudia was about to close down on her now.

'You make very good points,' she flattered Abby, 'but please trust me on this. At the very least I need Klaudia to know I'm there for her if she wants me to be. If she doesn't, I'll back off.'

Abby eyed her angrily. 'You just don't have a clue,

do you,' she sniped, tossing her head rudely. 'Whatever, I'll take the children. Just don't expect me to . . .'

When she stopped Leanne eyed her curiously. 'Expect you to what?'

Abby's face was tight as she turned away. 'Nothing,' and pushing past her mother she sailed back into the kitchen, all sweetness and light as she announced to the children that she'd been nominated to take them home.

Minutes later Leanne, Wilkie and Klaudia were seated around the table, their wine glasses refreshed and the dishwasher sloshing away like a stormy sea.

Klaudia's eyes were staring blankly at the crumbs on the violet-blue tablecloth, as though she'd lost a sense of where she was.

'You don't have to tell us anything,' Leanne began.

'Oh, she does,' Wilkie insisted.

Leanne shot her mother a look as Klaudia broke her trance and attempted a smile. 'Antoni's gone,' she informed them. 'He's had enough, apparently, so he left.'

Wilkie looked amazed. 'But he was here an hour ago.'

'Enough of what?' Leanne interrupted.

Klaudia shrugged. 'Me, the kids . . .' She took a breath. 'It doesn't matter, I'm not going to fall apart, I just need to get my head round it, that's all.' She took a sip of wine. 'We weren't suited really. I mean, in some ways we were, but . . . Well, if you'd heard what he said about Adam . . . I'd never want him back now, even if he wanted to come.'

Already bristling, Leanne said, 'What did he say about Adam?'

'That he's not right, that there's something wrong with him . . .'

'There's nothing *wrong* with him,' Wilkie protested hotly. 'He's a beautiful, sweet little boy who's not developing quite as quickly as some of the other kids his age.'

Klaudia's voice became angry as she said, 'I'm so disgusted with myself. I knew in my heart that Antoni wasn't the right one, but I kept hoping he would be. It's like I was desperate; one of those poor women who'd rather have the wrong man than no man at all. Oh God, I hate myself.' She started to sob, covering her face with her hands. 'What's the matter with me? I love my children more than anything in the world, but I kept telling myself I loved him too . . .'

As Leanne put a comforting hand on her shoulder she glanced briefly at her mother. In spite of it probably being a good thing that Antoni had gone if he couldn't cope with the children, Leanne understood only too well that feelings almost never disengaged when it would be right for them to. They just clung on, complicating things, making everything seem so much harder than it should be.

'I must say,' Wilkie piped up, 'now I know what he said about Adam I'm glad he's gone. We don't need him in our lives if he can't love our children.'

Klaudia's smile was tearful and grateful.

Leanne said, 'Do you know where he's gone?'

Klaudia dried her eyes. 'I guess he's at work tonight,

but his plan is to go to Germany. He thinks he'll be more welcome there. I suspect he's right.'

Wilkie's eyes darkened. 'Have people been turning on you again? I thought it had stopped.'

Klaudia shuddered. 'Not really. It happened today, as a matter of fact, but I think Antoni gets it more than I do.'

Leanne was remembering with distaste how some people in Kesterly, mostly from the notorious Temple Fields estate, but even some who'd known Klaudia for years, had started treating her differently after the referendum. Klaudia wouldn't ever repeat what had been said to her, but the news had been so full of the sudden surge of resentment that it hadn't been hard to imagine.

'You know if it happens to you,' Leanne said gently, 'at any time, and at any level, you must tell us. More than that, you need to report it.'

Klaudia shook her head. 'That would only make things worse,' she said, 'and it's not so bad really. It's only a few people . . .' She looked at the time. 'I should go and check on the children. I won't tell them about Antoni until they come home from school tomorrow. They won't expect to see him tonight.'

Leanne glanced at her mobile as a text arrived. It was from Abby, letting her know that the children were in bed. When was someone coming so she could go home?

Klaudia was at the door, already in her coat and scarf. 'Thanks for the meal, and the chat,' she said, going to embrace a woozy Wilkie. 'Glory used to say things never look so bad after you've slept on them, and we know Glory was always right.'

44

Wilkie's smile was bleary, her eyes half closed as she patted Klaudia's hand.

Leanne hugged her hard before she left. She'd have gone too if her mother wasn't going to require a little help getting up the stairs, and probably into bed.

The icy wind had gained new teeth as she struggled against it back to the barn. Reaching the porch her phone started to ring, but by the time she got inside the call had gone to voicemail. Whoever it was didn't leave a message, and as it was a number she didn't recognise she didn't bother to ring back.

Daniel Marks had seen his dad on TV earlier, but before he could hear what they were saying the woman whose house he lived in, Marcie, grabbed the remote and changed the channel.

'You shouldn't be watching that,' she scolded. 'Don't you have homework to do? Go on, off to your room. I'll call you when your food's ready.'

Doing as he was told, Daniel had walked slowly up the stairs and into the small room he shared with Timothy and Darren, foster boys like him, older by two and four years. They were out as usual. Daniel had no idea where and thought that probably Marcie didn't know either. They were always in trouble at school; sometimes they didn't even bother to go.

Daniel always went because he knew his dad would be upset and disappointed if he didn't. He tried hard in class; some of the teachers even seemed to like him and wanted to help him do well. He told his dad about them when he wrote and his dad sounded pleased when he wrote back. In his last letter he'd said, 'Mrs Christopher sounds kind and funny, I'm glad she makes you laugh. Do you like this school better than the last one?'

Daniel had written back to say yes, he did, but it wasn't true. He didn't like it any more than the other three he'd been to since they'd taken his dad away. He was picked on for being too clever, or for lying about his age because most boys of eleven were much bigger than him. Some didn't like him because he was fostered, or because he was shy, or simply because they didn't seem to like anyone at all. He didn't tell his dad any of that because he was afraid it would make him worry.

Daniel missed his mum and dad so much that it seemed to fill him up and make him feel so afraid and lonely that he prayed every night for them to come back. He knew his mum couldn't because she was dead, but his dad could. Once everyone realised he wasn't a bad person they'd let him go, and Daniel could live with him again instead of with people who didn't really want him.

He wondered why his dad had been on TV, and afraid he might know the answer he buried his face in the pillow so no one would hear him cry.

Chapter Three

There was something sublimely magical about the elegant vintage emporium of Glory Days. Most people sensed it, though no one could quite put into words the way it made them feel except to say it was good. These days most who came through the door were hoping to kit themselves out for themed parties and weddings, or a bit-of-a-laugh fancy dress. Glory had always been very good-humoured about that, in spite of the pride she'd taken in her vintage pieces. They might not be worth much in a monetary sense, but it mattered a lot to her that they were genuinely of their time. She'd even tell a little story to accompany a certain hat or stole or eye-catching brooch that the new owner could retell when showing it off. As for the coats and dresses, shoes, capes, flowing gowns and feathered turbans, Glory had marvellous tales to relate about them, from the grand garden parties and elegant balls they'd attended in their heydays, to the way they'd miraculously survived war, neglect, even fire to bring themselves to this new chapter in their lives.

With its Dickensian-style window and brass-accessorised black front door, it was a much larger shop than it appeared from outside. It was situated on the promenade, directly across from the main beach and just along the street from Kesterly's Seafront Café. Its side windows looked into Prince's Arcade, where a teddy-bear shop, fragrance boutique, two estate agents and an amusement arcade led to the quaint Inner Courtyard.

The idea of keeping Glory Days crammed with stock had been Glory's.

'People always feel they're going to happen upon a hidden gem amongst all the treasures,' she'd say, 'and they often do, because what might look like something ordinary to you or me could turn out to be something very special for someone else.'

So the walls continued to gleam and sparkle with costume jewellery made from crystals, amazonite, jade, garnet, topaz and aquamarine. There were necklaces, earrings, brooches, hair slides, bracelets, buckles, pendants and pearls. Frosted lights were draped across glass-fronted display cabinets, over hats, headpieces, fringed dresses and fake fur coats. (Glory had been a dedicated animal lover, so she'd always eschewed the glamorous minks, ermines and fox furs that had come her way.) The lovingly restored shoes were arranged in rows on shelves across the back of the shop, with Charleston flapper bags, jewelled plume purses and art deco vanity cases set decorously amongst them. The counter was a repurposed black-lacquered cocktail bar at the centre of the shop, with an elaborate chaise longue to one side of the spacious fitting room, and a bevelled pink, peach and copper framed mirror to the other.

Leanne was busily sorting through baskets of kid gloves and lace fans when the door suddenly banged open and Klaudia backed in with two takeaway coffees – and, Leanne remarked when Klaudia turned around, a rather satisfied smile on her face.

'So this is Friday at midday, right?' Klaudia declared, handing Leanne a latte. 'And he left on Wednesday.'

Leanne's eyebrows rose. 'Don't tell me you've already met someone else.'

Klaudia laughed. 'Unless you count Jolly Albert. No, it's taken Antoni all of two days to ask to come back and what did I say?'

Please don't let it be yes, Leanne willed, thinking of Adam.

'I said, *trzeba byc zartow.*'

'Which translates as eff off?' Leanne suggested.

'Which translates as you have to be joking.'

Same thing, just semantics. Pleased, though realising Klaudia had probably found it more difficult than she was letting on, Leanne said, 'So what happened?'

Klaudia settled herself on to the chaise longue and lifted one Victorian-booted leg over the other. 'He turned up just after Abby and the kids left for the school bus this morning,' she replied. 'I think he must have been waiting. Anyway, he said he'd made a big mistake and would I forgive him. I told him yes, of course I could forgive him, because there is no point in bearing a grudge. But then I said that I realised he wasn't happy here, so I thought it would be better if he pursued his plan to go to Germany, or wherever his new opportunity is, and I would be very pleased for him if he succeeds.'

'You're too good,' Leanne informed her. 'After what he said about Adam, I don't think I could have been so generous.'

Klaudia sighed and sipped her coffee. 'Well, at least he was honest. I don't have to like it, of course I hate it, but I don't believe he bears Adam any ill will. He just couldn't cope, and it isn't easy if the child isn't yours. Anyway, changing the subject, I just ran into your mother as I was coming out of the town hall. She was in such a hurry to get inside that she didn't tell me what she was up to . . . Any idea?'

'After this morning's news I'm going to guess that she's on a mission to make sure our local authority doesn't shut down the homeless centre. I'm sure we'll get to hear about it later, either at home or on the news if she manages to get herself arrested again.'

Klaudia laughed, although it wasn't really a joke, for Wilkie had a knack of ending up in a police cell for various infringements of the Public Order Act. She'd even, on one inglorious occasion, found herself in front of a magistrate for whacking a mounted officer with her banner.

They looked up as the door opened again and one of their regulars, Mr Gruber from the retirement village, was gusted in by the wind. His jowly, veined face was always merry, while his collar, tie, overcoat and trilby were invariably the smartest in town.

'Good morning, ladies,' he beamed, gallantly sweeping off his hat. He seemed not to realise that he'd dislodged his lacquered comb-over so that it was now hanging off to one side like a scoop, making him look for all the world as though he'd flipped his lid.

Struggling not to laugh as Klaudia drowned a guffaw in her coffee, Leanne said, 'Good morning, Mr Gruber. It's lovely to see you.'

'And to see you my dear,' he chuckled, coming forward. In spite of having fled Austria as a boy some seventy-five years ago, he still had a noticeable accent that seemed, in its way, to make him sound even merrier than he was. 'Blustery day out there,' he told them, 'but I had to come. It's Mrs Gruber's birthday tomorrow, and I was hoping you could help me to pick something out for her.'

Loving how devoted he was to his wife, who tragically didn't know who he was any more, Leanne was wondering if it would help or crush his dignity to mention his hair, when with one rapid swipe he had it back in place.

Klaudia snorted and shrank into the fitting room to compose herself.

Aching with the effort of suppressing her own mirth, Leanne said, 'I'll be delighted to help you. I think you got her a star sapphire bracelet for Christmas, didn't you, so how about we try to find a necklace, or perhaps a ring, to match it?'

Clearly pleased with the suggestion, he was soon inspecting the many pieces Leanne directed him to, while Klaudia sorted out some silk scarves as possible alternatives. In the end he bought a ring and a brooch, heavily discounted, because they knew that Mrs Gruber had willed all her jewellery to Glory Days. (Apparently once Glory had found this out she'd tried not to take his money, but he'd appeared quite offended by the suggestion, so Klaudia had been able to warn Leanne, when she'd taken over, not to try the same thing.)

Understanding that it might feel as though he wasn't buying his wife anything if he didn't part with cash, Leanne smiled and waved to him through the window as he set off along the promenade, one hand clutching a black and purple Glory Days bag, the other clamped to his head to keep hold of his hat.

After parcelling up three Internet orders to take to the post office, Klaudia was on the point of leaving when Marian Kent from the Temple Fields estate, whose sons were known for all the wrong reasons – petty theft, hard drinking, gang fights – came in.

'I thought you didn't work here on Fridays,' she said tartly to Klaudia, as though Klaudia was somehow tricking her by being there.

Used to the woman's abrasiveness, Klaudia said, 'Good morning, Marian. How are you?'

Marian scowled and started looking for her phone as Leanne's rang.

'Can I help you with anything?' Klaudia offered, as Leanne took her call.

'No, I don't mind waiting for her,' Marian retorted, nodding towards Leanne. 'I'll have a look round till she's ready.'

'Well, I'm sure she won't be long,' and with a friendly smile Klaudia went on her way.

After jotting down the details of a telephone order, Leanne rang off and smiled past her dismay as she watched Marian Kent poking around a row of flowery tea dresses close to the door. Though unable to imagine the raven-haired woman with her tattoos and thick legs in a dress at all, never mind one that was jaunty and elegant, Leanne said, 'Are you looking for something special?' *Something you can bring back tomorrow*, she didn't add, for Marian Kent almost always found fault with her purchases.

'Not really,' Marian retorted, turning her nose up at a pale green polka dot shirt-waister with pink chiffon trim. 'I just came in to say,' she turned around and fixed Leanne with pale blue eyes, 'that I think it's about time you gave the girl the heave-ho.'

Leanne frowned, not sure what she was meaning.

'Her,' Marian said, jerking a thumb towards the door. 'It's not right employing foreigners when there's plenty of English people looking for jobs.'

Leanne's eyes widened.

'I've held my tongue long enough,' Marian rasped on, 'but someone had to say it. Things have changed now, and it's time you did something about it.'

Tightly, Leanne retorted, 'Are you saying . . .'

'You know what I'm saying. We're taking back control and if you know what's good for you, you'll get rid of the Pole. There, that's spelling it out for you,' and tearing open the door she returned to the street.

Leanne couldn't let it rest there. Racing after her, she

heaved open the door and shouted after Marian Kent's retreating figure, 'Don't bother coming back to this shop, it's closed to you.'

She was shaking with outrage as she went back inside, unable to believe the damned cheek of the woman, and that was before she got into all the hateful meaning behind what she'd said.

Knowing exactly who would understand and share her outrage she rang her mother, but Wilkie wasn't answering, quite probably because she was still giving out orders at the town hall.

Leanne stood quietly staring at nothing, feeling a rising disgust for Marian and her threat, for that was what it had sounded like. *'If you know what's good for you . . .'* How dare the woman come in here trying to tell her who she should employ? And if Marian thought for one single second that she, Leanne, would consider *her* as a possible replacement should Klaudia's application for permanent residency not succeed, she had to be out of her poisonous little mind.

In an effort to purge herself of the unpleasantness she searched out Glory's *Book of the Way*, hoping to find a little homily that might calm the fury brought about by Marian Kent's words.

It didn't take long and she was so satisfied with her discovery that she smiled a thank-you to her aunt, as though Glory herself had written the words, or at least guided her search.

Care about people's approval, and you will be their prisoner.

She continued flicking through the pages in the hope of finding something to steer her through the turmoil with Abby, until the phone rang again and she put the book down.

Not recognising the number she clicked on cautiously, expecting a telemarketer or, God forbid, another Marian Kent.

'Hi, is that Leanne?' a male voice asked.

'Who's speaking, please?' she replied.

'It's Richard York. Steve York's brother. We ran into each other a couple of . . .'

'Weeks ago,' she finished cheerfully. 'Of course. Sorry, I didn't . . . How are you?' She'd been at school with Steve. Richard was a couple of years older, but she'd remembered him instantly when they'd collided in the street during a downpour. It had been a great surprise, for the last she'd heard of him was that he was a surgeon with the Red Cross, doing his best to save lives in war-torn parts of the globe.

'Burn-out,' he'd told her then. 'It started getting to me, to both of us – my wife's also a doctor – so it was time to take a break and start a family of our own before it's too late.'

'So are you getting used to being back in Kesterly?' she asked.

He laughed. 'I admit it's taking some time, but Jan is loving it. You'll have to meet her. In fact that's partly why I'm ringing. We're organising a march on Saturday to try to force Dean Valley Council to openly welcome refugees. The official line is that it's under consideration, so we think they need a nudge. What do you say?'

Leanne almost laughed. 'Absolutely you can count

me in. In fact, I'm surprised you haven't run into my mother yet. She's very supportive of refugees so I can safely say she'll rally to your cause, and so will my friend Klaudia.'

'Excellent.'

Feeling unexpectedly energised, Leanne said, 'My mother is going to love seeing you again. Why don't you and Jan come for dinner next Friday? I'll invite a few more friends who I'm sure will be like-minded. You'll probably already know some of them, and hopefully they'll join the march on Saturday as well.'

'Count us in. Just text me the time when you're ready. If you're still at Ash Morley I'll know where to find you.'

After ringing off Leanne stood for a moment thinking back over the call, and how timely it had been coming right after Marian Kent's nasty little outburst. Except those sorts of incidents were happening all the time these days, not to her specifically, but the papers were regularly reporting anti-immigrant episodes – that was when their journalists weren't stirring them up.

It was a pity, she reflected, that Kate couldn't be there, given her dedication to forging a career in human rights. But more concerning for the moment was whether Abby would want to join the march, given that next Saturday was the first anniversary of her father's death. There was a chance she'd seize it as yet one more reason to detest her mother for even thinking about marking such a significant day by sticking up for other people, when she'd never done anything to stick up for Jack.

Your words, not hers, she reminded herself, but she couldn't help wondering if it was what Abby thought.

'Hello, Klaudia, my love, how are you today? Bit blowy out there, innit?'

'Just a bit, Dotty, but at least you're tucked up nice and warm in your chair.'

'Oh, I am, I am. Best I stay in here in the living room while the weather's like this, and not bother with the bedroom. No point heating two rooms when I can only be in one at a time.'

Touching an affectionate hand to the old lady's papery cheek, Klaudia took off her coat and began clearing away the empty tray that a carer had left next to Dotty's chair. She winced at the sound of a piercing scream outside, and went to the window to find out what was happening. No sign of anyone, and she wasn't inclined to venture into the street to check, for this wasn't the safest of neighbourhoods.

Someone of Dotty's age and fragility should have been moved to sheltered housing a long time ago, but with all the cutbacks and no family to plead her case it was doubtful she'd ever be rescued from these damp walls and draughty windows, never mind all the violence outside.

'So how are those lovely little kiddies of yours?' Dotty asked kindly. 'Behaving themselves, are they?'

'They're very well, thank you,' Klaudia replied, noticing that Dotty hadn't eaten all her breakfast. 'Not hungry today?' she asked.

Dotty's jerking head gave a shake. 'No, not very. You're welcome to it if you're feeling a bit peckish.'

Klaudia regarded the congealed porridge and dab of jam.

Dotty chuckled, and realising it was a joke Klaudia laughed. Dotty was such a dear old soul, with a mischievous sense of humour and most of her marbles still intact. Her wiry white hair clearly hadn't been brushed today, possibly not yesterday either, and there was a good chance her pad hadn't been changed this morning.

Klaudia didn't blame the carers for not seeing to these things. It was likely that Dotty had soiled herself after their first visit of the day, and given how little time was allocated to each case a great many things went undone. This was why Klaudia had contacted social services to volunteer to check up on the most vulnerable a few times a week.

After finding there was no hot water, she put a kettle on to boil, then tracked down the things she needed – cotton wool, Nivea cream, hairbrush and some face powder. A few minutes later she was back at Dotty's side, smiling at the way the old lady's knotted fingers were unconsciously smoothing the pretty patchwork quilt over her knees. Klaudia had found the quilt a couple of weeks ago at a rummage sale and had bought it for Dotty, along with a fleece jumper and a pair of navy slacks.

Dotty gave a murmur of pleasure at the feel of her neglected face being pampered. 'What about that poor woman over in Marstone?' she said, as Klaudia began to pat her dry with a towel. 'Did you see it on the news? Could break your heart, it could.'

'What poor woman was that?' Klaudia asked, putting the towel aside and reaching for the Nivea cream.

'You know, the one whose little girl was taken. That dreadful man is going away for the rest of his life, so why not put the child's parents out of their misery and tell them where she is. Unless he's sold her on to one of those paediatric rings.'

'Paedophile,' Klaudia corrected, shuddering at the very idea.

Dotty nodded absently. 'Course he's saying he didn't do it, but they always say that, don't they?' She sighed and blinked sadly, as though it was all too hard to think about. After a while her trembly fingers closed around Klaudia's. 'If they end up expelling all you people they'll have my death on their hands, so they will, and that's a promise.'

Klaudia's heart contracted at the reminder of her wait for permanent residency. That morning she'd received an email asking for the dates she'd been in Poland during her mother's illness and death. What did that mean? Were they going to hold it against her in some way? It had happened to others who, like her, had been in the country for over five years so had expected automatic residency. It was what it said on the government website, but the more she read in the papers and saw on the news the more worried she was becoming.

By the time Klaudia had finished reading aloud the first two pages of *Gone with the Wind* – Dotty's favourite – the old lady was fast asleep. So, making sure the TV remote was in easy reach, Klaudia left a bar of Dotty's favourite chocolate on the arm of the chair and let herself quietly out of the door.

The carers would be by later to give Dotty some dinner, and she, Klaudia, needed to get home in a hurry now to make sure she was there before the children's bus arrived at the drop-off.

To her relief she found the wheels were still on her car when she got to it, and there was no sign of the youths who often hung about this part of the estate. So today the going was good, but it wasn't always the case. The last time she'd been there a gang of five had decided to entertain themselves by refusing to let her get into the car, and when they finally did they enjoyed a little more sport by sitting on the bonnet so she was unable to drive off. They'd kept her there for at least half an hour as they'd chatted and smoked and occasionally pulled ugly or threatening faces at her through the windscreen. She'd have called the police if she'd thought it would help, but others in her position had already found to their cost that this wasn't a good move.

If it weren't for Dotty and Jolly Albert she'd never come to this estate again, but she didn't have the heart to abandon them when they had so little company or joy in their lives.

Half an hour later she was driving the children up to Ash Morley, listening to Mia chatter on about her day, while Adam gazed out of the window seeming to be in a world of his own.

'So did you have a good day too?' she asked him as they trundled over the cattle grid and in through the gate.

'Miss Gibbs went to a meeting,' he replied.

Klaudia glanced in the rear-view mirror. 'Was it an important one?' she asked.

He shrugged, then pointed towards the stables saying, 'Look who's there.'

Klaudia's heart leapt with hope even as it twisted with dread. The postman was getting back into his van after making his deliveries. Had he brought a letter from the Home Office at last? Unlikely, of course, given the email she'd received that morning.

She needed to deal with that this evening, look up dates and details of the flights she'd taken to and from Krakow during the distressingly emotional time of losing her mother. And while doing it she had somehow to restrain the fear that they were trying to find a way to deport her.

It was just after seven by the time Leanne let herself into the barn, almost dropping her laptop in her haste to get out her phone.

'Hey, Mum!' Kate cried down the line. 'At last. I thought you might be avoiding me.'

Thrilled to hear her elder daughter's happy voice, Leanne piled her computer and handbag on to the bar that divided the kitchen and dining table, and perched on a high stool. 'And there was me thinking the same thing,' she scolded. 'How are you? Tell me what's new in your world.'

'Oh God, where to start,' Kate laughed. 'It's going crazy this semester. I've hardly got a minute to myself, but here's some good news. It's been confirmed that I'll be in Edinburgh this summer for the Creative Writing and Contemporary Literature course. So I thought I'd come a week early and spend some time with you guys, if that's OK?'

Both delighted and disappointed by the long wait to see her, Leanne said, 'Of course it's OK. You don't need to ask. We'll be counting the days. Any news yet on an internship?'

'Oh yes, I am so excited about it. That's really why I'm calling. You remember I applied to Amnesty International, ACLU and Human Rights Watch? Well, ACLU have accepted me at their affiliate in New Mexico . . .'

'ACLU? Remind me?'

'American Civil Liberties Union.'

Of course. Wilkie would be ashamed of her for forgetting.

'Anyway, I had a call from Amnesty International today and they've invited me to DC for an interview. I so want that one to happen. Washington's the place to be right now. It's all going down over there. Wilkie wouldn't know which way to turn first, there's so much to march about.'

Both thrilled and alarmed by the idea of her daughter being caught up in the conflagration of political, legal and media wars in the US capital these days, Leanne said, 'So tell me all about it. Who exactly rang you? When do you fly over there? Is Dad going with you?'

For the next few minutes Leanne listened with a mix of pride and trepidation as Kate filled her in on everything, from where she'd actually been when she'd taken the call – the Chesh, which Leanne remembered was a campus coffee shop – to how she'd have to go to DC and back in one day so she didn't miss out on too many lectures, and how both her father and stepmother were going with her.

What Leanne wouldn't have given to be there too, but it was hardly worth her crossing the Atlantic for the very short time Kate was going to be available in Washington. And she was so busy with her courses at IU that there would be no point going on to Bloomington either.

' . . . analysing politics,' Kate was saying, 'which is like so cool. It's one of my favourite classes, so I don't want to be late, but I've still got a few minutes. Oh God, I didn't tell you, did I? For my advanced nonfiction I've chosen Kurt Vonnegut and American Postmodernism. It'll be totally mind-blowing, but more on that later. I need to know how things are with Abby?'

Stifling a sigh, Leanne wondered if Abby was in her room or had stopped off at Tanya's and not come home yet. Just in case she was in earshot, Leanne kept her voice down and tone neutral as she said, 'More or less the same. Do you have anything to tell me? You could start with how she's getting on at school, because she won't talk to me about it.'

'OK, she doesn't say much to me either, but from what she does say I'm getting the impression that

63

things aren't great. Usually she just wants to change the subject, or she'll say it's a waste of time, or it all sucks, something along those lines. Maybe you need to talk to her pastoral care tutor, to find out more.'

'I will. Anything else?'

'Well, she's definitely mad as hell with you, we've known that for a while, even if we don't know why. She got really worked up when I FaceTimed her a couple of days ago. She kept saying you never listen, you're not interested, you're all about yourself. She's got it into her head that you have no idea what's going on in her world, but even if you did know it wouldn't make a difference because you don't care.'

Closing her eyes, Leanne said, 'She knows that's not true, of course I care, and I do listen – or I would if she'd only speak to me.'

'OK, well I reckon she only tells me these things so I'll pass them on to you. Actually, I'm sure she does because there wouldn't be any point otherwise, except to bitch and it definitely goes deeper than that.'

'She's still grieving,' Leanne said, echoing her mother, while knowing it to be true. 'She's never really talked about what happened, at least not to me, and we're not at all convinced the counsellor did any good.'

'I have to agree with that, but I'm sorry, I have to go now. I'll try you again at the weekend. Oh, hang on, Grandma said in one of her emails that you're staging a demonstration in support of refugees. Great cause. Hope it goes well. Love to everyone there. Love you. Miss you,' and before Leanne could echo the final words she'd gone.

Hanging up too, Leanne went to find out if Abby was in her room, eavesdropping, studying or even sleeping. No sign of her. Nor was there a note or a text to say where she might be. Understanding that this was a deliberate omission to make her worry, Leanne took out her mobile and sent a message saying, *Are you coming home for dinner?* Then just to be on the safe side she called Tanya's mother to find out if she was there and was told that both girls were with another friend, Becky, over in Westleigh Park.

Since she knew Becky, and Westleigh Park was one of the better neighbourhoods, Leanne put it out of her mind for the moment in order to focus on invites and food for Friday evening. Klaudia had already offered to make a *chlodnik* – a Polish beet soup – for starters, with a cranberry and Brie wreath as an alternative, and her mother was sorting out the appetisers and a dessert, so she needed to come up with a suitable main course.

Ignoring Glory's shelf full of cookbooks, she opened her computer to begin an online search for inspiration. So far they were going to be ten if Abby decided to join them, thirteen if the three friends Wilkie had invited confirmed they could make it.

Noticing a handful of emails in the Glory Days inbox, she clicked on to find out if anything was urgent, before continuing her recipe search.

They turned out to be from customers with the usual sorts of enquiries, one from the bank promoting a new style of account, and another from the local paper with an offer of reduced rates for regular advertisers. The most recent message to arrive had been sent from a Hotmail address comprising a random selection of letters and numbers, with *YOU NEED TO READ THIS* in the subject line.

Ordinarily she'd simply delete something like that, but for some reason she clicked on and found a message of four badly typed lines from someone who hadn't given their name, but who'd managed to make themselves perfectly plain.

Sickened, Leanne quickly closed it down, as though the venom of the words might break through the screen and contaminate her. It hadn't been meant for her, she realised, it was meant for Klaudia who could just as easily have opened it, but thank God she hadn't. It couldn't have been more full of hate if it had come from someone whom Klaudia had harmed savagely and unforgivably. As it was, Leanne was certain that Klaudia would have no more idea who the sender was than she did.

Not wanting to read it again, and certainly not wanting Klaudia to see it, she took a moment to decide what to do. In the end, deciding she couldn't just ignore it, she rang Kesterly police station and asked to speak to PC Barry Britten. She and Barry had been at school together, and since being back she'd run into him several times around town.

Luckily he was on duty, and she had only got as far as reading him the first part of the email when he said, 'You need to send it me so we can find out if it's one of our regular arseholes. If it isn't . . . Well, we'll need to see it anyway.'

'You're making it sound as though this is happening a lot,' she told him, after typing in his email address. She knew it was, of course, it was on the news all the time, and on her Facebook feed.

'It's definitely been on the increase these last few months. Let's say people with those sorts of views are feeling emboldened. Luckily, there aren't too many of them, but who was it who said, "all we need for evil to prevail is for good men to do nothing"? Or something like that anyway.'

'Edmund Burke,' she murmured.

'That's him. So, you didn't do nothing, you rang me, which is good, but how far we can go with it remains to be seen. Has Klaudia seen it?'

'No, do you think I should show her?'

'Probably. Not that I'd expect this scumbag to carry out any of the threats, they're what we call keyboard warriors – those who hide behind computers and false identities, cowards in other words – but she ought to know they're out there so she can stay vigilant.'

After ringing off, Leanne carried her laptop across to the stables, the motion-sensor lights coming on as she went, and the sound of her mother driving her shiny Morris 1000 over the cattle grid rattling through the night. Guessing Wilkie was off to one of her many committee meetings, Leanne knocked on the stables' side door and let herself into the kitchen.

'Hi,' Klaudia smiled. 'This is a nice surprise.' She frowned. 'Or is it?' she added when she saw Leanne's expression. 'Is everything all right? You look . . . worried.'

'I am,' Leanne admitted. 'Are the children in bed?'

'Adam is. Mia's still in the bath. Would you like some wine?'

After she'd filled two glasses Leanne sat down at the table and opened the laptop. 'You need to see this,' she said, and clicking open the email she turned the screen to face Klaudia.

As she read Klaudia's face tightened.

'Have you received anything like it before?' Leanne asked.

Klaudia nodded. 'Once or twice,' she said. 'I try to ignore it.'

'But this . . . *person* . . . is threatening to harm you.'

'I know, but I'm not the only one receiving these emails. It's happening all over.'

'And it needs to be stopped.'

Klaudia could hardly disagree. 'Luckily, the authorities seem to be taking it seriously, and I think most people are like you, they find it objectionable and want nothing to do with it. But there are obviously some who feel afraid, or angry, or apparently in a big hurry for us to leave.'

Appalled that someone as gentle and kind as Klaudia was being targeted in such a hateful way, Leanne said, 'You shouldn't keep these messages to yourself. OK, I understand that they're mostly sent by sad, ignorant people who have nothing better to do, but you don't know how far they might go. The bad feeling that's out there these days is spreading into some hearts and minds and turning people into the worst versions of themselves.'

Klaudia's smile was flat.

Leanne cried, 'If you won't think of yourself, then think of the children. All children. They're the ones we need to worry about, and there are so many of them who are suffering in ways . . . Well, never mind what kind of ways, the point is they shouldn't be suffering at all.'

*   *   *

Dear Dad,

I've moved again. The address is at the top of the page. It's quite a long way away from Marstone, near to London, but Carolyn, my social worker, said it was best for me to be out of the area for a while. This is because someone found out that my real name is Daniel Marks, not Daniel Fields.

Daniel paused, wondering whether he should cross that out, or throw the page away. It would upset his dad to be reminded that he couldn't use his real name any more. He definitely wouldn't tell him that he'd been beaten up because of it; his dad didn't need to know that, especially when there was nothing he could do about it. Lucky a teacher had come along when she had or he'd have suffered a lot worse than cuts and bruises, the way they'd been laying into him.

Daniel hated not being able to use his real name, but Carolyn had said that he'd make it much easier for himself if he just did as he was told. She hadn't said it in a nasty way, more like she was giving advice, and Daniel hadn't argued because he'd known that he wouldn't win.

He used to argue back to his mum and dad, not over

big things, just silly stuff like him not tidying up his room, or staying at his friends' too late when they were expecting him home. They always made up before they went to bed; it had been one of his mum's rules.

He wasn't in touch with his friends any more. They probably hated him because of what they thought his dad had done. Daniel didn't understand why anyone believed it. His dad had never hurt a fly and they'd all thought he was really cool before.

He started writing again.

This time they were going to call me Daniel Craig, then they remembered it was James Bond's name. Me and Carolyn found that funny. I thought you might too. Imagine me as 007. I wish it was true so I could find Kylie Booth and prove to everyone that they've got it wrong about you.

I'm Daniel Jones now, which makes me think of Mrs Jones who was my English teacher at St Jude's. I expect you remember her. She was really nice, so I'm OK with having her name, even though I'd rather have my real one.

The new family I'm with are quite nice. They never miss any meals the way the last family did so I'm not so hungry any more. Yesterday we all went to the ice rink, which was good fun. Even though I've never done it before I only fell down twice. There's another girl here, being fostered. Her name's Alice, she's twelve, and she's a really good skater. Lennie, who's taking care of us with his wife, Trish, has promised to take us to watch Arsenal play if he can get tickets. I told him I was a Man U fan so he said he'd try to get some tickets for one of their games too if he could afford them.

Alice and I are sad that we can't stay here for long, but we've already been told that it's only temporary. Lennie and Trish don't do long term. We're hoping wherever we go next we might go together. I haven't told Alice about you because I don't want her to think you're a bad person. Her dad's dead and her mother's on drugs, so that's why she's being fostered, but she thinks her mum will have her back soon.

I wish they'd let me come to see you.

Can you do something to make them?

Love Daniel

PS: I came top in maths before I left the last school, and also in science.

PPS: Lennie let me use his computer yesterday so I went on YouTube and watched some videos about there being two suns. It was really interesting. Apparently no one will admit that the second one exists, but even NASA has shots of it.

Daniel put down his pen, folded the letter and picked up the envelope Trish had given him. There was a mailbox at the end of the street, where he could post the letter himself. It wasn't that he didn't trust Trish, he'd just rather do it himself when he could. He felt more confident then that his dad would get it. He wished he could ring him up, but that wasn't allowed either. He couldn't see him or speak to him. Carolyn had said he should really forget all about him, but Daniel was never going to do that.

Chapter Four

It was Friday evening and the dinner guests were due to arrive at the barn any time soon. Abby was staying at Tanya's for the night, having explained to Wilkie, in Leanne's hearing, that they were going to be making their banners for the demonstration tomorrow. This was often how she communicated with her mother when she had something reasonable to say. Leanne had made no comment, but had felt relieved that Abby wanted to join in.

Klaudia was upstairs settling the children into what used to be Leanne's room when she was young and was now Kate's when she was here, while Wilkie created appetiser art in the kitchen. Two large dishes of lamb shanks in red wine (no vegetarians at tonight's meal) were slow roasting to perfection in the oven, filling the room with such a mouth-watering aroma that even the most weary taste buds would surely leap to life at first scent of it.

At the far end of the large, high-ceilinged room a wood-burning stove was flaming in the hearth, with a dozen or more candles casting a romantic glow all around it. Leanne was putting finishing touches to the dining table, wishing Glory was there to see it, for everything belonged to her aunt: the matt gold chargers, Stuart crystal glasses, antique silver cutlery and tartan napkins. Glory had loved to entertain.

It had been a long time, Leanne was thinking as she stood back to admire it all, far too long in fact, since she'd felt such sparkles of anticipation for the evening ahead. In the later years of her marriage she'd lived in dread of how Jack might behave when they had friends round. He'd often be drunk even before they arrived, and would then proceed to find fault with everything she served, what she said, or even what she didn't say. He never seemed to notice, or perhaps he hadn't cared, how uncomfortable his criticisms made their guests, and woe betide anyone who attempted to disagree with his rants against just about everyone in his profession. Unsurprisingly they'd soon found themselves with no guests at their table, and the once endless flow of invitations that used to come their way hadn't taken long to dry up either. Though he regularly blamed Leanne for their lack of friends she hadn't bothered to argue, it wasn't worth wasting the energy on it. When he was in one of those moods the only person he ever heard was himself.

Now, not having to worry about his abusive outbursts, or Abby launching some sort of attack on her, Leanne was feeling almost childishly excited by the prospect of old friends and new gathering around her table. It was a table that had hosted so many joyous occasions over the years it had belonged to Glory that it felt like a charmed entertainer in itself.

'There, that does it,' Wilkie declared, standing back in her turn to admire her tray of home-made arancini balls, caramelised onion tarts and truly scrumptious-looking mini bruschettas. 'And just in time, because I can hear someone arriving.'

With a leap of pleasure Leanne prepared to greet the first guests, who turned out to be Richard York and his heavily pregnant wife Jan. Jan was as tall as Richard, with warm blue eyes, a dazzling smile and the trace of a Dutch accent that for some reason made Leanne like her all the more. Richard, with his slicked-back hair, keen navy eyes and bushy beard, appeared so delighted to be there that Leanne hugged him especially hard. Klaudia swept in to offer drinks, while Wilkie tempted them with appetisers and Leanne greeted the next couple, Jenny and Blake Leonard, who had part ownership of Ogilvy Antiques in the Inner Courtyard. Blake was an exceptionally handsome man with large friendly eyes and a smile that was always infectious, while Jenny was as polite as she was petite, with a humour that was so quietly mischievous it was sometimes missed. Next came Bel and Harry Beck, a striking couple, due to Bel's stunning blonde hair and Harry's unmistakable Indian heritage. Harry was one of the region's most prominent breast cancer surgeons, and had taken such good care of Glory during her time in his clinic and operating theatre that he had come to feel like part of the family. Bel, his wife of only one year, was a successful property developer and interior designer, and, while not as pregnant as Jan, was probably only a month or so behind.

Last to arrive were Wilkie's friends, seventy-year-old Bill Simmonds and his sixty-something girlfriend Pamela Owen, with Pamela's adorable sister Rowzee Cayne. Rowzee was known to just about everyone in town since she'd taught most of them English and drama during her forty years at Kesterly High, and Leanne still remembered how much fun Rowzee's classes had been. She'd more recently become known as the Miracle Lady, for the brain tumour that had been diagnosed and treated over two years ago still hadn't carried her off, when it was supposed, in Rowzee's words, 'to have done for me in less than six months'.

Thrilled to have Rowzee here, Leanne embraced her warmly, saying, 'I'm not going to get enough of you tonight, so promise you'll meet me for coffee soon.'

'You just tell me when and I'll be there,' Rowzee twinkled, her enchanting heart-shaped face and floaty curls more or less restored to former beauty following her most recent treatment.

As she was whisked away by Richard, another of her ex-students, to be introduced to his wife, Leanne took a glass of wine from Klaudia and went to make sure that Blake and Jenny Leonard had been introduced to those they didn't already know.

By the time everyone sat down to eat and Klaudia served her delicious *chlodnik* the conversation was flowing as freely as the wine, and the sound of laughter was making Leanne feel so happy that she simply couldn't stop smiling. This was no time for guilty thoughts about Jack, although they tried to kick in once or twice as the evening progressed, but she was having none of it. She was starting a new life now, these people were her friends and not one of them would even dream of treating her the way he had.

'You don't seem to be saying much,' Klaudia murmured as she and Leanne prepared the main course for serving. 'Are you OK?'

'I'm loving every minute,' Leanne assured her. 'I just want to listen and watch and absorb how eloquent and funny and interesting everyone is.'

Giving her a quick hug, Klaudia carried a dish of greens to the table, joining in the laughter as Blake Leonard finished telling a story about a customer who'd tried to palm him off with an iPhone 4, claiming it was an antique.

'I hope it's all right to ask you this, Harry,' Wilkie piped up at one point, 'but are you having any problems about staying here?'

Klaudia's throat dried as Harry's eyes twinkled. 'Don't worry about me,' he replied, 'I was born here, but I'm afraid I'm finding myself being told to return to India rather more often now than I used to.'

Wilkie and Rowzee shook their heads in dismay.

'Do you ever answer these people?' Klaudia asked.

'Not if I can help it. It's not an argument worth getting into. Are you having trouble?'

Klaudia nodded. 'I read today about a German neurosurgeon, or maybe he was a scientist. Anyway, he's been here for years, apparently, but the Home Office have just told him to start making preparations to leave.'

'On what grounds?' Harry demanded.

'I think it was something to do with health insurance.'

Leanne's heart twisted with concern as the others murmured disapproval and dismay. 'It'll be an administrative screw-up,' she assured Klaudia. 'No one's going to be sending EU nationals home, I'm sure of it, especially not those who have jobs and families here.'

'Leanne's right,' Wilkie declared. 'It will be sorted out . . .'

'Well I hope it's soon,' Pamela interrupted, 'because what I saw at the doctor's today I don't want to see again, ever. This poor woman, I've no idea where she was from, but she was laid into by some horrible old man telling her to get out and stop taking decent people's places in the queue. He ranted on and on until she burst into tears and walked out.'

'Didn't you do anything about it?' Rowzee demanded, clearly appalled that her sister might have remained silent, especially with Pamela being so famed for her feistiness.

'Of course I did. I punched him on the nose, and sent the receptionist to get the woman back.'

'You actually *hit* him!' Jenny cried as her husband started to laugh.

Leanne said, 'I hope you did.'

'She didn't,' Rowzee declared knowingly.

'OK, I gave him a very sharp piece of my mind,' Pamela conceded, 'and I told the doctor when I went in that he needed to do something to stop that sort of thing happening again in the waiting room. He agreed, how could he not, but we both knew it would not matter what we said.'

'Please let's change the subject,' Klaudia asked. 'We're

having such a lovely time and I don't want to be responsible for bringing things down. Wilkie, have you heard any more about the theatre closing? I think we need to put it next on our list of causes if it is going to happen.'

'No, I haven't heard,' Wilkie replied, 'but absolutely we need to try to keep it open. Which reminds me, there's a new reporter at the *Kesterly Gazette*. I can't remember his name offhand, but he's a bright boy, really excited about giving us plenty of coverage for the march for refugees tomorrow. We could probably enlist his support for the theatre too.'

'What happened to Heather Hancock?' Pamela asked. 'Not that I've ever been a fan, but she's been there for years.'

'The paper's just gone under new management,' Wilkie told her, 'but whether that means the dreaded Heather has lost her job, we'll have to wait and see.'

It was well after midnight by the time everyone finally left to go home, saying affectionate goodnights and all eager to see one another again in the morning. Wilkie and Klaudia stayed behind to help Leanne to clear up, but once the first dishwasher load was under way Leanne insisted that they should go to their beds too. Mia and Adam were all right where they were, and she was actually quite looking forward to being on her own for a while, not only to relive the highlights of the evening, but to give more thought to an idea that was forming in her mind and finding no obstacles so far to its development.

By the time she was ready to blow out the candles and go up to bed she knew what she was going to do. She'd definitely made up her mind about it, and nothing, she told herself happily, was going to stand in her way.

When two great forces oppose each other, victory will go to the one who knows how to yield.

Some encouragingly profound words from the *Book of the Way*, Leanne decided the next morning, that seemed wholly appropriate for the day ahead. The people versus the local authority. Who would win by yielding? As far as she could see it, it would be a win-win if it was the council.

Then Abby came home, and the dynamic changed as Leanne took one look at the banner she had made for her and gaped in disbelief. 'What on earth is that?' she spluttered, hardly able to get the words out, she was so shocked.

'It's for you,' Abby retorted, standing firm in front of Tanya, who wasn't looking happy at all.

'Have you lost your mind?' Leanne cried. 'Why would you do something like that?'

'It's a joke!' Abby shouted angrily. 'You always have to take everything so seriously.'

Leanne was still struggling to make sense of it. 'I don't understand what's funny about *Go Back to Where You Belong*,' she stated. 'You surely realise I'd never carry a banner saying that at the kind of march we're going on this morning?'

Abby's face was crimson. 'Shut up!' she shouted furiously. 'Just shut up and leave me alone.'

'What's going on in here?' Wilkie demanded, coming through the door at that moment.

'She's picking on me again,' Abby sobbed.

Leanne directed her mother to the banner.

Clearly astonished, Wilkie turned to Abby.

'I can never do anything right in this house,' Abby wailed, tears starting down her cheeks. 'You all hate me . . .'

'Stop that now,' Wilkie chided. 'You know it's not true, and for heaven's sake you must have known this wouldn't get a good reaction.'

'I told you not to do it,' Tanya said quietly.

Leanne looked at the girl, relieved that at least her sense of humour wasn't flawed.

Wilkie pulled Abby into her arms and gave Leanne a meaningful look.

'OK, I'm sorry I got angry,' Leanne sighed, not really meaning it, but realising that both her mother and daughter needed to hear her say it. 'I just don't get why . . .'

'It's done,' Wilkie interrupted. 'It's backfired and now we'll chop it up to burn later and be on our way with proper banners. OK?'

'I don't want to go,' Abby sniffled. 'Not with *her*.'

'Then come with me in my car,' Wilkie replied.

Leanne didn't argue; as far as she was concerned her mother was welcome to Abby right now. She'd take Klaudia and the children instead, and by some miracle she'd have worked out what the heck was going on in her daughter's head by the time they got into town.

Fat chance of that.

'I've had an idea,' she told Klaudia as they headed out of Ash Morley. 'Actually, I'm quite excited about it,

I think you will be too, but I should probably discuss it with Mum and Abby first.' Realising how Abby might react to it, she felt her heart sink. What an upsetting start to the day it had been for them, and now here she was thinking only of herself when Abby was probably still upset.

'She was attention-seeking,' Klaudia stated, after Leanne finished telling her about the banner. 'And it sounds as though it's what she got, with both barrels.'

'But why do it like that? She must have known it would get a bad reaction. Even Tanya said she told her not to do it. Of all the things . . .'

'She got it wrong,' Klaudia came in gently, 'she knows that now and it won't help matters if you keep going on about it.'

Having to accept that was true, Leanne sighed and waved to some neighbours from the estate who were clearly heading into town for the same reason they were.

'I'll have a talk with her later,' she said, as they turned on to the coast road. With all her heart she wished she could wrap Abby in her arms and absorb all the pain and confusion that was tormenting her, but it had been a while since Abby had even come near her. Why was she so full of hate towards her? It was as though she, Leanne, had hurt her in some deep and terrible way without knowing how or when, although it was surely tied up with losing her father. Grief made people do strange things, everyone knew that, but to have produced such a banner . . . It wasn't making any sense at all.

Maybe Kate could talk to her.

What a pity Kate wasn't here today. She'd feel so energised by the crowds closing in on the town from all directions, so proud of her grandma who was preparing to speak, and so passionate about the cause, that knowing her she'd probably get up and speak too. She was so like Wilkie, and her father, for Martin was a vocal advocate for human rights. What kept worrying Leanne was the way Abby seemed to have inherited some of Jack's bitterness, especially when it came to Leanne.

Half an hour later, having located the rest of their group, all twenty of them were at the front of the two-or-more-thousand-strong demonstration singing 'All You Need Is Love' or chanting 'Open the Doors', or 'Our Town Welcomes Refugees.' Adam was riding Blake's shoulders, and Mia was holding tight to Abby's hand, waving her banner that said, 'Suffer the Children to Come unto Me'. For her part, Abby was putting great energy behind her own banner that said, 'Our Home is Your Home,' while doing her best to avoid Leanne's eyes.

'She wants to engage,' Klaudia murmured in Leanne's ear, 'but then she doesn't.'

'It's like trying to read a foreign book,' Leanne responded, 'except that knows what it's trying to say.'

'Oi, you!'

Leanne and Klaudia turned round.

'Yeah, you.'

It was a pink- and lime-haired woman in her late forties with a rash of freckles, several rows of gold chains about her neck and a tattered leather jacket.

'You think you're superior to the rest of us,' she told them, 'talking about welcoming people in, behaving like we're morons for not understanding that they need homes. Well we do understand it, all right? But tell me this, have you counted the homeless on Kesterly's streets lately? How often do you get down to the food banks, or the refuges? I'm telling you, you want to start concerning yourselves with what's on your doorsteps before you go round getting all moral on those of us who *do* care about what's happening to the worst off in our community. And we put them first. Tell me what's wrong with that?'

'They come first for us too,' Leanne told her heatedly, 'and we know the figures, we visit the food banks and refuges. We do everything we can to help everyone in need, we just don't cut off those who are further afield and don't have a way to speak for themselves.'

'Oi, Mum, come away,' a lad in his early twenties interrupted, grabbing the woman's arm. 'You don't want to start getting into this, not here. It's not the time or the place.'

'I'm not doing no harm,' she insisted, shrugging him off. 'I'm just making my point. I want my boy here having a job before some foreigner gets it,' she told Leanne and Klaudia. 'Don't he have a right to one? He's done his studies, he should be earning by now, but no one wants to pay him a decent wage.'

'Wages are for the government to sort out,' her son insisted. 'Now come on with me. We shouldn't even be here,' and taking her more forcefully this time, he drew her into the crowd before she could say any more.

'They are just the sort of people we need to know,' Leanne told Klaudia. 'They have a point, a really good one,.and we need to debate this sensibly so that we can start understanding each other better.'

'Marvellous!' Wilkie cried from behind her. 'I'm going to use those words in my speech, because you're right. The last thing we want is to alienate our neighbours. We want to do what's right for everyone, if we can . . .'

'Wilkie! You're up next,' Richard York shouted over to her.

A local councillor had been banging on for the last five minutes about health and safety and the importance of *peaceful* demonstrations, while a small group of individuals milled around behind him.

'Ah, Richie,' Wilkie called, waving hard in the direction of someone to the side of the platform. 'That's him,' she informed Leanne, 'the new reporter. I remember his name now. He reminds me of your boy, Matt,' she told Blake. 'Yes, on my way,' she shouted to the handsome young Richie. 'Come up there with me,' she urged Leanne and Klaudia. 'Let's stand together. Three women, two generations and one cause. And our cause is . . .'

'Kindness for All,' Leanne and Klaudia chorused rousingly.

There was something so invigorating, even intoxicating about being amongst so many people whose reason for being there was the same as theirs. They could feel the energy of it propelling them all the way to the platform, where they arranged Wilkie between them and looked out on a sea of faces and banners that filled the square and many of the small streets either side.

Richard was at the mic now. 'I realise Wilkie Emmett is well known to most of you,' he was saying. 'She's been a terrific force for good in this community. She is passionate about her causes, and plenty of you have supported them down the years, but I happen to know that nothing matters more to her than the plight of the underdog, especially when it comes to children. I know she has many things to say that will inspire and touch you, and hopefully bring us all much closer together as a community. My friends, Mrs Wilkie Emmett.'

As the applause erupted, Leanne watched her small mother with her big heart, peach-fluffy hair and burning soul step forward, and felt herself sob with pride. Beside her Klaudia's eyes shone with tears. In front of her, Abby, Mia and everyone in their party leapt up and down, cheering and waving as though Wilkie might be a celebrity Second Coming.

Wilkie was at the mic, holding up her hand seemingly to calm down her fans, but Leanne knew, as did most people there, that she wouldn't even be thinking about herself at this moment, probably hadn't even engaged with how popular she was. All that mattered to her were the councillors she needed to reach today, and those in war-torn lands, or refugee camps that were desperate for help.

She gave a smile, thanked everyone twice and waited for silence to fall before taking a breath to begin.

No one saw the brick coming; the whisper of it passing overhead as silently as an arrow registered nowhere.

The first anyone knew of it was when its harsh trajectory was broken by the front of her head.

She went down so fast that even Leanne and Klaudia weren't quick enough to catch her; that fell, quite literally, to someone standing behind them.

'It was meant for that bitch next to her,' someone shouted from the crowd, but Leanne and Klaudia barely heard it. They were on their knees beside Wilkie. Her eyes were closed and blood was pooling around the gash in her forehead.

'Mum,' Leanne cried urgently. 'Mum, can you hear me?'

'Someone get a medic,' the man holding her shouted.

'I'm a doctor,' Richard called, pushing his way through.

'Grandma! Grandma!' Abby shrieked, coming after him.

'Mum!' Leanne urged again. 'Can you open your eyes?'

Wilkie's eyelids fluttered.

'Can I have some space here,' Richard said, dropping to his knees.

Leanne and Klaudia stood up and drew back inches. The stranger holding Wilkie received a signal from Richard to stay where he was, cradling Wilkie's shoulders in his arms.

Feeling someone pinching her, Leanne turned to see Abby's stricken face. 'It's OK,' she said, drawing Abby against her. 'She'll be fine.'

Wilkie's bleary eyes moved between Richard and the stranger holding her.

A couple of paramedics mounted the platform and Richard moved aside.

Klaudia murmured, 'Oh no, please tell me this isn't happening.'

Leanne turned around and to her horror she saw that bedlam had broken out at the far end of the square. People were screaming and running, banners were flying, police were moving in fast. This was supposed to be a peaceful demonstration, but something horrible was happening that involved forces she'd never seen in Kesterly before. Youths had arrived with black sun flags and swastikas painted on their jeering faces.

'Leanne,' Richard said softly in her ear. 'We're going to take your mother to hospital.'

Leanne spun round. Wilkie's eyes were fully open; her hand was reaching for her daughter's. Leanne fell to her knees and took it. 'We'll come with you,' she said, meaning her and Abby.

'Did you see him?' Wilkie asked hoarsely.

'Who?'

'Him. The man who was there.'

Leanne looked up, but the stranger had gone. 'Do you mean the man who caught you?' she asked. 'Who was he?'

Wilkie had no time to answer. The paramedics were ready to move her.

Chapter Five

Klaudia was in Leanne's kitchen, making sandwiches and drinks for everyone who'd found their way there following the attack that had brought their demo to a shambolic end. No one had wanted to go home; given the chance, they'd probably have piled into the hospital to show their support for Wilkie. However, realising this, Klaudia had been quick to suggest they head to Ash Morley to wait for some news.

It hadn't been long in coming and Wilkie was soon back amongst them, with a large padded dressing over the stitches in her forehead and her eyes as bright as if she'd just walked into a surprise party. Which, Klaudia had to concede, she had in a way, and there was no doubt at all that the best medicine for Wilkie was to be surrounded by friends.

As everyone expressed relief that she was all right, and exclaimed over and over how shocked and sickened they were to have had their demo invaded by an ultra-Right mob who'd apparently come down from the Midlands, Klaudia felt her emotions overflow as Abby gathered up Mia and Adam and took them to her room. Abby had realised this was too much for them, that they were probably more scared than Klaudia had wanted to admit, so she'd come to the rescue.

'Are you OK?' Leanne asked as she started to open some wine.

'Yes, yes of course,' Klaudia replied, smiling fondly in Wilkie's direction. She was truly loving being the centre of attention, and almost certainly hadn't a clue that the offending brick had been 'meant for that bitch next to her'. Klaudia wondered if Leanne had heard the shout. In the shock and chaos of the moment it was unlikely, but Klaudia had, and she was in no doubt that whoever it was had meant her.

She felt racked with guilt as she filled a tray with more snacks. It was terrible knowing that she was putting the people she cared most about in danger; the people who'd made her feel as though she belonged in their family, who loved her children, who included her in everything with never a thought for the fact that she was foreign. And this was how they were being repaid for their kindness. A flying brick knocking Wilkie to the ground, and that might have done so much more damage had it been another sort of weapon.

'Did you happen to see the bloke who caught Mum?' Leanne asked, lining up wine glasses ready to fill.

Klaudia frowned. 'Kind of,' she replied. 'Do you know who he was?'

'No, I haven't seen him before, and Mum doesn't seem to remember him now, so I don't know how we're going to thank him. She'd have crashed right off that platform if he hadn't been there.'

89

Wincing at the thought of it, Klaudia handed a tray to Jenny Leonard as she came to help.

'Did you recognise the man who caught Mum?' Leanne asked her.

Jenny shook her head. 'It all happened so fast I'm not sure I even knew someone had caught her. I just remember things turning ugly, so we quickly grabbed Klaudia's kids and got them out of there.'

'Thank you so much for that,' Klaudia said warmly. 'I had an awful fright when I realised I didn't know where they were. Then Bel and Harry came to get me and ... Well, thank God for friends, is all I can say.'

Giving her a fond smile, Jenny carried away the tray while Klaudia opened another bottle to help Leanne fill the glasses.

Speaking in a low voice, Leanne said, 'I suppose the police will want to talk to us at some point.'

'And the press.'

Leanne laughed. 'My mother's going to love that part of it. You know what she's like, never one to miss an opportunity to further a cause. She'll probably make it a condition of talking to them, that they speak up for refugees. Now, I'd better start passing these around.'

As she moved into the gathering, Klaudia was about to take a second tray when Richard insisted on doing it for her. She stood alone in the kitchen watching the party, and for the first time in her years at Ash Morley she felt like an outsider.

* * *

Spotting Klaudia heading for the downstairs bedroom and sensing something was wrong, Leanne was about to go after her when her mobile rang.

Seeing it was Kate she immediately clicked on.

'Mum! What the heck?' Kate cried. 'Why haven't you called me?'

'I'm sorry, darling,' Leanne replied, pressing a finger to her other ear to block the noise. 'It's been pretty crazy since it happened. Don't tell me it's made the news over there?'

'No, I was on Facebook and it came up on my feed. Grandma's been hurt and you didn't even text.'

'I'm sorry. It all happened so fast and I didn't give a thought to how it would hit social media before I had a chance to speak to you.'

'So is she all right?'

'She's fine. I promise. Three stitches in her forehead . . .'

'*Three stitches . . .*'

'It's not the end of the world, as she'd be the first to tell you. She's here now, at home. Would you like to speak to her? Actually, before you do, are you going to be around tomorrow? There's something I'd like to discuss with you.'

'Sure. I've got a couple of things on, so let's say we speak around midday my time?'

'Great,' and pushing through the throng around Wilkie, Leanne pressed the phone into her hand, shouted 'Kate,' and headed for her desk in a nook under the stairs.

'Any more news?' Bel asked, coming to join her.

Leanne was watching the screen. 'I'm not sure, but my daughter in the States just saw it on Facebook, so it appears we've gone global. Yes, here we are,' she confirmed as her newsfeed downloaded.

They watched the shaky and fast-panning footage recorded on personal smartphones showing various angles of the square, and even the smaller streets leading down to the beach. The others began gathering around them, mostly searching for their own faces in the crowd until Wilkie mounted the platform, and things on the screen and in the room grew quiet. Leanne felt her mother sneak in under her arm and held her close as the awful moments of the morning played out. The brick hitting Wilkie's head, the gasp of horror that Leanne hadn't been aware of at the time, then the voice shouting who the brick was meant for.

Leanne stopped watching the playback and looked around at the others. Whether or not they'd heard it at the time, it was clear that every one of them had heard it now.

'Where is she?' Wilkie whispered to Leanne.

'In Abby's room,' Leanne answered.

'I'll go to her.'

Klaudia looked up in surprise as Wilkie knocked, then let herself in.

'Hey Grandma,' Abby said, eyes fixed on the computer game she was playing with Mia.

'Bad head,' Adam announced from Klaudia's lap. 'Ouch!'

Wilkie had to smile. 'Ouch indeed,' she agreed.

Klaudia pressed a kiss to Adam's hair and got up from the bed. 'Are you OK?' she asked Wilkie.

Wilkie batted it away. 'Listen, I heard the shout,' she said quietly.

Klaudia frowned.

'I've just watched it on Facebook. You mustn't blame yourself for this. I know that's what's happening, because I know you, but if you do, they've won, and we can't have that.' Her face softened. 'Can we?'

For a long moment Klaudia simply looked at her, aware of the children's eyes on her as she came to realise that merely being in the same room as Wilkie could make her feel stronger, more able to cope. There was absolutely no reason to feel ashamed of who she was. It was another form of self-pity, and she was damned if some stranger full of hate and ignorance was going to push her into being someone she wasn't. She had courage, she had integrity, she also had the resilience and determination Wilkie expected of her. 'Sometimes,' she said, meeting Wilkie's steely gaze, 'I wonder why we need the *Book of the Way* when we have you.'

Wilkie broke into a smile, and reaching for Klaudia's hand she said, 'Come on, there's a party going on out there and everyone's missing you.'

It was early evening by now and everyone had gone home, satisfied that Wilkie was living to fight another day and relieved to hear that some arrests had been made earlier, though whether they included the brick-thrower hadn't been clear.

Klaudia had taken the children home a while ago,

Abby had gone over to Tanya's for an hour, and Wilkie was upstairs lying down on Leanne's bed. Leanne had coaxed her to stay at the barn tonight so she wouldn't have far to go if she didn't feel too good.

Now, with a cup of tea beside her, Leanne was going through her emails, which were mostly expressing concern for her mother, until she came across one that made her heart sink.

Eileen, Jack's mother, was rarely in touch, and when she was it was almost never with anything good to say. This message didn't prove any different.

Leanne, I've just seen the news and to my horror I caught sight of Abby in that unruly crowd. What on earth did you think you were doing taking my granddaughter to such a dangerous place? She could have been seriously injured or worse. This in itself might be bad enough, but the fact that this is how you chose to spend the anniversary of my son's death has left me cut to the heart. I can only wonder why you'd be so thoughtless and cruel. Perhaps it was foolish of me to hope that you'd respect his memory by at least encouraging my granddaughter to contact me today. A visit, I realise, would have been far too much to expect.

Eileen

Leanne's eyes closed in dismay. Well, at least she didn't accuse me of causing his death, she was thinking dismally. It was what had happened the last time they'd met, which was why Leanne hadn't bothered visiting her again.

'You did nothing to help him,' Eileen had raged. 'You knew how difficult he was finding things, but all you ever did was make them worse.'

Had Leanne not understood that Eileen was a mother grieving for her son, her response might have been different. As it was, she'd bitten down on her temper and said, 'I'm sorry you think that, Eileen, because it isn't true.'

'But you know that it is. You were never really there for him. You didn't care that his life had become intolerable . . .'

'Actually, Eileen, I did care. I cared a lot, even when he was hurting and humiliating me, threatening to leave me and take Abby with him. I knew he was in a bad place, that he wasn't thinking clearly, but loving him, trying to get through to him was never enough for him. It wasn't me he wanted, it was the fame and acclaim . . .'

'So that's how you're letting yourself off the hook?' Eileen had snapped savagely. 'I might have known. Turn it around and make it his fault, why don't you? After all, it can't possibly be yours.'

'He took his own life,' Leanne cried, 'so how can it not be his fault? It was his decision. I didn't make him do it.'

'But you could have stopped him.'

'How? I had no idea he was going to do it. It was only when I walked into . . . into his study . . .' She'd been unable to go any further; her emotions were in far too much turmoil to be able to handle any more of her mother-in-law that day. And she hadn't felt up to it since.

On the other hand, she should have at least sent a card today and persuaded Abby to call. It might have helped Eileen to know that she was being thought of on this painful anniversary, and where was the harm in that?

Opening up a screen to compose a reply, she took a sip of her tea and tried to think what to say. The fact that Eileen hadn't bothered with a Dear at the beginning of her message, or a best wishes at the end, wasn't irritating her anywhere near as much as the fact that Eileen hadn't even mentioned Wilkie. It was clearly beyond the woman to say she was sorry to hear that Wilkie had been hurt, or to ask how she was. It was all about Eileen, and how aggrieved she was feeling for offences that would never have been caused if she only made an effort to be pleasant.

Dear Eileen,

I am very sorry we haven't been in touch today. As you already know events ran away with us this morning and we're all still feeling a little shell-shocked by it. Abby has gone to spend an hour with a friend, but I will be sure to ask her to message you as soon as she comes back.

You might find it hard to believe that I've thought about Jack today, but I have, a lot, and of course I've thought about you too and how difficult it has been for you this past year. I wish I could find words of comfort, but as we know it takes a lot more than words to heal the grief of losing someone, especially in that way.

Should she really say *especially in that way*? It might come across as a barb. In Eileen's book it almost certainly would, so she took it out.

> You know you are always welcome here if you feel like a change of scene. There is plenty of room and perhaps it would be a good opportunity for Abby to get to know you better than she does now.

Deciding she had to remove the invitation too, not only because she simply wouldn't be able to tolerate it if, by some ghastly chance, Eileen accepted, but because Abby would never forgive her if it happened, she tried again.

> I know how busy you are with your job at the opticians and all your other commitments, so I hope that they in some way help to fill the gap …

She was really getting stuck now, and becoming condescending, so it was a great relief when her laptop started to beep and she saw it was Kate FaceTiming her. She could hardly click on fast enough.

'Hi my darling,' she smiled, loving the mere sight of her daughter's beautiful, lively young face and wanting to hug the screen for lack of anything else to hug. 'I thought we were speaking tomorrow.'

'We were,' Kate grinned, clearly delighted by the surprise she'd given her mother, 'but I decided, why wait?'

'I'm glad you didn't, because right now I'm in need of a Kate-fix. Is everything OK?'

'Sure. So why in need of a fix? Is Grandma OK?'

'She's asleep and Abby's gone to a friend's for an hour.'

'I keep meaning to ask, did you make an appointment to see someone at the school?'

'Actually, I did. I'm meeting her pastoral carer on Wednesday at five. She doesn't know, and I'm not sure whether or not to tell her. Any thoughts?'

Kate's tousled head, full of her mother's honey-coloured curls, tilted to one side as she considered it. 'I'd say keep it to yourself for the moment, but when you go ask the carer about the talented and gifted.' She drew quote marks around the last three words. 'Unless you already know about it.'

'No, I don't,' Leanne replied, intrigued. 'What is it?'

'As far as I can make out, some kind of elite group that Abby probably doesn't belong to. She only mentioned it once, and didn't go into any detail, but it could be worth an investigation.'

'OK. I'll be sure to bring it up when I'm there. Thank you, my darling. I don't know how we'd manage without you. So now, tell me about you and what you're doing today.'

'We'll get on to it, but first you said earlier that there was something you wanted to run past me. So, here I am, start running.'

With a smile, Leanne picked up the laptop and carried it to the fridge. She'd only had one glass earlier, so another now was perfectly fine, and considering what she wanted to discuss it deserved a little celebration, or maybe she was getting ahead of herself and what she really meant was Dutch courage.

By the time she'd finished explaining her plan Kate was clearly torn between feeling astonished, thrilled and worried. 'Mum, I think it's a totally brilliant idea and you should do it,' she declared. 'But before you do, you know you need to discuss it with Abby.'

'Of course, of course. How do you think she'll take it?'

Kate shook her head, apparently not at all sure how to answer that. 'Tell you what,' she said, 'it might be a good idea if Grandma's there too.'

'I thought the same,' Leanne confided. 'And she'll definitely be up for my plan, don't you think?'

'Of course she will. She's Wilkie, how could she not be? I'm just . . . Well, see what Abby has to say and if she doesn't go for it . . . Actually, if she doesn't what will you do?'

'I haven't worked it out yet. I guess I'll have to cross that bridge when I come to it.' She added, 'It's a year ago today that Jack died.'

Kate grimaced. 'Of course. Has Abby mentioned it?'

'Not to me, but with all that's happened . . . I had an email from Eileen.'

'Oh God, was it bad?'

'It wasn't great. I can't think how to answer it.'

'Well, I'll have to leave that one to you. Dad's just turned up. He wants to say hi.'

Leanne's smile widened as she watched Kate scoot over so Martin could share her chair. When his round, slightly ruddy and dear face filled the screen she found herself starting to laugh. 'You're looking good,' she told him.

'Not half as good as you,' he countered. 'Kate told me what happened at the rally today. Wilkie's OK, is she?'

'She's enjoying having a war wound, and before she went upstairs to lie down I heard her on the phone granting some journalist an exclusive provided he or she is pro her cause and makes it known.'

Martin's laugh had a wonderful ring. 'That's the Wilkie I know. Don't forget to send her my love. I can't imagine what she'd be up to if she was in the States right now. There are so many rallies going on she'd never have time to sleep. You know, the three of you should get yourselves over here this summer. We'd love to see you.'

'Except I'm going to be in Edinburgh,' Kate reminded him.

'Sure, but not for the whole time.'

'And I'm off to Buenos Aires after, remember?'

Leanne frowned. This was the first she'd heard of Buenos Aires.

'Well, you don't have to be around,' Martin informed his daughter. 'The world still turns without you, and Matty and I would love to see you guys,' he told Leanne.

Leanne wanted to ask about Buenos Aires but Kate was already saying, 'I'll explain everything next time we speak. It's a fantastic opportunity and I know you're going to be thrilled for me.'

'You'll love it,' Martin assured her. Then to Kate, 'Does this mean we're going off air now?'

'It does,' Kate confirmed, 'or we're going to be late. Bye Mum, love you. I'll try calling again tomorrow.'

'Bye Leanne, love you too,' Martin grinned, and before Leanne had the chance to respond they'd gone.

Feeling very glad of her glass of wine now, Leanne took a sip and tried not to be down when there was nothing to be down about. She didn't mind about Kate going to Buenos Aires. If it was going to be a great opportunity then she'd never stand in the way of it, and before that Kate was coming to the UK. As for Martin's invitation, Leanne knew that his wife, Matty, would be as sincere about it as he was, because they were like that, very easy-going, always welcoming and they never allowed themselves to get bogged down by issues that belonged to the past. And that was what she, Leanne, was, an issue that belonged to the past.

Oh for heaven's sake, she said to herself sharply, *what you're really feeling is sorry that you let Martin go, so why not be honest about it?*

It was true, she was sorry, but a lot of years had passed since the painful time of their parting, and she had to ask herself, if she could change things, would she? Maybe in some ways, but if she'd gone with him to the States Abby wouldn't have been born, and in spite of how difficult things were at the moment she would never, ever wish for that. Nor would she wish for an ocean and several time zones between her and Wilkie.

No, she was happy where she was, and glad that Kate was doing so well at IU, and Martin was such a good father, which, on today of all days, felt more important than ever. Her heart twisted with love and pain for Abby, whose father probably hadn't even stopped to think of how his suicide would impact his daughter. As far as Leanne could tell all he'd thought about then was punishing his inadequate, infuriating and useless wife.

Remembering she'd been in the process of emailing Eileen she went back to the screen, but after reading what she'd already written she realised she simply didn't have the right words to continue. What was concerning her more was the plan she'd just discussed with Kate, and how she was going to present it to Abby.

Daniel was travelling in the front seat of his social worker's car. The bag containing his stuff was in the boot, and the letter he'd started to his dad last night was in his pocket. He'd written:

Dear Dad,

As from tomorrow I'll have a different address again. Carolyn says it's somewhere in Bedford. That will make six addresses since you left one year two hundred and forty-three days ago.

I wish I didn't have to leave Trish and Lennie. They're really kind, but they don't ever take children in for long. Alice, the other foster girl I told you about, has already gone. Her social worker came for her yesterday. She said she was going back to her mum, but I don't know if that's true.

Man United won their game against Chelsea yesterday. It was a really good match. Did you see it? You said in one of your letters that you've got TV where you are, but not all the channels. When I watch football I pretend you're there too and I talk to you in my head saying things like, oh great goal or how did he let that go? I can remember you saying those things, and how you used to swear sometimes and it made me laugh.

That was as far as he'd got when Trish had brought him a letter from his dad.

Dear Dan,
Remember how I told you that I love you double now that Mum's gone? That is so big you can't even begin to imagine it. It will always be with you in ways you can't see or hear; you won't even be able to touch it, but if you stay quiet for a moment you will feel it.

Now I'm going to tell you something you won't want to hear, but I believe it'll be for the best. You have to stop writing to me, son. You must do as they say and settle into a new life, and I think that'll be easier for you if you try to let go of me.

Be strong, my boy, embrace the world that is good, and please forget the one that has done us wrong.

Dad

As Daniel remembered the words a tear rose up in his eye and dropped on to his cheek. He really, really wanted his dad, more than anything in the world, and he didn't care what anyone said, he wasn't ever going to stop writing to him.

Chapter Six

Wilkie, complete with purplish bump beneath a fresh white dressing on her forehead, was in jubilant spirits following her interview with young Richie, the *Kesterly Gazette*'s newest reporter. She'd chosen him for her exclusive because he was just starting out – Wilkie was a big fan of helping young people on their way – and because he was, he'd claimed, a strong supporter of hers, and of helping refugees.

'Can you believe that?' she cried, after waving him off and coming over to the barn for a late breakfast with Leanne and Abby. 'He knew who I was before yesterday's debacle even happened.'

So it was a debacle now, Leanne thought wryly. 'If he's good at his job,' she said, putting a mug of coffee and plate of pancakes in front of her mother, 'he'll have read up on the community, and I think it's safe to say that you've featured in the *Gazette* more than most over the years.'

Wilkie chuckled and spooned a generous amount of honey on to her plate. 'He was telling me about the plans for the paper,' she continued, glancing up as a sleepy Abby, still in pyjamas and dressing gown, padded in to join them. 'They might even take it completely online with no hard copy at all. I shall feel sorry about that, if it happens. On the other hand, I can't remember the last time we bought one.'

'Oh, that's easy,' Abby yawned, sliding into a chair and shoving her hair back from her face, 'it would have been the last time you were in it, which was, let me see, about three weeks ago during the women's march.'

Wilkie grinned. 'I think you're right. We were all in that one with our pussy hats and posters. What a day it was! One to remember. You'll be able to tell your grandchildren about it one day, Abby. You can say you took part in one of the biggest marches the world has ever known, because it was a global event, I'm sure you realise that. I feel so proud to have been a part of it, and we'll be out there again on International Women's Day, so make sure it's in your diaries.'

'Are you going to have pancakes?' Leanne asked Abby. 'Or cereal and fruit?'

'What time are we having lunch?' Abby asked, reaching for her orange juice.

'Not until late. Klaudia and the kids are joining us, but she's taken them to a fair over at Mulgrove and won't be back until fourish, so we'll probably eat around five. I've invited Rowzee Cayne to come too. Pamela and Bill have other plans.'

'Oh, lovely,' Wilkie beamed, wiping a dribble of honey from her chin. 'I shall look forward to discussing the audio version of *The Woman in White* with Rowzee.' This was one of Wilkie's favourite books;

she'd even held on to the shortening of her maiden name – Wilkinson – in honour of the author, Wilkie Collins. 'I wonder if she's finished it yet,' she continued. 'You know, book clubs are all well and good, and I enjoy mine immensely, but there's nothing like a good one-to-one with Rowzee Cayne when it comes to literature. It's very stimulating and enlightening, because I can't tell you how often she's made me see things I had no idea were there. I hope I've told her that. I shall make a note to, just in case.'

'I wish we had her as a teacher,' Abby complained, while checking her phone as a text arrived. 'She's really cool.'

'She was the best,' Leanne confirmed. 'So. Breakfast?'

After a long wait for Abby to look up from her phone, Leanne asked again.

'No, I don't want anything,' Abby answered.

Leanne was about to protest when she sensed that something in the text Abby had received had upset her. Should she ask and risk getting her head bitten off, or just leave it?

Putting her phone down with a pinched, even defiant look, Abby said, 'Grandma, I think you should let me draw a peace sign on your dressing.'

Wilkie's eyes lit up. 'What a marvellous idea,' she cried excitedly. 'And you should do it in pink. I think I shall call my new friend Richie when it's done to ask if he'd like a photo to accompany his article.'

'I bet he will,' Abby decided. 'It'll look great and send just the right message. You are still all about peace, even though some moron lobbed a brick at your head.' Her eyes suddenly rounded. 'Oh my God, I just remembered. Me and Tanya . . .'

'Tanya and I,' Wilkie corrected.

'Whatever, we were watching it back last night and did you know that someone yelled out that it was meant for the person – that's not the word they used – next to you?'

Wilkie's expression turned grave. 'Yes, we do know that and so does Klaudia. I'm afraid it's the kind of thing she has to put up with rather a lot these days.'

Abby was puzzled. 'Klaudia? I thought they meant Mum.'

Leanne gulped on her coffee.

'Why on earth would anyone want to throw a brick at Mum?' Wilkie protested.

Leanne's eyes narrowed as, unable to hide a smile, Abby began pouring honey on to her pancakes.

They were quiet for a while, only half listening to *Sunday Morning Love Songs* on the radio and the rain pattering the windows, as Leanne tried to find the right words to begin rolling out her big plan.

After setting more pancakes on the table she sat down with her coffee and found herself saying, quite casually, 'I've had an idea.'

Wilkie was immediately interested.

Abby apparently wasn't.

'I'm very excited about it,' Leanne pressed on, 'and I think, I *hope* you will be too. It'll probably mean some big changes . . .' Abby's head came up at that, and Leanne realised she was feeling anxious. Abby had

107

had enough changes this past year, she obviously wouldn't welcome any more, unless they were presented in the right way. 'What I'm saying,' she continued hastily, 'is that I think we should open our home to a child who needs one.'

Wilkie looked about to cheer, until she registered Abby's expression.

Leanne met Abby's scowl. 'To put it more clearly,' she said, 'I'm going to follow in Aunt Glory's footsteps and look into becoming a foster parent.'

'Oh right,' Abby retorted, 'because you're such a great mother?'

'Abby!' Wilkie snapped.

Abby rounded on her. 'Well you wouldn't know, because she's not *your* mother, is she? And frankly I don't think she should be inflicted on anyone else. I mean, what did they do to her?'

Wilkie wasn't impressed. 'You're being ridiculous now,' she stated in an unusually firm tone for her. 'You have a wonderful mother who loves you a lot more than you deserve at times, and if we, as a family, can give love and security to a child who doesn't have it, I for one am behind it. Aunt Glory's fostering brought a lot of joy to our lives, as well as to the children who came to her.'

Leanne watched Abby's mouth tighten as her eyes went down. She wasn't used to being scolded by Wilkie, but that wasn't the worst of it. She was so mixed up and angry and at odds with herself anyway that she didn't have a clue how to make her argument, whatever it might be.

'If you're set against it,' Leanne said gently, 'then I won't do it.'

Abby's head snapped up. 'Oh, so then I'll be to blame for some poor kid somewhere not getting a decent home when it could have had one here? Great. Just make it my fault, because everything always is,' and slamming down her napkin she stormed off to her room.

Taking a breath, Leanne looked at her mother.

Wryly, Wilkie said, 'Underneath all that I think she's not really objecting to it, but because of the place she's in right now she can't bring herself to be agreeable. Have you talked to anyone official about it yet?'

'No, but I will. I wonder if Jack's suicide might work against me.'

Wilkie shook her head. 'They're so desperate for foster carers these days that I'm sure they'll welcome you with open arms.'

Suspecting that might be true, Leanne said, 'Do you remember Wendy Fraser from my schooldays? She was a couple of years ahead of me.'

'Well, of course I know Wendy. She's pretty high up in social services these days.'

'Indeed, which is why I've made a tentative appointment to go and see her on Friday of this week. I thought, if things didn't go well with Abby and we decided to wait a while, I could always postpone until a later date.'

'Of course, but I think she'll come round. In fact I know she will, because she'll want to make a difference to a young child's life just as much as we do.'

Encouraged by her mother's support, Leanne got up to hug her. 'Thank you,' she smiled. 'And I'm sure you're right about Abby . . .'

'Oh, don't mind me,' Abby spat, coming back into the room. 'You just do whatever you want; it doesn't make any difference to me. I mean no one ever listens to what I have to say anyway.'

Leanne watched her return to the table, still in dressing gown and pyjamas, and clearly fully aware of what had been discussed in her absence. After a moment she said, 'So do you have something to say?'

'No-oooo!'

'Then shall I take it you're happy for me to start things rolling?'

'I already told you, do what you want.'

Understanding that in Abby's current frame of mind this meant she agreed, Leanne was about to speak when Abby said, 'I don't see why I'm the only one who should suffer having you as a mother.'

Leanne's eyebrows rose, but before Wilkie could step in, she said, quietly but firmly, 'I surely don't need to remind you that you have a sister.'

Abby flushed and rolled her eyes. 'Yeah, like who's totally perfect and can never do anything wrong. I suppose you've already discussed it with her? Yeah, of course you have, because you always talk to her before you talk to me about anything. It's your way of making sure she knows she matters the most.'

Leanne inwardly reeled. Her eyes went to her mother, who was looking pretty stunned herself. 'Is that what you think?' Leanne asked Abby carefully.

'That Kate matters more to me than you? Because if you do . . .'

'It's what I *know*, all right? But that's OK, I've lived with it all my life, so I'm used to it. So go right ahead and foster some stranger, then you can make them more special than me.'

With a glance at Leanne, Wilkie said, 'Abby, you're talking nonsense . . .'

'No I'm not, but I don't care. I'll be glad to have someone around here who's closer to my age. At least then I might have a friend who doesn't think I'm a waste of space.'

'Now then,' Wilkie chided, 'you know very well that no one thinks of you that way . . .'

'Yes, Mum does.'

'Listen to me,' Leanne cut in forcefully. 'I love you and Kate equally. I always have and I always will, so . . .'

Abby flared up. 'Then you've got a funny way of showing it,' she cried, 'the way you never stop going on about how perfect and brilliant she is. And she is, we all know that, and I'm not a bit like her. That's what you're always thinking. What a shame Abby can't be more like Kate. Well, FYI I'm never going to be like her, because I'm not clever like she is, or pretty, or popular . . . I'm just me, the one who's dumb and ugly and who doesn't have any friends, because *you* made us leave London,' she seethed at her mother. 'It didn't matter what I wanted. It was all about you, because it's always about you, unless it's about Kate. So, you just go on and do what you want. Bring whoever you like into the house, it makes no difference to me. I've always got Grandma. She's the only one who really loves me, *not like you*,' and off she stormed again, leaving Leanne with her head in her hands and Wilkie with puzzled dismay written all over her face.

Minutes passed.

Out of desperation, Leanne went to take Glory's *Book of the Way* from her bag and randomly opened it.

When they think that they know the answers, people are difficult to guide.

Wasn't that the truth!

She showed it to Wilkie, and turned to stare past the rain on the windows, out across the fields to the mist-shrouded golf course way in the distance. 'She's never talked about Kate like that before,' she said eventually. 'I wonder if this is something new, or if she's been bottling it up for a long time.'

Wilkie sighed. 'My guess is it's a build-up of the confusion and angst she's been suffering since she lost her father. Everything has felt wrong for her this past year, and maybe this is yet more proof that the counselling didn't work.'

Leanne considered the truth of that and felt wretched for Abby that she hadn't been blessed with a father who loved her more than himself, who always put her first and was there for her whenever she needed him. Kate had had that. So had Leanne. It seemed so unfair that Abby should be deprived of a father's devotion when she deserved it as much as any child. Instead she was now living with the devastating truth – and for her it would no doubt feel like a truth – that her father hadn't loved her enough to stay.

'I need to talk to her,' Leanne said, feeling a sudden and overpowering need to be with Abby.

'OK, I'll clear things away here and be on hand in case you need me,' Wilkie replied.

There was no sound coming from Abby's room as Leanne approached down the hall, no music or tears, no TV or angry chatter on the phone.

Fearing she'd crept out and gone to Tanya's, Leanne knocked softly and waited.

Receiving no reply, she pushed the door open and felt a fierce rush of emotion when she saw Abby lying on the bed staring at nothing. Her face was tear-stained and blotched, her hair was mussed and her eyes swollen.

Leanne wanted to go straight to her and wrap her tightly in her arms, but she wasn't sure Abby would welcome that. 'Can I come in?' she said quietly.

Abby didn't answer.

Taking the lack of a response as an invitation, Leanne went to sit next to her on the bed and gently pushed the damp hair from her face. 'You don't really believe that I love Kate more than you, do you?' she asked soothingly.

Abby's eyes remained tormented and lonely.

'If you do you couldn't be more wrong. I love you both so much that nothing in the world matters more than you, and I'm sorry if I've ever given the impression that . . .'

'It's all right, I don't care,' Abby interrupted hoarsely.

'Yes you do, and so do I . . .'

'I get that she's everything I'm not, that she's a daughter you can feel proud of . . .'

'Abby, I've always felt as proud of you as I do of Kate, but you're comparing yourself with her in the wrong way. She's older than you, way ahead in her studies and ambitions. She wasn't as sure of herself when she was your age. If you remember, she was very conflicted about what she wanted back then . . .'

'So she chose to go and live with her dad. Well lucky for her that she has one, is all I can say, especially one who cares. And what about us? Why didn't she want to stay with us? It was like we didn't matter at all. She never stopped to think about how much we were going to miss her; she just went and look at her now. She'll never come back, I hope you know that, and she couldn't care less that we're stuck here in the middle of nowhere having a crap life while she's got a dad who gives her everything, a boyfriend who's crazy about her, loads of friends . . .'

As she started to sob, Leanne folded her tenderly into her arms. 'Ssh, ssh,' she soothed gently.

'It's not fair,' Abby wailed. 'I don't have anyone . . .'

'I know you don't rate me very highly right now,' Leanne responded wryly, 'but I'm sure you don't think Grandma's no one, or Klaudia, or Tanya and the friends you've made here. You've done so well the way you've settled in . . .'

'No, I haven't. I hate it here. I hate my school, and I hate my friends and hate you for making us come.'

'But my darling, you know we didn't have a choice. The house wasn't ours any more . . .'

'But we could have sold this one and stayed in London.'

Leanne's heart tightened with the irrefutable truth of that. 'Would you really have wanted that?' she asked, knowing it was the last thing either she or Wilkie would have wanted. Which meant they'd put themselves first, and not given enough thought to what might work best for Abby. 'This was Aunt Glory's home,' she whispered, feeling the specialness of the place, all the memories and dreams that had gone into making it tugging at her as though afraid she might forget. 'You've always loved it here . . .'

'Yeah, but not to live all the time. This isn't where I grew up, it's where *you* grew up, and I'm not you. I'm not anyone any more, because I've lost my home and my friends, and I don't have anyone here . . .'

'But sweetheart, think how Tanya and the others would feel if they thought you didn't value their friendship . . .'

'They wouldn't care.'

'I'm sure they would.'

'Just stop! You think you know everything, but you don't know anything.'

'Then tell me. You know I'll do anything to make you happy.' *Just please, please don't ask me to sell this barn.*

For a long time Abby said nothing, simply lay with her head on her mother's shoulder, her crumpled pyjamas and torn tissue seeming to mirror the hopelessness inside her.

In the end, Leanne said gently, 'You know, we haven't really talked since Dad died . . .'

Abby stiffened. 'I told you before, I don't want to talk about him,' she said bitterly.

'But I think . . .'

'I said I don't want to talk about him. It won't make any difference, he's not coming back and I . . . I . . .' As more sobs engulfed her, she turned her face into Leanne's neck as if to bury herself right inside her mother's skin. 'I know you don't want him to come back anyway . . .'

'Abby . . .'

'It's true. You're glad he's gone and so is everyone else . . .'

'Oh, sweetheart, that isn't true. No one wanted him to die, especially not in the way he did . . .'

'But he did and it was horrible and I hate him for it.'

'You know he was in a very bad place. He hadn't been happy for a long time . . .'

'I can't ever tell anyone what happened to him, but they know anyway because he was *famous*.' She spat the word with such disgust that it shook her whole body. 'They think there's something wrong with me, that he did it to get away from me.'

'Oh, Abby, I promise you no one would ever think that. Has anyone ever said it?'

'No, but I know it's what they're thinking, because it's what I'd think if I were them.'

Swallowing the resentment she felt towards Jack for the trauma he'd caused his daughter, Leanne said, 'I know it's hard to think about what happened, but we need to discuss it . . .'

'No we don't. I just hope he's happy now and looking down and feeling terrible for the way he treated us.'

Leanne continued to hold her, feeling the depth of her misery as though it were her own.

Minutes ticked by as Leanne leaned back against the padded headboard and closed her eyes. Her mind was in a turmoil of troubled thoughts, her heart was aching with guilt. She was failing her daughter on so many levels, and couldn't think how to change things without disrupting their lives again by selling the barn. Even without considering what it would mean for her mother, who would certainly be devastated, the very idea of it made Leanne feel so wretched inside that she simply couldn't allow herself to consider it now.

Now was about Jack and Abby and the complex, complicated relationship they'd had that was far more responsible for Abby's despair than the move here could ever be.

'Did you know,' Abby whispered throatily, 'that it was a year ago yesterday?'

With another twist of guilt tightening her heart, Leanne said, 'Yes, I did. I'm sorry, we should have marked it . . .'

'I didn't want to. I was glad when you didn't bring it up, but now I feel bad about it and sorry for Grandma Eileen, because we didn't even call her.'

Remembering that she still needed to respond to her mother-in-law's email, Leanne said, 'That was my fault. I meant to, but with what happened to Wilkie . . .'

'She sent me a horrible message,' Abby interrupted.

Leanne tensed, hoping she hadn't heard that right.

'Grandma Eileen sent you a horrible message?' she said, feeling a dull thud in her head. 'What did it say?'

'She accused me of not caring about anyone but myself. She said Dad would be ashamed of me if he knew I wasn't even thinking of him on such a significant day, but it isn't true. I did think about him . . .'

'Listen to me,' Leanne interrupted, gathering her in closer, 'Grandma Eileen had no right to make you feel bad for not behaving in the way *she* thinks you should. You don't have to answer to her, or to anyone else about the way you feel. Your grief and the way you deal with it is between you and me, and probably Wilkie, because Wilkie and I love you far more than we love anyone else in the world, apart from Kate who we love the same. Grandma Eileen is a different sort of person, and if this is how she treats you I'm going to tell her I don't want her to be in touch with you again.'

Abby said meekly, 'So I don't need to answer her?'

'After a message like that, certainly not. I'll contact her myself and until she's ready to apologise we don't need to think about her again.'

Abby seemed to relax a little after that, and as she turned on to her back she gazed at the star-stickered ceiling for a while. 'I don't really want to leave here,' she whispered. 'I know you love it, and I do too, I just wish . . .'

Muting her relief, Leanne said, 'What do you wish?'

Abby shook her head and looked away.

Hazarding a guess, Leanne said, 'That Kate was here too?'

When Abby didn't answer Leanne realised with dismay that she might have been off the mark.

'I wish I didn't feel so useless and stupid and like everyone hates me,' Abby muttered, tearing up again.

'Sweetheart, nobody hates you and in your heart you know it.'

'No I don't, and I don't blame them, because I hate me too.'

As she turned back into her mother's arms, clearly seeking the love and comfort she knew was there, Leanne understood that an outpouring of emotion was what she needed right now, no matter how illogical her words. To try to reason with her would be a waste of time while she was still unable to face the true horror of what her father had done. What really mattered was that she never failed to understand how much her mother loved her, even if she wanted to reject it at times.

Time ticked by, with the rhythmic beat of rain on the low roof and gentle sough of the wind circling the courtyard finally lulling them into an unsteady sleep. They were exhausted by the emotions they were still finding so hard to cope with, but at least this talk was helping to strengthen the bond between them.

It was after two by the time Leanne finally opened her eyes and found Abby's face on the pillow next to her, watching her. She smiled. 'What are you thinking about?' she asked softly.

Abby did a teenage shrug.

'Do you want to talk some more?'

Abby shook her head.

Leanne continued to gaze into her troubled young eyes. Their talk might only have scratched the surface of where they needed to go, but at least they'd begun, and this short time of closeness would surely prove to Abby that she really was loved and valued in a way that it would be hard to convey in words.

'Would you like to invite Tanya for our late lunch?' Leanne suggested.

Abby's eyes went down. 'She won't want to come,' she replied.

Leanne found herself thinking back to the text that had arrived over breakfast. 'Why not?' she asked carefully.

'She's at Becky's today.'

Suspecting Abby had been left out of something she would have enjoyed, and feeling the hurt for her, Leanne said, 'Then invite them both.'

'No. It's OK. They're doing stuff, and I just want to chill out here at home. What time will Klaudia be back with Mia and Adam? I've got some new games I want to show them.'

Sensing it would be best to end it there for now, Leanne said, 'Unless I'm greatly mistaken, someone's just driven over the cattle grid, so they might already be here.'

As they sat up and gave one another a spontaneous hug, Abby said, 'By the way, if you're going to foster someone, I mean, I think it's good if you do, I'm definitely up for it, but if you do, I think I should be able to have a dog.'

Leanne gave a laugh of surprise. There hadn't been

any talk of a dog since way before her father had died, and Jack had never been keen. 'OK, I'll agree to it,' she said, 'provided you understand that I don't want you to have one because you think I'm going to duck out on you in some way.'

Abby was quick to reassure her. 'No, I don't think that. I just think that whoever he or she is, I mean the child who comes to us, might like a dog as well. They're really good at helping people to make friends.'

With love and admiration for how Abby had clearly thought this through in a very short time, Leanne said, 'Then let's do it this week. You decide what kind of dog you'd like . . .'

'A rescue,' Abby came in, without hesitation. 'We have to get one who's been badly treated and needs someone to love him. Just like the child, I guess.'

Leanne had to smile, and embracing her she was about to praise her for being so kind and insightful when she glanced out of the window and saw that it wasn't Klaudia's car that had rattled over the cattle grid after all.

'Oh my goodness,' she murmured, with a jolt of unease. 'Why are *they* here?'

Chapter Seven

The last time Leanne had received a visit from the police had been the day Jack had taken his life, so the sight of a marked car and uniformed officer getting out of it transported her straight back to the horror of that mid-January morning. However, quickly pushing those awful memories aside, she left Abby to dress, and finding herself shaking slightly went to warn her mother.

'Yes, I saw the car pulling up,' Wilkie replied cheerily. 'Isn't it lovely?' and throwing open the back door as the policeman stepped into the porch she cried, 'What a nice surprise, but what on earth are you doing here on a Sunday? Come in, come in, I've already put the kettle on.'

'We work on Sundays,' the officer informed her, removing his cap as he came into the kitchen. 'A cup of tea will be brilliant.'

Seeing it was her old friend Barry Britten, his boyish face grinning with the pleasure of seeing them, Leanne relaxed. He certainly didn't appear to be the bearer of bad news, which meant the sudden fear that something had happened to Klaudia and the children could be calmed. And Abby was here, so no harm had come to her either.

'So to what do we owe this honour?' Wilkie was asking, as she urged him to sit down on one of the bar stools.

'Well, I could say I was here to make sure you're all right,' he replied, with a nod towards Wilkie's dressing. 'Are you?'

'Never better. Abby's going to paint a peace sign on it. Don't you think that's a marvellous idea?'

'Couldn't think of a better one,' he agreed, returning the warmth of Leanne's smile. 'No, I knew it was going to take more than a brick to bring our Wilkie down.'

'But it did! She hit the deck,' Abby reminded him, coming to join them.

'I meant in the long term,' he explained.

'Do you know who the bloke was who caught her?' Abby asked, climbing on to a stool opposite his. 'We want to thank him.'

'I didn't see any of it at the time,' he replied, 'and when we came to study the footage we could get our hands on, we were focusing on the crowd to find out who bunged it.'

'I heard you'd made an arrest,' Leanne said, dropping tea bags into the pot.

'Actually, we've made a few, but it's the one concerning the bunger that I've come to talk to you about.'

'So you got him?'

'We did.'

'That's great,' Abby cried. 'What are you charging

him with? Grievous bodily harm, I hope. He'll get a nice long sentence for that.'

Barry's eyes twinkled as he looked her way. 'You're right, he would, if we could make it stick,' he replied, 'but I'm afraid it's not very straightforward, which is why I'm here. I volunteered to come and talk to you, seeing as I've known the family for so long.'

Clearly intrigued, Wilkie set a plate of biscuits in front of him and heaved herself on to the stool next to Abby's – not so easy with her short legs. 'What's the lad's name?' she asked.

As he started to answer there was a sudden commotion outside, children laughing, someone shouting, followed by running footsteps and the outer, then the inner doors banging open. Mia and Adam burst in.

'We've got a new friend,' Mia announced, her creamy cheeks flushed with cold and excitement.

'It's a girl or a boy,' Adam laughed delightedly.

Abby went to scoop him up, while Mia jumped up and down in joyful anticipation as a man's voice shouted, 'Make way, make way, Mrs Doubtfire coming through.' And a moment later a six-foot tailor's dummy, frayed around the edges and a long time unwashed, but sporting an iron foot stand and coat-hanger head, came through the door, with Blake Leonard's strong arms clasped about its middle.

'We found it at the flea market,' Mia explained. 'Mummy said it would be perfect for the shop, but our car isn't big enough.'

'Then we ran into Blake and Jenny,' Klaudia continued, sailing through the door with Jenny close behind, 'so they very kindly offered to bring it in their van. What's the police car about?'

'It's mine,' Barry replied.

'Oh, Barry, I didn't see you there. I'm sorry, we're interrupting . . .'

'Not at all,' Barry corrected, 'because you're another reason I'm here.'

'We should get out of your hair,' Jenny Leonard declared.

'No, stay and have some tea,' Wilkie insisted. 'It's almost ready.'

Leanne's eyebrows rose as she filled a second kettle and put it on the Aga to boil. In all likelihood her mother would invite everyone to join them for a Sunday roast any minute, so just as well the joint was big enough to feed a small army. The freezer could probably be relied upon to yield up more veg and a few desserts.

'Do you need any wood bringing in for the fire?' Blake offered, tugging off his gloves.

'You are an angel,' Leanne told him. 'The empty basket is in the porch, and when you're done you can light it if you like.'

'My pleasure.'

'We brought cakes from Mrs Jellow's stand,' Mia announced, going to rummage in her mother's basket.

'I chose a chocolate one,' Adam said proudly. 'And we got you a lemon one,' he told Abby, 'because that's your favourite.'

Squeezing him hard, Abby said, 'Fancy you remembering that.'

Adam's blue eyes went worriedly to his mother.

'It's all right,' Klaudia whispered. 'It's a good thing that you remembered. Abby's very pleased, aren't you?'

'It's the best present anyone's ever bought me,' Abby assured him. 'Shall we unpack them all and put them on the coffee table in front of the fire?'

'There's not a fire,' Adam pointed out.

'But there will be, because Blake's lighting it,' Mia explained, and taking Klaudia's heavy basket she dragged it across the flagstones, in between the rugs and up over a sofa arm to land it on the cushions, where Abby and Adam joined her.

'Barry was just telling us about the person who's been arrested for throwing the brick at Mum,' Leanne informed Jenny and Klaudia.

'So you got him,' Jenny declared. 'That's good. What's going to happen to him?'

Barry took the mug Leanne was passing him. 'Well, that all depends on Wilkie. You see, he's someone who's been in trouble before, so we know him quite well. The problem is, he's not all there in the upstairs department. He's a good kid really, but he's got in with a bad crowd and sometimes they use him to do their dirty work. It makes him feel important, I guess. He doesn't quite realise that what he's doing is wrong.'

Thinking of Adam and how one day that could be him, Leanne, Jenny and Klaudia turned to Wilkie, each of them knowing exactly what was coming.

'Well, I hope you're not thinking of charging him in that case,' Wilkie protested. 'If he's mentally incapacitated he can't possibly take responsibility.'

Barry smiled. 'I told the inspector that's what you'd say, but we had to be sure.'

'So is anyone going to face charges for it?' Leanne asked.

'We know who shouted out that it was meant for someone else,' he replied, glancing at Klaudia, 'but that's not a crime, so there's nothing we can do about that.'

'What were the other arrests for?' Wilkie asked.

'Various, under Section 4 of the Public Order Act. A couple will walk, others won't. What concerns us is the bunch of toerags over on the Temple Fields estate who've got themselves hooked up with some right-wing element – it might be EDL, or Britain First, we're still looking into it. On their own these wasters aren't organised enough to get a piss-up going in a brewery, but they can use the Internet and that's how this sort of call to action begins these days, as you know. They obviously heard about your demonstration and decided to come and stir up some trouble. Lucky no one was hurt – apart from you, of course, which brings me back to the kid we've got for it. Are you sure you don't want to press charges?'

'Certainly not if he's been used in such a despicable way,' Wilkie responded. 'Does he have a mother?'

She's about to offer, Leanne was thinking, putting a hand to her head.

'He does, and a father. They're good people, but he's twenty now and a big lad. He's hard to keep control of.'

Suspecting her mother was already plotting how she might help the family in some way, Leanne said, 'You mentioned you wanted to talk to Klaudia. I'm afraid this place isn't great if you want to be private . . .'

'I have no secrets,' Klaudia declared rashly.

Barry glanced towards the children. They were chattering away so eagerly and loudly with Abby that they were clearly oblivious to what was happening in the kitchen. Nevertheless, he kept his voice low as he said to Leanne, 'Just to confirm, you told Klaudia about the email you forwarded to me?'

Leanne's eyes went to Klaudia as she nodded.

Klaudia's face paled.

'It turns out,' Barry said, 'that it was sent by some tosser who lives above the Chinese takeaway on Beach Road. We've traced stuff to him before, mainly because he's too much of a dumbass – pardon my language – to know how to cover his tracks. I'm just glad for you you didn't have to see him when we went in. He's definitely not one of your more elegant species of life. In himself he's harmless; I don't think he gets out much, but the kind of stuff he spews out of that computer of his . . . Anyway, charging him's not as easy as it should be. He's falling into the category of hate incident, rather than hate crime, so there's not much we can do apart from issue a warning. One of the sergeants came down pretty hard on him while we had him in custody, so I don't think he'll be doing it again for a while.'

'What I'd like to know,' Wilkie said, going to close the door behind Blake as he came in with the wood, 'is how to stop him doing it again.'

Barry shook his head doubtfully. 'Winning hearts and minds is more your territory than mine,' he replied, 'but if you had to deal with some of the lowlife that crawls across my path, you might not feel any more optimistic than I do.'

Looking unusually downcast by that, Wilkie said, 'Well, we're not giving up trying to do the right thing, even if others might want us to. They're not in the majority, we are, so we'll definitely keep going. Are you doing something to stop these extremist bullies finding their way here?'

'That would be a bit like trying to filter scum off a sewer,' he replied, 'but everything's being done that can be, and not just at a local level, because obviously it's a national problem. As one of our DIs commented the other day, cancer starts with just a few cells going rogue, and look at the devastation it can end up causing when it spreads.'

Klaudia shivered.

Leanne felt suddenly depressed.

Collecting herself, Wilkie announced, 'OK, time for a change of subject. Who's going to stay for a Sunday roast? It's beef with goose-fat potatoes and Yorkshire pud. I hope you're not going to turn us down,' she said to Barry.

'Still on duty,' he grimaced, 'or I'd definitely take you up on it.' To Klaudia and Leanne he said, 'Any more emails like the last one, or anything at all you know isn't right, we'd like to hear about it.'

Klaudia nodded, but Leanne could tell that she was worried about the harm it might do should it be discovered that she'd gone to the police.

'Thanks for the tea,' he said, getting up. 'Sorry it

wasn't better news, but I don't think it was all bad, was it?' Before anyone could answer, his phone rang. 'Better take this. Don't worry, I'll see myself out.'

As he left Rowzee Cayne arrived, all swaddled up against the cold in her pink pussy hat and matching scarf. 'Was that Barry Britten I just saw driving off?' she asked, digging into her pocket for something. 'Ah, here it is. Wilkie, dear, you left this in my car the other day. I only spotted it this morning.'

Taking the crumpled letter she was holding out, Wilkie frowned as she tried to recognise the writing. Then, shrugging, she tore it open, and her expression turned to one of sadness.

'It's from Kylie Booth's parents,' she said, handing it to Leanne. 'I never imagined they'd thank me for the letter I sent, but they have.'

' "Dear Mrs Emmett," ' Leanne read aloud, ' "it was very thoughtful of you to take the time to be in touch with us to express your sympathy for the loss of our beloved little girl. We miss her more than words can say, and we always will, but our pain is helped a little by people like you who have the kindness in their hearts to reach out to us at this difficult time. Thank you for that. With our best wishes to you and your family, Jill and Steve Booth." '

Klaudia went to hug Wilkie as, with tears in her eyes, Wilkie said, 'No one should ever have to lose a child the way they did. There are too many bad things happening in the world. Just far too many, and I'm starting to feel afraid of what might happen next.'

*　　*　　*

130

'Come in, Daniel, and sit down.'

Mr Green was smiling, but Daniel still felt nervous as he tried to think of what he'd done wrong.

Going to close the door to his office Kevin Green, the school's sports teacher and football coach, went to perch on the edge of his desk, closer to Daniel, but not too close.

Daniel looked up at him and away again. Mr Green had chosen him for the lower school football team and yesterday he'd said that Daniel was turning into a star player. Daniel had told his dad that in a letter he'd started last night.

Gently, Kevin Green said, 'Can you tell me how you got those marks on your legs, son?'

Daniel flinched, as though the question had brought the sting of his injuries back to life.

'Did someone do that to you?' Kevin Green prompted.

Daniel lowered his head. He didn't want to tell tales, but he didn't want to stay with his foster carer either. He was afraid of him, and didn't want to be beaten again.

'I think I can guess what's happened,' Kevin Green said, 'so I'm going to contact your social worker. Is that OK with you?'

Daniel nodded. 'Can I stay with you, sir, until she comes?' he asked.

After dropping the children, including Abby, at school Klaudia headed straight for the Seafront Café to pick up a takeaway coffee. At last the rain and wind had died down, but the sky was leaden grey and the waves in the bay looked restless and forlorn.

She hurried along the promenade, dodging dog-walkers and hasty commuters until she reached Glory Days, with its romantic window displays and feeling of home.

After flipping the door sign from Closed to Open and turning on the lights to do away with the gloom, she set her coffee down on the counter and took off her coat. She knew already, thanks to a quick check on her laptop before leaving the house, that a couple of orders had come in overnight, along with a complaint from a client in America, and there were also about half a dozen requests to receive the shop's newsletter. It was amazing how many people were signed up for their bimonthly bulletin – the last time she'd checked it was almost two thousand. Their popularity, she knew, was largely due to the special offers the circulation usually contained, and since Leanne had introduced a competition to win an item of jewellery the numbers had swelled to proportions that would have made Glory beam with amazement.

Sadly, the same hadn't happened with the orders.

Everyone wanted something for nothing, or at least a great bargain, and who could blame them? Klaudia was no different. It would just help to balance their books a little better if someone would follow up their windfall of a prize or amazing bargain with an order or two. Better still would be if someone were to throw a spectacular twenties- or thirties-style wedding party in one of the local hotels, or a lavish fancy-dress do in support of some deserving charity. Actually, even the sale of a couple of original flapper dresses would help; however she wasn't holding her breath for anything expensive and unique to fly out the door any time soon.

She hadn't broached the subject of their finances with Leanne recently. Given the time of year they expected things to be slow, but with the threat of business rates rising and inflation tightening purse strings, they'd have to discuss it soon.

Luckily, Klaudia had some ideas, which she had to confess weren't entirely her own, but as they'd originated from Glory she had every confidence they'd find a home with Leanne.

Surprised to hear the door opening this early in the morning, she turned to greet the newcomer, but when she saw who it was she felt a quick beat of unease strike her heart. A solid, almost brutal-looking woman was glaring at her across the shop as if she'd like to punch her.

Managing to keep her voice steady and friendly, Klaudia forced a smile as she said, 'Can I help you?'

The woman didn't smile back; her whiskery face showed no expression as she put down the large bag she'd brought in and loosened her scarf. 'You're her what looks out for Dotty and Jolly Albert over on the estate, aren't you?' she demanded.

Klaudia's breathing was shallow as she nodded.

'Well this is for you,' the woman said, pointing to the bag, 'from everyone on Sellerton Street. We saw what happened at the weekend and we know that brick was meant for you, not the woman it knocked over. So we lot clubbed together and got this because we want you to know how grateful we are that you take the time to look out for the old folk. Not everyone would, and we're shamed that we don't do enough ourselves. We're just busy, is all, but it shouldn't be down to some foreigner to make us recognise our duty.'

Klaudia merely looked at her, unsure of where this was going.

'Don't think we have a grudge against you for anything,' the woman continued crossly. 'As far as we're concerned you're welcome here,' and turning on her heel she walked out of the door as abruptly as she'd come in.

Klaudia was so thrown by the unexpectedness of it, never mind the bizarreness, that for a moment all she could do was watch the woman disappear past the window. Then she lowered her gaze to the bag. It was an old Tesco recycler, cracked and scuffed and held together by a string bow tied around the handles. For all she knew this was some horrible prank, and as soon as she opened it something would blow up in her face. However, she couldn't just stand there looking at it, she had to do something, so steeling herself she took a pair of scissors from the drawer and went to cut the string.

When she saw what was inside – six cellophane-wrapped bunches of tulips with a card saying, *Thanks Klaudia, from residents of Sellerton Street. YOU'RE WELCOME HERE* – she felt tears fill her eyes.

Well, she was thinking as she lifted the flowers out of

the bag, it just goes to show how wrong it can be to judge someone by the way they look. Never would she have expected this touching gesture of support from the woman who'd just come in here.

Deciding to use the exquisite art deco vase they had for sale in the window, she plucked it from the display and began arranging the short-stemmed, multicoloured buds as beautifully as if they were a Valentine gift from a lover.

It was as she placed the vase on the small table beside the chaise longue that she noticed someone hovering outside the shop. His shoulders were hunched, and his hands dug deeply into the pockets of his workman's jacket.

Realising who it was, she went to the door and beckoned for Antoni to come in. It was too cold to leave him standing where he was, and he presumably had something to say to her, or he wouldn't be there.

'I thought you'd already left for Germany,' she said, closing the door behind him and hoping he wasn't in need of money. 'Are you . . .' She broke off suddenly as he turned to look at her. His face was swollen and cut, bruised, stitched and looked so painful she could feel herself wincing. 'What happened?' she cried.

'It doesn't matter,' he said, the rasping of his voice telling her that he probably had other injuries. 'I needed to see you. I want you to understand . . .' He seemed unable to get his words out in the right order. 'I made a big mistake . . . I mean, about us. I just don't know what anything's about any more. It's like . . . I can't think straight. The things that are happening . . . I've got no idea who my friends are . . . People I thought I could trust have turned against me . . .' He attempted a breath and gasped. 'I was there on Saturday when that brick hit Wilkie. I heard what was said, that it was meant for you. I couldn't let them get away with it. If that brick had hit you . . . Bad enough that it hit Wilkie . . .'

Realising what had caused his injuries, she tried to interrupt, but he stopped her.

'This isn't a good place for us any more, Klaudia. I'm definitely going to Germany and my brother's said we can stay with him until we get a place of our own, if you want to come too. He's got kids, older than yours, but he can make room for us. Listen!' he cried, as she raised her hands and backed away.

'Stop!' she protested. 'Please stop. I'm sorry this has happened to you, but getting into fights will only make things worse. I know this is a horrible time. We're being made to feel like second-class people, and we don't deserve it, because no one does. But not everyone feels that way. You've seen kindness as well as . . .'

'You're making excuses,' he shouted. 'The bleeding hearts you live with up at Ash Morley aren't typical of the general . . .'

'Yes they are! OK, I'll admit that some people have been hateful to me, but something happened before you came in, something that was special. See those flowers?'

He barely glanced at them. 'Just tell me this. Have you got your permanent residency yet?'

Klaudia could only look at him.

'Eighty-five fucking pages,' he exclaimed furiously.

'It took you a month to fill out that joke of a form, and you still haven't had the decency of a reply, much less the legal status you're looking for. And shall I tell you what, you won't get it.'

'You don't know that!'

'Yes I do. It's in the papers all the time, bankers, doctors, professors . . . people in top jobs are being told to make plans to leave every day, some have already been deported. So what makes you think it'll be any different for you? It won't count that you have British-born children, because some of them have too. And even if they end up giving you the right to stay, do you really think that's going to change the way people feel? No, it'll get worse because they'll say they haven't got their way . . .'

'Antoni,' she broke in sharply, 'I don't want to listen to any more . . .'

'I'm telling you for your own good. I care about you, Klaudia, I don't want to see people hurl bricks and abuse at you. You don't deserve that. You're a decent person, ten times more decent than those arseholes out there with swastikas on their faces whose only purpose for being alive is to stir up trouble. Go and talk to your friends at the Polish Centre, they'll tell you they feel the same. They love it here, just like you, they want to stay, but what's the point in being somewhere you're not wanted?'

How could she shut out his horrible words and make him go away? 'Please stop this, *now*,' she cried. 'Believing in the bad side of human nature is no better than running away . . .'

'It's not running away, it's starting a new life in a place where we're wanted.'

'*But I don't want to,*' she shouted over him. 'I'm staying here for as long as I can, and if in the end I'm told I have to leave . . . Well, I'll just have to cross that bridge when I get to it.'

His eyes were glittering with frustration. 'I'm trying to do my best for you,' he told her gruffly. 'I want to protect you, be with you . . .'

'That's not what you said the night you left.'

'Please, Klaudia, at least think about what I've said.'

She was shaking her head. 'Whatever happens in the future, it's over between us, Antoni. I'm not going anywhere with you, least of all Germany, and I couldn't take you back even if I wanted to, not after what you said about Adam.'

He threw out his hands in angry despair. 'I knew you'd bring that up, but you know I didn't mean it. Everything was getting to me at the time, so I couldn't see clearly. I was lashing out like a fool. Listen, I'm sorry. I swear I didn't mean to hurt you, or Adam. It's the last thing I'd want . . .'

'But you did,' she told him fiercely, 'and it made me see what I should have seen a long time ago, that it's better for us to go our separate ways. Germany is waiting for you. I hope it works out for you . . .'

'Klaudia!'

'There's no more to be said.'

'Then, as a friend, will you just let me come and stay until I go?'

As the truth of what this was really about slid

138

horribly through her, she eyed him coldly as she said, 'I'm sorry, Antoni . . .'

'Please,' he cried. 'I've got nowhere else. I slept rough last night . . .'

'Stop! Don't try to guilt-trip me. You've got friends . . .'

'They've already gone, and I need to get some money together so I can go too.'

'Then talk to Mr Chlebek at the Polish Mart on Clyde Lane. He's always looking for help, and he has rooms above the shop.'

Despite her resolve it wasn't easy watching him leave. His head was down trying to hide the injuries he'd claimed to have got for her, his shoulders hunched in a miserable, lonely defeat.

Going to pick up the phone as it rang, she put on a cheery voice as she said hello.

'Hello, dear, it's Mr Gruber here. I'm afraid I've caught a little chill or I'd have come by the shop to tell you in person how happy Mrs Gruber was with the beautiful gifts you helped me to choose for her. They made her birthday very special, you know, and she looks quite the lady in them. I told her, she could be twenty again. Now that would be enjoyable, wouldn't it?' he chuckled in his throaty way. 'If we could all be young again. God bless you and Leanne,' and without giving Klaudia a chance to respond he rang off.

As Klaudia replaced the receiver she felt so bemused she wasn't sure whether she wanted to laugh or cry. What a morning. She was almost afraid to wonder what next.

To her relief – although she'd have welcomed some customers – there were no more dramas or upsets over the next couple of hours, only a passer-by asking for directions to the station and the postman with yet more information on the rise in their business rates.

And no emails arrived from gov.uk following up on the one they'd sent acknowledging receipt of the information she'd provided regarding her trips to Poland four years ago.

'We could do with some good news around here,' she commented to Leanne when she arrived with two take-out lunches from the Seafront Café. 'I'm starting to feel as dismal as the weather.'

'Well here's something for us to feel excited about,' Leanne smiled, taking off her coat. 'I had a call from Wendy Fraser at social services about an hour ago. Because she knows me personally, and because of Aunt Glory's history of foster care, they're going to start all the checks on me now, before I even go for an interview.'

Klaudia's eyebrows rose. 'They must have a lot of children they need to place, if they're moving ahead so quickly.'

Leanne nodded agreement. 'I left Mum sorting out the bakery in the hope we can offer it to a family, should things go that way.'

Klaudia laughed. 'She's never been one to do things by half.'

Wryly, Leanne said, 'She's also sent off a letter to Kylie Booth's parents, inviting them to come and stay if they feel like a break at any time.'

Klaudia was still smiling. 'How does such a big heart fit inside such a little body?' she wanted to know.

With twinkling eyes, Leanne said, 'Dad used to tease her that one day all those good works of hers would end up getting her into trouble, and do you know what she used to say? What's the point of life if you can't make trouble?'

Chapter Eight

'Hello? Am I speaking to Leanne Delaney?'

For some reason Leanne's heart jolted as she stopped feather-dusting a jewellery case and said, 'Yes, you are. How can I help you?' It'll be a telemarketer, she quickly decided, needing a rejection fix.

'My name's Tom Franklyn,' the man informed her in a cultured voice that was neither friendly nor remote, but, she thought, intriguingly engaging. 'Your Aunt Glory and my mother, Helen, were friends.'

Helen Franklyn. Of course, Leanne remembered her, more by name than actual acquaintance. 'I didn't know your mother well,' she said, 'but my mother and I were very sad when she passed.'

'Thank you, we received your card. The words were very touching.'

Leanne was surprised. Did he really remember them? He must have received hundreds, for Helen had been very popular; was known to many as the lovely lady who lived on the hill.

'How is your mother after the incident at the march?' he asked.

Guessing he'd seen it on the news, she said, 'Much better now, thank you for asking.'

'That's good.' There was a moment's pause before he said, 'The reason for my call is to inform you that my mother didn't change her will after your aunt died, so her collection of twenties and thirties memorabilia is still bequeathed to Glory.'

Leanne couldn't think what to say to that.

He continued, 'I believe you're running the shop now, and I'm sure my mother would be very happy for her bequest to go to you. This is, of course, if you'd like to accept it. There is no obligation – I will understand . . .'

Slightly stunned, Leanne said, 'If it was meant for my aunt, then of course I'd love to accept it on her behalf, but only if you're sure there isn't someone else in your family who'd like it.'

'I'm sure,' he replied without hesitation. 'The dresses won't fit me, and as for the shoes . . .'

Leanne laughed. She might not have seen Helen's collection, but it was easily imagined as extremely flamboyant and feminine – and whatever her son might be like, he certainly didn't sound either of those.

'So how should we go about this?' he asked. 'I'm not sure you're going to want everything, some of it looks in sorry condition to me, but you're the expert, so I'm happy to take orders.'

Thinking that he didn't sound like someone who took orders – though what that particular someone did sound like she had no idea – she said, 'Perhaps I should come and take a look at it. It will save you bringing it here, and if we decide that some things ought to be let go of, we can do it right away.'

'Fantastic. I was hoping you'd say that. Do you know where the house is?'

'Of course.' Everyone in Kesterly knew Villa Tramonto, with its shimmering white walls and elegant Italianate columns. It stood at the top of the Mount, overlooking most of the town and the bay. 'I've never actually been there,' she admitted, 'but I'm guessing I wind up over Monkton Hill to the top, and then there's a private road?'

'Track would be a more accurate description,' he remarked drily. 'You should then go past the first gates on the right as they're for tradesmen – that is a joke, by the way, but I guess they once were. They're not in great shape these days, but you'll soon see a second set of gates, tall, black, with artful patches of rust and lazy hinges. Through them, along a short drive and you'll be at the front door. In case you're unsure, *Benvenuto* is carved into the stone above the porch. That's a bit of a giveaway, I reckon.'

Enjoying his humour, she said, 'Provided you speak Italian?'

'Which I don't, and nor did my mother. However, she loved all things Italian and who can blame her for that? So tell me when is convenient for you, and I'll work my day around it.'

Leanne glanced at the clock, as though it were showing her diary.

'Actually, if you're free now,' he suggested eagerly, 'I could offer you a cocktail of your choice, because even the Ritz would be hard put to beat the selection in my mother's bar. You'd never guess she was a teetotaller.'

In spite of how inviting it sounded, Leanne had to say, 'I'm afraid I have an appointment at my daughter's school in half an hour, and I'm not sure how long it will go on.'

'OK, no problem. It was just a thought. I'm getting a bit lonely up here on my own, you see, and the temptation of this cocktail bar . . . Well, let's not get into my character flaws. So when will suit you?'

'I could come tomorrow, around three?'

'Perfect. Do you have this number in case you get lost or need to reschedule?'

'Yes, it came up, thanks. I'll call if there's a problem, otherwise I'll look forward to seeing you.'

'Likewise. *À demain*, as the Italians would say if they were French.'

Laughing as she rang off, Leanne wondered if she'd just been flirting with Helen Franklyn's son, or not. It kind of felt like it and she had to admit she'd enjoyed it. However, there wasn't time to stand around thinking about it; if she didn't leave now she'd be late at the school. So going rapidly about the business of closing up the shop, she texted her mother to remind her she'd be late home, and set off to the car park, still thinking about Tom Franklyn and enjoying that as much as she had the call.

Half an hour later she was glaring at Abby's pastoral care tutor in furious disbelief. 'Let me get this straight,' she cried, trying to keep her voice calm and not succeeding, 'you have a select group of students in each year known as the talented and gifted, and it's never occurred to you that this might cause all kinds of problems for the kids who don't make the grade, mine being one of them?'

'I understand your frustration, Mrs Delaney,' Ruth Caber responded, her fair complexion flushing to a fiery pink, 'and I can see why you . . .'

'It's so divisive, so utterly elitist,' Leanne raged, 'that I can't believe you're even trying to defend it. Surely other parents must have complained before this? No one wants their child to feel excluded, or stupid, and that's exactly what this sort of madness achieves. And in case you've forgotten, my child is still trying to get over the death of her father and at the same time settle into a new school that clearly doesn't have every student's needs at heart. I want to see the head. This can't be allowed to continue. You do realise, I hope, the damage you're doing . . .'

'Mrs Delaney, if you'll please let me speak, I'm trying to tell you that I agree wholeheartedly with your objection. I don't think this programme is in any way helpful to all students, but I was outvoted when it was proposed three years ago. Of course there are those who've benefited from it, but for those who aren't considered to be at that level . . . I mean, it can be aspirational for some, but on the whole I agree, it can have a negative effect on others, so we need to work on finding a better way to reward and encourage.'

Feeling slightly embarrassed by her outburst, Leanne said stiffly, 'So what are you doing about it?'

'We're looking for parents, such as yourself, to make their objections known. So far we have over twenty families calling for an end to the scheme, but given the school's high population that still isn't enough, and our current head is quite committed to it. The fact that she's away on long-term sick leave isn't helping, but that shouldn't stop us putting our case to the acting head.'

'Who's Kenneth Sunderland, I believe?'

'That's correct.'

'Good. You can leave this with me. I'll be in touch.'

'One minute, before you go. Please remember that you'll be accused of self-interest when it becomes known that Abby isn't one of . . .'

'Of course it's self-interest. What the hell else do you expect when she's my daughter? And for your information, she was a grade A student before coming here. What she needs is a sensitive and intelligent integration into this school that would help her confidence and keep her grades up. Instead, you're cutting her off from the friends she's made by telling her that she's dumber than they are and so can't be in the top group that presumably enjoys all kinds of privileges not available to the *untalented* and *ungifted*.'

'As I said, Mrs Delaney, I'm on your side, and I would urge you to speak to Mr Sunderland in just the same way as you've spoken to me.'

'Don't worry, it'll happen. Is he in his office now?'

'I'm not sure. I can check.'

As the pastoral carer made the call, Leanne stepped outside the office and connected to her mother.

Wilkie listened quietly, saying nothing until Leanne had finished. 'OK, don't go and see him now,' she advised. 'I'll bring it up at the next governors' meeting, and by the time I'm done we'll have all the support we need.'

Finding the place empty when she got home, Leanne decided to have a little whirl around Google to see what she could find out about Tom Franklyn. However, she got no further than typing in his name before the outer door of the barn banged open and a moment later a fuming Abby crashed into the kitchen.

'What the hell were you thinking?' she raged, slamming down her schoolbag and looking as though she'd like to do the same to her mother. 'You've made me a laughing stock going in there and kicking off like that. Everyone heard you shouting. You're like a madwoman telling them how to run their school, going on about my problems and making out like I'm some kind of mental case who can't speak up for myself. Did you stop to think what'll happen if you get your way? Everyone who's in the talented and gifted will blame me for it falling apart, and I had nothing to do with it. I didn't even tell you about it because I knew you'd go off on one, but I never dreamt you'd show me up like this. I hate you; I hope you realise that. I hate you so much I can't even stand to look at you,' and grabbing her bag she tore past Leanne so furiously that she almost knocked her over.

Wincing as the bedroom door slammed shut behind her, Leanne put her hands to her head and groaned out loud. What a fool. What a ridiculous, hotheaded, menace of a mother she was. Instead of thinking things through and even discussing them with Abby, which she could see now that she should have done, she'd just fired off at Ruth Caber like some heat-seeking missile, and without giving a thought to who might be able to hear. Yes, it was a lousy scheme, she was in no doubt about that, but the last thing she wanted was Abby being blamed for its closure.

What on earth was she going to do to make this right?

Chapter Nine

The following morning Tom Franklyn texted to say he was sorry, he'd been called away unexpectedly, but would be in touch as soon as he returned.

Though Leanne knew it was ridiculous to be disappointed when she didn't even know him, it was how she felt. She even found herself spending far too much time over the next few days wondering what had called him away, and when he might be back. This was when she wasn't trying to make her peace with Abby, and a week after her disastrous intervention at the school she still wasn't having much luck with that.

However, everything else was pushed to the back of her mind when she received a call from Wendy Fraser asking if she could go into the main social services hub for a meeting.

So here she was sitting alone in a fourth-floor conference room, waiting for Wendy to join her. It was clearly the child protection area, given the toys piled up in one corner, a small rack of DVDs and plenty of books to colour or read. Leanne thought about the families that came in here, the traumas they were suffering, and felt her heart churn with pity. So many tragedies playing out as the rest of the world went about its business, stories most never got to hear about but that turned lives inside out.

Surely there were some happy stories too.

Her mobile buzzed.

Any news yet? Kx.

Still waiting, she texted back.

Moments later, *What's happening?* It was her mother.

Will let you know soonest.

Leanne turned off the phone and gazed out of the window to where the cluttered red roofs of Abby's school were glinting in the late-morning sunlight. Abby, at this moment, was sitting the religious studies exam she'd been revising for via FaceTime with Kate this past week, while making sure her mother knew she was excluded from the call. In fact, the only time Leanne had been allowed out of Coventry lately was when she and her mother – in Abby's presence – had discussed the summons from social services. Though Abby hadn't said much, she hadn't been difficult either. However, Leanne's renewed attempts to apologise for the blunder over the talented and gifted had met with a furious 'Just stay out of it from now on.'

Having already decided that would be the best course until things settled down a little, Leanne had called Ruth Caber to explain that although she fully supported the cancelling of the scheme, she couldn't allow Abby to be considered responsible for it. Ruth Caber had understood and promised to do her best to smooth things over at her end. How successful she'd

151

been, Leanne had no idea. All she did know was that she probably wasn't the right person to be sitting here right now applying to foster a child, when she was getting it so badly wrong with one she already had.

By the time Wendy came in, Leanne had all but made up her mind that she really couldn't go through with it. It simply wouldn't be fair to bring an innocent child into the combative atmosphere she and Abby were embroiled in. The poor thing had probably already suffered enough and was by now in desperate need of safety and calm. Although they'd be safe at the barn, she couldn't say the same for the calm. And actually, she really should consider the tensions in town and how they were likely to affect a newcomer. God knew it was bad enough for Klaudia, who spoke English fluently and had in every significant way integrated into the community. What would it be like for a small child who might not speak the language, had possibly lost one or maybe both parents, or who might have suffered the most awful abuse?

'Leanne,' Wendy announced with the mild aggressiveness Leanne recalled from the uppity young teenager she'd once known. Her hair was flecked with grey now, but still cut in a severe bob, and her skin remained as pallid as a winter sky.

'Wendy, how are you?' Leanne asked.

'I'm very well, thank you. I hope you are too, and your mother after her incident at the refugee march.'

'She's fine. The stitches are out, and dressing off, which she's a bit sorry about because my daughter decorated it with a peace sign.'

Wendy nodded as she sat down and opened one of the files she'd brought with her. 'Thank you for coming at this short notice,' she said. 'Has anyone offered you a coffee?'

'Yes, and I'm good, thanks,' Leanne assured her.

Wendy studied the file in front of her, apparently engrossed, until she finally looked up and regarded Leanne with her sharp grey eyes. 'The reason I asked you to come in now,' she said, 'is because we have urgent need of someone to take care of a little boy, and I thought you might be the one to do it. He's eleven, very bright I'm told, and very much in need of the right home.'

Quietly stunned by such an abrupt and unexpected start to the meeting, Leanne regarded her steadily.

'His name is Daniel,' Wendy continued, 'and he's been in care for just over a year. Unfortunately none of his placements have worked out.' Her eyes stayed glued to Leanne's as though challenging her to ask why.

'Is he violent?' Leanne asked. 'Is there a drug problem?'

'Nothing like that. In fact, considering what he's been through he's being reported as a very well-balanced boy. His mother died of cancer when he was eight and his father's in prison. I'll explain about that in a moment. Before I do I should mention, in case it influences your decision to take him, that he's black.'

Leanne started, then sat back in her chair in shock. 'What on earth kind of difference does that make?' she cried. 'If you know anything at all about my family, you must know that would never be an issue for us.'

Wendy's smile was small, but genuine. 'Yes, I do know that,' she confirmed, 'but I wanted to hear you say it. So now we know that doesn't present an obstacle, I'm going to assume that you'll pass all the usual checks and tell you a little more about him.'

Leanne waited, already certain she was going to take this boy no matter what Wendy said next.

'His father is Patrick Marks,' Wendy stated, 'the man who is serving a life sentence for the murder of five-year-old Kylie Booth.'

Leanne's breathing stopped.

'I'm afraid Daniel hasn't been well treated by a number of foster carers,' Wendy confided. 'One or two have seemed to blame him for his father's crime. I suspect that will make no sense to you; it doesn't to me either. After all, he's just a child, but there's no accounting for how people react to things. You'll remember that there was a lot of publicity around the search for Kylie until Patrick Marks was arrested. The fact that he pleaded not guilty in spite of the evidence against him, and put the parents through the distress of a trial, didn't help at all.'

Leanne wasn't sure what to say, so continued to listen.

'Daniel remains devoted to his father and believes him to be innocent,' Wendy went on. 'He'll tell you that if you ask, and it's largely this that has caused him problems with his carers.' She studied Leanne intently, seeming to expect a comment on this.

Though Leanne recalled hearing on the news that Patrick Marks was trying to appeal his sentence, her first thought was for the lonely little boy's faith in his father. It touched her deeply, but she said nothing, simply waited for Wendy to continue.

'There have also,' Wendy said, 'been incidents at school. Not many, but if the other children find out who he is they beat him up, steal his books, throw his bag in waste bins or rivers, throw stones at the windows of his foster families ... To date he's had eight different placements in half a dozen or more areas around the country.' She paused to let that sink in. 'We were contacted a few days ago by our colleagues over in Marstone, where he was originally taken into care, to ask if we could help with a placement in Kesterly. I thought of you because I know how open-minded you and your family are.'

Although Leanne's head was spinning, she quickly said, 'So where is he now?'

'He's in a temporary placement just outside Marstone. He's scheduled to leave there at the end of next week and at the moment there's nowhere else for him to go, apart from residential care which is something we're trying to avoid.'

Leanne was thinking so fast that it was becoming a blur. The end of next week was ten days away. Marstone was on the other side of the county, the only other local authority in Dean Valley and where Patrick Marks's trial had taken place. Was that significant? She had no idea. She only knew that she felt as though she was being pushed into making a decision that she should be finding easy, but for some reason wasn't.

'I realise you'll want to talk this over with your family,' Wendy stated.

Of course. That was what she needed to do next, and relieved that Wendy wasn't expecting an answer today, she got to her feet.

When they reached the lift Wendy put a slim file into her hand. 'Give this a read,' she said. 'It'll tell you more about him.'

'Whatever it says,' Leanne responded, 'I want you to know that if it were only down to me I'd say yes right away. My mother would too, but we have to consider Abby. She's fourteen and in a difficult place at the moment.'

Wendy nodded her understanding. 'Because of her father's suicide?'

Thrown, Leanne said, 'You know about that?'

'It's my job to know,' Wendy replied, pushing a button to summon the lift. 'And your husband wasn't exactly unknown.'

'And you don't think it's an issue?'

Wendy turned to her. 'Unlike the children who come into care, your daughter, whatever her difficulties, is in a stable and loving home. I know that both you and your mother have her interests very much at heart, so if you don't think there's an issue I see no point in creating one.'

Leanne wasn't sure what to say, though she realised this was proving the desperate need for carers.

'You have my number,' Wendy said as Leanne stepped into the lift. 'Any questions or clarifications you might need, just give me a call, and of course the necessary checks of you and your family will continue. I see no problem presenting itself.'

'You've got to be kidding me,' Abby murmured, clearly stunned by such an unexpected turn of events. 'He's *Patrick Marks's* son?'

Leanne nodded and looked at her mother.

'Well we can't hold that against him,' Wilkie declared, gazing at a picture of the boy from the file Leanne had brought home. As determined as she sounded, she was evidently worried.

'I know what you're thinking,' Leanne said. 'It's the invitation you sent to Kylie Booth's parents to come and stay if they want to.'

'Amongst other things,' Wilkie agreed. 'What on earth would we do if they accepted?'

Though it was an answer that made Leanne no more comfortable than her mother, she said, 'He'll have a different name.'

Wilkie's eyes flicked to hers and back to the file. They couldn't enter into that sort of deceit and they both knew it.

'There's something else we need to consider,' Klaudia put in. 'If he does become a target for hate, in the way I am . . .'

Wilkie said, 'If the boy is going to be discriminated against for things that are no fault of his, and we shall hope he isn't, no one will understand better than you, Klaudia, what he's going through. We, he, will need you.'

Klaudia smiled as she said, 'That's what I was about to say, but perhaps not in those words.'

'I think it's right for him to come here,' Abby decided, surprising Leanne, although it was likely Abby would change her mind again in a moment. 'If he turns out to be a psycho like his dad I'll just go and live with Grandma.'

There were times, Leanne was thinking, when treating her daughter like a grown-up didn't always seem wise.

Wilkie appeared not to have heard. She was reading the file on Daniel Marks again and looking graver by the second. 'It says here,' she told them, 'that one of his male carers beat him with a belt as a punishment for what his father did.'

'Oh for God's sake,' Leanne murmured. 'What is wrong with some people?'

'It seems a teacher at his school realised quite quickly what was happening,' Wilkie continued, 'so he contacted the social worker. Sadly, it doesn't look as though what he went on to was much better.'

'Surely not every one of his carers was a monster,' Klaudia protested.

'No, actually there seem to be more good than bad, but they were either temporary homes to begin with, or they couldn't put up with the attacks on them and their properties when it was found out who he was.'

They fell silent, needing to digest that before continuing.

'I never realised that the children of murderers were made to suffer for what their parents did,' Abby said.

'I don't think it's normal,' Wilkie replied. 'It's probable that social services haven't done a good enough job of hiding his identity, because you don't usually hear anything about the families of killers after they've been convicted. Not the children, anyway.'

'What happened to his mother?' Klaudia asked.

'Apparently she died of cancer about a couple of years before her husband's arrest.'

'Oh God, that's really sad,' Abby wailed.

'Does it say anything about what sort of man his father is, or was, before he was caught?' Klaudia asked. 'Was Daniel abused at home?'

Having read that part already, Leanne said, 'There's no mention of it.'

'It says here,' Wilkie continued, 'that Patrick Marks managed a hot air balloon company near Marstone, but we know that from the news. He has a degree in economics from Sheffield . . .'

'If that's true he should have had a better job,' Abby decided. 'Don't you think it's spooky that he didn't? Maybe he was playing about with balloons because they got him near children.'

'Moving on,' Leanne said purposefully. 'What we do know from the file is that Patrick Marks had no previous record of violence, actually no criminal record at all before Kylie.' She looked at her mother. 'Wasn't there something about him touching a child inappropriately at some point?' she asked.

Wilkie was searching her memory. 'I seem to remember something,' she replied, 'wasn't it back at the time of his arrest?' She looked at Klaudia.

'I think so,' Klaudia responded, 'but I don't think I heard it mentioned again after that.'

Since there was nothing about it in Daniel's file, Leanne decided to dismiss it for now. 'He and his wife were still together when she died,' she continued. 'Daniel was eight and a half at the time. There's no mention of domestic disputes, or engagement with social services, until the time of Marks's arrest when Daniel was taken into care. Actually, Wendy told me today that Daniel believes his father is innocent.'

Abby's eyes grew so round they almost popped.

Wilkie said, 'There was a trial. The evidence proved that the girl was in his car, and hasn't the request for an appeal been turned down?'

Leanne hadn't heard that, but it wouldn't be difficult to find out.

'Actually, I don't blame him for thinking his dad is innocent,' Abby suddenly piped up. 'I mean, who'd want to believe their dad was capable of something like that?'

'No one,' Klaudia concurred, 'but what we have to ask ourselves is would it be right for Daniel Marks, or whatever they're going to call him, to come here?'

Leanne looked at her mother and daughter. She knew what her answer was, but she needed to hear theirs first.

'Actually, I think there's something you're all missing,' Abby declared, 'and it's pretty important. Or I think it is.'

'Go on,' Wilkie encouraged.

'It's like totally obvious, isn't it?' Abby replied. 'We're all female and white. So why would he *want* to come to us?'

Saddened by the answer she was about to give, Leanne said, 'I don't think he gets a choice about where he goes, but I definitely think that's a good question for Wendy.' She made a note of it, knowing it was pleasing Abby, and said, 'Do we have any others?'

'How much has he interacted with children younger than him?' Abby asked importantly. To Klaudia she said, 'I'm thinking of Mia and Adam.'

Leanne frowned.

'He's going to be interacting with them too,' Abby said spikily. 'So we need to know how well he gets on with small kids. Not me, because I'm older, but Mia and Adam are . . . What's that word? Impressionable. We don't want them turning into little . . .'

'Abby,' Leanne cut in sharply.

'I'm just saying,' Abby snapped.

Wilkie said, 'You're not putting your points forward in a particularly helpful way, Abby. However, we do want to hear them, because they're as valid as everyone else's. So, do we have any more?'

For a while no one could think of any, until Klaudia said, 'How soon did you say he'll be here?'

'*If* we decide to take him,' Abby put in.

Leanne said, 'If you have an objection, Abby, you must spell it out.'

'I'm cool,' Abby insisted, arms wide. 'Just bring the son of a psycho into my home and let's carry on like everything's normal. Sounds good to me.'

Leanne dropped her head into her hands.

'I think from that,' Wilkie said, 'we know we *can't* bring him here.'

Abby flared up. 'Oh, so like everything's my fault again, which is totally what I should have expected. In case you've forgotten, I'm the one who just said we should let him come if he wants to. That we should be open-minded and not blame him for who his father is, or give him labels he doesn't deserve.'

Leanne looked at her mother. Exactly when Abby had made these points had totally escaped her, and as her dear mother was clearly wondering if she'd just developed Alzheimer's, it was left to Klaudia to say, 'Abby, you've just done an excellent job of focusing us on how we need to go forward. Thank you.'

Clearly wholeheartedly agreeing with that, Abby sat back in her chair, apparently waiting for her mother to take over again.

'OK,' Leanne said, pulling herself together, 'I think two of us should start making a list of questions for Wendy, while the other two go and take a look at the bedroom he'll be using if he comes, to work out what we should do to make it boy-friendly.'

It was with no small relief that she watched Abby go upstairs with Klaudia, already full of what they needed to do to make Daniel feel welcome – when, no longer if, he came.

Wilkie said quietly, 'Are you absolutely sure you want to do this?'

Surprised by the question, Leanne said, 'I am. Completely. Why, aren't you?'

'There's no doubt in my mind, but do you have Glory's *Book of the Way* nearby? I'll be interested to know what it offers us today.'

Going to her bag Leanne took out the small book, and feeling oddly tense, she turned to a random page. The first words she saw were, *'The further out one goes, the less one knows.'*

What?

She looked at her mother.

Wilkie looked back, then said crisply, 'Well, no one ever said it works every time. We'll just have to woman up to our decision and see what fate has in store for us.'

Chapter Ten

A week later Leanne was sitting in a window seat of the Crustacean, one of Kesterly's better eateries, with Tom Franklyn. The mainly seafood restaurant was situated close to the marina on an outcrop of rocks that seemed to tumble slow-motion into the waves. In daylight it offered front-row views of the enormous bay; when it was dark, as it was now, there were only reflections of candles that seemed to float and flicker like fallen stars in the night.

She'd spent a good part of the afternoon at the Villa Tramonto, sorting through Helen Franklyn's bequest to Glory Days. To her surprise she'd recognised Tom the instant he'd opened the door to greet her; he was the man who'd caught her mother when the brick had hit her on the day of the march. Of course she'd thanked him immediately, and asked why he'd disappeared so suddenly afterwards, but because of the way he was looking at her she couldn't remember at the moment what his answer had been. Oh, that was right, he'd reminded her that she was the one who'd left, in an ambulance with her mother.

What she was remembering with far greater clarity was Helen Franklyn's spectacular collection of exquisite vintage dresses, all original, some even haute couture. Leanne had never seen gowns so beautifully crafted, and evocative of an era that Helen herself had been too young to enjoy. They included a gold metal lace and pure silk evening gown, a genuine pearl-beaded flapper dress, and even a Mariano Fortuny black silk peplos. It turned out that they had belonged to her mother and grandmother before her, and had been carefully, lovingly preserved down the years.

Though Leanne had known right away that she couldn't possibly accept these prized family heirlooms, she'd continued to admire them, unable to make herself stop. It was like stepping into a dream, or a movie, with music playing faintly in the background and the blurred images of dancers, cigarette holders and cock-tails slipping in and out of focus. She had been aware of Tom watching her as she'd carefully caressed the almost century-old fabrics that retained shimmer and glamour in a way that seemed to keep them alive. She'd sensed his appreciation of her reaction to treasures that had meant so much to his mother, and his amusement at how surprised and even embarrassed she was to know that they'd been left to Glory – and now her.

'You do realise,' she'd said to him eventually, 'that the Mariano Fortuny alone is probably worth around ten thousand pounds?'

When he didn't reply she turned to look at him and had to smile. Though tall and lean, he was a very masculine man sitting in a small dusky-pink wing-backed chair beside his mother's open armoire, one long leg folded over the other and his head propped on one hand as he watched her. His dark eyebrows rose, and his long, elegant fingers spread in a gesture of laissez-faire, apparently as comfortable with the news as he seemed with the attraction between them that was making her, at least, slightly light-headed.

Trying not to be conscious of the fact that they were in a bedroom, she continued to inspect the tissue-wrapped shawls and gloves he'd laid out on the counterpane before she'd arrived. 'Some of these things,' she murmured, 'are so valuable that I can't even begin to guess what they might be worth. I hope you realise that I can't possibly accept them?'

'But you have to,' he insisted. 'As the main benefi-ciary of Glory's will, which I take it you are, all these things are rightfully yours.'

Puzzled, she said, 'But surely there's a woman in your family who'd want them? You can't just give them away.' Did that sound as though she was dig-ging? Even if it did, it was a fair point.

He was shaking his head. 'No women, just me and my son and they're not exactly our style. Besides, as I've just pointed out, under the terms of my mother's will they already belong to you.'

She looked at them again and felt so beguiled by their enchanting femininity that she heard herself say-ing, 'I could never sell them . . . I wouldn't want to part with a single one, but they're so fragile, and far too small for most women these days.'

'Maybe you can offer them to a museum?'

Liking the idea of that, she said, 'I'll look into it. It's possible they could raise a good sum at auction. I mean for you, not me,' she added hastily.

He smiled, and she noticed again, as she had the first time she'd seen him, how his smile transformed his otherwise rather dark and heavy features.

'Join me for dinner,' he said abruptly.

Startled, she couldn't think what to say. 'But we haven't finished here,' she protested. 'You mentioned . . .'

'The jewels. Indeed,' and he indicated a japan chest with at least a hundred tiny drawers, nestled between an elaborate cheval mirror and a tall sash window that opened on to a private balcony. 'It's full,' he informed her, 'and could take days to go through. Most of it's paste, I'm told, but the lawyers think it should be carefully scrutinised in case something of value has found its way into one of the hidden compartments. It will still be yours, of course, but for insurance purposes I think it would be wise for you to be sure about what's there. So, are you free? I'm very hopeful you'll say yes, because I've already reserved a table at the Crustacean.'

Startled again, she took a quick decision not to make herself look foolish by accusing him of being presumptuous, or claiming not to be free when of course she was, but succeeded another way by saying, 'It's not even five o'clock.'

'As that's sounding like a yes, can I suggest I pick you up from Ash Morley at seven?'

Feeling both railroaded and swept off her feet, she

said, 'Why don't I meet you at the restaurant? It'll save you driving all the way out to our neck of the woods.'

'I wouldn't mind in the least, but if you'd feel more comfortable meeting in town, shall we say seven thirty?'

And now here they were, toasting one another with flutes of champagne and looking, she suspected, blissfully romantic in the soft glow of candlelight that was reflected in the window, and the glasses and even their eyes.

'This used to be my father's restaurant,' she told him after they'd taken a first sip of the Roederer.

Clearly surprised, he said, 'Tell me more.'

'Well, I'm talking a long time ago. It was called the Moonstone then, named after the Wilkie Collins novel that was one of my mother's favourites. I think it still is, but she can be fickle.'

He smiled. 'It's a wonderful name for a restaurant,' he decided. 'It must have been before my mother bought the house here, because I only remember it as the Oyster Catcher and then the Crustacean.'

'Yes, he sold it after my uncle, his brother, died in an accident. I think he lost heart for a while, but then he opened another place on the promenade, the Owl and the Pussycat after my favourite poem. Next came the Pea Green Boat which is now Joe's Diner in the old town.'

'And the Owl and the Pussycat?'

'Has been absorbed into the Royal Hotel. However, there's an Edward Lear lounge where the restaurant used to be, with various owl and pussycat prints and

168

paintings hanging on the walls. My mother loves that room, but it almost always makes her cry.'

He smiled again and she felt herself responding to it warmly. She was finding him so easy to be with, and so attentive in the way he listened, that she could believe he might be enjoying the evening as much as she was.

'How is your mother?' he asked. 'I mean apart from the bump on her head.'

'It's going down,' she assured him, 'and right now she's in Calais helping to feed the refugees that have started to gather again since the camps were cleared. If you know my mother at all, that won't surprise you.'

His eyes twinkled as he said, 'I don't know her well. We've probably only met once or twice, but I've heard a lot about her. My mother used to refer to her as truly remarkable and adorably crazy.'

Leanne laughed. 'That sums her up rather well. She's stopping in London on the way back,' she continued, 'to join a protest against NHS cuts. This is her last hurrah for a while, as she puts it, because she wants to be around to welcome the new member of our family.'

He was clearly intrigued.

'I'm becoming a foster parent for the first time,' she explained, a pang of nerves, pride and excitement catching her insides. 'We have a young boy coming to us who's been finding it difficult to settle since he was taken into care.'

His head tilted to one side as he regarded her carefully. 'Didn't Glory used to foster?' he asked.

Surprised and pleased that he knew that about her

aunt, she nodded. 'So you could say I'm following a family tradition.'

'It's a good tradition. I salute you for stepping up to it, and I feel glad for the boy that he's going to join such a fine family. Sorry, did that sound pompous?'

She laughed. 'Not at all. It just sounded . . . kind.'

'Now that's something he'll want a lot of, kindness, if he's been bumping around the care system for a while. What do you know about him?'

She hesitated as she wondered what to reveal.

Deciding to trust him with the truth, while hoping she wouldn't regret it, she confided it carefully and watchfully, wanting to gauge his reaction to her taking in the son of a convicted child-killer. It wasn't easy to read; however, his words were reassuring when he said, 'I must admit I don't know anything about the case. I spend so much time out of the country that I miss a lot of the domestic news. I think it's wonderful that you're prepared to take him in. I hope it works out for you all.'

'Thank you.' Leanne felt a sense of relief as her tension ebbed away. It probably shouldn't matter what he thought, but she knew that if he'd shown any sign of prejudice or judgement against an innocent boy, their new friendship would have been at an end.

They looked up as a waiter came to describe the specials and ask if they'd like more champagne.

'Would you?' Tom asked. 'Or perhaps you'd like to go on to wine?'

As Klaudia had dropped her here she was intending to take a taxi home, so she said, 'Wine?'

After asking the waiter to bring the list, Tom said, 'Do you prefer red or white? I know, it'll depend on what we're eating. Shall we choose?'

Deciding that to ask him to choose for her might create more confusion than romance, she felt quite pleased when he asked if she'd like to share a hot seafood platter. She'd had it here before and it was one of her favourites; she just needed to make sure she didn't get carried away and end up devouring more than her share.

'So tell me more about you,' she prompted, after they'd placed their orders. 'You said you spend a lot of time out of the country.'

'I do, which is both good and bad. Good in that I usually enjoy my work, bad in that I didn't get to see enough of my mother before she died, and still don't of my son. It was easier when Helen was dividing her time between London and Kesterly, because I usually stayed with her when I was in London, but after she moved here permanently there wasn't always the time to visit.'

'Did your son move here with her?' Leanne asked, puzzled because she couldn't remember Glory ever mentioning it.

'No, he was at school in Somerset, so not far away, but he did come for the holidays when his mother felt she could spare him.'

Understanding from that that he and his wife had separated, she glided past the happy rush inside and said, 'Where is your son now?'

Apparently amused, he said, 'Actually, you've met him. Or your mother has. Richie Franklyn.'

Leanne blinked in surprise. 'You mean the young reporter who interviewed her at the demo?'

He nodded.

'Of course. I should have made the connection when I realised his name was Franklyn. I wonder if she did.'

'It's not such an unusual name, so maybe not. I hope she was pleased with the way he told her story.'

'She was delighted. She was already a fan even before that; now she can't get enough of what he writes. Actually, he's gone to Calais with her and her merry band of activists so he can write about them, but I'm sure you know that.'

'I didn't, and I've been wondering where he was since I got back.'

'Does he live at the villa with you?'

'No, he has a studio flat in town, and I don't actually live at the villa myself. I'm just staying while I sort things out.'

Hoping her disappointment at the sound of impermanence didn't show, she said, 'So where do you usually live?'

'I have a base in London, just a pied-à-terre in St James's. The rest of the time, which is most of the time, I am to be found in various other parts of the world.'

'Doing what, exactly?'

His eyes were narrowed and dancing. 'I work for the government,' he told her.

Since that could mean almost anything, she ventured, 'At an embassy?'

'Yes, at embassies mostly.'

Teasing him, 'So you're an ambassador.'

He laughed. 'Try a little further down the food chain.'

He's a spy, she guessed immediately, and almost smiled at the thrill it would give Wilkie if it were true. She had to admit she might be quite excited by it too, if she believed it. 'I'm not sure of embassy hierarchy,' she confessed. 'Would you be a chargé d'affaires?'

'My title,' he said wryly, 'though it's not much used, is commercial attaché, which means I focus on promoting the economic interests of our country abroad.'

He's definitely a spy, she decided, and this was his cover. More likely he was one of the thousands of negotiators out there trying to keep Britain on the world stage. 'So where are you currently based?' she asked.

'I've been in Baghdad for the past two years, but the posting is coming to an end, at least for me, which is how I'm able to spend some time sorting out my mother's estate.'

Baghdad. Definitely a spy.

As the waiter arrived with the wine, Leanne waited until Tom had approved it before saying, 'Have you decided what you're going to do with the villa?'

'Mm, I've been thinking a lot about that,' he replied, staring down at his glass. 'I'm not sure I want to sell, but it needs a lot of work. I don't suppose you know anyone who might be interested in renovating it?'

Though unprepared for the question, she had no problem answering. 'There's a good friend of mine, Isabella Beck, we call her Bel. She's a very successful property developer, but,' she grimaced, 'she's about to have a baby so I'm not sure it's a great time for her. However, there's Graeme Ogilvy ... Yes, definitely,

Graeme. He owns the antique shop in the Inner Court-yard close to Glory Days, but he branched out into property development a couple of years ago and he's had some quite interesting projects. His partner in that particular field, also in life, is Andee Lawrence who you might know? She used to be a detective here in Kesterly?'

He shook his head. 'The name doesn't ring a bell.'

'People still call on her to help with cases the police have given up on,' she told him, 'but she's trying to establish herself as an interior designer. She and Graeme are away at the moment, I forget where, but I'm sure they'd love to take a look at the villa if you're still here when they get back.'

'Let's make it happen,' he declared, signalling the waiter to refill their glasses. 'Now, tell me more about young Daniel Marks. When is he coming to join you?'

Experiencing a pleasing surge of anticipation, she said, 'Next Friday afternoon, provided all the clear-ances have come through by then, and his name will be Daniel Davis. Apparently he doesn't like having to keep changing it, but the authorities insist that he does for his own safety. Much good it's done him so far, because someone always seems to find out – and now I'm worried because my daughter, Abby, knows who he is and I'm not sure she'll be able to keep it to herself.'

'How old is she?'

'Fourteen, going on forty today, ten tomorrow. We all agreed I had to tell her, especially my older daughter, Kate, who's in the US. As she said, think how much worse it would be if it does come out and she didn't know.'

'I agree with Kate,' he replied, 'but I understand your concerns. Does the lad have any contact with his father?'

'Only written, apparently. I'm told I won't have to take him for visits.'

'Does he go? With a social worker?'

'I don't think so. The decision seems to have been that it would be best for him to have no contact with his father.'

'Apart from writing?'

'Indeed.'

He frowned thoughtfully. 'Have you considered what you'd do if he asked you to take him to the prison?'

Her eyes fell to her wine, as the confusion she felt about that sobered her for a moment. 'I have, and I'm not sure how to answer. I mean the man is his father and from what I'm told Daniel is still very attached to him, but how I'd feel, coming face to face with a child-killer . . .' She shivered. 'I guess I'll just have to cross that bridge when, if, I get to it.' She took a sip of wine and decided to move to a different part of the subject. 'Abby, my youngest, is concerned about us all being female at Ash Morley, apart from six-year-old Adam, our neighbour's son, but luckily several male friends have already volunteered to try and step into that breech. Hopefully it'll make us seem like a bigger family for the lad to feel a part of.'

Apparently liking the sound of that, he said, 'I'm

sure I can speak for Richie when I say he'll be willing to lend his support. Me too, when I'm around.'

Moved and thrilled by the offer, Leanne raised her glass and touched it to his. 'Thank you,' she murmured, 'I'm sure Daniel would love that, and so would I.'

As their eyes held she felt an unsteady heat rising inside her, making her far headier than the wine she'd drunk. *You need to pull back from this,* a small voice was warning her, and yet right now she couldn't think of a good reason to try. It had been so long since she'd even flirted with a man that she'd all but forgotten just how liberating and joyous it could be. However, Jack had been a master flirt when she'd first met him so she mustn't forget just how unreliable her judgement had proved when it came to men.

They were the last to leave the restaurant, and as they walked outside into the icy, moonlit night, she was as afraid he might ask her to go home with him, as she was hoping he would. She had no idea what she'd say if he did; perhaps there would be no need for words. He'd just open his car door for her to get in, and they'd drive silently, expectantly to Villa Tramonto . . .

'I've enjoyed this evening,' he said quietly, turning to her.

'Me too,' she smiled. 'Thank you.'

'We'll do it again?'

'I'd like that.'

After gazing for a moment into her eyes, he signalled for a waiting taxi to come forward. 'I'll take the next one,' he said, 'and come back for my car in the morning.'

Deciding she actually liked him more for not trying to take their friendship further at this stage, which in its own way was worrying on more levels than she could even get her head round right now, she got into the cab and managed not to blow him a kiss as it drove off.

By the time she got to Ash Morley she was in such need of some grounding that she almost cheered to see Klaudia's lights still on. Quickly paying her fare, she ran across the courtyard to the stables.

'I feel like I've stepped into a fairy tale,' she gushed, as Klaudia demanded to know everything. 'He's so . . . *perfect*, which is scary, because no one is, we know that, but there's something about him . . . No, don't listen to me. I'm not to be trusted where men are concerned, history has taught me that. But honestly, I've only known him a day yet it feels like for ever. You know, I think he might be a spy.'

Klaudia burst out laughing. 'Are you serious?'

'I've no idea.'

'I can't wait to see what your mother thinks of that.'

Doing a convincing imitation of Wilkie, Leanne said, 'Oh, how marvellous. I wonder if he drives speedboats and jumps out of planes and blows up the bad guys.'

Still laughing, Klaudia took out two mugs and reached for the tea bags. 'Unless you'd prefer wine?' she offered.

'Honestly, I've had enough tonight. I'm on such a high I can't imagine how I'm going to sleep as it is. I wonder how he's feeling right now. Is he at home having a nightcap, thinking about me?'

'I have no doubt of it,' Klaudia assured her.

Giving a sigh of contentment, Leanne stretched out her arms and stifled a yawn. 'The timing of this isn't great,' she murmured, 'whatever *this* is. I need to be completely focused on Daniel when he comes, and I will be, I'm not at all worried about that . . . Actually, Tom said he'd like to play a role in the boy's life too, which would be wonderful, wouldn't it?'

Surprised, but starting to sound cautious, Klaudia said, 'I guess so.'

Tuning into the doubtful note in Klaudia's words, Leanne said, 'Are you all right?'

'Yes, yes of course, I'm fine.'

'No you're not. You think I'm getting too carried away . . . OK, I understand that. We know I'm starved of affection, male attention, sex even, and so I'm building things . . .'

'No, honestly, it has nothing to do with that.'

Leanne stopped and looked at her. 'Then what?' she demanded. 'Has something happened? Oh God, you've heard back from gov.uk,' she cried, already dreading the negative reply that would separate them.

Klaudia put the tea mugs on the table and suddenly started to cry. 'I am just being stupid, I know it,' she sobbed, 'but with some people being so kind, obviously you and your mother, and seeing you happy . . . I love you all so much. I really don't know what I'll do or where we'll go if we have to leave.'

'It's not going to happen,' Leanne told her fiercely. 'They'll work it out, I swear. Even if we have to lie down in front of the Prime Minister's car, or hurl flour bombs at MPs, we'll make them do the right thing. Remember that! We have the power, because we are the people . . .'

'But you're only half of the people. The other half . . .'

'No, we're far bigger than that! Believe me. Most people are kind and compassionate. They don't want to do harm to anyone, and they know we can't manage without all the lovely people like you who make our lives so much better. And we, as a family, absolutely cannot manage without you. So take it from me, you're here to stay.'

It was official. Leanne now knew that she was the worst, most neglectful mother in the world. Abby didn't have to tell her that any more, she was showing her instead. Three days ago Abby had come home with Wilkie and Richie carrying the cutest and sprightliest little champagne-coloured mutt to his new life.

'I knew you'd forget,' Abby informed her as Leanne gathered the ecstatic creature up in her arms, 'so I went to the refuge and took matters into my own hands.'

'With some help,' Leanne added with a sidelong glance at her mother and Richie, whom she'd only just laid eyes on since their return from Calais and London. Though Richie wasn't quite as tall or muscular as his father, there was a strong resemblance in looks. If this applied to his character she could hardly say, since she really didn't know either of them.

'We're calling him Juno,' Abby chattered on as Leanne was treated to a vigorous licking. 'We got a male because we thought Daniel might like that better, with us all being girls, but anyway, like Grandma said, Juno was sitting there waiting for us to come and rescue him. We could tell right away. He went wild when he saw us. He was so cute, well you can see. He's about nine months old, according to the vet, and he's got nothing wrong with him that anyone could find.'

'So what was he doing in the refuge?' Leanne asked, laughing as Juno tried to climb round her neck.

'He was abandoned on the moor,' Wilkie replied in her capacity as part-time carer at the animal refuge, 'and a couple of tourists brought him in. He had no collar, no microchip, no anything to tell us where he came from, and a dog matching his description hasn't been reported missing.'

'But here he is now,' Abby gushed delightedly, 'and he's ours.'

'Before you ask,' Richie piped up, 'we're told he's probably a cross between a lurcher and a poodle . . .'

'Making him a lurchoodle,' Abby giggled, 'or a poocher.'

'He's also perfectly house-trained,' Richie continued, 'and doesn't have worms or fleas, but obviously we haven't had time to test the house-trained bit yet.' He laughed as Juno sprang into his arms and treated him to a hilarious little howl that Abby instantly decided was Juno's howl of love.

It turned out that they'd shopped for everything on the way home with the dog: a blue and white striped lead with matching collar, plenty of food, a box full of toys and a bed that Abby was happy to have in her room, unless Daniel decided he'd like to have it in his, in which case they'd share. Then Mia and Adam came home with Klaudia, and to both children's breathless delight Juno sang out his little howl of joy all over again.

The puppy was so adorable that it didn't take Leanne long to wonder how they'd ever got along without him. He brought a smile to everyone's faces no matter what mood they were in, and he was clearly so happy to be there that Leanne didn't even want to think about how frightened he must have been up there all alone on the moor before the tourists had found him.

Their only problem turned out to be deciding who should have him during the day while everyone was at work or school. Wilkie was extremely keen for him to be with her, but so too were Leanne and Klaudia if they were at the shop. Richie was up for having him too, so the exuberant little dog was never short of company, and never had Leanne known herself, or the others, so eager to go for walks. The only person not taking part in the settling-in of Juno and preparation for Daniel to join their lives was Tom, who'd been called away the day after the dinner at the Crustacean. Neither Leanne nor Richie were clear about when he might return.

'This is so him,' Richie stated one evening as they all sat down at Wilkie's table for a delicious home-made shepherd's pie. 'It's what drove my mother mad. She never knew where he was or when we might next see him. He goes days without being in touch, sometimes weeks.' He shrugged. 'I've got used to it. I mean, it didn't make much difference to me when I was at school and uni, and the way I see it, he's a grown-up. As long as he doesn't go round making an arse of himself I'm prepared to cut him the slack.'

As everyone laughed, Klaudia said, 'So where is your mother now?'

'Oh, she's back in Argentina,' he replied airily, while serving himself a sizeable portion of pie.

Leanne wondered if he knew that she and his father had had dinner, or that she was inheriting his grandmother's twenties collection. If so, he appeared not to be engaging with it, and there was nothing she could read into that. She knew very well that young people were all about themselves, and their parents, while loved and appreciated on many levels, mattered not at all on others.

'Is that where she's from?' Abby was asking, clearly thinking Argentina exotic – as did Leanne.

'It's in South America,' Mia whispered to her mother.

Klaudia smiled and pressed a kiss to Mia's head.

'Yep, she's Argentinian through and through,' Richie told them. 'She got married again last year. Her new husband seems a cool enough bloke.'

'You've met him?' Wilkie asked, passing Abby a bowl of minted peas, and clearly trying to appear as uninquisitive as said peas.

Leanne could only feel grateful that Tom wasn't here, because she felt sure he'd see through it all.

'Just at the wedding,' Richie said. 'I haven't seen them since.'

'My sister, Kate,' Abby piped up, 'is supposed to be going to Argentina this summer.'

Richie made a show of interest, but Leanne could tell that he was only being polite, so rescuing him from having to hear about the plans of someone he didn't know for the next half an hour, she said, 'Tell us what brought you to Kesterly? I know your grandmother was here . . .'

'Actually, that had nothing to do with it,' he answered. 'There was a job going on the *Gazette*. Pure and simple. When I came for interview they told me the sort of changes they were planning and I thought it would be cool to get involved with them, you know, taking it digital and trying to build a bigger profile.'

'So is it a stepping stone,' Wilkie asked, 'or do you see yourself staying in Kesterly?'

'No, I want to go to London or New York. This is just to get some experience behind me, being fresh out of uni and all. There are all kinds of opportunities with online news media these days, but the competition's huge.'

'So what do you think of Kesterly so far?' Abby asked, slipping Juno a nugget of meat.

'Yeah, it's good. I'm learning a lot, especially hanging out with you guys. You're kind of *on it* in a way that's giving me lots of insights and contacts in useful places. Dad told me it would be a great gig for starting out, not that I always listen to him, but I guess he's been around a bit.'

'What does he do?' Abby asked eagerly, and Leanne could have kissed her.

Richie shrugged and picked up his beer. 'Something for the government,' he said. 'He never goes into it much, but it's something to do with trade. My mother used to say, who knows who your father is, because I certainly don't.'

As Leanne and Klaudia exchanged glances that said *spy*, Adam announced, 'I'm Spiderman.'

Richie's eyes widened in amazement. 'You know, I thought you were,' he whispered, 'because you're definitely a superhero type, and it's really cool that you're Spiderman.'

Adam beamed.

'He's just got a Spiderman outfit,' Mia explained.

'Will you show us, after tea?' Abby encouraged.

Adam nodded eagerly. 'It's in my bedroom. Can Juno come too?'

Eventually the youngsters trundled off to the stables, leaving Leanne and Klaudia clearing up while Wilkie went through the paperwork Leanne had been given by social services earlier in the day.

'It's not telling us much that we don't already know,' Leanne informed her. 'Just who our contact will be . . .'

'Not Wendy?' Wilkie asked.

'She's too elevated these days. There's a social worker from Kesterly assigned to his case, but as far as I can make out the one in Marstone oversees it, except she's just gone on sick leave, so they have to appoint someone else.'

'Do we know the Kesterly person?'

'Her name's Safiyo Dyer, but apparently we should call her Saffy. Wendy spoke very highly of her.'

'I don't recognise the name,' Wilkie stated, still

browsing through the papers. 'Do we know if Daniel has met her yet?'

'We don't, but obviously he will, because she's going to bring him here.'

Klaudia said, 'Speaking as someone who knows what it's like to be a part of your family, I can tell you – and I will tell him when I get the chance – that he is a very lucky boy.'

Going to hug her, Leanne whispered, 'Listen, if all else fails with the residency permit, I have a plan, so please don't worry, and don't be sad.'

'. . . we can only do our best,' Wilkie was saying, 'and Richie's doing a great job advising us on how to turn the spare room into a boy's own empire.'

It was true, for only this evening Richie had turned up with a couple of sailboat prints and an old oar for the walls that Blake Leonard had painted sky blue at the weekend. Last night Richie and Blake had hung a 3D solar system from the ceiling, while Abby had randomly stencilled lobsters and anchors and starfish over the wardrobe doors. They were being careful not to overdo it, for they didn't know yet what sort of things interested Daniel, but as they lived near the coast the nautical theme seemed a reasonable place to start.

Over the next couple of days Leanne shopped for what she hoped would be suitable bedding (plain navy – OK, clichéd but she wasn't about to try and make a PC statement right now), along with a football and a kite, a fishing rod and scarf and a bobble hat. She went to the school to discuss assimilation with his new form teacher and was told that reports from his previous school had been requested but not yet received.

'I've already chased it,' Mrs Johnson assured her, 'because without it we won't know exactly where to place him. Is he an A or D grade student? What are his favourite subjects, what sports does he like, if any? But don't worry, we'll get it sorted and do our best to see that he settles in well.'

'Who knows about his background?' Leanne asked warily.

'Only those who need to. Me, the head, and Mrs Bradley who teaches English and is our liaison with social services. She'd have been here today, but one of her children is sick so she had to go home. Have you met her before?'

Leanne shook her head. 'How many foster children do you currently have at the school?'

'I don't know the exact number, but probably six or seven. They're mostly in years eight and nine. Being younger, Daniel will join us in year seven. You have a daughter in year nine, is that correct?'

'Year ten. Abby Delaney.'

Mrs Johnson smiled. 'I haven't come across her, but I know she's fairly new to the school herself, so I hope she's settling in well?'

Suspecting Mrs Johnson knew more about the family than she was voicing, which probably included Leanne's outburst over the talented and gifted, Leanne simply smiled. She still felt so opposed to that madness that she might have brought it up again, were it not for fear of Abby's wrath. Besides, fighting Abby's battles clearly needed far more sensitive handling than she'd managed so far, and for the moment Daniel's integration was the priority.

Later in the day she dropped in at the health centre to register him with a doctor and to pick up a prescription for Wilkie. Then she drove on to the dentist to set up an appointment for Daniel, since no one seemed to know when he'd last had a check-up.

By Thursday evening everything was as ready as she could make it, with the bed made in the guest room, now Daniel's, fresh curtains hanging at the window and a small TV on the desk-cum-chest. Next to the TV was a colourful pile of envelopes containing cards delivered by many of her friends over the past few days. Abby, Mia and Adam had made a 'Welcome Daniel' sign that was now strung from the stair rail to one of the beams, and Wilkie had taken an Amazon delivery that day of a wooden plaque bearing Daniel's name to hang on his door. And it didn't end there, for Richie had popped by earlier with a poster to go over Daniel's bed saying 'Wake Up and Be Awesome' and Klaudia had brought over an iTunes voucher for him to download ten pounds' worth of his favourite music.

'We don't know yet if he has an iPod or anything like it,' Leanne was telling Kate on FaceTime after everyone had gone to bed, 'but if he doesn't we'll get him one.'

'He's going to be so happy with you,' Kate declared. 'I bet no one's looked after him this well since . . . Well, since his little life fell apart.'

The thought of that touched Leanne's heart. Forget

about the boy's father, just think of how much he must miss his mother, she reminded herself. 'I wonder how he's feeling tonight,' she murmured. 'I expect he's really nervous about being moved on to yet another home.'

'Probably,' Kate agreed. 'Question for me is, how are _you_ feeling?'

Leanne took a moment to think. 'Nervous too,' she admitted, 'but ready to do it.'

Kate smiled. 'The only thing that concerns me,' she said, 'is how attached you might become to him. It won't be easy if they decide to move him on.'

'I don't think they do that unless it's not working out, but I'm prepared for there to be difficulties. There are almost bound to be, given what he's been through. We aren't the types to give up on him easily, though.'

'That's true, but if it starts to negatively impact Abby . . .'

'We'll deal with it _if_ it happens, but right now it seems to be having the opposite effect, so let's try to look on the bright side.'

'Of course. Sorry. I'm just feeling a bit protective, I guess.'

Since that suggested Daniel might take after his father, Leanne simply stared at her daughter, letting her expression convey her disapproval.

Understanding she'd gone too far, Kate returned the stare until her eyes started to twinkle with a change of subject. 'OK, so I want to know about this date you went on last week,' she demanded.

Leanne gave a cry of surprise. 'You've obviously been talking to Grandma, and it wasn't a date.'

'So what was it?'

'A meal, with a friend. Actually, I can't even call him that, because I don't really know him.'

'So when are you seeing him again?'

'I've no idea. It's not something I've even thought about.'

'I don't believe you.'

Leanne laughed. 'There's a lot else going on around here, remember? And the last thing I need is a complicated relationship with a man who . . .'

'Why complicated?'

'Because from what I hear that's how it is with him. Anyway, I don't want a relationship, full stop.'

'So you're going to let the bad experience with Jack put you off ever getting involved again? Doesn't sound much of a plan.'

'I hadn't actually thought of it that way, but you could be right. I'm not keen on trusting my judgement after that, and anyway, I'm perfectly happy here with Mum and Klaudia. Now, tell me about you and what's new in your world.'

'Same old. Dad reckons you should meet someone else . . .'

'I don't care what your father thinks. It's my life. I'll live it the way I choose, thank you very much. So, back to you? What's happening in your love life?'

Kate sighed dreamily. 'Everything's totally cool. We're going to stay with his parents next weekend. But listen, your guy . . .'

'He's not mine.'

'Grandma says . . .'

'I don't care what Grandma says, and I don't want you two trying to push me into something I have no desire to do.'

'Seriously? I hear he's attractive, and you enjoyed the date . . .'

'It *wasn't* a date, and if you can't talk about anything else I'm going to ring off, because I've got a big day tomorrow and the last thing I need is to be distracted by . . .'

'OK, OK, I hear you. I just don't want you to miss out on something that might be wonderful, is all. Having said that, taking in a little boy and giving him love and kindness . . . I guess you can't get much more wonderful than that. By the way, I've put something in the mail for him. I hope it'll get there by tomorrow. Good luck. I'll be thinking of you. Call as soon as you can, and if you hear from Tom Franklyn . . .'

'Goodbye,' Leanne interrupted, and she promptly cut the connection.

It wasn't until she was putting her phone on charge before turning out the lights that she saw a text had arrived while she was talking on the computer to Kate.

Good luck tomorrow. I hope you're as happy with him as I know he'll be with you. TF

Chapter Eleven

Though the weather wasn't exactly auspicious on the day of Daniel's arrival, at least the rain held off, and from time to time the sun broke out in an extravagant blaze to dazzle the daffs and tulips around the courtyard. It was looking so pretty out there now, with the early spring flowers showing off their rainbow colours, and birds chirruping about the feeders, that a feeling of pure goodwill seemed to fill the air.

Earlier in the day Leanne and Wilkie had made a trip to Tesco for a mega shop, wanting to be sure there was enough variety in their cupboards to satisfy whatever tastes Daniel might have. Afterwards, they'd met Klaudia, Bel and Jenny for lunch at the Seafront Café, where the talk had been mostly of Daniel. Then Wilkie had popped into the town hall to make sure her latest project – a familiarisation course for newcomers to Kesterly – hadn't been forgotten.

Now they were back at the barn, Bags for Life unpacked and recipe books open as they prepared a veggie Wellington for dinner. Although there were no vegetarians at Ash Morley they didn't know about

Daniel, so had decided this was the safest, tastiest option.

'You shouldn't have deleted the text from Eileen,' Wilkie was saying as she caramelised the leeks in a cast-iron pan. 'I'd like to have read it.'

Leanne groaned. 'I told you what it said and I really didn't want to keep it.'

'Tell me again.'

With a sigh, Leanne chopped extra mushrooms as she précised the text she'd received this morning from Jack's mother. 'She wanted to know if it's true that we're allowing the son of a murderer into our home, and if it is she'll be taking steps to get her granddaughter out of here.'

Wilkie remained silent as she added thyme and garlic to her pan and continued to stir. 'What I'm asking myself,' she said, 'is how Eileen knows about Daniel. I'm sure Abby wouldn't have told her.'

'I've no idea, but here's my guess. Because she's Abby's grandmother, someone from social services contacted her to find out if there was anything they needed to know about *her* or our family before they placed Daniel into our care.'

Wilkie reached for the mushrooms and dropped them into the pan. 'I'll have a chat with her,' she said. 'She needs to have her mind – and her heart – prised open a little.' With an impatient scoff she added, 'There's nothing I can tolerate less than intolerance. Now let's get this in the oven and pour a nice big glass of wine to help ready ourselves for the grand arrival.'

Leanne looked at her sharply, certain she was joking, but needing to be sure.

If the truth were told Leanne wouldn't have minded some sort of steadier right now – though definitely not alcohol – for she was experiencing some last-minute concerns that wouldn't go away. They were to be expected, she realised that, but the trouble with her family was that they were all heart and no head when it came to kindness and compassion. Everyone was welcome; none were to be turned away. She felt proud of that, naturally, but she had to concede that they were as capable as the next person of getting things wrong, and where Daniel Marks was concerned she was acutely aware that they'd created the picture of him that they wanted to see, rather than waiting and allowing him to paint it for himself.

'But of course we have,' Wilkie protested when Leanne voiced her misgivings. 'If we were telling ourselves he was the Devil incarnate, we'd need our heads read for even considering taking him in. No, what we're doing is seeing things in a positive light, and that's exactly how we should continue. Positively and generously and . . .'

'Oh God, you're going to start singing "Kumbaya".'

Wilkie's eyes lit up at the suggestion.

Leanne was about to gag her when they heard a car crossing the cattle grid. They quickly removed pans from the heat before going to throw open the rarely opened front door, where they stumbled into a farcical moment as they tried to get out at the same time.

The car that drew up next to Leanne's was a shiny lime-green Mazda; the woman who climbed out was a merry bundle of smiles with jet-black hair, poppy-red lips and dangly earrings. The boy who remained in the passenger seat was no more than a shadowy presence for the moment.

'Mrs Delaney? Leanne?' the social worker beamed, reaching for Leanne's hand. 'I'm Saffy. It's lovely to meet you. I'm sorry I didn't come before. It's hectic at the moment, but here we are now. This is a fabulous place,' she added, looking around to take it all in. 'It's like something out of a magazine.'

Smiling at the overstatement, Leanne said, 'This is my mother, Mrs Emmett. Everyone calls her Wilkie.'

'Yes, I recognise you from the TV and papers.' Saffy warmly shook Wilkie's hand. 'So, let me introduce you to Daniel.' She dropped into a whisper. 'He's a little bit shy, but I think you'll like him.'

Leanne glanced at her mother as Saffy stooped and waved for Daniel to join them.

Obediently, he opened the door and as he came round the car Leanne had to fight an urge to go straight to hug him. She'd been told he was small for his age and he was, but surely he didn't have to be so thin or frightened-looking. His hair was cropped short to his head, his large eyes were the colour of beechwood, his child's mouth seemed to tremble as he tried several times to look at them, but failed.

'Hi Daniel,' she said softly. 'I'm Leanne. Welcome to Ash Morley.'

He mumbled an answer, then raised his head and

looked past her at the barn, all the way up to the high-est gable.

'Behind that window up there,' Leanne told him, 'is your room. On a good day you can look out and see the sea.'

Wilkie said, 'Hello Daniel, I'm Leanne's mother. You can call me Wilkie. It's lovely to have you here.'

His eyes went briefly to hers then fell away, almost as though he wasn't sure if he was allowed to look.

'Can we shake hands?' Leanne asked, holding out her own.

He lifted his cautiously, and feeling the fragility of his fingers she gave them a gentle squeeze, a gesture she hoped was reassuring.

'Shall we go inside?' she suggested. 'It's quite cold out here, isn't it?'

His eyes widened, showing alarm, and he seemed to take a step back before Saffy gently eased him forward.

'You'll be fine,' she whispered in his ear. 'These are lovely people. You're very lucky to be here.'

'We're lucky to have him,' Wilkie insisted, clearly not fully approving of Saffy's technique.

Leanne led the way inside and stood back proudly, hopefully, to watch Daniel's reaction to the Welcome banner.

He stared at it then looked at her, as though not quite understanding that it was for him.

'My daughter, Abby, made it for you,' she explained. 'She'll be home from school any minute with Mia and Adam. They live next door in the stables, and Wilkie lives the other side of here in the farmhouse. We're always in and out of each other's homes, like one big family, and we'd like you to feel a part of that too.'

Daniel was obviously listening, hearing, but it was impossible to know what he was thinking.

'I'll bring his things in,' Saffy said, and touching a hand gently to his head she returned to the car.

'Are you hungry?' Wilkie asked, gesturing towards the table. 'There are biscuits and cake . . .'

Daniel looked around the room, seeming unable to take it in. Then he gazed out through the windows across the fields to the far horizon.

Wondering what his previous foster homes, or parental home had been like, Leanne simply watched him.

He looked up at the banner again.

'Come and sit down,' Wilkie said from the table. 'Do you like tea or lemonade or squash?'

After a beat he said, 'Please can I have squash?'

Relieved that he'd spoken at last, and impressed with his good manners, Leanne led him across the room and held out a chair for him to sit down. 'I guess this is all feeling quite strange,' she said softly. 'It's awkward trying to get to know people, isn't it? But please feel free to ask us anything you like, and if you don't mind we'll ask you some questions too.'

His bony hands closed around the large glass Wilkie passed him, and tilting it to his mouth he drank deeply.

Wilkie smiled. 'I think you were thirsty,' she declared. 'I'll get you some more.'

Leanne turned round as Saffy came in carrying a

large black plastic bag. 'Do you need a hand?' she offered.

'This is it,' Saffy replied, dropping the bag at the bottom of the stairs.

All he has is a refuse sack, Leanne was thinking, appalled. Not even a proper holdall. 'A backpack or schoolbag?' she prompted.

'It's in there,' Saffy assured her. Then, glancing at her watch, she said, 'I'm sorry, but I have to be somewhere. I'm sure you guys are going to get along just fine,' and after giving Daniel a quick hug she returned to the door. 'If you need anything you have my number,' she said to Leanne. 'I'm told someone's already given you the care pack?'

Leanne nodded. 'Thanks for bringing him,' she smiled, going to see her out, and not knowing what else to say she simply stood at the door watching her drive away.

'So, Daniel,' she said, returning to the table, 'we need to find out what your favourite things are.'

His beautiful, anxious eyes came to hers.

Leanne felt a surge of emotion, and she saw that her mother did too. His reaction made her wonder when someone had last spoken a kind word to him, or shown an interest in the simple way she just had. 'Do you like music?' she asked, sitting down next to him.

He nodded.

'Which bands?'

When he didn't answer, she decided to let him come to it in his own time, and moved on. 'How about sport?' she ventured.

'Football,' he said quietly.

Wilkie chuckled. 'My husband was a keen football fan,' she told him. 'Which team do you support?'

'Man United, the same as my . . .' He stopped, dropped his head and Leanne realised he'd been about to mention his dad.

Unsure at this stage whether or not to encourage it, she said, 'Have you ever been to see them play?'

He shook his head. 'Only on the telly.'

'What about school?' Wilkie asked. 'Which subjects do you like best?'

He shrugged. 'Maths and science and PE.'

Leanne smiled. 'Perhaps you'll be able to help Abby, my daughter, with her maths. She's not very good, I'm afraid.'

His eyes remained down and she was asking herself if she should just show him to his room to give him some space for a while, when the sound of a car grinding over the cattle grid signalled a new arrival.

Moments later Abby, Mia, Adam and Juno were bounding in through the door.

'Is he here?' Abby cried, tearing off her coat. 'Oh, great, there you are. Hi, I'm Abby,' she declared, going to Daniel, 'and this is Juno . . . Juno, don't jump. Bad boy,' but Juno was already all over Daniel, licking, panting, pawing and in apparent raptures at meeting someone new.

Daniel patted the dog awkwardly.

'Do you like dogs?' Leanne asked, grabbing Juno's collar.

Daniel nodded, then started as Juno let out his howl of love.

'Don't worry,' Mia came in kindly, 'that means he likes you.' She held out her hand to shake. 'Hello, I'm Mia. I live next door with my mum and brother. That's my mum there. Her name's Klaudia.'

Coming to him, Klaudia took his hand as she said, 'It's lovely to have you here, Daniel.'

He appeared bemused, but said nothing, only watched as Klaudia manoeuvred Adam to stand in front of her. 'This is Adam,' she said, 'he's six. Say hi to Daniel, there's a good boy.'

Daniel looked down at Adam's bowed fair head and after a moment he tentatively put out a hand.

Adam looked at it, almost as if he didn't know what to do. Then he gingerly lifted his hand and put it into Daniel's. He gazed at their immobile handshake for a moment before tilting his head back to look up at Daniel's face. Then quite suddenly he broke into a dazzling smile.

Daniel said, 'Hey, Adam.'

Adam glanced at his mother, still holding on to Daniel's hand and appearing thrilled, as though someone had just given him the best imaginable gift. Then he turned back to Daniel and went on smiling.

Leanne had no idea if Daniel had realised right away that Adam was different, but whether he had or hadn't he'd been so gentle with the boy, and patient, and hadn't seemed to mind at all that Adam didn't want to let go of his hand.

He was upstairs now being shown his room by the others, leaving Leanne and Wilkie to carry on preparing dinner and Klaudia to pour the wine.

'He seems very nervous,' Wilkie was saying, as Leanne stood her aside in order to get to the Aga. 'I keep thinking about the man who beat him with a belt.'

'Me too,' Klaudia murmured, 'but I can't imagine he's afraid we're going to do the same.'

'Trust isn't so easily come by,' Leanne commented, 'especially when you've had your world turned upside down, and for all we know the man who beat him was nice to him at first.'

'I don't understand how anyone can hold a parent's crime against a child,' Klaudia remarked, keeping her voice low as footsteps thundered across the landing. Daniel was probably being shown the bathroom.

Leanne shook her head in dismay, sharing Klaudia's incomprehension. She glanced up as Abby came down the stairs, followed by Mia and Juno.

'Daniel's unpacking,' Abby informed them, 'and Adam's helping.'

'I'm here,' Adam said, following on behind, and going to his mother he whispered, 'Daniel doesn't have any toys.'

Klaudia scooped him up. 'He's older than you, so he probably doesn't want any.'

Adam rested his head against hers. 'Can he live with us?' he asked.

Klaudia smiled and smoothed his hair. 'He's going to be here in the barn, so you can see him as often as you like.'

Sliding his arms round her neck, he said, 'Can I see him now?'

'I'm sure he'll be down in a minute. Why don't you help Mia to set the table and you can sit next to him?'

Clearly happy with that, Adam went to his sister and cradled his arms ready for loading.

'You're weird,' Mia told him fondly.

'I'm weird,' he assured her.

Going to cuddle him, Abby said, 'Can I sit the other side of you?'

He leaned into Mia as he nodded.

'Who's that now?' Wilkie demanded as the cattle grid rattled again.

Checking out of the window, Leanne said, 'It looks like one of your delivery guys.'

'Oh lovely!' and off she went to sign or chat, or to make a new friend if it was someone she hadn't seen before.

She was back minutes later, looking thrilled. 'It's for Daniel,' she announced, holding up a heavily stamped box. 'And it's all the way from America.'

Abby turned to Leanne.

'Yes, it's from Kate,' Leanne confirmed. 'But no, I don't know what it is.'

'I bet I do,' Abby replied. 'Shall I take it up to him?'

Leanne felt torn. He could be feeling a little over-whelmed right now, and glad to have some time to himself. 'Let's keep it for when he comes down to eat,' she suggested.

By the time the veggie Wellington was out of the oven and drinks were poured, more than an hour had passed and there had still been no sight or sound of him.

'Maybe he feels too shy to come down,' Abby said, looking up from the coffee table where she and Mia were doing their homework.

Suspecting that might be the case, Leanne left Klaudia and her mother serving up while she went to find out.

'Daniel,' she called softly, knocking on his door.

When there was no answer she tried again. 'Can I come in?' she asked.

Still no reply, and for one awful moment she was afraid he might have jumped out of the window.

'I'm coming in,' she warned, and turning the handle she pushed open the door.

Daniel was lying on the bed with his face against the wall.

Feeling her heart contract, she went further into the room. 'Are you all right?' she asked. 'Food's ready, so time to eat.'

He didn't move, only continued to lie facing the wall with an arm circled around his head.

His unhappiness and loneliness were almost too much to bear.

'Not hungry?' she said softly.

Long minutes ticked by.

Unable to leave him like this, she went to sit on the bed.

At last he turned to look at her and she saw right away that he'd been crying.

Taking his hand in hers, she said, 'I know things haven't been easy for you, but we want to change that.'

His eyes didn't come to hers, but he didn't remove

his hand and nor did he show any sign of not wanting her there.

'We only have one rule here,' she told him, 'and it's not even a rule really. It's more of a request, or an invitation. We'd like you to think of this as your home and us as your family. Do you think you can do that?'

He didn't answer.

'It's OK, I understand it'll take some time for you to get used to us. We're all a little bit crazy in our ways, but I want you to know that I am here for you any time you like. You already matter a great deal to me, so if anything makes you unhappy or afraid or confused I want you to tell me so I can help you.'

His eyes flicked briefly to hers and away again.

'Would you like to come and eat now?' she asked.

For a moment it seemed he might speak, but his mouth only trembled, and no words came.

Wishing she could take him in her arms and make all his fear and pain go away, she said, 'A parcel arrived for you just now.'

He looked at her, and she saw a flicker of hope go through him. 'Is it from . . .'

Realising his first thought had been for his dad, she felt wretched as she said, 'It's from America.'

He was puzzled.

'It's a welcome present from my daughter, Kate. She's at university there.'

He looked away, his disappointment almost palpable.

'Would you like me to go and get it?' she offered.

He shook his head.

He doesn't want anything except his dad, she was

thinking, and it just about broke her heart. And what about his mum? She wondered if he'd ever been encouraged to talk about his parents and the terrible, devastating grief of their loss. If not, he needed help badly. Not only help, but understanding and love.

'Will you give us a go?' she asked gently. 'We'd like it very much if you did.'

His fingers seemed to twitch inside hers, and after what seemed an interminable time he started to get off the bed. She watched him go to the door, and realising, at least hoping, that he was going downstairs, she followed.

Though he started tentatively, as though not sure the food was really meant for him, Daniel was soon eating so heartily that even he, in spite of his embarrassment, began to laugh along with the others at his appetite.

'We'd have made two if we'd known,' Wilkie teased him, 'but don't worry, there's pudding. Do you like banoffee pie?'

He seemed not to know what it was, but then with the ghost of a twinkle, he said, 'I expect so.'

The touch of humour so delighted Leanne that she didn't realise how loudly she laughed until Abby kicked her.

'Ignore her,' Abby told Daniel, 'she's just weird.'

'I'm weird,' Adam reminded them. To Daniel he said, 'Are you weird?'

Daniel nodded. 'Definitely,' and everyone laughed again.

As soon as dinner was over Abby plonked the parcel from Kate in front of Daniel, with instructions to open it right away.

'Talk about bossy,' Leanne muttered.

'Sorreee, you didn't tell me you were saving it for a rainy day,' and turning back to a slightly flummoxed Daniel she said, 'I can guess what it is, but I'm not saying anything until you've unwrapped it.'

Mia and Adam crowded around, eyes wide as they waited for the surprise, appearing as excited as if it were going to be theirs. When Daniel pulled out what appeared to be a large hardcover book they all clapped their hands in delight. However, Abby was quick to realise that Daniel didn't understand.

'It's a keepsake box,' she explained. 'Kate's into that sort of thing. She's given us all one, me, Mia and Adam, and we store things in it that are special to us. You know, like photos – if you can be bothered to print them off – ticket stubs, programmes, pictures of your favourite celebrities . . .'

'I've got some seashells in mine,' Mia told him. 'And a bottle of perfume that Wilkie gave me – it's empty now, because I've used it all, but it still smells really nice.'

'What's in yours, Adam?' Klaudia prompted.

When he only blinked at her, she said, 'You've got some sweet wrappers and an ice-lolly stick . . .'

'Yes, and a Spiderman comic and a wriggly goldfish,' he cried.

'My diary is in mine,' Abby confessed, 'but there's a lock on it to stop prying eyes,' she informed her mother.

'Like your life is so interesting,' Leanne retorted.

'It's more interesting than yours.' She turned back to Daniel. 'We'll get your name printed on the front so everyone will know it's yours, and you don't have to tell anyone what's in it, unless you want to. It's like a box of secrets really.'

'I don't have any secrets,' Mia said. 'Do you?' she asked Daniel.

The colour deepened in his cheeks as he looked down at the box.

'You can have some of mine,' Adam told him, 'because I've got lots.'

Chapter Twelve

The following afternoon Leanne went to take over from Klaudia at Glory Days, while Wilkie piloted Daniel and Abby about town to search for the things they'd discovered Daniel needed. This ranged from pyjamas that fitted, a dressing gown and toothbrush, a new comb, shampoo and shower gel right through to a decent pair of trainers and a warm, waterproof coat. Though Leanne had promised her mother that she'd cover the cost, she knew already that Wilkie would refuse; however, when it came to a new laptop and smartphone Leanne had insisted that she'd already been provided with funds to cover the essentials.

'I don't think social services would class those things as essential, would they?' Wilkie had commented doubtfully. 'Maybe they do. Things are very different now.'

All Leanne knew was that a sum of money had been paid into her account, presumably for Daniel's food and clothing, but she was keen for him to be as much like the other kids as possible. So, in her book, a smartphone and laptop were essential.

'We'll go to the mall and get them after school on Monday,' she'd told Abby before the shoppers had set out on their mission that morning. 'And don't worry, you can be there to help do the choosing, but try to remember, it's for Daniel, not you.'

It was surprising, and touching, to see how involved Abby wanted to be in organising Daniel's new life; all that concerned Leanne was how long it would last. For the moment the boy was a novelty, the brother she'd never had, and, being Wilkie's granddaughter, a cause for her to claim as hers. She just hoped Abby's attitude wouldn't change towards him once she got bored and wanted to spend more time with her friends.

Looking up from the dismal accounts Klaudia had left for her to peruse, she checked to see who was calling her mobile and felt a jolt of surprise when she saw the name. For a moment she felt tempted not to answer, but that was absurd.

Just as absurd was the crisp way she said, 'Hi, Leanne Delaney speaking.' She didn't want him to think she was pleased to hear from him, or had in any way been waiting for his call, or had his number programmed into her phone, because . . . Well, because . . .

'Hi, Tom Franklyn here,' he said, drily matching her formality. 'How are you?'

Feeling herself smile, she said, 'Yes, I'm fine, thanks. How are you?'

'A little jet-lagged, but I'll get over it.'

He must be back. Cue butterflies and brain drain.

'So,' he went on, 'how are things going with the new member of your family?'

Sliding happily into that, she told him, 'He's still finding his feet, but Abby has him in hand, poor thing.'

There was a smile in his voice as he said, 'I guess he's not with you at the moment?'

'No, I'm at Glory Days. My mother's taken him shopping.' Would it come across as polite to ask where he'd been for the past two weeks, or inquisitive? Bypassing it, she said, 'I guess you're calling about your mother's things.'

'That, and to say I'm sorry for cutting out so abruptly a couple of weeks ago. I hadn't expected to be going away again for at least a month.'

'Oh, please, no apology necessary.'

For a moment neither of them spoke, and she couldn't think how to fill the gap. In the end, he said, 'Has Richie met Daniel yet?'

'No, actually, we haven't seen Richie for a few days.'

'Mm, I expect there'll be a girl involved somewhere, but you didn't hear that from me. So, what about . . .'

'We've got a new dog,' she blurted, and instantly wondered why that was relevant. 'He's a lurchoodle, or a poocher, take your pick. Very cute, a busier social life and fan club than my mother's. His name's Juno.'

'I'm quite keen on dogs.'

'This one howls if he likes you. It's quite entertaining.'

'Mm, an interesting technique. I must give it a try.'

She spluttered a laugh.

'So, what kind of things is Daniel into?'

'Well, he likes football. He's a Man United fan.'

'I guess we can forgive him for that. How about

209

Richie and I take him for a kick-around on the beach tomorrow morning, unless of course you already have other plans?'

How could she possibly say no when it was such an unexpected and kind offer – and when she didn't even want to? 'That's a great idea,' she said. 'We've already arranged to meet some friends at the Mermaid for lunch. Perhaps you and Richie would like to join us after the kick-around? We'll be about twelve, maybe fifteen.'

'Is that all?' he remarked drily. 'Count us in. I take it some of those friends are male, so would any of them be up for joining the kick-around?'

'Actually, I expect they would. I'll ask.' How was she going to introduce him? She didn't want anyone getting the wrong idea – whatever that might be – and how foolish was she going to look if she started blathering on about his mother's kind bequest to Glory Days. Too much information . . .

'Shall we say ten thirty?' he suggested.

'OK. Ten thirty at Hope Cove. It's a date.'

After putting the phone down she stood looking at it for a while, going back over the conversation and wincing at how bizarre she might have sounded. He hadn't seemed to notice, or if he had he'd been too polite to comment. However, she was tempted to call him back to be a bit friendlier.

Don't be ridiculous, she scolded herself as she returned to the accounts. *Exactly how are you going to manage that? Hi, Tom, it's Leanne again, just wanting to be friendly. So where exactly have you been for the last two weeks? Baghdad. Really? No, I've never been. How was the weather?*

She choked on a laugh. How was the weather?

Oh, and then you flew on to Berlin. No, I've never been there either, but it's on my bucket list. Do you have a bucket list?

She looked up as the door opened, and broke into a smile when she saw it was Andee Lawrence, her old friend from sixth-form college, and many other things to the community at large. 'Hi, what a lovely surprise,' she cried, going to hug her.

'I can't stop, I'm afraid,' Andee grimaced, 'I just wanted to let you know I'm back.' She was a tall, dark-haired woman with as much presence as elegance, and the most striking aquamarine eyes. Leanne remembered how all the boys used to go for her when they were young, and there was no doubt she continued to turn heads now.

'It seems everyone is coming back today,' Leanne quipped.

Andee appeared confused.

Leanne grinned. 'Never mind. Remind me where you were.'

Andee threw out her hands. 'Stockholm, Paris, Turin, back to Stockholm. It's been hectic, but we're here for at least the next month. Let's try to catch up sometime in the week. I'll give you a call, OK?'

'Great. I'll look forward to it. Actually, before you go, we're having lunch tomorrow, a crowd of us, at the Mermaid. If you and Graeme fancy joining us . . .'

'We'd absolutely love to, but my mother's keen for us to go there, and as we've been away for so long . . .' She broke off as her mobile rang. 'I should take this,' she said, 'but I'll be in touch soon, promise,' and a moment later she'd gone.

Leanne's smile faded as she turned back to the spreadsheet displayed on her laptop. There was no getting away from it, they were no longer breaking even – in fact they'd departed those shores quite some time ago. If she hadn't already stopped paying herself a salary she'd be cutting it now, but that saving hadn't helped much, and with so few customers coming in and the business rates going up ... One obvious saving was Klaudia's wages, but she could never bring herself to lay off her friend, not when she was already feeling so vulnerable and unwanted. Klaudia loved Glory Days as much as she did, she'd worked here longer, knew the customers better and put so much of herself into finding new stock as well as promoting what they had. However, they had to face it, if they carried on like this they'd end up having to close the shop altogether, and that would break all their hearts.

Klaudia was immersed in housework, cleaning bathrooms, changing the beds and piling in the laundry. Mia was outside playing hopscotch with a friend, while Adam slavishly threw a ball for Juno to fetch, appearing even more delighted than the dog that it could perform such a clever trick.

It wasn't until the washing machine ended its noisy spin cycle that Klaudia realised she'd missed several calls, all from the same number. It wasn't one she recognised, and whoever it was hadn't left a message, but since they seemed eager to get hold of her she pressed to ring back.

'Hello, it's Klaudia Marek here,' she told the man who answered.

'Ah, Klaudia, it's Peter Chlebek, at the Polish shop. Forgive me, I am using my wife's phone as I have mislaid mine. I have some sad news to tell you. Lena and I have decided to return to our home town of Lodz. I have a sister there and a nephew. They are helping us to find somewhere to live. We expect to go by the end of April. The reason I am calling you is to say that if there is anything you would like from the shop I will keep it for you until you can come to pick it up.'

'Oh, Mr Chlebek,' Klaudia murmured, tears starting in her eyes. She couldn't bear to think of Kesterly without him. He had been here even longer than she had, and was like a favourite uncle to so many, not just those of his own nationality. 'I am so sorry to hear this. I hadn't . . . I wish I . . .'

'Yes, we are sorry too,' he told her gravely. 'For many years we have considered this our home. We have always loved it here, but since the paint was thrown over our windows and the damage was done to my wife's car . . . It was very upsetting . . .'

'I didn't know about that,' she said. 'How horrible for you. Did you report it to the police?'

'Of course, and they were very polite, but what can they do? No one can say for certain who did the damage.'

Klaudia's breathing was shallow. She was so tense it was hurting her head. 'Did you . . . ? Did you apply for your papers?' she asked.

'Yes, we did, but there are so many questions, always something else, as though they are looking for an excuse to deny them. But even if we are permitted to stay, it is hard to see attitudes changing towards us. My wife is afraid they will get worse.'

Sharing the fear, Klaudia said, 'Thank you for ringing to let me know. I will come to see you during the week. Is the shop still open?'

'It is, but please ring this mobile first so I will know it is you and feel safe to open the door.'

As she rang off, Klaudia stood staring out of the window to where the children were playing. *Safe to open the door.* That poor, sweet man and his lovely wife were clearly cowering in their shop, too afraid to go out and worried about who to let in. They were being driven out of their home by thugs and criminals, and even by some people they'd once considered friends.

Her eyes went to Adam and once again filled with tears. She'd been told yesterday, by the school, that much of the funding for special needs children had been withdrawn as a result of budget cuts.

'As you know,' Victoria Gibbs had said sadly, 'we never did have funding for Adam, but the school wanted to help him anyway. Now, from September . . .' Her voice faltered. 'They're laying off five of us seven teaching assistants,' she confided, 'so I'll be leaving at the end of the summer term.'

Klaudia had felt a quick panic rise. 'But what about the children who need you?'

A spark of bitterness shot through Victoria's eyes. 'I

asked the same question and I was told that if they misbehave they'll be expelled.'

Shocked, Klaudia said, 'To go where? And Adam doesn't misbehave.'

'Of course he doesn't. He's the sweetest little soul. All I can tell you is that if parents want to work in the classroom, on a voluntary basis, the school will be open to it.'

'You mean as unskilled, unpaid teaching assistants?'

Victoria nodded.

Now, carrying the washing basket outside, Klaudia tried to collect her thoughts. She hated this feeling of helplessness, of being unable to make plans for the future, when everything depended on a decision that was completely out of her hands.

Leanne was laughing and clapping furiously as she cheered on the crazy five-a-side game on the beach at Hope Cove, with the unreliable Juno in one goal and a trying-very-hard Adam in the other. Wilkie – who knew next to nothing about football – had appointed herself referee, while Klaudia and Abby were eager subs. Leanne was supposed to be the official photographer; however, she'd got so carried away with supporting Daniel's side that Jenny Leonard had taken over.

The rest of Daniel's team comprised Tom and Richie Franklyn and Blake Leonard, while playing against them were Richard York as captain, his brother Steve, Harry Beck and Harry's eleven-year-old son

Neelmani. The score so far was twenty-eight to Daniel's side and sixteen to Richard's, mainly because Adam was a better goalie than Juno, who kept chasing the ball when he wasn't supposed to, or running off to meet other dogs.

Watching the delight and determination on Daniel's young face as he dashed about the sand with all the skill of a professional (at least to Leanne's eyes) was making her so happy that she felt she could burst with it. Only two days in and he seemed so settled already, even like a part of the family, or he certainly did this morning, engrossed as he was in the game. And heaven only knew what he'd been doing to make Abby and Mia laugh last night, but they'd been so close to hysteria that Leanne had had to go to Abby's room to tell them to calm down. Of course that had made them laugh all the harder, which in turn had made her laugh, and because she didn't know what she was laughing about they'd just about convulsed.

'Yes!' she and Klaudia yelled in unison as Richie kicked a ball gently towards Adam's goal and Adam caught it. To their great amusement Adam ran to Daniel for a celebratory hug.

'He's doing his best,' Klaudia laughed as Adam returned to his position and kicked the ball back to Richie. Daniel flew in from the side, snatched the ball with his left foot, saw off tackles from the opposing team and kicked it straight past Juno.

More cheers, more hugs and more photos.

By the time the game was over the score was thirty-five to Daniel's team, twenty to Richard's and three to

Wilkie, who'd managed to get in the way so the ball bounced off her and into goal.

Leanne didn't hold back when Daniel trotted up to her with Neelmani at his side, ready for a high five. It wasn't enough, she had to hug him, but to make sure he wasn't alone in his embarrassment she hugged Neel too, in spite of him being on the losing side.

'I wouldn't mind one of those,' Tom remarked, as he joined them.

Leanne looked up in amazement, already starting to colour, until he pointed to the trays of orange segments Misty had brought out from the pub.

Knowing he'd deliberately teased her, she narrowed her eyes and ignored Klaudia, who was murmuring some witticism that she didn't quite catch.

'OK, everyone to the pub,' Wilkie shouted, leading the way up the beach, arm in the air like a tour guide.

As everyone traipsed after her, the players covered in sand, the spectators too, Leanne and Klaudia went to grab Adam's hands to swing him along behind. However, Adam was having none of it, and wriggled through the crowd to get to Daniel. At first Daniel had no idea he was there and carried on reliving the game with Neel, until spotting him he dropped to one knee so Adam could climb on his back and ride all the way in through the pub door.

'What can I get you?' Tom offered as Leanne and Klaudia reached the bar.

Before they could answer Wilkie decided they should pop some Prosecco to celebrate the win, and no one was about to object to that.

The lunch turned into its own form of chaos, with so many of them crowded around the table that Misty's staff had set up along one entire side of the beach room, as the main bar was known. Sunday roasts were ordered all round, wine, beer, cola and water arrived, and because everyone was talking at once it was impossible to hear what anyone was saying.

After a while they began to fracture into groups with the children at one end of the table, the doctors, Harry and Richard, in the middle with Tom, Richie and Blake, and the women at the end closest to the door. Though Leanne was keeping an eye on Daniel, she was certain she didn't have to worry. He was so relaxed with the other kids – though with much less to say now he was no longer a captain shouting orders to his team – that he might have known them for a lot longer than he had.

'He seems to be off to a great start,' Jenny remarked, following the direction of Leanne's gaze.

'So far so good,' Leanne smiled, loving the way Daniel tilted his head so he could hear what Adam was saying. 'If you ask me I think he's been made to feel like a foster child until now, you know, kind of an outsider, or someone who has to be treated with kid gloves. We're just doing our best to make him feel like he belongs. Needless to say Mum's already spoiled him rotten. You should have seen all the things she bought him when they were out shopping yesterday.'

Overhearing, Wilkie said, 'Bless him, he didn't realise it was all for him until we got home. He thought he was helping to choose things for someone his size.'

'What I want to know,' Bel murmured in Leanne's ear, 'is more about Tom Franklyn. He's Helen's son, isn't he? So is he someone we're going to be seeing a lot more of, by any chance?' She was looking meaningfully at Leanne.

Klaudia said, 'Absolutely.'

Wilkie said, 'I certainly hope so.'

Leanne said, 'I shouldn't think so. He's just here sorting out his mother's house before selling it.'

With raised eyebrows, Bel said, 'He's selling Villa Tramonto?'

'Apparently, that's the plan, but he wants to get it into better shape first. I thought of you right away, but with the baby coming I wasn't sure you'd want to take it on.'

'I'd give anything to get my hands on that place,' Bel sighed, 'but I've promised Harry – and myself – that I'll take at least a year off to be a full-time mum. Has he spoken to Graeme Ogilvy? Graeme would be perfect for it.'

'Not yet, but now he and Andee are back I'll see if I can get them together.'

They looked up at a sudden explosion of laughter from the other end of the table. Leanne's eyes danced as she saw Daniel looking all innocence, with his hands spread as if he had no idea what was so funny.

'Come on, share the joke,' Richie called out.

'No way,' Abby called back. 'You wouldn't get it, anyway.'

Richie turned to Leanne.

She shrugged as if to say, don't ask me. 'Mum, who

219

are you texting?' she asked, noticing her mother engrossed in her phone.

'Not texting, ordering,' Wilkie replied. 'He could do with a new pair of football boots.'

'But shouldn't he choose them himself?'

Wilkie stopped and looked deflated. 'I wanted it to be a surprise,' she pouted, 'but I suppose you're right. Can I have another glass of wine?'

'Coming up,' Blake responded, passing a bottle of white her way. 'Anyone for red?'

'Oh, yes please,' Bel drooled.

Harry shot her a look. She poked out her tongue and picked up her soda.

For a while Tom and Richard seemed engrossed in intense conversation, making Leanne wonder if they'd met before, perhaps in some war-torn part of the world. Then Tom was teasing Daniel about his support of Manchester United, with Daniel giving as good as he got and Neel getting so carried away with it all that much to everyone's hilarity he fell off his chair.

Next thing they were naming their best holiday ever, with Bel and Harry deciding on Sicily where they'd been for their honeymoon; Blake and Jenny chose California, while Wilkie tactfully declared hers to be a week in Cornwall with Glory, Klaudia and the children. Leanne would have liked to change the subject as the children joined in, worried about how difficult it might be for Daniel, but he didn't even hesitate when it came to his turn. His best holiday ever had been a week in Florida when he was six.

So his parents had taken him to Disneyland. That

pleased Leanne so much she found herself wanting to ask about it, but Richie was saying, 'Dad's favourite holiday was on the Greek island of Paxos, wasn't it, Dad?'

Tom's expression turned wry. 'Thanks for bringing that up,' he retorted, giving the distinct impression that it had been anything but his favourite. 'What about yours, Leanne?' he asked, turning to her.

Had Abby not been there Leanne would have chosen a two-week drive through France with Martin when they were students, not only because it had been so romantic, but because it was when Kate had been conceived. For Abby's sake she said, 'I think it has to be the month we spent in Italy when you were ten, Abby. We have great memories of that time, don't we?'

Abby didn't disagree, which was a relief since it hadn't been without its tensions. Her top-rated holiday turned out to be a skiing trip with the school, noted absence of parents.

Time ticked on, with no one seeming ready to leave until eventually, well after three, Tom announced that Richie had to be somewhere and as he was the chauffeur . . .

Understanding from Tom's tone that 'a girl was involved', Leanne laughed and hiccuped at the same time and wished she was a person of more dignity. By then Klaudia was at the bar in earnest conversation with Misty about something or other, leaving the chair next to Leanne vacant so Tom came to sit in it on his way out.

'Great day, great kid,' he told her. 'Apparently he's into fishing, so Harry and I have promised to take him and Neel next weekend if he's free.'

'I don't see why he shouldn't be,' Leanne replied, feeling the others watching her and hoping the effect of his proximity wasn't showing on her face. 'I'm sure he'd love it, but he's got a week of school to get through first, so perhaps we can confirm sometime on Thursday?'

'I'll be in touch before that,' he told her, and helping himself to the chocolate that had come with her coffee, he waggled his eyebrows and got up to steer his son out to the car.

Leanne was stretched out on the sofa dozing in front of the fire when Abby and Juno wandered in from the downstairs bedroom.

Leanne yawned. 'Everything all right?' she asked, as Abby flopped down on the opposite sofa and patted it for Juno to join her.

'Yeah, why shouldn't it be?' Abby retorted.

Intuiting that it wasn't, Leanne said, 'I thought you were going over to Tanya's this evening to finish your homework.'

'I've already done it.'

Curiously, Leanne said, 'Have you two fallen out?'

Abby's eyes rolled. '*Nooo!*'

'Then what's the problem?'

'Who says there's a problem?'

'It's a feeling I'm getting, and you haven't seen her all weekend.'

'Because Daniel's here. I wasn't just going to take off, was I? Anyway, she's with Becky being all *talented and gifted.*'

Leanne's eyes darkened.

'Don't go there,' Abby snapped. 'You've already shown me up once, don't even think about doing it again.'

'But if it's upsetting . . .'

'It's not upsetting me. They can do what they want, I'm cool with it.'

Although that patently wasn't true, Leanne decided to back off before things got any worse. 'Where's Daniel?' she asked.

'In his room.'

'Is he OK?'

'How should I know?'

Stifling a sigh, Leanne said, 'If you've finished your homework, why don't you ask him if he wants to watch a video or play a computer game?'

'I already did, but he doesn't want to.'

Leanne frowned and glanced at the stairs. 'Do you think I should go and check on him?' she asked.

'Stop fussing,' Abby complained. 'He's not a baby. Anyway, don't think I don't know that your favourite holiday *ever* was one you had with Kate.'

Thrown, Leanne said, 'Actually, that isn't true.'

'But it wasn't the one you said, because you hated that time in Italy. You couldn't wait to get home.'

'Parts of it were good, usually when it was just you and me. We had a lot of fun.'

'But he ruined it, like he ruined everything.'

Leanne sat quietly watching her, not sure yet where to go with this.

'Now I suppose it's me who always ruins things.'

Leanne frowned in surprise. 'Why would you say that?'

'Because it's the way you make me feel.'

Guilt flooded Leanne on hearing this. 'I certainly don't mean to,' she said, 'because you don't ruin anything for me, not one single bit. I love you more than anything. In fact it's not possible for anyone to love someone more than I love you, and I think I keep proving that in the way I let you say such horrible things to me and get away with it.' She'd meant it as a joke, but apparently Abby didn't find it funny.

'See, there you are having a go at me again.'

'Abby, I was teasing.'

Abby didn't respond, just kept on stroking Juno's ears.

'I wish you'd talk to me,' Leanne said gently. 'I know something's bothering you . . .'

'It's not the talented and gifted, all right? So stop thinking that.'

'Then what is it? You know you can tell me anything.'

Abby didn't answer.

'Abby . . .'

'I'm fine, OK?'

Leanne took a breath, knowing that she probably didn't want to hear the answer to her next question, but she had to ask it. 'Are you regretting having Daniel here?' she said quietly.

Abby's eyes flashed. '*No!* He's cool. I like him. OK?'

Leanne wasn't sure that it was.

'Why are you looking at me like that?' Abby snapped.

'I just said he's cool,' and getting up from the sofa she stalked back to her room and slammed the door.

Daniel was sitting at the desk in the room Leanne and her family had done up with all sorts of things just for him. For a long time he'd been lying on his bed staring at the planets on the ceiling and the cards Abby had propped on his windowsill. He was trying to make sense of it all, because it felt like a trick, or a dream. Everyone was being so kind, and that didn't usually happen to him. They'd taken him shopping, bought him stuff that was really cool; they liked it when he ate a lot and laughed at his stupid jokes. He was having fun in a way he hadn't since his dad went away; the trouble was it didn't feel right having fun without him. It made Daniel feel guilty and sad, like he was letting his dad down in some way, even though his dad had told him that he should try hard to get along with the people who looked after him.

Usually they didn't seem to care whether he got on with them or not, but Leanne and her family were different. He really liked them already, and now he was scared that the social worker was going to come and take him away. She would, because she always did when things went wrong, and sooner or later they'd go wrong here.

He wished he could tell Leanne and Wilkie that his dad was a good person, that he hadn't done what everyone said he had, but he'd had instructions not to talk about him at all.

He didn't always stick to it.

'My dad doesn't lie,' he'd told the last foster carer he'd been with.

'But honey, you have to realise he wouldn't tell you the truth about something like that,' she'd replied. 'He's lied to everyone about it, not just you, because people who've done bad things and don't want to be locked up for them always tell lies.'

She'd offered to go online with him so they could read about the trial and how the evidence had all pointed to his dad, but Daniel hadn't wanted to. He didn't care what anyone said, or what proof they had, his dad would never hurt anyone, he knew that for a fact.

As a tear rolled down his cheek he looked at the piece of paper in front of him and tried to think what to write in his letter. His dad had told him more than once to stop writing, but he still did, and his dad always wrote back.

For some reason he was finding it difficult today. He knew he should be telling him all about Leanne and her family, their lovely home, the dog, and friendly friends, but the words just weren't coming. All he could do was cry like he was losing his dad all over again, and it felt so horrible he didn't know what to do. If only he could see him, talk to him, it would be all right. He'd know then for certain that his dad hadn't lied, and that he hadn't meant it when he'd said Daniel should forget all about him.

The next couple of weeks flew by so quickly that Leanne found herself losing track of it all, though there had been many highlights along the way, not the least of which was the day she'd driven up to Villa Tramonto expecting to go through more of Helen's collection.

When she'd arrived she'd found the front door open and the house filled with a rousing performance of a Mendelssohn concerto – at least she thought it was Mendelssohn, but she was no expert.

Assuming it was coming from the radio or a music system she went in search of Tom, and to her astonishment found him seated at a grand piano in a magnificent, though much faded, drawing room, play-ing his heart out.

Spotting her, he kept his eyes on hers as he continued the stirring performance, swaying with the music, seeming to feel it right through to his soul, until he got up to greet her and the piano carried on playing.

She blinked, and burst out laughing.

'An old family joke,' he told her.

They went on to spend the next hour sorting through

227

some of his mother's jewellery and ended up deciding, before the first dozen drawers were emptied, that she and Klaudia should return at the weekend to start cataloguing and photographing it all. As none of it was precious or, apparently, of sentimental value, it made sense to try and sell it online.

It wouldn't solve their financial difficulties by a long stretch, but the more stock they had the more chance there would be of at least bringing in something. The dresses and hats were a different matter. With some of them worth thousands of pounds they really could help turn things around, but Leanne still wasn't comfortable about accepting them. The problem for her was that they were such a special and romantic part of his family history that it just didn't make sense for him to allow her to auction them off to the highest bidder, who'd know nothing about where they'd come from.

Tom was far less sentimental; however, for the moment he wasn't pressing her to take them, understanding that they were safer where they were until they'd reached an agreement.

Something else she remembered from the past fortnight with some pleasure was the lunch she'd had with Andee Lawrence, who'd assured her right away that she and Graeme would be keen to talk to Tom about Villa Tramonto. With that decided Andee had wanted to know all about Daniel, and to her own amusement Leanne had found herself running on about him with such pride that he could have been one of her own.

There was no doubt he'd settled into school well. He was already, Abby had informed Leanne before his teacher had, part of the talented and gifted in his year ('Go and kick up a fuss about it now,' Abby had challenged, which of course Leanne hadn't). He'd also been drafted into the lower school football team and, to his clear delight, he'd been invited to join the choir.

'I can't sing for toffee,' he'd told her when he'd come home with the news, but he could. In fact he had a beautiful voice, which, he said after wowing them all with a solo of 'One Day I'll Fly Away', he probably got from his mum. This was the only time he'd mentioned her so far, but when Leanne had tried to coax more from him he'd clammed up.

She could hardly bear to think of how much he missed his parents, especially his mother, who she knew from his file had been a professional singer until cancer had done its worst. When it came to his father . . . Well, they hadn't discussed him at all, not even when Daniel gave Leanne letters to post, or when she'd handed him the one that had come yesterday. All she knew about the contact was that Daniel wrote at least twice a week, and last night, presumably after reading his dad's letter, he hadn't even come down for dinner. She'd stood outside his door for a while, knowing he was crying, but when she knocked he'd asked her to leave him alone.

This morning he'd been as eager as he had the previous Saturday to go fishing with Tom, Harry and Neel, so Leanne had dutifully got up at five a.m. to wave them off when they'd come to pick him up. They'd taken Adam this time, after he'd begged his mother to let him go, because he was a big boy now.

'I'm not sure who to be the most worried about at the moment,' she said to her mother when a tousled and bleary-eyed Wilkie wandered in just after nine. 'Actually, I might put you top of the list, you look terrible.'

'Thank you for that,' Wilkie croaked, going to help herself to coffee.

'Are you hung-over, or coming down with something?'

'Both,' Wilkie decided. 'I overdid it a bit last night with Rowzee and Pamela. Rowzee doesn't drink, because of her medication, but Pamela and I made up for it.'

'Where did you go? And please don't say a disco.'

Wilkie chuckled. 'I was at their place up at Burle Crest. We were supposed to be having a meeting about the future of the theatre . . . Actually we did, but I can't remember much of it now. Don't worry, I didn't drive home. Bill brought me, so I'll have to ask you to take me back there later to get my car. So, who else are you worried about?'

'In no particular order, Abby, Daniel, Klaudia.'

'So let's take them in that order. Abby first.'

'Talking about me again?'

Leanne looked up as Abby came into the kitchen, dressed and apparently ready to go out. 'Where are you going?' she asked.

Abby's eyes narrowed with annoyance. 'I told you last night that I'm taking Mia to the toy sale down on the estate. You never listen to anything I say.'

'I'm sorry, it slipped my mind. Would you like me to come too?'

'Why?'

Leanne shrugged as she glanced at her mother. 'I just thought . . . It doesn't matter. I'm taking over from Klaudia at the shop at lunchtime if you fancy coming into town with me.'

'I just told you, I'm looking after Mia.'

'Well obviously she'll come too.'

Abby flipped back her hair and reached for a piece of toast.

'Is that a yes or a no?' Leanne prompted.

'It's a maybe, I'll let you know,' and after treating Wilkie to an affectionate hug, she went to jam on her boots before picking up an extra scarf on her way out.

Finding herself thinking of Jack and his mother, Leanne said, 'You were going to talk to Eileen.'

'Mm,' Wilkie nodded, 'I've arranged to see her the week after next. I thought I'd drive over there and do it face to face. It should have more of an impact.'

Leanne couldn't help but smile. 'Your lovely little face always has an impact,' she teased.

'Apart from today. Anyway, what's worrying you about Daniel?'

Leanne tried to decide where to start. 'I don't want to force him to talk about his parents,' she said, 'but he's got it all bottled up inside, and I'm afraid he's an even bigger explosion waiting to happen than Abby.'

Wilkie looked equally concerned. 'I'm starting to wonder if the farmhouse is far enough away,' she grunted.

Leanne shot her a look.

Wilkie twinkled and sipped her coffee.

231

'There's nothing in his file about counselling,' Leanne continued, 'so he probably hasn't had any – and he needs it, for the loss of both parents.'

'It'll be the cutbacks,' Wilkie decided. 'Look what's happened to Adam, and then there's how far they got – or didn't get – with Abby. No one's receiving the help they should any more.'

Depressed by the truth of that, Leanne said, 'If we're going to help them we ought at least to try and do something.'

Wilkie didn't disagree. 'Just don't push them,' she advised. 'Make sure they know you're there for them, the way you always do, and I'm sure they'll come to you in their own time. Meanwhile, they're striking up quite a bond between them, and friendship can be a very helpful kind of therapy.' She turned to the table and eyed the toast dubiously. 'Now, what about Klaudia?' she asked.

Leanne sighed deeply. 'Yes, indeed, what about Klaudia?'

Klaudia wasn't prone to violent reaction, but right now she wanted to scream and shout and throw her laptop across the shop in sheer frustration – and dread. Apparently her application for permanent residency could not be processed until she provided evidence of a valid Comprehensive Sickness Insurance.

She should have known that was coming, everyone in her position was talking about it, but for some insane reason she'd been telling herself that it wouldn't apply to her.

Apparently it did, and now, because she didn't have it – like everyone else had never even heard of it until a few months ago – there was a good chance her status was in jeopardy.

Knowing she couldn't face responding to the email now, she slammed down the lid of her computer and went to the window, willing herself to think of something else in the hope of calming herself down and clearing her head.

It was a dismal day. There were so few people around that it was no wonder Glory Days was struggling. Everyone's business was, and not only thanks to the season and weather; inflation and a general sense of unease were taking a toll too. Still, looking on the bright side, she'd sold a rose-pink flapper dress earlier that morning for just over two hundred pounds, which had earned them a profit of a hundred and eighty-three. She'd found it at a vintage sale a few months ago, torn and faded and obviously not worn or looked at in years. Since then she'd painstakingly restored it to its former glory, sourcing beads and crystals, silk and lace from the Internet, and using skills she'd barely known she'd had until she'd started working here.

Despite having been here for so long, there were still times when she found it hard to get her head around just how different her life was now to what it had been before. It was as though she'd stepped out of a drab, difficult existence into a world full of colour and plenty. There was so much here that was different, vibrant, absorbing, that she could barely remember a time before it. But she could, of course, because she'd never forget the beatings her mother had suffered at the hands of her drunken husband, the lack of support from local authorities, the way other women had turned aside, not wanting to get involved. Nor would she forget the poverty of their village, where any form of luxury and hope had been in equally short supply. She supposed it was different now, money had been pumped into the economy, but she knew that in spite of this government's cutbacks, Mia and Adam would never receive the kind of care or opportunities in Poland that were their birthright here.

Hearing a text jingle on her phone she turned back to the counter, and broke into a smile when she found a picture of Adam – from Daniel's phone – beaming all over his dear little face. He was holding up an impressively large fish. *Look what I caught.*

She didn't doubt for a minute that he'd had help, and not only because this was his very first fishing expedition, but because it was too big for him to have landed it on his own. She wouldn't have been at all surprised to discover that the stronger hands belonged to Daniel. He was such a remarkable boy, so kind and patient with Adam, never seeming to mind when Adam wanted to tag along, or sit next to him, or copy the things he did or said. If anything he seemed to encourage him, and for his part Adam was already showing small signs of a confidence Klaudia hadn't seen in him before.

Heaven only knew what it was about Daniel that Adam had taken to right from the start, but whatever it was no one could deny that there was a bond between the two boys that transcended all their differences, to make them as happy in each other's world as if they'd been sharing the space for years.

Starting as another text arrived, she saw it was from Misty at the pub and clicked on.

Next meeting confirmed for Thursday at 2. Hope you can make it.

Klaudia's insides clenched with unease. This was not a meeting she wanted to attend, or even know about, if the truth were told. As far as she was concerned these groups shouldn't even be necessary, at least not for the reasons they'd been formed.

'We need to help one another as much as we can,' the group leader had told her on the phone after Misty had passed on her number. Misty didn't have a problem herself, she was British born, but having been subjected to all sorts of abuse while growing up, thanks to her colour, she was as keen as Wilkie was to help anyone she felt was being treated as though they were in some way inferior or unwelcome.

Klaudia had only been to one meeting so far, and it had made her feel separate from the community at large, rather than an integral part of it. She wasn't sure this was the right way to go, forming groups who got together to share their fears and frustrations – kindnesses too, it had to be said – so they could advise one another on how to handle verbal, and in some cases physical, attacks. This particular movement was part of a nationwide effort to link people from all communities, so they could be assured that they weren't alone.

Klaudia already knew she wasn't alone, at least not

in that sense, but listening to people talking about the way they'd been treated hadn't made her feel any less insecure. If anything, it had increased her anxiety, for she now knew that the immigration authorities had swooped on a Romanian woman somewhere in Devon and taken her to a detention centre outside London. Apparently she was the mother of a British-born child, who'd been taken into care. How much truth there was to the story Klaudia had no idea, she hadn't been able to find any mention of it online, but, as someone had pointed out to her at the meeting, not everything got reported.

Since this was the era of fake news, she'd been trying to convince herself that the raid was apocryphal, a rumour that had sprung from fear of the worst and somehow turned itself into a believable scenario. But what if it wasn't a myth? What if they came for her in the same way, carried her off because she'd spent too long out of the country during her mother's illness and didn't have the right insurance? What if they locked her up and snatched Mia and Adam away? Though she had no doubt that Wilkie and Leanne would fight for the children, and would, please God, win, it just about broke her apart to think of the terrible fear and confusion her babies would be forced to suffer at the hands of the authorities before things could be sorted out. And what about her? How long would it be before they deported her? Would she be allowed to see her children before she went, or would the sight of them make the separation even harder?

Stop, she told herself forcefully, *just stop.*

To her relief the door opened at that moment, and seeing Leanne she instantly felt calmer.

'Hey, how's everything going?' Leanne asked, wiping her feet on the mat. 'I guess I've missed the rush?'

Klaudia smiled. 'You couldn't move in here an hour ago,' she quipped, and spotting Mia outside with Abby she felt her heart contract. As wrenching, even devastating as it would be for them all, maybe it was time for her to start thinking seriously about where she and the children could make a new life. Not Germany with Antoni; he'd found someone else, he'd told her in a recent email, but he'd wished her well.

Realising Leanne was waiting for an answer to something, she quickly pulled herself together. 'Sorry, I was miles away.'

'I said, I take it you've seen a picture of the fish,' Leanne repeated, going to hang up her coat.

Klaudia smiled again and held up her phone. 'He looks so pleased with himself, doesn't he?'

'And so he should be. Apparently they're all having a good day, so their catch, whatever it is, is on the menu tonight. Tom's offered to cook.'

Klaudia's eyebrows rose.

'Don't go there,' Leanne warned. 'It doesn't mean what you seem to think it does.'

'And what would that be?'

Leanne slanted her a look.

Klaudia's eyes were still twinkling as she got herself ready to go and take Abby and Mia shopping. If anyone deserved a little romance in their lives, after what she'd been through with Jack it was Leanne. And if

anyone needed to get a grip on herself and start thinking more positively, it was her. 'I'm going over to Mr
Chlebek's to pick up my order,' she said, already feeling the sadness of saying goodbye to her old friend.
'I'll see what he has left for dessert. Do I need to go to
the supermarket as well?'

'You probably should. We thought baked potatoes
and ratatouille to go with the fish. Mum would have
gone, but she's nursing a hangover.'

Klaudia smiled as she pictured a bleary-eyed Wilkie
with a glass of orange juice in one hand and her phone
in the other, so she could keep a check on the world
and its woes.

Remember to live in the moment, she told herself
firmly, as she left the shop. If you don't, all these special times with these very special people will pass you
by and you'll never get them back again.

Leanne wasn't entirely sure how many they now were
for dinner, as Blake and Jenny had dropped in while
passing half an hour ago and had been persuaded to
stay. Then Rowzee had driven down to check on Wilkie
and had also been coaxed into joining them. Richie had
just rung to say he was on his way (apparently it was
all off with the latest girlfriend), and Bel was bringing
Harry's older son, Josh, plus her niece and nephew
who were spending the weekend with their aunt.

'Mum, how many are we supposed to be laying the
table for?' Abby demanded, rummaging in the cutlery
drawer.

'I've no idea,' Leanne replied, laughing as she and

Tom danced around one another in the kitchen to get to where they were going. 'Just pair up all that we have and we'll hope for the best. Don't forget the napkins.'

'How are we doing for wine?' Wilkie wanted to know, peering worriedly into the fridge.

'I'll call Richie,' Tom responded, 'and get him to raid my mother's cellar on his way.'

'Does anyone want a glass now?' Wilkie offered hopefully.

'I thought you'd never ask,' Leanne told her. 'Tom, where did you put the scissors . . . Ah, there they are. How many fish do we actually have?'

'Seven.'

'*Seven!*'

'Don't worry, I shall perform something biblical,' he promised. 'Daniel!'

No reply.

'Daniel! Where are you?'

'Here,' Daniel cried, half running, half sliding down the stairs, with Neel close behind.

'You're in charge of games,' Tom informed him.

'What games?'

'The ones we're going to play after we've eaten.'

Daniel's eyes went briefly to Leanne and he started to grin. 'But I don't know any.'

'Yes you do,' Abby protested.

'Yeah, like football and cricket . . .'

'No, like that charades thing you showed us the other night. And there's the word stuff . . . Mum, you've got to see . . . Mum! What is that . . . ? Oh my God,' she exclaimed, and as everyone burst out laughing she quickly snapped a photo of her mother looking utterly bewildered with a trout's head on her shoulder.

'What is it?' Leanne demanded. 'What have I done?'

'There's a fish head on your shoulder,' Mia shouted.

Leanne looked at it, jumped and hit the thing on to the floor. 'Was that you?' she challenged Tom as he picked it up.

'Totally innocent,' he assured her.

'It was Wilkie,' Adam told her, clapping his hands.

'You're a grass!' Wilkie laughed.

'I'm a grass,' he cried proudly, leaping up and down.

Catching him, Daniel began play-fighting him on to the sofa with Juno, while Neel and Abby threw more logs on to the fire and Blake went round with the wine.

In no time at all they were enjoying one of the craziest and funniest evenings Leanne could remember in a long time – and that Klaudia could ever remember. There was so much banter and laughter that there wasn't a single moment of quiet, even when they found somewhere to perch to eat. There was also a little flirtation under way, Leanne noted, as Abby and Josh kept looking at each other and colouring up or trying to impress.

When the games started it was as though Christmas had broken out in early March.

'Do the word thing,' Abby urged Daniel excitedly. 'Mum, it is hilarious. You wait.'

Within minutes the adults were all breaking up with laughter, not because Daniel's 'word thing' was funny, but at the sight of the younger ones doubled up with mirth.

'OK, here's another,' he declared, apparently enjoying the limelight as his eyes flicked to Leanne to make sure she was still watching. 'I tried to catch some fog but I missed.'

There was a moment's confused silence before Mia cried delightedly, 'M-I-S-T.'

Why that was so side-splitting Leanne had no idea, but off they all went again into gales of hilarity, and the way Daniel's lively brown eyes seemed both thrilled and disbelieving made Leanne's heart swell with pride.

'Velcro! What a rip-off,' Daniel grinned.

Another explosion of laughter, followed by another when he said, 'I didn't like my beard at first, but then it grew on me.'

He seemed to know so many of these silly lines, and though Abby, Mia and Adam had clearly heard some of them before, they kept calling for more.

'Do the maths trick,' Neel challenged. 'The one you did in class the other day. None of you will get this right,' he promised. 'Even the teacher didn't.'

'I think she was pretending,' Daniel told him.

Neel shrugged. 'Do it again, whatever it was.'

'I can't remember. Was it, how many times can you take two from one hundred?'

'No, but it'll do.' Neel looked around, waiting for someone to work it out.

Leanne looked at Tom. He knew, she could tell, he just wasn't going to steal Daniel's thunder.

'I've got it! I've got it!' Abby declared. 'Fifty.'

Daniel regarded her sadly. 'Once,' he stated, 'because

after you've done it the first time it's not a hundred any more.'

Throwing a cushion at him as everyone applauded, Abby cried, 'Give us another.'

His eyes went briefly to Leanne again as he said, 'OK. How many sides does a circle have?'

'I know that one!' Josh shouted. 'An inside and an outside!'

Everyone cheered and jeered and Adam grabbed Daniel in a headlock trying to wrestle him down, while Abby gazed at her new heart-throb as though he were an intellectual god.

'You have to get really tough now,' Neel instructed Daniel. 'Do that one, you know, it had a third in it.'

'Oh, right.' Daniel sat up straighter, glanced at Leanne again and began. 'OK, so here goes. Nine minus three divided by a third plus one equals what?'

Wilkie's eyes crossed.

Harry said, 'We have to write this down.'

Mia said, 'I bet you know, don't you, Mum?'

Klaudia said, 'I might.'

'My mum's good at maths,' Mia told Daniel. 'She does accounts and things.'

'Do *you* know the answer?' Leanne asked Daniel, making him laugh.

'Sure I do,' he replied.

'This is like two plus two for him,' Neel informed her. 'He's a total genius.'

'He does all my maths homework,' Abby put in.

Leanne slanted her a look.

'Just kidding.'

'OK, so who knows the answer?' Bel demanded. 'Anyone?'

No one put a hand up.

'It's one,' Neel told them, 'but he'll have to tell you how to get there.'

Daniel went through it so swiftly that Leanne doubted anyone was the wiser, but it didn't matter. It was just fun watching how much he was enjoying himself; how thrilled he clearly was to be there.

The entertainment continued on into the evening with the performance of some ludicrous charades, notable for Wilkie trying to be clever with an imitation of *Batman Returns*, and Klaudia falling over Juno when attempting to *Climb Every Mountain*. Then there was freeze-dancing which Tom won, followed by some sort of quiz that Leanne was by now too tired and tipsy to follow, and then an entertaining selfie session broke out that most of them were probably going to regret in the morning when they went on to Facebook.

Eventually Tom and Richie carried a sleeping Mia and Adam over to the stables, followed by a merry Klaudia, while Wilkie and Leanne said a sleepy goodnight to the others, and those who were staying disappeared off to bed.

'There's plenty of room at the farmhouse,' Wilkie told Tom when he and Richie came back, 'if you guys would rather not drive.'

'That's kind of you, Wilkie,' he said, drawing her into an embrace, 'but believe it or not I've only had one glass, and I have to be on the road early in the morning.'

'Where are you going?' Richie demanded, playing an idle game of catch with Juno.

'Only to London. I'll be back on Tuesday, Wednesday at the latest.' To Leanne he said, 'Thanks for a fabulous evening.'

'It was the best,' Richie informed her, giving her a hug. 'I'll catch a ride with Dad and get someone to bring me back for my car tomorrow, if that's OK.'

'Of course,' she assured him.

'Come with me,' Wilkie said, linking Richie's arm and practically frogmarching him outside, 'I have something to say to you.'

As the door closed behind them Leanne turned to Tom. 'That was subtle,' she commented.

He laughed. 'I'll take it.' He was gazing into her eyes in a way that was making it hard for her to breathe properly. 'I meant it,' he said. 'It was a really special evening. Thanks.'

'Thank *you*. You not only caught the dinner, you cooked it. And supplied most of the wine.'

His eyes were still on hers, and feeling the colour rising to her cheeks, she said, 'There's still quite a lot of jewellery to sort out. I can . . .' She broke off, not sure what she wanted to say.

'Let's continue on Wednesday or Thursday,' he said. 'I'll call you.'

As he took out his keys and went to the door she didn't know whether she felt relieved or disappointed that he was going without something more. Disappointed. Yes, definitely disappointed, but also relieved.

Hearing a sound behind her she turned round,

expecting to see someone there. No sign of anyone, but she suspected that Abby and Daniel had been watching and listening.

Tom's eyes were shining with laughter, but he said no more as he opened the door and went out into the night.

Half an hour later, after putting a second load into the dishwasher and straightening up stray throws and cushions, Leanne was on her way along the landing to her bedroom, yawning and wondering if she could leave her mascara on just this once, when Daniel, looking even smaller than usual in his pyjamas, came out of his room.

'Hi, are you OK?' she asked fondly. 'I thought you'd be asleep by now.'

'I was waiting for you,' he told her. 'I just wanted to say . . .' He shrugged, awkwardly. 'I really like it here.'

'Oh, Daniel,' she murmured, going to embrace him, 'you are so welcome here. You've fitted in amazingly well, it should be me thanking you.'

Though he wasn't quite hugging her back, he didn't try to break away, until finally with a catch in his voice he said, 'You remind me of my mum sometimes,' and turning away he disappeared back into his room.

Chapter Fourteen

Abby was pushing frantically through the crowd in the school yard, not caring about the angry protests and thumps she was receiving as she thrust her fellow students out of the way.

'What is it?' someone cried. 'Abby! What is it?'

Seeing it was Josh she grabbed his hand. 'I think it's Daniel,' she panicked. 'We have to get to him.'

Being taller and stronger, Josh Beck forged a path through the chanting mob, seeming oblivious to the insults and threats that followed them. When they reached the inner circle Abby saw to her horror that Daniel was on the ground being kicked and mocked by Ed Foster, a renowned and sadistic bully. Foster's mates were cheering him on, so were some of the crowd, while others screamed for it to stop.

Abby and Josh exchanged a glance, read one another perfectly, and recklessly threw themselves on top of Daniel in an effort to protect him.

Luckily for them a whistle was already blowing and the crowd was parting for Mr Philbert, the head of PE, to come through.

'Foster! My office, now!' he barked, taking next to no time to assess the situation. 'Abby Delaney and Josh Beck, on your feet.'

As they got up Mr Philbert dropped to his knees to check on Daniel. 'Are you all right?' he asked, making it sound more of a command than a question.

Daniel managed to nod, but blood was pouring from his nose and one eye was already too swollen to open.

'Let's get him to First Aid,' Mr Philbert instructed Josh and Abby. 'Can you stand up?' he asked Daniel.

Daniel forced himself slowly to his feet, wincing at the pain in his back and ribs, reaching out for his bag.

Abby grabbed the bag, and put an arm around him. 'What happened?' she whispered as they started across the yard to the main school building. Many eyes were following them, but with the drama over, most were drifting off home.

'Nothing,' he replied, using a hand to wipe the blood from his nose. 'It's OK.'

'Mate, you're hurt,' Josh protested. 'What made them lay into you like that?'

'I'll talk to you later,' Philbert told Daniel as they reached the door. 'See that he gets to the nurse,' he instructed Abby and Josh.

'I'm OK,' Daniel insisted after Philbert had gone. 'I don't need the nurse.'

'Yes you do,' Abby argued.

'It'll just complicate things. Let me clean up in the toilets and we can go home.'

'I've got rugger practice,' Josh grimaced. 'Are you sure you're going to be OK?'

'I'll stay with him,' Abby declared.

'Text me later,' Josh urged, and after lifting Daniel's face to inspect it more closely, he said, 'Lucky we came when we did.'

After Daniel had disappeared into the toilets Abby paced up and down the corridor, phone in hand, trying to decide whether or not to call her mother. Ordinarily she wouldn't have hesitated, but the way Daniel was treating this was making her hold back, at least until she'd spoken to him again.

By the time he came out she was sitting on a bench next to a row of lockers, tapping a foot on the ground and still clutching her phone. She sprang to her feet. 'OK?' she asked, offering him his bag.

'Yeah, I'm good,' he assured her, taking it.

He definitely looked better now he'd washed the blood from his face, but the bruise around his eye was turning into a shiner.

'So what happened?' she asked as they started back down the corridor.

He shrugged.

'They didn't attack you for no reason, so . . .'

'Apparently Foster's pissed off that I'm good at maths,' he interrupted. 'He wanted to teach me a different kind of lesson.'

They walked on quietly, out through the gates and along to the bus stop. 'Mum'll want to know how you got the black eye,' Abby pointed out.

'Let's say it happened in football.'

She gave it some thought and decided she'd feel better about keeping his secret if she knew what lay behind it. In the end, steeling herself, she said, 'Did it have something to do with your dad?'

He looked at her quickly and away again.

Her heart started to thud. 'It did, didn't it?'

He still didn't answer, and as she didn't have the courage to say any more she let it go.

'So you know about my dad,' he said, finally.

Feeling a bit blindsided, she tried to think what to say. 'I know he's in prison,' she said eventually.

'And do you know why?'

She swallowed drily as she admitted that she did. 'But it wasn't you who did it. No one should be trying to blame you.'

A long silence followed. He kept his head turned away, but she could sense how tense and miserable he was.

'How did they find out?' she asked worriedly.

'They didn't. It wasn't about that, but I expect they will find out. Sooner or later.'

'So why did they pick on you?'

He shrugged. 'I'm good at maths, I'm fostered, I'm black, take your pick.'

Feeling terrible for him, she took his arm as she said, 'You have to tell Mum. They can't get away . . .'

'No,' he protested, and tears filled his eyes.

'Why? She'll talk to the head . . .'

'I don't want her to. I just want . . .' His voice caught on a sob and he shrugged her off.

'Dan, talk to me. Tell me why . . .'

'They'll make me go somewhere else if they know I'm being beaten up,' he growled.

'But Mum won't let that happen. I promise you.'

'She won't have a choice. The school won't want any more trouble, and once everyone knows who I really am they'll start saying they don't want their kids mixing with me. It's going to happen anyway. They'll take me away . . .' He couldn't say any more, he was trying too hard not to cry.

'Listen,' Abby said, 'you don't know my mother and grandmother very well yet, but they absolutely will not let it happen. I swear it.'

He swallowed hard and put his head back as though to sink the tears. 'I still don't want them to know,' he said. He turned to her. 'Promise not to say anything.'

Hoping she was doing the right thing, she nodded. 'OK, I promise, just this once. If it happens again . . .' She wasn't sure what she'd do if it did, so she let it drop.

A while later, as they sat side by side on the bus going through town, he said, 'Doesn't it put you off me, knowing about my dad?'

'No,' she replied honestly. 'It wasn't you who did it.'

Neither of them spoke again until the bus turned on to the coast road and started towards Ash Morley.

'He didn't do it,' Daniel said quietly.

Abby sat very still.

'If you knew him,' Daniel said, 'you'd know he didn't do it.'

Abby was thinking about what she'd seen on the news.

'I'm not lying. It wasn't him.'

Feeling she had to say something, she said, 'So who was it?'

His eyes went down and she could see how tightly he was holding his bag, forcing back his pent-up emotions. 'I only know that it wasn't him,' he replied.

Understanding why he didn't want to believe it, she decided not to press him any further, and in an effort to try and make things more normal she took out her phone and opened a game.

'What happened to *your* dad?' he asked suddenly.

Abby's throat turned dry. 'We don't ever talk about him,' she said.

'Why not?'

'We just don't.'

He looked at her and away again. 'Do you ever see him?' he asked.

'I can't, he's dead.'

'Oh, sorry.'

'It's OK.'

After a while he said, 'Are you upset about it?'

She shrugged. 'Kind of, but not in the way you think.'

'Then in what way?'

'It doesn't matter.'

Letting it go, he watched her playing for a while, then said, 'I'd like to see my dad, but no one will let me.'

Without thinking about it, she said, 'That's just mean.'

He nodded, and took her phone to show her the fastest route to the next level of the game.

*   *   *

251

'Right now,' Leanne was saying to Tom on the phone, 'Klaudia and I are on our way to see Jan and Richard York's new baby. It arrived a couple of days ago. A healthy bouncing boy. Everyone doing well, I'm happy to report. So where are you?'

'On the M4 heading in your direction. I've got a meeting in Bristol on the way, which will probably drag on, so it's likely I'll stay over. Please pass my congratulations to the new parents.'

'Of course. I'm sure they'll be thrilled. Did you hear from Graeme Ogilvy or Andee Lawrence yet about fixing up the villa?'

'Graeme and I have arranged to meet sometime next week, details TBC. Apparently Andee's in Stockholm for the next few days, so we're not sure yet if she'll be joining us.'

'Yes, I heard she was away again. I was supposed to be meeting up with her, but I'm sure we'll catch up soon.' Waving frantically towards a parking space before they passed it and gasping at how fast Klaudia crossed the traffic to grab it, she said, 'We've just arrived, so I should probably go. Have a good meeting.'

'I'll try. Before you ring off we should set a date for you to come and inspect more jewellery.'

'Just let me know what works for you and I'll try to schedule things around it. Klaudia says hi, by the way.'

'Hi to Klaudia.'

After ending the call Leanne grinned. 'I knew you'd have said it if you'd thought of it.'

'Absolutely,' Klaudia agreed, and checked her phone to find out who'd rung while she was driving.

'Mia,' she declared, and went through to the message. 'They're making banners at Wilkie's ready for the science march,' she told Leanne, 'and they'll be having tea there.'

'Are Abby and Daniel with them?'

'Apparently yes, because she sent this. Brace yourself.'

It turned out to be a photo of Daniel with a swollen and deeply purple eye.

Instantly worried, Leanne asked, 'Does she say how he got it?'

'Football, apparently.'

Leanne looked again, not sure she believed it.

'You can quiz him later,' Klaudia reminded her. 'For now let's go and meet baby York.'

With Richard and Jan's spacious apartment being at the heart of the new marina complex, it took them a good few minutes to walk through the pedestrian zone to the snazzy modern block with its filigree balconies and expensive views.

'So,' Klaudia said once they were safely through the security gate, 'am I right in guessing that Mr Franklyn is on his way back to Kesterly?'

Leanne tried to sound nonchalant. 'You are,' she confirmed.

'And you're feeling quite excited about that?'

Leanne tried for a shrug, but only managed a laugh.

'I think he's keen,' Klaudia informed her.

Leanne's insides fluttered like a teenager's as she said, 'He's just being friendly.'

'Right.'

They walked on for a while, both of them trying not to laugh.

'Being serious for a moment,' Leanne said, 'I know we're trying to avoid this, at least I am, but there's no getting away from the fact that our financial situation could be much improved if we were to auction some of the dresses his mother left to Glory.'

'It's true, but you're worried about using them that way.'

Leanne didn't deny it.

'I don't think he was expecting you to keep them and wear them,' Klaudia pointed out. 'In fact, I'd go as far as to say I imagine Helen left them to Glory so that Glory could sell them.'

'Mm,' Leanne responded thoughtfully. 'It seems such a pity to let them go out of the family though, doesn't it?'

'It does to me, but apparently she was happy about it and if he is too . . . Of course, we don't know yet how much we can actually get for them. Or how long it might take to sell them.'

'So we need to come up with something p.d.q. to help us out of the disastrous slump we've fallen into.'

'Correct. And I've had some thoughts. I'll go into more detail on the way home, but in a nutshell, I think we should try out some of the ideas for expansion Glory herself had before she took ill.'

Leanne was intrigued. 'I didn't know she had any,' she confessed.

'I'm not sure how serious she was, or how well they'd work, but she suggested staging some party-type fashion shows at local hotels, and vintage teas for birthdays or hen dos or any other sort of special occasion. She thought businesses might even be interested, if they had some kind of event going on.'

Already feeling uplifted by the possibilities, Leanne said, 'It's definitely worth thinking about. Let's talk it over with Mum when we get back. She's sure to have something worthwhile to add, and given it's Glory Days she'll want to be in the loop.'

Minutes later they were fussing around Richard and Jan's new son, Joel, keeping their voices down so as not to wake him.

'He's been so good,' Jan told them with a tender smile.

'And the baby hasn't been too bad either,' Richard added, passing them both a drink.

Jan's eyes shone with merriment as she looked at her husband, the bear-like man whose enormous, skilful hands had saved more lives in the fields of conflict than probably even he knew.

'So, tell us all about Daniel and how he's settling in,' Jan said, as Leanne sat next to the crib and felt nostalgic for when her own had been that size.

Leanne needed little encouragement to boast about how funny and clever he was, and was just getting round to the black eye when Richard's phone rang.

'Sorry. I'll take it in the bedroom,' he said.

As the door closed behind him Jan put a hand on Leanne's to still her, and turned to Klaudia. 'What's the latest on your permanent residency?' she asked softly.

Klaudia's expression sobered as she said, 'I've just

emailed to admit that I don't have the Comprehensive Sickness Insurance that everyone in my position is supposed to have. The fact that most of us had never even heard of it before the referendum probably won't help our cases, and apparently we can't just take it up now. We have to show that we've always had it, and as that's not possible all I can do is wait to see what they say. Best case is that they'll decide it doesn't matter. Worst, is deportation.'

As the word fell like some awful knell between them, Jan's expression showed her shared agony. 'It's a horrible position to be in,' she said. 'As you know, Richard is British and obviously so is our son, but with the way things are we have no idea if I'll be allowed to stay, especially when I've been here less than a year. Nor do we know if Richard will be given residency in the Netherlands where most of my family is, so it isn't possible to say we can settle there either.'

Feeling helpless and even ashamed, in spite of knowing she wasn't responsible for the angst, Leanne said, 'I can't imagine anyone's going to negotiate a deal that will end up breaking families apart.'

'We hope not,' Jan responded gravely, 'but at the moment we have no idea what will happen, and that is very difficult, very stressful for everyone who is in our position.'

Leanne's eyes went to Klaudia, whose face seemed as unreadable as her future as she gazed down at the baby. With a flush of embarrassment, Leanne remembered telling her that she had a plan if things didn't work out, but Jan's words had just reminded her that her airy notion of them recreating Ash Morley in Ireland wasn't a possibility either. Even if her mother were willing to go, and of course she wouldn't be.

So, for the moment, there was absolutely no way round this. In spite of having British-born children, and in Jan's case a British husband, both Jan and Klaudia had no choice but to go on living with the strain of not knowing what the future might hold. At least Jan had Richard, and all the contacts they'd made around the world. Somehow they'd work something out. But Klaudia only had them, so what on earth could they do to help her?

The following evening Leanne was about to go and collect Daniel from choir practice when Abby wandered into the kitchen, looking troubled.

'What is it?' Leanne asked, trying not to glance at the time.

'I've just been FaceTiming Kate,' Abby replied, 'and she said I needed to talk to you.'

Curious, and pleased with Kate's advice – and the fact that Abby was apparently taking it – Leanne decided it wouldn't matter if she was a few minutes late, and put down her keys.

'It's about Daniel,' Abby said, perching on a bar stool.

Leanne stilled. 'What about him?'

Abby's eyes came to hers, flicked about the kitchen and went down again.

'What about him?' Leanne pressed.

Abby was knitting her fingers. 'He really wants to see his dad,' she said.

Thrown, as much by this as by the fact that Abby and

Daniel must have discussed it, Leanne said, 'He told you that?'

Abby nodded.

Leanne swallowed. 'What else did he sa,.

Abby shrugged. 'Nothing really.'

There was more, Leanne could tell, so she waited in the hope that Abby would get to it.

In the end, Abby said, 'I think it's mean not to let him see his dad.'

'But you know what his dad did. The decision has been taken for Daniel's own good.'

Abby's face was pale; she was clearly unsure of her ground, though apparently felt the need to speak up for Daniel. 'Do you really believe it's good for him not to see his dad?' she asked. 'As far as we know he never did anything bad to Daniel.'

But he did to Kylie, Leanne wanted to say.

As though reading her mind, Abby said, 'He doesn't believe his dad did it.'

Wishing she felt better prepared for this, Leanne said, 'How did the subject of his dad come up?'

Abby shrugged and looked away. 'I can't remember. It just did.'

Leanne's suspicions closed in. 'Would you like to try that again?' she suggested.

'What do you mean?'

'You do remember, so why not tell me?'

Abby's eyes flashed. 'Because it doesn't matter, OK? I just thought you should know that he wants to see his dad,' and leaving it there she went back to her room.

* * *

The following afternoon Leanne was at Villa Tramonto, sitting on the floor of Helen's high-ceilinged, ornate bedroom with her back against the side of the bed and Tom sitting beside her. They were surrounded by tiny drawers that he'd taken from the japan chest and laid out for them to inspect in a more comfortable position than standing.

So far nothing particularly valuable had come to light, though there were some exquisite lapis lazuli earrings, a very grand garnet necklace and several art deco-style bracelets that she'd put up on the bed ready to be photographed and posted on their eBay shop.

Though she was acutely aware of how close he was, especially when his hand touched hers to give or take a gemstone, or he leaned across her to pick up another drawer, she was just about managing to stay focused on what they were doing – and what they were discussing.

'So have you spoken to Daniel about it yet?' he asked, as he gave up trying to piece a broken cameo together.

'No. I thought I should talk to his social worker first, so I've left a message for her to call me.'

'And if it gets the go-ahead, how are you going to feel about taking him to the prison?'

'Not great, but it might be that someone from social services has to do it.'

He nodded thoughtfully, and reached for a silvery mesh bag. 'Do you know which prison Marks is in?' he asked, emptying a dozen or so clip earrings into his palm.

'Sellybrook. So it wouldn't be too long a drive.

However, the prospect of visiting that place even without the added horror of who we'll meet there . . .' She let her words trail off.

He said nothing more as he tried to match the earrings and she continued to untangle a string of black pearls. 'It's hard to know,' he remarked eventually, 'whether it's the best thing for a child to be denied contact with a parent when the parent is Patrick Marks.'

'They do have contact,' she told him. 'They write quite regularly.'

Seeming surprised, he said, 'Have you ever read the letters?'

'No. Daniel hasn't offered to show me, and he doesn't seem to want to discuss them either.'

With a sigh, he tossed three stray earrings into the junk pile and placed four pairs back in the bag for her to take away. 'It'll be interesting to hear what social services have to say,' he commented, and taking the pearls she was still trying to unravel he tossed them across the room.

She laughed, and picked up another drawer. Inside was a fraying velvet choker decorated with a trio of fake emeralds in bezels of dull crystals. More stones to be released, before adding the ribbon to the junk pile.

Speaking over one another he said, 'Changing the subject,' as she said, 'On another note.'

'You first,' he insisted.

'No, you.'

'I was only going to ask if you'd like some more tea.'

Not entirely believing it, she slanted him a look.

'I've only just finished the last one,' she reminded him, 'so I think I can hang on for a while. Unless you want some.'

'No, I'm good. So, what were you going to say?'

She was fiddling with the clasp of a rhinestone brace-let, not entirely sure, now she had the opportunity, that she wanted to take it. Deciding she would, she said, 'Well, I was wondering what happened on Paxos.'

He seemed perplexed for a moment, then apparently recalling the favourite-holiday conversation at the Mermaid, he said, 'Ah, yes. So typical of my son to bring it up the way he did. He gets a kick out of embarrassing me.'

After a moment, she remarked, 'I got the impression that it actually wasn't your favourite holiday.'

He laughed. 'No, it certainly wasn't that,' he confirmed. 'It was where my marriage came to an inglorious end in spectacular fashion.' He used his teeth to break a knotted thread and caught a dozen blue beads in cupped hands as they fell. 'We'd rented a villa,' he continued, 'three families, all with kids of the same age, twelve or thirteen – actually Richie was fourteen by then. Luiza, my wife, managed to convince herself that I was having an affair with one of the other wives. I wasn't, but Luiza was never someone to let the truth get in the way of something she wanted. And what she wanted, on that holiday, was an excuse to sleep with the Adonis of a pool boy. So she did, and told me after that she wouldn't have done it if she hadn't been so upset about my affair.'

Picturing Luiza as a tempestuous, erotic siren with

smouldering eyes and juicy red lips, Leanne said, 'How did you know that she slept with him?'

His tone was wry as he said, 'Actually, I don't think much sleeping was involved, but taking your point, we walked in on them. All of us. We'd been out sailing for the day, and when we got back there she was, stark naked on the veranda, riding the boy so vigorously that she didn't even realise we were there until he scrambled out from under her.'

Wondering if he really found it as amusing as he seemed to, Leanne said, 'So Richie saw it?'

'Oh yes. I think the image emblazoned itself so vividly on the poor kid's mind that he was in his twenties before he could blot it out sufficiently to indulge in the exercise himself. From what I can tell, he's making up for lost time.'

Understanding that no child ever wanted to find a parent in flagrante, or even think about it come to that, Leanne said, 'Were you upset? I guess you must have been.'

'At the time I was more embarrassed and angry than the kind of upset you're meaning, but I did still love her, in spite of how impossible our marriage had become. It was always going to end, I just didn't envisage it happening like that.'

'And she's in Argentina now, Richie tells me.'

'With a new husband, God help him, and surrounded by family, which was what she always wanted.'

'Where did you meet?'

'In Buenos Aires. I was working at the embassy there, her father was – still is – a prominent businessman. We were introduced at a cocktail party, and I guess you could say it was love at first sight. We were married within the year, Richie came along soon after, and when I was recalled to London she was happy to come too. She loved London, and Paris where I was posted next, but when less glamorous locations – at least to her mind – started coming on to the agenda she didn't want anything to do with them. So, she stayed in London, had numerous affairs I'm sure, and I confess I'm not entirely innocent myself, but what mattered to us both was that she wouldn't be far away if Richie needed a parent. He didn't live with her, he was at Millfield by then . . .' He broke off as his mobile rang, and seeing who it was his eyebrows rose. 'Speak of the devil,' he drawled drily and clicked on. 'We were just talking about you,' he said, getting to his feet and stretching his legs. 'Where are you?'

Realising it was Richie, not Luiza, Leanne carried on sorting the trinkets in her lap, only half listening to the conversation until Tom gave a shout of laughter. 'You have to be kidding,' he cried, sitting down on the bed. 'Listen to this,' he said to Leanne, 'he's at the dog pound and there's a Labrador-cross he thinks we should give a home to. Richie, my son, how much longer are you going to be in this job? A year at most, and once this house is up together and sold I won't be here . . . No, I can't have it in London with me, I'm not there often enough, and I can't take it anywhere else either. A dog needs a proper . . . I hear what you're saying, but I'm telling you if you want a dog it will be your responsibility . . .' They apparently moved on to another topic then, because he said, 'Hang on, I think I saw it downstairs. I'll go and check.'

As he left the room Leanne got to her feet and began packing up the jewellery they'd put aside for the shop, her movements stiff and slightly awkward. His conversation with Richie had been a timely wake-up call for her to remember who he was and how he saw his future. Of course he'd never said that it was going to be here in Kesterly, so she couldn't accuse him of misleading her. Nevertheless, it hadn't stopped her from harbouring hopes that something might change his mind. Now she felt foolish and angry with herself for even thinking she might feature somewhere in his plans. Clearly he had no more intention of entering into a relationship with her than he had of getting a dog.

By the time he'd found whatever he was hunting down for Richie, she was at the front door with her coat on.

Finding her there, he gave a start of surprise. 'Are you going already?' he asked, putting aside his phone.

'I should,' she replied, hoping she sounded friendly. 'I'd forgotten I promised to take over from Klaudia at four. She's just texted to find out where I am.'

Eyeing her curiously he said, 'Am I . . . ? Did I say something?'

She gave a laugh. 'No, of course not. I'm sorry. I just . . . Thanks very much for this.' She held up the box of his mother's gemstones. 'We'll get them photographed and displayed by the end of next week. I'll send you a link to our store.'

As she turned to go out he said, 'Leanne?'

She pretended not to hear, and quickly getting into her car she gave him a cheery wave before heading down the drive.

She hadn't got far before he rang, but she let it go to messages. She couldn't speak to him now. She needed to collect herself first, and remember that she wasn't the kind of person who could enter into a torrid affair with no strings attached and come out unscathed. Presumably that was what all the flirting had been about, or why would he have bothered?

She'd reached the coast road by the time the phone rang again, and seeing it was the school this time she quickly clicked on to the handsfree.

'Mrs Delaney. It's Carol Hodge from Kesterly High. I'm ringing to let you know that Daniel is on his way to A & E.'

Chapter Fifteen

Daniel was sitting quietly beside Leanne in the front seat of her car as she drove them over the cattle grid into Ash Morley and parked next to a bush of blooming camellias. Since Wilkie had gone to see Jack's mother today, and Abby was at Bel's where she was staying for tea with Neel and Josh, Leanne and Daniel should have the place to themselves until Klaudia got home with the children.

Following Daniel into the barn, Leanne closed the door and turned off her phone. She'd already texted Klaudia and her mother to let them know that the blow to Daniel's head hadn't turned out to be serious – no fractures or concussion, just a nice big swelling to replace the one going down around his eye. He'd acquired this new injury, she'd been told by the school nurse who'd gone with him in the ambulance, from falling off a chair. Why he'd been standing on a chair in the first place Leanne had yet to find out.

'Are you hungry?' she asked, as he paused in the kitchen to fuss an ecstatic Juno.

'No thanks,' he mumbled.

'Thirsty?'

He shook his head.

He started towards the stairs, Juno at his heels, but stopped when she said, 'We need to talk.'

Keeping his head down, he turned around and came to sit in the chair she was holding out for him.

She put a glass of squash in front of him and sat down too. 'So what really happened?' she asked firmly, but gently.

He shrugged and seemed to twitch nervously.

'Two injuries in the space of a week,' she said. 'Coincidence? Or is there something I need to know?'

He didn't move, just continued to stare at his drink.

Sitting forward, she said, 'Daniel, you must know that you mean a great deal to me already, and I want you to understand that anything you tell me can stay between us if you want it to.' She allowed a moment for that to sink in, then went on, 'Let's start with the black eye. I'm guessing you didn't get it playing football. Am I right?'

He nodded.

'Someone hit you?'

He didn't deny it.

'Do you know why they hit you?'

He shrugged again.

'Something must have been said.'

'It doesn't matter.'

'It does to me.'

'It's just stuff. It doesn't bother me.'

'Was it about your father?'

He swallowed noisily and shook his head again.

Not sure whether to believe it, she decided to leave it there for the moment and said, 'Tell me why you were standing on a chair today.'

His breath shook slightly as he inhaled. 'Because the teacher told me to.'

Confused, she said, 'Why?'

His cheeks were reddening as he said, 'He got angry because I kept putting up my hand to answer questions. He said I should give someone else a chance.'

'So did you?'

'Yes, but no one else knew the answers, so I put my hand up again. That's when he made me stand on a chair. He said if I was so clever I should be in a place where everyone could see me.'

Shocked, and furious, she said, 'And how did you come to fall off?'

'It happened after the bell went. He said I had to stay there until everyone left the room. They started going out and he went with them, then someone came up behind me and pushed me.'

Aching at the mere thought of it, she said, 'Did you see who it was?'

'No.'

'Did the teacher know it had happened?'

'I don't think so. I got knocked out when my head hit the desk so I don't know.'

Sitting back in her chair, she took a moment to try and work out the best way to handle this. In the end she said carefully, 'If you think any of this is to do with your dad . . .'

'It's because I'm fostered,' he broke in quietly. 'Sometimes that's enough to make other kids pick on you.'

As saddened by that as she was reluctantly prepared to believe it, she said, 'Has anyone mentioned your dad?'

'No.'

'Are you sure?'

'I'm sure.'

Wondering if the teacher who'd made him stand on the chair knew who he really was, she made a mental note to find out.

'Can I go now?' he asked. 'I've got loads of homework.'

Touched by how diligent he was in spite of everything, she said, 'You know, if you want to talk about your dad . . .'

'It's OK,' he interrupted.

She hesitated, but when he didn't get up she decided to press on. 'Or your mum,' she added.

At that he turned his head away, but she could see that he was struggling not to cry, and mindful of all that was bottled up inside him, she pulled him into her arms and held him as close as she could make him come.

He didn't try to get away, but he didn't embrace her either, he just held his hands to his face as he sobbed and sobbed as though he might never stop. She could feel the power of his grief racking his slender limbs, and breaking his heart. She wondered if he'd ever cried like this before, with someone trying to hold him together as he struggled to cope with his world falling apart. Not yet twelve years old, and he'd already experienced life at its cruellest. First his mother, then his father, then the terrible upheaval, insecurity and bullying that had followed.

It was breaking her heart too.

Many minutes passed before he turned aside with his head still down. Gently she asked, 'Do you have any photos of your mum?'

He shook his head and more tears ran down his cheeks. 'You can see her online,' he said. 'She was a singer. She used to sing to me and my dad all the time.' He gasped as he sobbed again. 'I can show you if you like.'

Smiling, she said, 'Yes, I'd like that very much.'

Taking the laptop from his bag, he typed in his password and went straight to a picture of a young, almost patrician-looking woman with long black hair in a single plait over one shoulder, and turquoise paint colouring the lids of her almond-shaped eyes. From the pose and lighting it was clearly some kind of publicity shot, but the next photo he clicked to showed her laughing in a way that brought a smile to Leanne's lips. She wasn't only beautiful, she was vibrant and carefree; someone who seemed so at ease with herself and in love with life that Leanne felt overwhelmed by the tragedy of her early death.

'She's lovely,' she whispered.

'My dad said she was the most beautiful woman in the whole wide world and I was lucky to have her as a mum.'

Having to swallow, Leanne said, 'I think he was right.'

'Do you want to hear her sing?'

Leanne nodded eagerly. Moments later they were on YouTube listening to the soft, smoky sound of Gracie Marks performing a jazz rendition of 'Isn't She Lovely', except she'd changed the lyric to 'he'.

'She recorded this when I was born,' Daniel told her. 'It's my favourite.'

Wanting to sob and howl and hug him again, she had to take a steadying breath before she could say, 'I'm not surprised.'

'She used to sing with bands in pubs or different concert places, and sometimes she'd sing on her own. She recorded lots of backing tracks for famous people.' He named some and he was right, they were famous. 'No one knew her name, but my dad used to say that everyone would one day.' His head went down. 'But then she got sick and she couldn't sing any more.'

Leading him to the sofa, Leanne sat down with him and encouraged him to tell her more. So he did, tentatively at first, but then with growing enthusiasm as he tried to remember everything in the right order. There was so much and it came tumbling out of him with such eagerness and joy that Juno's head tilted wildly from side to side as he tried to understand. Daniel laughed and hugged him, told him that his mother had loved dogs, and had promised he could have one . . . Then the words ran out and he sat looking empty and bewildered, and sadder than any child should ever have to be.

Leanne pulled him to her again, and wasn't surprised when, within minutes, he was fast asleep. After the blow to his head and the emotional outpouring he was clearly exhausted.

After a while she settled him more comfortably, put a throw over him and went quietly back to the kitchen where she turned on her phone, finding several missed calls and messages from Abby, Wilkie, Klaudia and the school.

Deciding to answer them all by group text so she wouldn't wake Daniel, she sent a few lines letting them know that he was now at home and sleeping.

Then she sat down at her computer to compose a letter to Patrick Marks.

At Eileen Delaney's neat semi-detached in a suburb of Reading, Wilkie was allowing her reluctant hostess to talk down to her in a way that seemed to come naturally to Eileen. 'But the boy's father is a murderer,' she was saying, as if Wilkie didn't already know that. 'And for all we know he's a paedophile too.'

'No charges were ever brought for paedophilia,' Wilkie pointed out patiently.

Eileen's prim features tightened. 'I read the papers; I know what happened as well as you do, and the idea of my granddaughter being in any way associated with that family . . .' She shuddered, words apparently failing her.

Wilkie decided not to remind her that Abby was also *her* granddaughter, and said, 'I haven't come here to argue with you, Eileen. We both know that you can't take Abby away from Leanne, which is why you haven't tried. You'd gain nothing from it apart from alienating her further, and I don't believe you actually want that.'

Eileen's whole demeanour remained taut, though Wilkie felt certain it wasn't what she wanted. 'All I care about is doing the right thing for my granddaughter,' Eileen stated tersely, 'which is apparently more than I can say for you.'

Letting the ludicrous jibe sail past her, Wilkie said, 'The reason I'm here is to try and bring some perspective to the situation, and I was hoping this would help.'

Eileen's flinty eyes flicked towards Wilkie's hands as she reached into her bag and brought out an iPad.

'I want you to see for yourself,' Wilkie said, handing the tablet to Eileen, 'that he's just like any other boy . . .'

'But he *isn't*,' Eileen protested.

'Yes he is. We're none of us responsible for what our parents have done. Not me, not you, and certainly not him.' She was looking at a shot of Daniel playing football on the beach, and holding it so Eileen could see it too if she cared to. She hadn't asked if Eileen would consider Abby to be guilty of what her father had done, but hoped that on some level the question was reaching her.

Suddenly getting to her feet, Eileen walked around to the back of the sofa, as if trying to distance herself from the iPad, or perhaps from Wilkie. 'I know you think you're some kind of saint,' she declared, 'put on this earth to try to make the rest of us look small or lacking in some way, but your holier-than-thou nonsense doesn't work with me. Abby should never have been exposed to a child like that, and I blame you and your daughter for making it happen. You've only done it to try and bring some sort of glory down on yourselves. Well, it's going to backfire on you with this boy, mark my words.'

Carrying on as though the ridiculous outburst hadn't happened, Wilkie said, 'Eileen, why don't you just look at him? He's very sweet, and he's good at so many things.' She swiped the screen. 'Look, you can see him here fixing up his fishing rod; and here he is with Adam, who's six and has a little developmental issue. He's mad about Daniel and Daniel's very good with him. And here he is with Abby. Have you ever seen two kids laughing so hard? They're enjoying themselves so much. Oh, this one is adorable; he's fast asleep with the dog, and still in his school uniform. I guess he must have worked especially hard that day. He's very clever, you know.'

'You can put it away now, thank you.'

Wilkie looked up. 'He's a *child*, Eileen, and nothing you say will convince me that you'd really turn your back on him.'

Eileen was nothing if not stubborn. 'I would on that child,' she insisted, 'and you should too. Let someone else take care of him. One of his own people. I'm sure he'd be much happier there.'

Wilkie's eyes flashed. 'One of his own people?' she repeated.

'You know what I mean.'

Sorry that she did, Wilkie hid her distaste and said, 'The reason you're getting so worked up about this is quite transparent to me, but I wonder if it is to you.'

Eileen's nostrils flared.

'You're sad and grieving for your son, and you're upset because as far as you're concerned Leanne and Abby aren't doing the same. This business with Daniel is no more than a cry for attention. You're angry and hurt and you want be heard. More than that, you want to be cor dered and understood. And frankly, I think you s uld be. As a mother myself I feel very deeply fc what you've been through, and I also think that Leanne and I could have done a lot more than we have to help you deal with your loss.'

'You certainly could.'

Ignoring the interruption, Wilkie said, 'We've been far too focused on ourselves and settling Leanne and Abby at Ash Morley, but I'd like to try and put that right. I'd like you to feel included as an important member of our family.'

Eileen's expression showed that whatever she thought of that, it wasn't much.

Undaunted, Wilkie continued, 'There's plenty of room at the farmhouse if you'd like to come and stay . . .'

Eileen turned her head away.

'Before you make up your mind against it,' Wilkie pressed on, 'why don't you consider the alternative for a moment? You're here in this house, all alone, with no family nearby and no real reason to stay.' *If I invite her to come and live at Ash Morley Leanne will kill me,* she was thinking. 'Why don't you look into taking a holiday cottage near us for a while so you and Abby can spend some time together?' *Now Abby's going to kill me, but*

275

really this has to be done. 'She's Jack's daughter and I know you don't want to lose touch with her . . .'

Eileen's voice shook with emotion as she said, 'It's only happening because of you and her mother.'

'I'm afraid, Eileen, it's happening because of you. Don't you realise that it's your attitude that's driving her away? She's a lovely girl with a beautiful heart, but it hasn't been easy for her either. Losing her father to suicide . . .'

'That her mother drove him to.'

Wilkie's patience was starting to thin. 'You know that's not true, so please don't say it again. I told you just now that I didn't come here to argue with you. I just want you to understand that behaving the way you are towards us is hurting you a lot more than it's hurting us. And we don't want it to be like that. I'm sure you don't either, not really.'

Eileen stared at her. Of course she didn't, but Wilkie could see that she'd be damned before she'd admit it any time soon.

'There is so much you could be involved in if you came to Kesterly,' Wilkie encouraged. 'You'd make lots of friends and find a way to rebuild your life that doesn't appear to be happening here.'

Eileen said nothing.

'We need some help to save the old theatre,' Wilkie continued off the top of her head. 'I think that's a project Jack would wholeheartedly approve of, don't you? And if we had his mother on our committee . . . The Delaney name could carry a lot of weight.'

'He didn't work for years,' Eileen reminded her. 'That worthless community turned their backs on him.'

'It is indeed a fickle world,' Wilkie agreed, 'but he did some great work in his day, and wouldn't you rather he was remembered for that than what came later? We could even rename the theatre if you wanted to and call it the Delaney Playhouse, or Delaney Court, or something that includes his name.'

Though Eileen didn't respond to that, Wilkie could see that she wasn't shutting out the suggestion, and that she might even be willing – after Wilkie had gone – to consider it. There was also a good chance that showing her the photos of Daniel hadn't left her as unmoved as she'd tried to appear. She was human, after all, much as she might pretend not to be.

Deciding it was time for her to go, Wilkie picked up her bag and walked to the door. 'I hope I hear from you,' she said softly, as Eileen came to see her out.

Avoiding her eyes Eileen mumbled something that Wilkie didn't catch, but it didn't matter because Wilkie felt quietly confident that her mission hadn't been an entire waste of time.

Hearing her mother's car on the cattle grid, Leanne picked up her laptop and let herself and Juno out of the house. Abby and Daniel were in their rooms, but she didn't want to risk them overhearing the conversation she wanted to have with Wilkie. It was best had in the farmhouse.

Instead of drafting a letter to Patrick Marks as she'd

intended earlier, she'd spent some time Googling him instead. It turned out that the appeal against his conviction had not yet been heard; the date kept being changed for various reasons and so far she'd found no mention of when it might happen.

She read about the police investigation again, and was struck by how quickly it had come to a conclusion after six months of getting nowhere. She wasn't sure why that bothered her, though she remembered finding it curious at the time. His old boss suddenly gets in touch to point the finger? What exactly had prompted him? How long had he been suspicious? The police would presumably have asked the same questions, and apparently they were satisfied with the answers, so why shouldn't she be? Maybe she would be if she knew what they were.

No doubt because of her chat with Daniel, she'd found herself seeing Marks rather differently to the way she had before. To begin with, while the police mugshots made him look wild-eyed and sinister, earlier shots – pre-Kylie – showed him to be quite a handsome man with strong, well-defined features that closely resembled Daniel's.

The way Daniel told it, they'd been a happy family with no demons lurking within or secrets to be ashamed of. He clearly remembered his childhood until his mother's death as being close to idyllic. His parents had put him at the centre of their world, and as far as he seemed aware they had adored each other as much as they'd adored him. Leanne got the feeling that the reason he worked so hard in school was for them.

They'd been proud of him, had urged him to do well, and he wanted them to stay proud of him. For all she knew, his father's letters encouraged him to carry on doing his best.

Patrick Marks had no previous convictions that she could find. His own parents (now deceased) had been a bus driver and a nurse in the Midlands, and his boss at the media design company he'd worked at for eight years after leaving uni had insisted in court that he'd never believe Patrick would harm anyone, least of all a little girl.

The only disturbing incident in Marks's past that Leanne could find had been brought to light by one of the tabloid papers. Apparently Marks had touched a six-year-old girl inappropriately while helping her into a basket at the hot air balloon company where he'd worked during the three years before his arrest. This had happened a few months after Gracie Marks had died.

Leanne had continued to search, just in case there were similar incidents that she hadn't heard about at the time of the trial or read about in Daniel's care notes. Finding none, nor any further mention of the first one, she began scrutinising the time Marks had become a suspect in Kylie's disappearance more closely. The press coverage had been even more intense and inflammatory than she'd realised, in some cases it had been almost hysterical, but in essence they were all saying the same thing.

'He took her,' she said to her mother as Wilkie read through the excerpts Leanne had bookmarked for her, 'no one seems to be in any doubt about that. The trouble is . . .'

Wilkie sat back and rubbed her tired eyes. 'The trouble is what?' she prompted.

Leanne shrugged. 'OK, I know this is going to sound crazy, but my gut is telling me that something's not quite right about this. We know Marks is appealing his sentence – actually it's not the sentence he's appealing, it's the actual conviction – and the way Daniel believes in him . . .'

Instead of reminding her that the case had been in front of a jury who'd come back with a unanimous verdict, Wilkie nodded thoughtfully.

Tensing, Leanne said, 'Are you agreeing with me?'

Wilkie was still reading. 'I'm not disagreeing,' she replied, 'but I need to look at it again in the morning. Meantime, I think you should go ahead and be in touch with Marks, because he's the only one who can tell you if your instincts about him are right.'

Chapter Sixteen

More than a week had passed since Leanne had started a letter to Patrick Marks, and she still didn't feel she was approaching it the right way. Wilkie wasn't sure she was, either, and until they were convinced that Leanne was striking the right notes with her questions they weren't happy about asking them.

Since Saffy, Daniel's social worker, hadn't returned any of Leanne's calls, Leanne had emailed Wendy Fraser this morning in the hope of moving things along. What she wanted to know was the official reason why Daniel wasn't allowed to see his father, and if that reason or ruling could be overturned if she, Leanne, felt it to be in Daniel's interest.

She hadn't mentioned anything to Daniel yet. It would be cruel to get the boy's hopes up if, in the end, she decided it was likely to do more harm than good for him to know she was in touch with his father.

Meantime life was going on with its usual ups and downs; she'd finally received an apology from the school for the way Daniel had been made to stand on a chair, and they'd all joined Wilkie for the science march in Bristol last week. She'd had a few, friendly chats with Tom on the phone; in fact she'd seen him a couple of times, once when she and Klaudia had gone to pick up his mother's dresses and accessories, and again at a charity jazz event at the Mermaid.

'I'm getting the impression you're avoiding me,' he'd told her, having to raise his voice to be heard over the music.

'You're imagining things,' she'd assured him with an airy smile.

His eyes narrowed. 'What did I do wrong?'

She looked at him in amazement. 'Nothing,' she insisted. 'There's just a lot going on at the moment – I'm sure there is for you too. It's lovely to see you this evening.'

'Can I see you tomorrow, or the next day?' Before she could answer he added, 'I'd like to talk.'

'I'd love that,' she agreed enthusiastically. 'We've got a full weekend ahead of us, but you and Richie are more than welcome to join us for lunch or dinner on either day.'

Of course she'd known very well that he'd intended it to be just the two of them, but as much as she might want that she wasn't going to let it happen.

He's not staying in Kesterly, she kept reminding herself, *his life is elsewhere, so before you get yourself in any deeper it's time to return to the shore.* The fact that she seemed caught in a riptide of emotions that kept landing her in imaginary conversations and situations with him that were often too entertaining, or more often thrilling, to relinquish, was neither here nor there. She was determined to fight this. If she didn't she was going to end up with a broken heart, and that was something no sane person subjected themselves to if they could avoid it.

'So, as far as I know,' Andee was saying over lunch at the Duck and Bill in the old town, 'he's considering all three proposals and he'll get back to us when he's made a decision.'

For an embarrassing moment Leanne realised she'd lost track of what they were discussing. Then, remembering that Andee's partner, Graeme, was working on plans for Villa Tramonto, she said, 'I shall be fascinated to see what Tom ends up doing with the place. His mother loved it, as I'm sure you know, but I don't think Tom or Richie feel the same sort of attachment. My mother thinks we should always be in that state of mind, ready to let go.'

Andee laughed. 'Your mother is my mother's idol, do you know that, but I'm afraid mine still struggles with the less esoteric goals in life.'

'Believe me, so does mine, but she talks up a good story. Anyway, you've been in Stockholm again? Was that business?'

Andee gave an ironic smile. 'Not exactly,' she replied. 'It's a long story for another time. Let's get back to you and Patrick Marks. Tell me again why you want to write to him.'

Feeling slightly uncomfortable, even foolish, now she was having to put her instincts into words, Leanne said, 'I've read a lot about him in the last couple of weeks, and I . . .' She started again. 'He pleaded not guilty, as you know, and now he's appealing his conviction. OK, I know you're going to tell me all convicts do that, but I honestly think there's a chance he didn't do it. If indeed it was ever done. Well, obviously the little girl was abducted, I'm not disputing that, but was there really a murder? The body's never been found.'

Andee's lovely eyes narrowed with puzzlement and interest.

Leanne took a breath. This wasn't easy when she had nothing substantial to support her, but she pressed on anyway. 'I've read a lot about the case in the last couple of weeks . . .'

'So you'll know about the evidence that damned him?'

'Of course, and I can't exactly explain why I think there's something wrong with it, or something missing, or . . .'

'His lawyers will have tried taking everything apart,' Andee assured her, 'and they obviously couldn't.'

'I understand that, but how hard did they try? Did the police ask the right questions? What's holding up the appeal? OK, I get that you're the expert here, and that I have almost no idea of how these things work, but I've come to a decision.' She put down her fork. 'I've decided that instead of trying to put my questions in a letter to Patrick Marks, I should go to see him, if he'll allow it. That way he'll have to answer me straight away, and I might have a better chance of knowing whether or not he's telling the truth.'

To her surprise Andee didn't seem to have any argument with that.

'Obviously,' Leanne continued, 'if I come away believing that he isn't guilty, or that something has gone wrong somewhere, it's unlikely I'll be able to carry out any sort of investigation on my own.'

Andee's eyes held to hers, showing that she now fully understood where this was going. 'I won't be around much from the end of next month,' she said, 'but if you can talk to Marks in that time and you still feel convinced that his conviction isn't safe, we should speak again.'

Leanne was at the shop with Klaudia, trying to hide her impatience as a customer took her time paying for a frivolous tricorne hat from Helen's collection. It suited her so well that she decided to wear it right away, so all the complimentary reassurances were given, along with a highly desirable Glory Days hat-box (a practice that would no longer exist once the current supply ran out, thanks to their dismal finances).

As soon as the happy musketeer was on her way, Leanne related the details of her lunch with Andee. 'So what I need to do now,' she declared, opening up her laptop, 'is write to Marks and ask him to put me on his visitors' list. If he agrees I should get clearance within three days of an online application, or so it says on the website.'

'I'll be happy to go with you as moral support,' Klaudia offered. 'We'd have to ask Wilkie to take care of the shop, but I'm sure she will.'

Leanne looked up with a smile. 'I'm sure she will

too,' she said, 'and it would be a big relief not to have to go there alone.'

A week later, experiencing a mix of so many emotions that she could barely connect with one of them, Leanne was sitting in the driver's seat of her car staring at the forbidding exterior of Sellybrook Prison. There wasn't a single part of her that wanted to set foot in a place that housed violent criminals, much less psychopaths and paedophiles, but here she was.

'Are you OK?' Klaudia asked worriedly.

Leanne's gaze moved to the people walking by, dodging the potholes and puddles as they headed for the iron-gated entrance between two towering barbed-wire fences. There was no knowing how far anyone had travelled to get here – for her and Klaudia it had been just over sixty miles – nor any way of telling whom they were here to visit. She wondered how many of them felt as self-conscious as she did right now – and ashamed, she had to admit, for anyone to think that she had any sort of connection to the offenders inside.

Realising how narrow-minded and snobbish that was, she turned to Klaudia and put on a smile. 'There have been things I've looked forward to more,' she said drily.

After opening the car door she added, 'Wish me luck.'

Picking her own route around the muddy ruts and puddles towards the entrance, she kept her eyes down, trying to remind herself of why she was there and what she hoped to achieve. For some reason a sense of unreality was prevailing, throwing a kind of fog over her motives for coming. She suddenly felt very unsure about everything, apart from the fact that she was about to meet the man who'd been convicted of abducting a little girl, and still wouldn't say what he'd done with her.

Overcome by an urge to turn around and leave, she thought about Daniel and what this would mean to him, to everyone, if her instincts proved correct. Those instincts were nowhere in evidence today, it had to be said. It was as though they'd dumped her and left with no forwarding address.

Reaching the back of a short queue to go in, she kept her eyes down and deliberately didn't listen to the conversations going on around her. The sight of some of the visitors was warning enough to mind her own business. More assumptions, prejudices, judgements based on the fact that some people had tattoos, bad teeth, piercings, shaved heads . . . *Get a grip, Leanne. If nothing else, try to be your mother's daughter.*

She wondered what Patrick Marks was doing now, if he was in a cell, psyching himself up for a rare social occasion? She felt suddenly sick at the thought of him planning to flirt with her, or play mind games that she didn't understand. She tried to imagine what he might be expecting from their meeting. The letter she'd sent asking to be added to his visitors' list had said only,

Dear Mr Marks
I am Daniel's foster carer. I am glad to tell you that he is doing very well and we are enjoying having him as part of

our family. I would be most grateful if you could put me on your visitors' list so we can talk.

Yours truly,
Leanne Delaney

A note had come back three days later saying,

Dear Mrs Delaney,
Your name is on the list.

Patrick Marks

She wasn't sure what to read into the fact that he hadn't asked what she wanted to talk about; except of course he'd presume it was Daniel. They had nothing else in common, wouldn't even know of each other's existence if it weren't for the boy – or Kylie Booth's disappearance.

Remembering that, she felt a warning twist deep in her heart. In spite of what she'd been trying to tell herself over the past two weeks, that he was the tragic victim of injustice who needed to be saved from a lazy, incompetent or even corrupt system, she mustn't forget that the full process of law had shown him to be so far beyond the realm of decency and good conscience that he was exactly where he needed to be. *And remember,* she told herself with mounting dismay, *he didn't even ask if you were going to bring Daniel.* Although he presumably knew that the only contact he was permitted with his son was by letter.

'I'm sorry no one's got back to you before about this,'

Wendy Fraser had said when Leanne had eventually got hold of her by phone. 'Saffy is on sick leave and should have handed over her mobile, but apparently didn't. Anyway, I've been checking with my colleagues over at Marstone, and I'm told it will take a court order to reverse the ruling of no contact. I can put that into motion if you'd like me to, but naturally we need to keep Daniel's best interests at heart. Do you really think he would benefit in some way from seeing his father?'

Leanne said, 'Maybe not at this stage, but how long would it take for the order to be granted if we did apply?'

'Presuming it is granted, a lot would depend on the court schedule. It could take weeks.'

If she felt it was the right thing to do after meeting with Marks, she'd do everything she could to bring it about. Until then, it was only right that she went along with the decisions that had been made to keep Daniel safe.

With the ordeal of entering the prison, which had included a humiliating body search and even a check in her mouth for drugs, finally over she was now seated at a small, scratched table in the visitors' hall gazing off to one side, still reluctant to engage with anyone other than the person she was here to see.

'Mrs Delaney?'

She looked up to find Patrick Marks standing over her. Her heart gave a sickening lurch as she half rose and held out her hand. He was taller, far more muscular than she'd expected, and his expression wasn't friendly.

He shook her hand, and she wondered with horror if this was the same hand that had been used to take an innocent child's life.

He gestured for her to sit down again, and took the chair facing her. He seemed confident, unabashed, but not as threatening as she'd initially thought, more guarded in fact. Though he was still in his thirties his hair was quite grey, and his eyes, his whole expression now she looked closer, seemed haunted, withdrawn in a way she found slightly unnerving.

'Thank you for seeing me,' she began, having to clear her throat.

'How's Daniel?' His tone was devoid of emotion, yet the fact that it was his first question did him credit.

'He's fine. I'm not sure what he tells you in his letters, but he's doing very well at school, and he seems to have settled in well with us.'

He nodded, but didn't smile. 'He's told me about you. Thank you for taking care of him. He deserves to be with people who understand his needs.'

Leanne swallowed drily. 'I know we don't have very much time,' she said, 'so I should come to the point of why I'm here.' She was starting to feel slightly queasy and light-headed, as nerves and tension were almost overwhelming her.

'You want to adopt him,' he said shortly.

She blinked in surprise, not because the thought had never crossed her mind, for it had, but because of how angry he'd sounded. 'Would you object if I did?' she asked.

His eyes went down to his tightly bunched fists. His hands were so large, so strong that it was impossible not to think of what they could do – had already done? In the end he said, 'I want what's best for my son.'

Thinking of his wife, Gracie, and how unafraid she'd seemed of this man, how tender he'd looked in the family photos, Leanne said, 'Then we want the same thing, but I'm not here to ask if I can adopt him, I'm here because . . .' Words were starting to fail her. She couldn't think how to continue without making herself seem absurd. 'I've read a lot about you lately and I was wondering . . .' She broke off as a mean, impatient look flashed in his eyes.

'Please don't tell me Daniel's been put with someone who gets off on murderers,' he growled. 'If that's why you're here this meeting's over.'

Shocked, and offended, she said, 'I'll try to overlook how insulting that was and . . .'

'You've got the wrong guy if that's why you came,' he told her harshly. 'You want yourself a killer, look around the room, take your pick . . .'

'Stop!' she cried angrily. 'I am not some sort of sick groupie who gets off on . . . Actually, I don't have to defend myself to you. I don't even have to stay here, but before I go let me tell you this. I came because I believe there's a chance you're not guilty of the crime you were convicted of, and *one* of the reasons I think that is because I'm getting to know Daniel, and I've also read about your wife. To my mind it doesn't make sense that someone with such a beautiful family, and who has no record of harming anyone, would randomly go out and kill a little girl.'

His eyes were watching her carefully; a vein throbbed in his forehead. Long minutes passed until in a rough, merciless tone he said, 'They found child porn on my computer and her DNA in my car. How are you managing to reconcile that with things not making sense?'

'I admit I can't, but I'm hoping you can.'

His eyes didn't move from hers. More time passed. She was dimly aware of the other voices in the room, shouts of laughter and anger, children yelling, chairs scraping. In the end he leaned towards her as he said, 'All I can tell you is that you're right, I didn't kill her. Frankly, I don't even know if she's dead. They've never found a body, and if there is one, I've got no idea where it is.'

Leanne's throat was dry, her breath was shallow as she absorbed what he'd said and tried to decide what she needed to say next. 'So what made the police suspect you?' she asked.

'You'll surely have read that they followed an anonymous tip-off.'

'Who turned out to be your boss at the balloon company?'

His bitterness seemed edged with sadness, or was it confusion, as he said, 'That's right.'

'Why would he do that if . . . ?'

'Whatever the reasons,' he broke in abruptly, 'it still led them to finding her DNA in my car.'

'So how did it get there?'

His smile had no humour. 'He was a good friend,' he said. 'I couldn't believe – still can't – that he'd ... He just wouldn't make things up. Not stuff like that. He knew me. He knew my family and he was there for me when Gracie died.'

'Yet he pointed the finger at you. Why would he do that if he was such a good friend?'

Marks shook his head, rigid and nonplussed.

'Do you think . . . You must have thought that maybe he was the one who abducted Kylie and tried to shift the blame to you?'

'Of course I thought that, but I swear even now I can't see him . . . If you knew him . . . He's a good guy. I'd have trusted him with my life. Now I ask myself, do you really ever know someone?'

It was a good question, but a philosophical discussion wasn't for now. Moving on, she said, 'Is there anyone else who might have a grudge against you? Someone who might have gone to him with information he felt he had to act on, even if it wasn't true?'

He was shaking his head, as though genuinely bemused. 'I've always been a pretty placid sort of guy,' he said. 'I didn't make enemies, or none that I knew of.'

She was losing direction, grabbing at threads, but quickly brought her mind back to what she knew. 'The porn on your computer?' she queried. 'Do you think someone put it there?'

'It's the only way it could have got there, because I sure as hell didn't download it.'

Her head was starting to spin. She was trying to deal with too many thoughts at once, hardly knowing which to run with first.

He sat forward again and said, 'Does Daniel know why you're here?'

'No. I didn't tell him I was coming. I didn't want him to feel bad about being left behind, and it wouldn't be fair to get his hopes up either.'

He nodded. 'That's good. Whatever you do, don't mess with him. He's been through enough.'

'I feel as strongly as you do about protecting him. I just wish you could tell me something that I could use to help you.'

He looked suddenly dejected, beaten. 'All I can tell you is what I just have, which is the same as I told my lawyers and the court.' His eyes came to hers, bleak, bitter and, she thought, uncomprehending. 'Yet here I am,' he said, and to her frustration the visit was brought to an end.

'Yes, I still believe he didn't do it,' Leanne told Klaudia as they started the journey home with Klaudia at the wheel, 'but I don't know whether that makes me gullible or delusional or what the heck it says, because the jury obviously didn't come to that conclusion.'

'Did you ask about his appeal?'

'I didn't get the chance, but I think the reason it's not going anywhere is because there's no new evidence.'

Klaudia gave that some thought. 'Going back to the jury,' she said. 'They didn't have a one-on-one with him the way you just did. Maybe, if they had they wouldn't have ended up beyond a reasonable doubt.'

'So have I been suckered in, or have my instincts managed to connect with something no one else's have?'

Klaudia glanced at her. 'What are your instincts telling you now?'

Leanne gave it some thought and sighed. 'Frankly, they're all over the place, but if he didn't do it then surely I can't be the only one who's in doubt. What about his lawyer? He'd have talked to him dozens of times in a confidential situation, so does he or she think an innocent man is paying for a crime he didn't commit?' Taking out her phone, she said, 'I need to call Andee and fill her in on what's happened.'

A few minutes later, after going through everything again, she was listening to Andee on the speaker as she said, 'We should get together. I can't make it for the next couple of days, but I could come to the shop on Friday. Better still, why don't I drive up to Ash Morley? The shop is too public and we won't want any interruptions.'

Leanne glanced at Klaudia and received the thumbs up to say that Klaudia could rearrange her schedule to suit. 'OK. Come about eleven?' she suggested.

'Great, but before I go, I want to remind you of something you pointed out to me yourself, which was that every guilty person claims they're innocent – and from what I remember of you, Leanne Delaney, you were always extremely good at seeing how wonderful things could be in spite of how wonderful they weren't. It comes from being your mother's daughter, of course.

You have a little boy with you now who I'm sure you're already half in love with, if not completely, and you'd like nothing more than to fix things for him so that his life is whole again.'

Leanne sat mutely with that, absorbing the unexpected insight into her character. 'His mother's dead,' she said in the end, 'so I could never make things whole again.'

'No, but you can try the next best thing,' Andee responded. 'I'll see you on Friday at eleven.'

Moments after she rang off the phone rang again. It was Kate.

'Mum, I've got some news. I can't wait to tell you. Are you sitting down?'

More curious than cautious, Leanne said, 'I'm in the car.'

'Driving?'

'No, Klaudia is.'

'Hi Klaudia. How are you?'

'I'm great, thanks. It's lovely to hear you. If your news is private . . .'

'No, you can hear it too, then you can calm Mum down once I've told her. Has she just gone white?'

Leanne thought she might have. 'Kate, come to the point,' she scolded.

'OK. It's brilliant news, honestly. I'm so excited. I know you're going to be too.'

Leanne listened in mute astonishment as Kate revealed the change to her plans. When she'd finished Leanne still didn't know what to say, couldn't even get her head around what she'd just heard.

She looked at Klaudia and laughed, almost hysterically. There was nothing like a perspective check to get a person thinking clearly, or laterally, or even madly. And nothing like children to prevent life from ever becoming dull.

Chapter Seventeen

Martin had finally rung back after a hectic and bewildering two days, during which Leanne had struggled hard not to overreact as she tried to get hold of him.

All restraint went out the window the instant she heard his voice. 'Uganda and Rwanda!' she shouted. 'What the heck happened to all her other internship plans? How and when did genocide and conflict resolution get on to the table? You surely can't be supporting this. If you are . . .'

'Hold up, hold up,' he cried, laughingly. 'I swear I felt the exact same way you do when I first heard about it, and I still can't say I'm thrilled, but you need to have all the information. I've just emailed you the links, but in short the organisation she's signed up with is highly reputable. It helped support the early Peace Corps and, frankly, it's a great programme that's going to stand her in very good stead not only for her course, but for future employment in her field of interest.'

Since Leanne couldn't offer an opinion on that yet, she said, obstinately, 'I should have been consulted before a decision was made.'

'She's twenty-one,' he reminded her, 'she doesn't have to consult anyone.'

'But you have to finance it, so you're the one who should have told me.'

'We decided it wasn't worth worrying you until we knew for certain that it could happen. And you know I'd never finance anything if I thought it carried any undue risk.'

'We're talking Africa, the whole damned continent is a risk.'

He laughed. 'That doesn't sound like you.'

'I can assure you it is me, and I don't approve of this.'

'Read the email, then call me back when you've had time to think it over.'

So that was what she did, and in the end, in spite of still wishing it wasn't happening, she had grudgingly to admit that it was a great opportunity, and Kate would undoubtedly excel in her handling of it. Nevertheless, she wasn't going to sleep a wink the entire time Kate was there.

'OK, the wars might be over,' she ranted to Wilkie and Abby when they sat down to discuss it, 'but bad things still happen in those countries.'

'Bad things happen everywhere,' Wilkie pointed out, though Leanne could tell that she wasn't impressed by the idea either. 'Africa doesn't have an exclusive.'

'And on the bright side,' Abby put in excitedly, 'she's going to stop off here for a whole two weeks on her way through.'

That was certainly helping to make it more appealing, though Leanne was already aware of how wretched she was going to feel when it came time for Kate to fly off again – to *Africa*.

Still, it all remained a good three months off, so now wasn't the time to get worked up about it, especially when there was another daughter to fill that space.

She'd been worried – more worried than usual – since the night she'd come back from visiting the prison. She hadn't meant to eavesdrop; in fact she wouldn't even have known the conversation was taking place if she hadn't woken with a start from a nightmare about Patrick Marks drowning, with her trying to push him under. She'd felt so rattled by the struggle that she'd been unable to go back to sleep, so she'd gone downstairs to make a hot drink and had heard voices coming from Abby's room.

Presuming it was the TV or YouTube, she'd been about to knock and remind her of the time when she'd heard Daniel saying, '. . . but you have to tell your mum. It's crazy not to.'

'You don't understand,' Abby protested. 'She's the last person I can tell.'

'Why? She's your mum, and she's a really good person . . .'

'That's what you think, it's what everyone thinks, but you don't know her like I do. She can be really mean at times.'

'In what way?'

There was an awful pause before Abby said, 'It happens in ways you can't see.'

Leanne had felt so thrown and upset by that that she hadn't known what to do until Juno made the decision for her and came to scratch the door. She'd quickly run back up the stairs to her own room, and had lain awake for most of the night wondering how she was being mean to Abby in ways no one could see.

Of course her mother was having none of it.

'She's talking nonsense,' Wilkie insisted after Leanne confided what she'd heard. 'Kids make things up to try and sound more interesting or tragic or . . .'

'I understand that, but there's obviously something she's not telling me, or Daniel wouldn't have said what he did. Do you think I should ask him what it is?'

'No, certainly not. She's told him in confidence, and it wouldn't be fair to try and get it out of him. This is between you and Abby.'

'So what do I do?'

Wilkie's expression showed that she was as worried as Leanne, and equally confounded. 'Give it some more time,' she advised, 'and if she hasn't taken Daniel's advice by, say, the end of the week, we'll talk again.'

Unfortunately her mother's counsel hadn't prevented Leanne from asking Abby, while Daniel was at football training last night, if there was anything she wanted to talk about.

Abby's eyes narrowed. 'You were listening the other night, weren't you? I knew it! That's why Juno went to the door . . .'

'I didn't hear anything . . .'

'You are such a *spy*!'

'Abby, please come back. You have to know . . . Abby,' she called through Abby's closed door, 'please tell me why you think I'm being mean . . .'

'Go away!' Abby shouted. 'I don't want to talk to you, and I don't want you standing out there *spying* on me.' Her music went up so loudly that there was no way Leanne could make herself heard.

Now, here she was on Friday morning waiting for Andee Lawrence to arrive, still worried about Abby, trying not to think about Kate's Africa project, and wanting with all her heart to do her best for Daniel. She would immerse herself in his problems as soon as Andee arrived, but apparently there was another issue to get through before that, because Tom Franklyn was calling her mobile.

Should she answer?

Deciding to grow up, she clicked on with a snappish hello.

'Hi, you're sounding a little . . . stressed?' he dared to venture.

'Just a bit,' she admitted. 'There's a lot going on at the moment.' Attempting a quick centring, she continued in a less harried tone, 'How are you?'

'I'm fine, thank you. It feels too long since I saw you.'

'I'm sure you're surviving,' she countered. Had that come across as sarcastic? What the heck, she'd said it now.

'I guess I am,' he agreed, his amusement sounding a bit too smug for her liking. 'Actually, I'm ringing to let you know – in case you're interested, and I will understand perfectly if you aren't – that I'm leaving on Sunday, and it's unlikely I'll be back until after the summer.'

At that her heart gave such a tremendous lurch that

she wanted to thump it for its treachery. 'That's a long time,' she commented smoothly. 'Can I ask where you're going?'

'Beijing, mainly.'

Oh, not far. 'Have you been there before?'

'A few times. Anyway, the reason I'm calling is that I have something for you, and I was hoping you might agree to have dinner with me before I leave so I can give it to you.'

As her mind whirled into a bizarre slideshow of what it could be, she heard Andee's car on the cattle grid, and quickly tried to think what to say. She found him far too attractive, was still having imaginary conversations with him all the time, and seeing him again was not going to make the fantasy go away. So the answer had to be no. 'OK,' she said. 'When were you thinking?'

'Tomorrow night? Shall we say the Crustacean at eight? There's a reason for choosing that location which will become clear when I see you.'

After she'd rung off she stood staring at the phone, trying to imagine the reason, but she was so agitated by the conflict going on inside her that in the end she just laughed.

'Hi, seems I've caught you at a good time,' Andee commented, coming in through the open door.

'I don't know about that,' Leanne responded, going to embrace her. 'Would you like some coffee? I've just made it.'

'Sounds lovely. Thanks.'

Minutes later, with the usual chitchat about family

and mutual friends out of the way, they were seated at the dining table talking earnestly, with Andee making notes on her laptop as Leanne once again related details of her visit to Sellybrook Prison.

When she'd finished, Andee sat back and picked up her coffee. 'OK, that's more or less as I remember it from our phone call,' she said, taking a sip. 'I just wanted to make sure I'd understood everything correctly. Do you have any plans to visit him again?'

'Not at this stage.'

Andee reached for a biscuit. 'Since we spoke I've been in touch with some ex-colleagues in Kesterly CID and as I expected it's not likely that anyone in Marstone will agree to release the files, much less reopen the case when no new evidence has been found.'

Though Leanne had expected as much, it was still disappointing to hear. 'So is there anything we can do?' she asked.

'Apart from obtaining a transcript of the trial and going through it line by line searching for some kind of discrepancy or clue or peculiarity, there's not much *you* can do. However, I've had a chat with the lawyer who handled Marks's defence. Frankly, if he hadn't been so brusque with me I might not be as concerned as I am now.'

Leanne was immediately intrigued.

'He seemed annoyed that I was asking about Marks, which led me to wonder if he was completely comfortable with the way he'd handled the case. I didn't put that to him, but I did ask about the appeal and he told me, again quite brusquely, that in spite of Patrick Marks

trying to make it happen it couldn't without the existence of new evidence, and as there was none I should,
for the sake of Kylie's parents, leave things alone.'

Leanne grimaced. 'Well, I guess I can see his point on
that front,' she had to admit.

'Indeed, if you're someone who's convinced Marks
did it, then you would want to leave it alone.'

'So you think he's convinced of Marks's guilt?'

'What I think is that he's afraid of having his own
shortcomings – presuming they exist – brought to
light.'

'Which isn't the same thing at all.'

'No, it isn't, and now I've read everything you've
read I've naturally put it together with the responses I
received from Marstone police and the lawyer, and
come to the same conclusions you have, that this needs
a closer look.'

Leanne experienced a surge of hope.

Andee said, 'Let me do some more asking around.
With any luck it'll give us a clearer idea of what needs
to be done next.'

The following morning when Leanne brought in the
mail she saw there was a letter for Daniel from the
prison. As usual she left it on his bed so he could read
it in private when he returned from his football training. He would then, she knew, pop it into the memory
box Kate had given him.

Though she hadn't expected Marks to write to her
too, she felt slightly surprised that he hadn't. Wasn't he
interested to know what she'd been thinking since their

meeting on Tuesday; didn't he have any more to ask or say? For her part the concern about his guilt was never far from her mind, or her conscience, for she'd becor acutely aware of how distressing it would b lie's family if they were told that Patrick Marks's conviction was being questioned, and not only by Marks.

As usual, when Daniel came home, he grabbed a snack from the fridge and went up to his room where he stayed for a while, presumably reading his letter and possibly writing one in return. When he came down again he made no mention of it, so it would appear that his father hadn't told him about Leanne's visit, which was a relief to her. She didn't want Daniel to find out about it that way, and she wasn't ready to tell him herself until she felt more certain of what to say.

'So when is Andee likely to be in touch with you again?' Tom asked that evening after Leanne had surprised him with the events of her week. He was looking especially attractive tonight, she thought, which was no surprise, only unsettling and even slightly annoying. How freeing it would have been to come here and wonder why she'd taken such pains getting ready for a date that wasn't actually a date at all.

'She didn't say,' she replied, 'but I know she won't keep me hanging on unnecessarily. She'll call as soon as she has something.'

Looking intrigued and slightly concerned, he said, 'I guess you've already thought about the fact that if Marks didn't do it then whoever did is still out there?'

'And given that a body's never been found, there's a

chance the little girl is still alive,' she added. Her conscience burned again for Kylie's family. However, they, more than anyone, deserved the truth, and if it brought their daughter back . . . 'If she is still alive,' she said, 'I don't even want to think about what's been happening to her all this time.'

'Then perhaps you should tell yourself that she was stolen and is being looked after by someone who loves her. Romantic maybe, but it's as possible as any other scenario. What did Andee say about the DNA evidence and computer porn?'

'She didn't mention it yesterday, but obviously she'll be looking into it.'

'I'm starting to wish I was going to be around to find out what happens.'

Deciding to turn his comment into a change of subject, she said, 'So, you're leaving tomorrow?'

He nodded, and paused as the waiter came to refill their glasses. 'I'll probably take off around ten,' he said. 'Richie's coming with me to spend a few days in London, then I'll fly to Berlin where I'll be for a couple of weeks before going on to Beijing.'

Making a good job of sounding wry, she said, 'So *are* you a spy?'

He was clearly amused. 'Nothing so dashing, I'm afraid. Just a plain old diplomat with a PhD in economics who brokers international trade deals on behalf of Her Majesty's government.'

Nothing special then. 'It's a good cover,' she remarked.

He didn't deny it.

'You're teasing me now,' she accused.

He laughed. 'I promise you I am not working for the intelligence services – at least not directly. Indirectly, there isn't much they're not involved in, but I don't report to any of their agencies.'

'It sounds like a complicated world.'

'It is, but not in a particularly fascinating way. Something that's much more fascinating, at least to me, is your inheritance from my mother. I know you've taken most of the collection now, but I wanted to give you a key so you can return to the villa any time you like to pick up the rest.'

So that was what he had for her, a key to his family home. Under other circumstances she might have read all sorts of things into that; under these she simply felt grateful and, she had to admit it, disappointed. 'Thank you,' she said, as he put it on the table between them. When her eyes returned to his she found him watching her curiously.

Trying not to be drawn in by his expression, she said, 'Have you decided what you're going to do with the place yet?'

He sighed. 'Not really. Graeme's come up with some interesting ideas that I'm still considering.'

'Can I ask what they are?'

'Of course. In no particular order, it could become a boutique hotel, or luxury apartments, or remain as a very large family home. Whichever comes up favourite it'll be sold when the renovation or conversion is complete, not before.'

'Don't you feel any kind of attachment to it?'

'Of course, I've had some very happy times there,

but it's way too big for me to rattle around in on my own, especially given how infrequently I'd be there . . . On the other hand, if we go the apartment route, I might be interested in taking one as a holiday rental investment. At the moment I think the hotel is favourite. Still a lot to be decided, but I've promised Graeme I'll give him an answer sometime over the summer.' He tilted his head to one side as though intrigued to know what she was thinking. 'You're looking . . . sad?' he ventured.

She forced a smile. 'Not sad, just reflective,' she corrected. The way he was discussing leaving Kesterly with apparently no regrets wasn't doing much for her ego, that was for sure.

Leaning forward, he said softly, 'Listen, I think there's a chance I might have given you the wrong impression about . . . Well, about us, and if I did, I'm sorry.'

Her cheeks burned. 'I don't . . . I'm not sure I follow,' she stammered, indignation rising up hotly inside her.

'I'm just saying . . . Well I guess what I'm saying is that with all the travelling I do I'm not really relationship material . . .'

'I never thought you were,' she informed him tartly. 'I hadn't, there wasn't . . .' She had no idea what she was trying to say, only knew that she was more embarrassed and more furious than she'd ever want him to know.

Grimacing, he said, 'I guess I misunderstood. I'm sorry . . .'

'No, really, you haven't misunderstood.' Yes he had.

No, he hadn't . . . For heaven's sake, why couldn't she think straight? 'I've only ever thought we were friends,' she blurted. 'I hope we still are.'

He smiled. 'I hope so too.'

She'd have given the world to leave right then, but how could she without looking like she was off in a fit of pique?

He said, 'I hope you know how attractive I find you . . .'

'Please, stop now,' she interrupted. 'I don't think either of us needs to dig ourselves in any deeper.'

Thankfully their food made a timely arrival, allowing them some moments to draw back and try to find an easier way to get past the excruciating muddle they were in.

'You might remember I mentioned on the phone,' he said, 'that I have something for you.'

She regarded him with surprise. 'I thought it was the key.'

He looked at it. 'Oh, no,' he laughed. 'I mean the key is for you, obviously, but there's something else. I found it in my mother's bedside cabinet a couple of days ago and I . . . Well, I couldn't think of a more fitting home for it than with you.'

Curious, she watched as he reached into an inside pocket and drew out a small velvet box. 'Open it,' he invited.

She did, and blinked in amazement when she saw what was inside.

'It's a moonstone,' he told her.

It certainly was, heart shaped and probably a genuine

antique – and nestled in a bed of what looked very like real diamonds. 'I thought,' he said, 'given the name of this restaurant when it belonged to your father . . .'

'Tom, I can't accept this ring,' she murmured, closing the box. 'It's far too precious. I mean, if those stones are real . . .'

'They are,' he confirmed. 'I've had it checked and valued. You'll need to get it insured, presuming you decide to keep it. I kind of hoped you would.'

She was shaking her head. 'Really, I can't,' she protested. It had to be worth thousands of pounds, and he'd found it in the bedside drawer, not the japan chest, so it hadn't been meant for Glory. 'Tom, this was your mother's ring. It will have meant a great deal to her . . .'

'I really want you to have it,' he insisted.

She pushed the box gently towards him. 'Thank you, but if you're doing this to make yourself feel better . . .'

Astonished, he said, 'Why would it make me feel better? Other than knowing it's going to . . .' He stopped suddenly and his face darkened. 'If that means what I think it does, you're completely wrong. I want you to have the ring because it's a moonstone and . . .'

'It's very generous of you, but it's far too expensive a gift to ease your conscience with . . .'

'That's not what it's about,' he cried indignantly.

' . . . when it doesn't need to be eased. I wasn't expecting anything from you, Tom. As I said just now, I thought we were friends, but if you try to make me take this that won't be possible any more.'

Appearing genuinely perplexed, he said, 'Why would this stop us from being friends?'

'I think you know why, so please, put it away and let's pretend this never happened.'

Still seeming at a loss, he pocketed the small box and picked up his wine. 'I've made a complete mess of this evening, haven't I?' he said glumly. 'I think I can see how, but I'm afraid you'll need to tell me what to do to put it right.'

Managing a smile, she said, 'You don't need to do anything apart from eat your meal and drink your wine, because we're having a perfectly lovely time, and when this evening's over we shall say goodbye as friends and wish each other well.'

To her dismay, that was more or less what happened.

Klaudia said later, 'So how do you feel?'

Leanne sighed. 'You mean apart from stupid and like I really want to ring him and say . . . I don't know what I want to say, I just . . .'

'So ring him.'

Leanne regarded her sideways. 'And make an even bigger fool of myself? I don't think so. No, like I said, he'll be gone tomorrow, and we won't stay in touch because there's no reason to. He was just a little crush that I won't have any problem getting over . . .'

'This is me you're talking to.'

'And if I can't talk BS to you, who can I talk it to?'

Smiling, Klaudia folded her into a sisterly embrace. 'If he doesn't realise how close he came to being the luckiest guy in the world, then he really isn't the intelligent man we all took him for.'

Leanne had to smile. 'Even if he had felt tempted,

Kesterly's not big enough for him. He's an international high-flyer with an exotic past and exciting future, whereas I'm just a small-town shopgirl with one crazy daughter on her way to Africa, another troubled one on her way to driving me nuts, and a foster son whose convict father is quite possibly going to take over our lives in the coming weeks.'

It was only as she was about to leave that she belatedly remembered Klaudia's issues. Feeling terrible, she turned back. 'I'm sorry,' she said. 'I should have . . .'

'Still no news,' Klaudia told her with a smile, 'but if it's going to be bad I can wait.'

Chapter Eighteen

Three days later Leanne was in the visiting hall of Sellybrook Prison, facing Marks across the same scratched table as before. Andee was beside her, explaining the reasons they were there. As he listened he was staring at the photos Leanne had brought of Daniel, his thick fingers not quite steady. His heart, she felt sure, must be breaking inside his father's chest. However, he was paying attention to Andee, Leanne could see that, for when he finally looked up there was a flicker of something – hope? – juddering into light behind the wariness in his eyes.

Still keeping her voice down, Andee said, 'So we need to know how *you* think the porn got on to your computer, if you didn't put it there.'

Shaking his head, he said, 'I'm no expert on how these things work. Maybe I got an email I shouldn't have clicked on . . .'

Andee said, 'Who had access to your computer?'

His dark eyes seemed so sad as he said, 'To be honest, I never tried to deny anyone access. As far as I was concerned I had nothing to hide and no reason not to trust anyone.'

'So your colleagues at the balloon company . . .'

'All used it from time to time. We used one another's.'

Leanne glanced at Andee to see what she was making of this, but her expression was hard to read.

Moving on, Andee said, 'Did the police ever ask you how *you* thought Kylie's hair could have got into your car if, as you say, you never knew her, or saw her?'

He didn't have to think about that. 'No, they didn't ask me. I kept trying to tell them that it couldn't be possible, but they weren't listening.'

'You were asked again in court?'

'Yes, I was.'

'And you said?'

'That I had no idea how it could have got there, because . . .' He swallowed and dropped his eyes before he said, hoarsely, 'First of all I wondered if *they* put it there. The police, I mean. I couldn't think of anything else. They needed to solve the case, to get someone for it, but then I had to ask myself why me? As far as I knew I wasn't even on their radar until suddenly I was.' He took a breath and stared down at the photos again. 'You find yourself with a lot of time to think things over when you're waiting for trial. So much time that you can end up convincing yourself of something just because you want it to be true.'

Leanne's gaze remained fixed on his as she waited for him to continue. Next to her Andee sat very still.

'I told you before,' he said to Leanne, 'that I thought he was a friend. I never would have dreamt he'd do me wrong . . .'

'We're talking about your old boss, Ed Fairley?' Andee said, spelling it out.

His eyes stayed down as he shook his head in a bewildered, defeated sort of way. 'He had to know I'd never hurt a child, especially not like that.'

'Do you think he put Kylie's hair in your car?' Andee asked bluntly.

He looked so wretched, and so like Daniel in that moment, that Leanne almost reached for his hand. 'It's the only way I can think of,' he replied.

'Did you ever tell the police this?'

He nodded. 'Of course. I had to. I don't know if they interviewed him, but I'm guessing they did because he's never wanted anything to do with me since. He wouldn't even look at me when we were in the court. He didn't say anything bad about me, he praised me all the way, but he was behaving all the time as if he thought I was guilty and had tried to shift the blame on to him.'

Andee nodded thoughtfully. 'And of course you've discussed all this with your lawyer?' she said. 'I mean both before the trial and since, while preparing for the appeal?'

'Yes, I have,' he replied.

'And what does your lawyer say?'

Marks shrugged. 'Just that he's working on it.'

Andee's expression was still inscrutable, but Leanne sensed she'd received the answer she'd expected.

'To be honest,' Marks said, 'I don't think he's interested. I've tried to find someone else to represent me,
but no one wants to take it on.'

Seeming unsurprised by that, Andee said, 'Tell us
about the incident where you touched a little girl
inappropriately.'

Marks appeared to flinch. 'I didn't even know about
it until it came out in the press,' he replied hoarsely.

'So it never happened?'

He shook his head. 'No way.'

'In which case there won't be any record of it?'

'I can't see why there would be, unless one was
made up. But if it was checked out . . . Listen, I know
how this is all looking, God knows it's stared me in
the face all this time, but Ed Fairley was properly
there for me and Daniel after Gracie died. They invited
us into their home. He gave me all the time off I
needed . . . It's why I never really considered him when
I was first asked who else had access to my computer
and car. Of course he did, but . . . Doing something like
that . . . ?'

Andee sat back in her chair, a fist bunched to her chin
as she thought.

Leanne said, because she had to, 'Do you think
there's a chance Kylie might still be alive?'

There was a harrowing sadness in his eyes as he
turned them to her. 'I don't know,' he replied, 'because
I've got no idea what happened to her.'

'So what are you thinking?' Leanne asked as she and
Andee returned to their cars.

After a moment Andee said, 'I need to talk to my ex-DI. We might not have any new evidence, but after today . . . When we put it together with the way I've been blocked by CID in Marstone, and how Marks's lawyer is no longer returning my calls, I think we can put on enough pressure to get a look at the files, even if we can't get the case reopened.'

'But it will reopen if it turns out that there's even a chance the wrong man is in jail?'

'If we can create enough doubt, then quite possibly.' Coming to a stop next to her car, Andee turned to Leanne and said, 'I'm going to pay a visit to Ed Fairley at the hot air balloon company tomorrow.'

'Would you like me to come with you?'

Andee thought about it. 'I think it's best if I go alone. Two might come across heavier than one, and I don't want to put him on the defensive if I can help it.'

'Is there anything else I can do?'

'I'll let you know if there is; for now just hang tight and wait for my call.'

Somewhere Leanne really hadn't expected to find herself three days later was outside Kesterly police station, talking to PC Barry Britten as she waited for her mother to be released from custody.

'Don't worry, she hasn't been charged with anything,' Barry was assuring her, 'she just got caught up with the mob.'

'You mean the mob she was leading,' Leanne responded wryly.

'Unless you tell me she's joined the English Defence

318

League I can pretty much guarantee she wasn't leading.'

'The EDL. What the heck was she doing with them? No, don't tell me, she was trying to get them to see reason – or her version of it. I hope she didn't get thumped for her trouble.'

'Not thumped, but she caught a shedload of abuse, that's for sure. Lucky she wasn't in the thick of it when things turned really ugly, or she might have copped a stabbing like the poor bloke who got rushed off to A & E. That's basically why everyone had to be hauled in. It's bedlam in there, and you know Wilkie better than me, so you can guess how vocal she's being. I expect she'll be out any minute just so they can get rid of her.'

Right on cue, out Wilkie marched, as puffed up and pink in the face as only she could be after a rousing confrontation with opposition forces.

'What are you doing here?' she demanded the instant she saw Leanne.

'You rang me,' Leanne reminded her.

'Oh, so I did. Barry, you look so scrumptious I could eat you on toast. How are your lovely twins?'

'They're doing fine thanks, Wilkie. Taking after you in some respects, that's for sure.'

Wilkie appeared delighted.

'They like nothing better than a good duff-up,' he explained.

As Wilkie and Leanne burst out laughing, Barry was called back into the station, so after saying their good-byes they got into the car.

'I'm parked over by the station if you can take me there,' Wilkie instructed.

'Of course, why else am I on this planet other than to bail you out and run you around?'

'Yes, I've always said it's useful having children.'

Unable not to laugh, Leanne turned out of the Quadrant and headed towards the promenade.

'What news from Andee?' Wilkie demanded, as soon as she'd finished checking her mobile.

'Nothing since yesterday, when she rang to let us know that the detective chief inspector at Marstone was on maternity leave during the hunt for Kylie.'

'So we don't know yet why that's significant?'

'No. I left a message earlier, but I'm still waiting to hear back.'

'Oh, this is all very frustrating and worrying . . .'

'Mum, she's already warned us that it could take a while, and as much as we want to think Daniel's father is innocent, we have to keep reminding ourselves that there was an investigation and a trial and . . .'

'And a conviction. Indeed, but if he's in prison . . .'

'. . . for a crime he didn't commit, we need . . .'

'. . . to know who did commit it.' Leanne took a breath. 'Top of the list is the ex-boss, who's not helping himself one bit with the way he's giving Andee the runaround. First he's free to see her, then he isn't. Then he'll meet her somewhere, but gets held up . . .'

'So she still hasn't spoken to him?'

'Only on the phone, when she asked about the person who'd complained that Patrick Marks had touched her child inappropriately. He told her it was history, he didn't want to discuss it, and no, he wasn't prepared to give out any details about the woman or the child.'

'Mm, I call that suspicious, don't you? But as my whole *raison d'être* is to make sure we don't rush to conclusions or judgements about people . . .'

'Which doesn't exclude opinions, and as far as I'm concerned – Andee too – the hot air balloon guy is full of his own stuff.'

Wilkie frowned. 'What would that be?'

Leanne rolled her eyes. 'Hot air?'

'Oh, I see. I completely agree. You can drop me anywhere here.'

As Leanne pulled in at the entrance to the station car park, Wilkie got out and leaned back in through the open window. 'Try to remember,' she said, 'that serious issues, and of course this is one, have a habit of taking over to the exclusion of all else.'

'Meaning?'

'That you need to lighten up a little, because the children in your house are starting to pick up on your stress.'

Leanne immediately felt bad. It was true, she'd become fixated on this business with Patrick Marks, unsurprisingly given how important it was, but it was no excuse to neglect those who mattered most. She looked at her mother again.

'Just saying,' Wilkie grinned, and with an airy little wave she vanished into the maze of parked cars.

By the time Leanne reached home she was ready to suggest all sorts of family activities for the coming weekend from a picnic on the moor, to an afternoon at the cinema, to an all-day Sunday at Watermouth Castle and theme park. However, there was only a note to greet her, letting her know that Abby and Daniel had taken Juno on the bus to an agility class and were meeting Klaudia and the children after for a pizza at the Mermaid, where dogs were allowed.

Going to make herself some tea, Leanne checked her emails and found one from Abby's pastoral care tutor.

She read it quickly, found her mouth dropping open in astonishment and read it again.

'. . . in the light of which we're considering moving Abby into the talented and gifted group. However, knowing your feelings on this matter, I thought I should check with you before taking any action.'

Now there's a dilemma, Leanne thought wryly. The best part of it, of course, was that Abby's grades had improved enough for her to earn the recognition – and this had happened since Daniel's arrival. Was there a connection? It was hard to say with any certainty, but she wasn't going to dismiss it.

Emailing back, she said, 'I need to discuss it with Abby. Have you mentioned it to her?' After sending it she was about to text Klaudia to say she'd meet them at the pub when Andee called.

'I've just spent the last couple of hours with Kylie Booth's parents,' she announced. 'To say they were relieved to hear that we're looking into the police investigation is an understatement.'

Sitting down with a thud, Leanne said, 'Does that mean they don't think Patrick Marks is the right man?'

'Let's say they have their doubts, not least of all because of a letter they received from Marks himself.'

'He's written to them? Why didn't he mention it?'

'Possibly because he never heard back. Apparently they wrote begging him to tell them where their daughter could be found, and since getti﹐ ; his reply they've been asking themselves over and ﹐ er if he was telling the truth.'

'So what did he say?'

'He swore on his dead wife's ɡᵣave that if he had the answer he would have told them right away. He said he was truly sorry for everything they've been through, and that if there was anything at all he could do to help alleviate their suffering he would do it.'

'Did you see the letter?'

'I did and it's impressive. Very convincing, in fact. It would definitely have swayed me, maybe not into believing him, but into asking more questions.'

'So have they done anything about it?'

'They took it to the police right away, but they were reminded of the physical evidence against Marks and were advised to have no further contact with him. Killers can be very manipulative, they were told, and it would only make things worse for them if they didn't accept the verdict.'

'Which is why they didn't write back. I take it they spoke to the original investigating officer?'

'They did. Detective Inspector Barnwell. I don't know him personally, but he's been in the job for a long time and as far as I'm aware he has no blots on his record.'

Feeling a brick wall approaching, Leanne said, 'So what next?'

'Helen Hall, a lawyer based in Kesterly, is going to request the police files on the grounds of there being a cause for doubt in the investigation. She'll outline the doubt in a way that'll make it difficult for them to refuse, although I'm sure they'll try.'

Thrown by this, and uplifted, Leanne said, 'How long is it likely to take?'

'How long is a piece of string, but if they don't play ball, and Ed Fairley the balloon man continues to avoid me, I might have a chat with a reporter I know. There's nothing like a bit of media pressure to get things moving.'

'If you involve the press I'll have to tell Daniel. I don't want him finding out like that.'

'Of course not, but don't worry, I'll be sure to let you know first if I decide to go that route. With any luck the threat of it might be enough.'

Two days later Leanne was still waiting for news from Andee when she sat Abby down to discuss the talented and gifted. Though she remained strongly opposed to the scheme in principle, she accepted that this had to be Abby's choice, not hers.

'I know what you're going to say,' Abby declared before Leanne could begin.

'Oh good, then it'll save me the trouble.'

'Great. Can I go now?'

Leanne almost laughed. 'Are you sure you know what I'm going to say?' she asked.

'Of course. It's about the talented and gifted. Miss Hawks told me she'd put my name forward. I don't think she was supposed to, but it was too late once it was out.'

Leanne regarded her closely. 'And what do you think about it?' she ventured.

Abby shrugged. 'Same as you, I guess, that it's elitist and stupid, and really mean towards those who aren't in it, but then I talked to Daniel about it and we decided it would be easier to speak out against it if we're in it. It won't look like sour grapes then. Well, it wouldn't for him, because he's already in it, but if I'm in it too we can try and get a group of T&Gs together to see if we can come up with something that works more fairly for everyone.'

Leanne regarded her in pride and amazement. 'You're definitely Wilkie's granddaughter,' she smiled tenderly.

'Duh! Was there ever any doubt?'

Leanne shook her head. 'So I have to email back and say that I have no objection?' she asked.

Abby nodded. 'But don't let on that we're going to try and sabotage it. We need to do that ourselves, and we don't need any help from you, thank you very much. Can I go now?'

Later that same evening Leanne found Daniel outside on the veranda, scraping mud off his football boots. 'Is everything OK with you?' she asked, going to sit on the step beside him.

He glanced up at her and nodded as he turned back to his task.

'Anything you'd like to talk about?' she invited casually.

He shrugged. 'I'm cool,' he replied. 'Abby told you about our plans for the T&Gs?'

'Yes, she did. Was it her idea or yours?'

'Hers, really, but I definitely think it's a good one. We just have to find some T&Gs from other years to join us, so we've got everyone covered.'

Leanne watched him for a while, thinking of his father in prison and how he would give anything in the world to be sitting here now, chatting with his son, helping to clean his boots and perhaps giving him fatherly advice on his schooling. Reaching out, she smoothed a hand gently over Daniel's short dark hair.

He turned to her and when he broke into a smile she felt almost overwhelmed by emotion.

'You're a very special young man,' she told him softly. 'I hope you know that.'

'Sure,' he replied in a way that made her laugh.

'I like it here,' he said, still looking at her. 'It's the best home I've ever had after my real one.'

The following day Leanne received a letter from Patrick Marks that moved her to tears.

Dear Mrs Delaney,

I want you to know how much I appreciate your belief in me. Being in a place like this can make you forget what human decency and kindness is like, I even forget to practise it when it used to come naturally to me. The only time I am myself now is when I write to Daniel. He is all that matters to me, much more even than my freedom, but I'm sure it goes without saying that I pray every day for the chance to be with him again.

I know you've read about his mother, Gracie, so I'm sure you understand how much Daniel meant to her. It would be hard for a mother to love a son more, especially when she'd been told before his premature birth – that's why he's so small – that she would never have children. He is our miracle. She died knowing that I would always be there for him, and would do everything in my power to make sure he had a good life. It was what gave her peace at the end. Neither of us would ever have dreamt that fate had such a cruel hand in store for him, ripping him away from me and putting him into the care of strangers.

I know from Daniel's letters that you don't feel like a stranger to him. You've treated him with the kindness and understanding that all children deserve. I think having lost his mother and then his father makes him even more deserving than most.

Thank you, Mrs Delaney, from the bottom of my heart for believing in him.

Yours sincerely
Patrick Marks

There were tears on Klaudia's cheeks as she handed the letter back to Leanne. 'What really stands out for me,' she said, 'is that he's not asking for anything. He's only saying thank you and letting you know how much his son means to him.' She paused to dab her eyes. 'Most people in his shoes would be thinking only of themselves and how desperate they are to get out of jail.'

'I'm sure he is desperate,' Leanne responded, 'but I agree, the way he makes it all about Daniel is really touching.'

Klaudia frowned at the tone of her voice. 'What is it?' she prompted.

Leanne sighed and shook her head. 'It's just me being cynical, I guess, or overprotective . . . I don't know . . . I guess I can't help thinking about what the police told Kylie's parents, that killers can be very manipulative.'

Astonished, Klaudia said, 'Are you saying you no longer believe Patrick Marks might be innocent?'

Leanne shook her head. 'No, not that, but . . . Heck, I don't know what I'm saying or even thinking half the time. I suppose I'm just afraid of it all backfiring on us in a way that'll end up hurting Daniel even more than he's already been hurt.'

Klaudia reached for her hand. 'That's not going to happen,' she told her gently. 'I understand why you're feeling so anxious and restless, God knows waiting for news can drive you half out of your mind.'

Coming to her senses, Leanne quickly said, 'I'm sorry, Mum warned me I was obsessing. I keep doing it, and it's so unfair to the rest of you. The decision you're waiting for is every bit as huge, as life-changing . . .'

'Forget about me,' Klaudia interrupted. 'I'll be fine. After all, I have my freedom and my children, and that's what really matters.'

'But you won't have the freedom to remain here if things don't go that way.'

Klaudia's eyes darkened. 'And Patrick Marks won't

have the freedom to be with his son if things don't work out for him.'

'But we know for certain that you haven't done anything wrong. Can we honestly say that about him?'

Klaudia regarded her carefully. 'Can we?' she prompted.

Leanne thought about it again and finally nodded. 'Yes,' she said, 'yes, I'm sure we can.'

Chapter Nineteen

Leanne, Wilkie and Klaudia were seated around Wilkie's kitchen table, listening in appalled fascination to what Andee was telling them.

'To say the investigation was shambolic is putting it mildly,' Andee confided, gesturing her agreement to the wine Wilkie was offering. 'We know that because Helen Hall has managed to get her hands on the police files. The problem, in her view, seems mostly to have been created by the pressure the detectives were under – as much from their bosses as from the media – to bring the case to a conclusion. It's because of this that the right procedures were shortcut, evidence wasn't properly processed, questions that should have been asked weren't, and not all information was followed up on.'

Stunned, Wilkie said, 'And we always have such faith in the police.'

Andee glanced at her, clearly not sure whether she was joking or not. 'I've been through parts of the case files myself,' she continued, 'and frankly, the interrogation of Ed Fairley was hardly short of farcical in the way it barely scratched the surface. It's like they'd decided they had their man, so they just wanted it wrapped up and over with. As far as we can make out, he wasn't even asked what made him point them in Patrick Marks's direction. That is such a shocking oversight, not only on the part of the police, but also the Crown Prosecution Service who referred the case for trial, that there are grounds right there for an appeal.'

'So what is Marks's solicitor doing?' Leanne asked. 'If you can find this out so easily, surely to God he can.'

'It's a very good question,' Andee told her, 'and I might be able to answer it if the man would return my calls.'

'Why would he avoid you?' Klaudia wanted to know.

'Because he clearly hasn't done his job properly either,' Andee replied.

'And the barrister?' Wilkie wondered. 'He surely brought it up in court.'

'He did,' Andee confirmed, 'however, if you look at the transcript you'll see that it wasn't done in a particularly meaningful way. He simply put it to Fairley that a lot of time had elapsed between Kylie going missing and him contacting the police with his suspicions. It wasn't even a question, so Fairley didn't answer.'

'He wasn't asked what made him suspicious?' Leanne cried in disbelief.

'He was, and Fairley replied that he became concerned when he saw how fixated Patrick Marks seemed to be with the case. Then he got to thinking about the incident with the little girl that Marks was supposed to have touched inappropriately when she was getting into a hot air balloon. The problem with that is, after a check, which I'll tell you more about in a minute, it turns out there's no record of any such incident.'

As they regarded her in astonishment, Klaudia said, 'You're making it sound as though anyone can come forward with a suspicion about anything and the police will just believe them.'

'I'm glad to say,' Andee responded, 'it doesn't usually work that way. What's happened here, in my opinion, is that Patrick Marks has been set up by someone he trusted and then profoundly let down by the system that's supposed to protect him. And the jury, apparently in as much of a hurry to condemn him as everyone else appeared to be, went along with it.'

After a while, Leanne said quietly, 'Do you think it might have been different if he weren't black?'

Andee regarded her sadly. 'Who knows, but the thought has crossed my mind. Anyway, to continue, three days ago I got a call from an officer who'd worked on the case. He'd heard I was asking around, and he was willing to talk to me, he said, on condition I didn't reveal his name. When we got together he told me that all hell was breaking loose in the department. The DCI who'd been on maternity leave was now back and demanding to know why questions were being asked about the Kylie Booth case that had nothing to do with where the little girl or her body might be found, but about *who* had abducted her. As far as she was aware, the case had been solved during her absence and the right man was in prison.'

Leanne had no experience of police investigations, but thinking of the Marstone force being in chaos enabled her to cling to a small sense of justice.

'According to Kylie's parents,' Andee was saying, 'their daughter had never come into contact with Patrick Marks that they knew of, although she'd been for a balloon ride at Fairley's about a month before she disappeared. There is the connection, or it might have been if Marks had been working that day.'

Leanne's heartbeat was slowing.

'How do you know he wasn't working that day?' Wilkie asked.

'By the time our friendly detective spoke to me he'd already checked, and had it confirmed by a secretary at the balloon company, that Marks had not been in at all that week. At the same time he established that there was no record of any inappropriate behaviour concerning Marks. Both very simple enquiries that should have been made during the initial investigation, but apparently weren't. It seemed everyone was happy to take Fairley at his word, and for reasons best known to herself, the secretary didn't offer up this important information at the time of Patrick Marks's arrest.'

Wilkie said, 'Do you think she was involved somehow? Trying to protect someone?'

'It's possible,' Andee conceded. 'We'll know more once the investigation has gone to the depths it should have in the first place. Something else that didn't happen when it should have was a full check of how the DNA had got into Marks's car. Obviously the first assumption would be that Kylie herself had been there, but no one bothered to find out if it might have been put there. That's certainly what Marks claimed, not only during his interrogation but again in court. This was never followed up. It was just assumed, as soon as confirmation came through that it was Kylie's hair, that Marks had abducted her. Apparently he doesn't have an alibi for when she went missing, so that was all they needed to make an arrest. Then his computer was checked, the porn was found and as far as Marstone CID was concerned his guilt was sealed. The CPS agreed and the case was sent for trial.'

After a pause, Wilkie said, 'I feel outraged by this.'

'You have good reason to,' Andee told her. 'I'm not defending anyone, but the police hear offenders shouting their innocence all the time, the way Patrick Marks did, so it doesn't hold much sway with them, particularly if they're already convinced of someone's guilt. And remember the system is set up in such a way that they have to believe a person is guilty before they present the case to the CPS.'

'So in their eyes,' Wilkie said, 'someone is guilty and has to prove themselves innocent.'

Andee nodded. 'Of course that's not the way the courts work, although any trial starts with a presumption of guilt or the offender wouldn't be there.'

Leanne's hands were pressed to her cheeks as she thought of Patrick Marks locked up in that awful prison. Two long years he had been shut away for a crime he hadn't committed, suffering only he knew what at the hands of other inmates as punishment for what he was supposed to have done to Kylie. 'So to get this straight,' she said, 'we are assuming that it was Ed Fairley who took Kylie?' She was thinking of what Marks had told her about the man's kindness at the time of Gracie's death. It was all too horrible, too twisted and distressing even to begin to understand.

'On the face of it,' Andee replied, 'that's a reasonable assumption. He directs the police to Patrick Marks in order to save his own skin – or,' she looked at each one of them in turn, 'to save someone else's.'

Leanne sensed everyone's intake of breath as they waited for Andee to continue.

'Ed Fairley has a fifteen-year-old son,' Andee said. 'By the time I left Marstone earlier both the boy and his father had been taken in for questioning.'

Leanne sat back in her chair, feeling as though she'd been struck.

After a while, Wilkie said, 'So what you're saying is that in order to try and protect his son he was prepared to destroy the life of an innocent man and a dear, sweet little boy who'd already lost his mother.'

Andee put a hand over Wilkie's. 'It's looking that way, but thanks to you and Leanne and the way you've believed in Daniel, and his father, we now have a good chance of putting things right.'

It was just after lunchtime the following day that Leanne went to the school to collect Daniel. Andee had called to warn her that Ed Fairley's son was about to be charged with Kylie's abduction, and that heavy digging equipment was already in a field next to the Fairleys' home.

Leanne had felt so upset when she'd heard about the

equipment that she'd found it hard to speak through her tears. All through the night she'd kept hoping and praying even against all the odds that Kylie was hidden away somewhere, and the police would soon rescue her and take her back to her parents. Did those poor, devastated people know yet about this new search for their daughter? No one deserved such torment, such unimaginable heartache. How on earth were they going to get through it?

Wishing there was something she could do for them, while knowing there was nothing, she switched her concerns to Daniel and his father and what these new developments were going to mean for them.

Since Daniel hadn't mentioned anything about his father during the drive home, Leanne felt confident that the news, via social media or some kind of kids' network, hadn't yet reached him. However, he was clearly anxious about being taken out of school, and realising he could be afraid that she was going to tell him he had to leave, she wasted no time in putting his mind at rest.

'It's all right, you haven't done anything wrong,' she told him with a tender smile as she sat down with him on the sofa. 'I came to get you because I have something to tell you.'

His deep brown eyes held fast to hers, as though if he let go he might fall.

'It's about your dad,' she said softly. 'Don't worry, he's fine, nothing's happened to him, but . . .'

'Can I go and see him?' Daniel jumped in eagerly. 'Please say I can see him.'

With a lump in her throat, Leanne said, 'You will . . .'

'He didn't do it,' Daniel cried, tears rushing to his eyes. 'The things they said he did, he didn't do them.'

'Ssh,' she whispered, smoothing his cheek.

'Please believe me, Leanne,' he begged. 'He doesn't lie . . .'

'I do believe you,' she interrupted.

'. . . he told me he didn't do it, and he never tells lies.'

'I do believe you,' she repeated.

Finally registering her words, he regarded her with enormous, doubtful eyes.

'Things have been happening,' she told him, 'and they're about to break on the news, which is why I came to get you. I wanted you to hear it from me first. You see, there's a very good chance your daddy will be coming home.'

Still he could only look at her, as though trying to understand, then suddenly he was sobbing so hard that he couldn't catch his breath. 'Daddy, Daddy,' he gulped, his hands going up and down to his head. '*Daddy*,' he cried desperately.

Folding him into her arms she rocked him back and forth, feeling his whole body trembling and shuddering as he tried to cope with the news.

Heaven knew she was finding it hard too, for to see so much grief pouring out of him told her how much he'd been bottling up all this time.

It was a while before he drew back to look at her. His sweet face was soaked in tears, and flushed crimson with heat. 'When?' he asked hoarsely. 'Will it be soon?'

Sitting him down again, she said, 'I'm not sure. We'll find out more as the day goes on, but for now you need to know that the police are talking to Ed Fairley, your dad's old boss . . .'

'Ed knows he didn't do it. He should have told them before . . .'

'He didn't,' she said gently, 'because it's looking very like it was his son who took Kylie.'

Daniel's face stilled in confusion. 'You mean Maurice?'

Leanne nodded. 'The police think that Ed Fairley set things up to make it look like your dad was guilty, when all the time he knew that Maurice had taken Kylie.'

Daniel swallowed, looked away and back again. She could tell this was too much for him and wished she could have taken more time to break the news, but she needed to prepare him for the media storm to come. And come it would once they found out who and where Daniel Marks was, but for the moment, thank goodness, his identity and location were still a secret. 'So what did he do to her?' he asked uncomprehendingly.

Taking a breath, she said, 'They're searching for her now, but I'm afraid they're not expecting to find her alive.'

Apparently having real difficulty with that, he looked around the room as though he might find a way to process it, or even to explain why Leanne had it wrong. In the end he turned back to her and said, 'My dad's a good person. He wouldn't have hurt her . . .'

'We know that now.'

'But I don't understand why Ed or Maurice would . . .'

'None of us understand it, but the important thing is to put them out of your mind and think about you and your dad.'

He nodded, almost absently, then suddenly animated, he said, 'I want you to meet him. I know you'll like him. Will you be able to?'

'I've already met him,' she replied gently. 'I've been to the prison twice. I didn't tell you because I didn't want to get your hopes up.'

Clearly stunned by this news, he said, 'So did you make it happen that he's coming home?'

She smiled. 'Not exactly. The police and lawyers will do that, I just went with a friend of mine who used to be a detective to have a chat with him . . .'

'Did you like him?'

'Yes, I did.'

His face lit up. 'I wish I could tell my mum. She'd be really pleased.'

Wishing he could tell her too, Leanne said, 'I'm sure she would, in fact I expect she does know, because I'm sure she's watching over you both.'

He nodded, seeming to like the sound of that. 'Can we go to the prison now?' he asked.

'Not yet, but as soon as we can we will.'

He sat with that for a moment. 'Then can we,' he said tentatively, 'have a look at your *Book of the Way*?'

Touched that he should think of it, while secretly hoping this wasn't going to be a mistake, she went to get it and handed it over for him to open.

With eyes closed he lifted a finger, hovered for a moment then touched it down on the page.

'*Blessed are new beginnings,*' he read out loud. He gave a small gasp and looked up at Leanne, eagerness and hope shining in his eyes. Then quite suddenly he threw himself at her and hugged her with all his might.

By the end of that week Kylie's remains had been found in a shallow grave close to one of Fairley's storage sheds, while both Fairleys and the company secretary had been charged on several counts, including abduction, child rape, murder and perverting the course of justice. The press and social media were so full of the shock discovery that Leanne was eternally grateful for the fact that no one had yet found out that Daniel Davis was in fact Daniel Marks, son of Patrick Marks. Nevertheless, she'd kept Daniel and Abby home from school just in case they were unable to stop themselves bursting out with the news.

It was still too early to know when Patrick might be released, but Helen Hall, who'd been recommended by Andee to act as his lawyer, had already referred the case to the Criminal Appeal Court.

'There will be a swift application for bail pending a full court hearing,' she'd told Leanne on the phone yesterday, 'but as yet it's not clear when he'll be allowed to leave.'

'But he will be?'

'He will.'

'Does he know that yet?'

'I spoke to him just before I called you. He sounded quite subdued; I think it's taking a time to settle in. How's Daniel?'

'Excited, fearful, euphoric, can't stop talking one minute, fast asleep the next. He keeps begging me to take him to the prison, but Patrick hasn't made it possible yet.'

Having no explanation for that, Helen Hall had rung off, promising to call again as soon as she knew more.

Around midday two letters arrived from the prison, one for Leanne and one for Daniel. As usual Daniel ran upstairs to his room with his, while Leanne sat down with Abby and Wilkie to read hers.

Dear Mrs Delaney,

One day I might find enough words to express how thankful I feel for the way you've believed in me, and helped to right the wrong I have suffered. I'm afraid today isn't that day, as I am still too overcome by all that is happening. I think I've taken it in, but until I walk out of here I know I will keep doubting, and feeling afraid that it is all a dream.

I have already written to Daniel to tell him how proud I am of him for the way he's come through this, and how much I'm looking forward to seeing him. As the time is drawing close for us to be together again I would like it to happen outside of this place rather than inside, so I have asked him to come and pick me up, not to visit. Seeing me in here is not a memory I want him to live with.

I hope you understand, and that he will too.

With kind regards

Patrick Marks

PS. I will also be writing to Andee Lawrence to thank her for everything she's done to help me to regain my freedom.

*   *   *

When Wilkie and Abby had finished reading, Leanne smiled at the tears glistening in their eyes.

'I understand why he wouldn't want Daniel to see him there,' Abby said, 'but I wonder if Daniel will. He can hardly wait . . .' She broke off as Daniel came charging down the stairs.

'It's OK,' he said, his eyes red-rimmed and still swimming in tears, 'I understand too. I just want him to come home like now.'

Holding out a hand for him to join them, Leanne said, 'It'll happen soon enough, I promise, and meantime maybe we can sort out a lovely homecoming for him.'

'It might be too much to throw a party,' Wilkie stated, clearly thinking of Kylie and her parents, 'but we could do a nice family meal here at the barn . . .'

'Where are you going to live?' Abby cut in. 'I mean, when he comes out where will you go?'

Daniel shook his head. 'I don't know. Do you think we can go back to our old house?' he asked Leanne.

Having no idea what had happened to the property, Leanne said, 'All that will be sorted out before we go to get him.'

His eyes rounded with surprise. 'Does that mean you'll come with me?' he asked.

Wondering how on earth he thought he'd get there on his own, Leanne pressed a kiss to his forehead. 'Of course I will,' she whispered.

'I was wondering,' Wilkie said with a twinkle, 'if you and your dad might like to spend the first couple of weeks in the bakery. There's plenty of room, you'd have a bedroom each and . . .'

'. . . and you'd still be with us,' Abby rushed in eagerly. 'That would be brilliant, wouldn't it?'

Daniel nodded, but he seemed uncertain.

Noting this Abby's face fell, and Leanne could tell she was worried she might have said the wrong thing.

'I'm going to write to him now to ask if we can do that,' Daniel said.

As he went upstairs Leanne could see that Abby was still baffled, and when Juno came to put his chin in her lap she got up and went off to her room.

'She's got used to him being here,' Wilkie said, after hearing Abby's door close. 'We all have.'

'It's a good idea about the bakery,' Leanne told her. 'I don't suppose there'll be any official objection to it. I mean, he should be free to do as he wants after his release.'

'Indeed, and they'll both need a period of adjustment, so just in case, I don't think I'll put the bakery back up on the website for summer rentals until we're sure of what Patrick wants to do.'

It was much later in the day, as they were about to set off to join Klaudia and the children in town for a Chinese, that Leanne made a quick check of her emails, just in case there was more news about Patrick.

There wasn't; however, her heart did a severe flip when she saw there was a message from Tom.

Deciding it could wait until she came back, she put her phone away, then took it out again and opened the message. It didn't take long to read, because there wasn't very much of it.

* * *

343

Hi Leanne,

Very glad to see that you were right about Patrick Marks. It's causing quite a sensation, I believe, although Richie tells me your name has been kept out of it. This is wonderful news for Daniel. How fortunate he is to have found you.

I think of you often,

Tom

Determined not to fall into the trap of analysing that last line, she closed the email and picked up her keys. There was no need to reply to it; he hadn't asked her to, he hadn't even said where he was or what he was doing, though she wasn't entirely sure why that made a difference.

No, she wouldn't bother sending a message back.

Hi Tom,

Yes, we're all very pleased. There couldn't have been a better outcome for Daniel, though Patrick hasn't been released yet. Expecting it to happen within the next couple of weeks.

I hope all is well with you,

Leanne

Chapter Twenty

Two extremely tense weeks followed as they waited for the application to overturn Patrick's conviction to be confirmed, unopposed. As both Fairleys had now given full confessions that apparently absolved Patrick from blame, there was no doubt that he would be released, it was just a question of when.

The call finally came late on a Friday afternoon, just as they were giving up hope of hearing anything more that week.

'You can go to pick him up at nine thirty on Monday,' Helen Hall told Leanne. 'An official announcement is being held back until after the event, so you shouldn't have to face any press interest. However, you should prepare yourself for a bombardment once they find out where he is, and of course they will.'

Deciding she'd have to deal with that when it happened, Leanne put the phone down and called her mother from the farmhouse and Klaudia from the stables to share in the news. So much cheering and celebration followed, with Daniel veering from stunned to excited to full-on ecstatic, that Leanne didn't notice right away that Abby wasn't seeming quite as thrilled as everyone else.

'Is everything all right?' Leanne murmured so no one else could hear.

Abby snapped, 'Nothing's wrong with me apart from *you*.'

Deciding not to spoil this evening for Daniel, Leanne let it go, and went to take her phone from Klaudia, who'd answered it for her. 'Who is it?' she asked.

Klaudia simply grinned at her.

Thinking immediately of Tom, Leanne put the phone to her ear. 'Hello?' she said tentatively, hopefully.

'Mrs Delaney?'

Recognising the voice instantly, she felt her heart skip with surprise and joy. 'He's right here,' she said softly, 'I'll put him on.'

As she held the phone out to Daniel he appeared confused, then apparently understanding he leapt forward so urgently to grab it that he almost fell.

'Dad?' he whispered, once he'd righted himself. 'Dad, is that you?'

As he turned away everyone had tears in their eyes. This was such a special moment for Daniel, and for Patrick, that it was impossible not to feel overcome by it.

Father and son didn't talk for long and all Daniel said was, 'yes', 'no', 'yes', and 'we'll definitely be there.' At the end he said, 'I love you too,' and Leanne actually sobbed as he passed the phone back to her. 'He wants to speak to you,' he told her.

'Hello, Patrick,' she said, dabbing her eyes. 'This is

very good news. Like Daniel said we'll be there on Monday, so don't go without us.' She saw Daniel grin as his father said, brokenly, 'We don't want to be a burden on you . . .'

'Please don't say that. The bakery is ready, we'll put some supplies in over the weekend . . .'

'Mrs Delaney . . .'

'Leanne.'

'Leanne, I wish I knew how to thank you.'

'It's us who should thank you for letting us have this time with Daniel.' Hearing her own words she groaned aloud. 'That was such a stupid thing to say, I'm sorry, I . . .'

'It's OK. I get what you mean.' There was a smile in his voice that made her feel even worse. 'I have to go now,' he said, 'but I'll see you on Monday.'

It was in the middle of Sunday afternoon that everything came to a head with Abby, and Leanne could only feel thankful that Wilkie had taken Daniel to Bel and Harry's so he could break the news of who he really was to his friends Neel and Josh.

'I don't understand why you didn't want to go too,' Leanne ventured, as Abby sauntered in from her bedroom just after Wilkie had driven off. 'I thought you might have wanted to see Josh.'

Abby's eyes flashed. 'Why would I want to see *Josh*?' she challenged tightly.

Realising she'd launched herself straight into a minefield, Leanne quickly tried to back out. 'No reason.'

'Yes there is. You wouldn't have said it otherwise.'

'Well, it's just that you two seem to get along and . . .'

'So what if we get along? It doesn't mean I have to go and see him.'

'No, it doesn't.'

Abby helped herself to an apple and bit out a chunk.

Leanne continued washing Glory's valuable collection of bone china, taking great care with it as she always did. She hadn't decided yet whether she and Klaudia should use it for their vintage teas – if they managed to launch the venture – but being as pretty and authentic as it was, it would make quite a statement.

'Anyway,' Abby said, 'if Daniel's going to tell Josh and Neel who he really is why would they want me there?'

Puzzled, Leanne turned to look at her. In spite of it being three in the afternoon Abby was still in her pyjamas, with the belt of her robe hanging loosely and her hair uncombed.

Realising that she needed to give this some proper attention, Leanne reached for a towel to dry her hands and leaned back against the sink with her arms folded. 'That's an odd thing to say,' she commented carefully. 'I'm sure they do want you there . . .'

'I just said they don't, OK?'

Frowning, Leanne said, 'Have you had a falling out with one of them?'

'*No-ooo.* Just leave it, why don't you?'

Knowing that Abby wouldn't have brought it up if she really wanted that, much less be hanging about the kitchen, Leanne watched her, hoping she'd say more.

She didn't, but as she tried to make a show of reading a colour supplement Leanne saw a big fat tear drop on to the page.

'Oh Abby,' she murmured, going to her.

Abby backed off, holding up her hands to stop her coming any closer.

'What is it?' Leanne pleaded. 'Why won't you tell me what's upsetting you?'

'*Why* don't you know?' Abby shouted, and before Leanne could stop her she ran to her room.

Going after her, Leanne tried the door and to her relief found it unlocked – a sure sign that Abby wanted her to go in.

Abby was on the bed, sobbing into Juno, who was doing his best to lick away the tears.

'Abby, what should I know?' Leanne asked, going to sit beside her. 'Please tell me.'

'Why should I? If you're too stupid to guess that Josh has got a girlfriend, then you're even dumber than I thought.'

Inhaling deeply, Leanne put a comforting hand on her shoulder, and when it wasn't rebuffed she started to rub. 'I'm really sorry to hear that,' she said, understanding and almost feeling the depth of a first rejection. 'Does Josh know that you like him?'

'I don't *know*. Who cares? It's not about him anyway.'

Although she wouldn't have brought it up if it weren't an issue, Leanne could guess what else was upsetting her. 'It's Daniel, isn't it?' she asked gently.

'No! Go away. I don't want to talk to you any more.'

'You're afraid he's going to leave us.'

'Well he is, isn't he? Now his dad's coming out he won't want us any more. He'll just go off like we never existed and that's just mean, because we've been really nice to him.'

'I don't think it's going to happen like that,' Leanne soothed. 'Remember, they're going to be just across the courtyard in the bakery for a while.'

'But they'll go eventually, and I don't . . . I don't want him to go. Oh Mum, why does he have to go? Please make him stay here with us.'

As she threw herself into Leanne's arms, Leanne held her close and smoothed her hair. 'Surely you want him to be with his dad, Abby,' she said.

'Yes, but . . . No. I don't really. I want him to be with us.' She raised her head and Leanne's heart contracted to see so much anguish and pain. 'Everyone leaves me in the end,' she wailed. 'Nobody likes me, and I don't blame them because I'm horrible and mean and ugly and . . .'

'Hey, hey,' Leanne interrupted gently. 'You're none of those things. You're beautiful, kind and generous and I happen to be very proud of . . .'

'No you're not. You don't even take any notice of me. It's always about Daniel. You love him better than you love me.'

'That isn't true and you know it.' There was no point getting into the contradictions when she was obviously too stricken with misery and confusion to know what she was saying. What was evident, and Leanne felt wretched for not considering this sooner, was the fact that Daniel was about to be reunited with his father and for Abby that was never going to happen.

Leanne ached with the sadness of it, and searched rapidly for a way to broach the subject with words that wouldn't send Abby into a fury again.

Abby suddenly said, 'Daniel's dad really loves him. He's not going to kill himself just to get away from him like mine did.'

Leanne had to take a moment before she could respond to that. It was so big and so tragic that she hardly knew where to begin. 'Abby, I swear to you that's not why Dad did what he did,' she said. 'It had nothing to do with wanting to get away from you . . .'

'Yes it did!' Abby shouted. 'You don't know anything. He wanted to get away from me . . .'

'Stop!' Leanne cried, trying to grab her as she dashed out of the room.

Hurrying after her, she almost fell over Juno as she reached the door. By the time she got to the kitchen Abby was tearing up magazines and newspapers in a frenzy of rage.

'Abby, listen to me,' Leanne cried, struggling to get hold of her. 'Please, just listen. I promise you, Daddy didn't do . . . Abby!' she gasped, as Abby raced to the sink and began smashing Glory's precious china. 'Please don't do that, sweetheart. Please. It's very special and . . .'

'Everything's more special than me!' Abby seethed. 'Everything and everyone and I don't care . . .'

Grabbing the teapot, Leanne caught her in a single-arm embrace and tried to hold on to her. 'Abby, calm down, please,' she begged. 'Breaking things isn't going to help. You need to talk to me, to understand that Daddy loved you . . .'

'No he did not!' Abby screamed into her face, and tearing herself free she ran back to her room. *'He did not, he did not,'* she seethed, banging her hands into the bed.

Taking her by the shoulders, Leanne turned her into her arms and held her close. She felt so shaken by the violence of the outburst that it was several minutes before she could assimilate her thoughts, and even then she wasn't sure of the right thing to say.

Eventually Abby stopped muttering, but she was still sobbing, horrible wrenching spasms that tore right through Leanne's heart.

'Ssh,' Leanne soothed, stroking her hair and kissing her. 'Everything's going to be all right, I promise you. We just need to talk about Daddy and what happened . . .'

'I don't want to talk about him. I hate him. I wish he wasn't my dad.'

Still holding her, Leanne rested her head on hers and closed her eyes. In that moment she sorely wished Jack was there to see what he'd done to his daughter. Hadn't he thought about her at all before he'd climbed on to that chair with anger, revenge and heaven only knew what else in his heart?

'Daniel said I had to tell you,' Abby said brokenly. 'I don't want to, because I know you'll blame me for everything. He says you won't, but he doesn't understand.'

Realising she must tread very gently now, Leanne said, 'I don't know what you've been telling yourself, or Daniel, but I swear there's nothing you could say or do that would make me blame you for anything.'

'Yes, there is.'

She was so adamant that Leanne felt almost afraid of what Abby had been telling herself all this time. *She's mean in ways you can't see*, she'd said to Daniel. What on earth had made her say that? 'I know,' she said, almost chattily, 'why don't you tell me what it is so I can prove you wrong?'

Abby took a breath that turned into a sob. 'I can't,' she gasped.

Leanne feigned surprise. 'Is that Wilkie's granddaughter I hear saying *I can't*?'

Though Abby didn't laugh she managed another breath, but still the words wouldn't come.

Leanne gave her some more time, still holding her and feeling how desperately she was clinging on, without seeming to realise it.

In the end she sat up and pushed the hair from her face. 'Actually, I don't care if you hate me. I'll be leaving home soon . . .'

'Abby, please just say it.'

'All right, if you must know, he killed himself because of me. I told him, the night before he did it, that I hated him and that we would be better off without him and I wished he was dead.'

As she broke down again, Leanne quickly and firmly

returned her to her arms and pressed her face to her chest, feeling more love – and fury – than she had ever experienced in her life. That he could have done what he did, right after what must have been a blazing row to have forced his thirteen-year-old daughter to say what she had, was so cruel and unforgivable that if Leanne had the chance she'd kick the chair right out from under him.

'Listen, sweetheart,' she said, far more gently than she'd thought herself capable of, 'I promise you, what you said had nothing to do with Daddy killing himself.'

'But I . . .'

'I understand why you think it did, but the truth is he probably wasn't even listening. You remember how we always used to accuse him of that . . .'

'But I know he heard me, because he said I should be careful of what I wished for.'

Stunned, Leanne tightened her hold on Abby's trembling body. Was it possible to despise him more? 'That's something else he was always saying,' she reminded Abby. 'Every time I told him to go away and leave us alone he'd say it. If I said he ought to get help he'd say it.' Pulling back, she took Abby's tear-ravaged face between her hands. 'I've told you this before,' she said, 'and I want you to listen very carefully now as I say it again. Daddy was sick. He was an alcoholic. He could hardly think straight at times, much less behave the way the rest of us do. He didn't even remember half the things we said, and I know he'd have forgotten what you said long before he shut himself in the study. You see, it wasn't about you or me, it was all about how much he had come to detest himself and how incapable he was of getting his life back in order. The demons got such a hold on him that he wasn't even willing to try, because he couldn't see beyond them. It was tragic, and we should feel sorry for him, because he'd gone past the point of being able to help himself. I swear, if he'd still been the Daddy you knew when you were little he'd never have done what he did, and you would never have had a reason to say what you did.'

Abby was still, but tense, and Leanne could tell she needed to hear more.

'He provoked us both, all the time,' she continued, 'so horribly sometimes that we couldn't stop ourselves lashing out with the most hurtful things we could think of. I don't know what made you say what you did that night, but whatever it was I don't blame you for it, and you must not blame yourself.'

Abby's head drooped a little, but she was still pressed hard to her mother. 'I said it,' she confided brokenly, 'because of how mean he'd been to you. He was always saying cruel things to you, trying to make you look small, and I couldn't stand it any more. But the really bad thing is that I meant it when I said it, I did hate him and I wanted him to die, or not die, but to go away and leave us alone.'

Was it possible to feel any worse for not knowing that Abby's suffering had come out of defending her? Her poor baby had seen too much, had lived through more anguish and torment than any child ever should, and she, as her mother, had let it happen. How was she ever going to make it up to her?

'I ought to have left him long before he killed himself,' Leanne murmured, as much to herself as to Abby. 'Pitying him and feeling afraid of what he might do if we went didn't help him, or keep him alive, all it did was subject us to more and more abuse, and hurt you in ways that . . . that I was too blind, too foolish to see. I'm sorry, my darling, I'm so, so sorry.'

'No, Mum, it wasn't your fault,' Abby insisted, sitting up to look at her. 'You didn't make him drink or be like he was. You always tried to be nice to him, but he just kept on being horrible.'

Smiling at the way Abby was defending her, Leanne cupped Abby's beloved face in her hands again and gazed into her eyes. 'Please tell me you understand that he was sick, that what he did wasn't your fault or mine.'

Abby's eyes went down.

'You know it's true,' Leanne whispered.

Abby looked at her again and gave a small, shaky nod.

Beside them Juno whined, letting them know that he understood too.

With a spluttery laugh Abby reached out to fuss him, but her head remained against Leanne.

Leanne could hear her mobile ringing, but she let it go to messages. There was still so much to say, and it had been far too long since she and Abby had been this close. She thought of how angry Abby had been with her all these months and realised that on some level she'd been blaming her for not understanding, or *knowing* what was happening to her. She'd felt so ashamed of what she'd said to her father, and so horrified by what he'd done, that it had taken her all this time to be able to confess it. How tragic and heart-breaking that she'd believed no one could love her once they found out what she'd said.

Recalling the conversation she'd overheard with Daniel, Leanne said, very gently, 'Do you remember the night you and Daniel were up late talking? I heard him saying that you should tell me something. Was this it?'

After a moment Abby nodded.

'So *he* knew I wouldn't blame you and that it wouldn't change how much I love you?'

'I guess so.'

'And when you said I'm mean in ways you can't see?'

Abby didn't answer.

'It's OK, you can tell me. If you don't, I won't be able to put it right.'

Abby mumbled something that Leanne couldn't hear.

'Can you try that again?' Leanne encouraged.

Abby's face was still hidden as she said, 'I made it up.'

Leanne's eyebrows rose.

'I wanted Daniel to believe me,' Abby confessed, 'so that's why I said it.'

'And did he?'

Abby's bloodshot eyes came up. 'You know how brilliant he is,' she said, 'he works things out much better than I ever can.'

Leanne smiled. 'Sometimes it's easier to see things from the outside, but I guess Daniel is pretty special.'

Abby's voice was tearful again as she said, 'I don't want him to go, Mum, I really don't.'

Feeling the same sadness, Leanne said, 'Remember, it's not going to happen immediately, and by the time it does . . . Well, who knows what might have happened?'

It was just after nine the next morning when Leanne, Abby and Daniel arrived at Sellybrook Prison. They'd allowed far too much time to get there, but Leanne would never have forgiven herself if she'd made Daniel late for this very special reunion. Not that there had been much chance of that. She'd heard him get up at six, and when she'd gone downstairs at seven she'd found him in the kitchen with Abby, getting ready to take Juno for a walk.

As soon as he saw her he'd said, 'Can Abby come with us today? I know it'll mean her missing school, but I'd really like her to meet my dad.'

Leanne smiled. How on earth could she refuse that? She didn't even want to try. 'Yes, of course,' she replied, and then laughed as she was treated to a double hug from them followed by a howl of love from Juno.

Now, as they sat in the car staring at the gate in the formidable fence, and a faint spring breeze blew stray leaves across the tarmac, Leanne could feel Daniel's tension building. It was charging the air, sparking in his eyes and laying siege to all their efforts to hang on to some semblance of self-control. They were past speaking now, not wanting to do anything more than wait for the gate to open and Daniel's dream to come true.

At nine thirty-three Daniel got out of the car. He was so restless and afraid that something would go wrong that he couldn't stay still. Leanne and Abby got out too. They stood slightly behind him, watching and waiting, until finally the gate opened and Patrick Marks stepped through.

Daniel caught his breath, started forward, stopped, then ran with arms outstretched towards his waiting father.

Patrick dropped his bag, held out his arms and caught his precious boy as he flew the final distance straight into them.

Even from where she and Abby were standing, Leanne could tell that father and son were sobbing and laughing and holding one another so tight it seemed they might never let go. Daniel's skinny limbs looked so tiny and fragile in Patrick's muscular embrace, so protected and loved. She could only begin to imagine the depth of feeling they were experiencing right now, the rush of hope and relief that their terrible separation was finally over.

Realising there were tears on her cheeks, Leanne put an arm round Abby and heard Abby's breath catch on a sob.

'This is a really special moment, isn't it?' Abby murmured, her voice strangled by feeling.

'Yes,' Leanne whispered, 'it really is.'

Eventually Patrick returned Daniel to his feet and, scooping up his bag, he put an arm round his son's shoulders as they shared his first steps to freedom.

Smiling, as they drew closer Leanne held out a hand to shake Patrick's.

'Thank you,' he said softly, as he took it. He looked

tired, uncertain and slightly dazed, but there was a light she hadn't seen before struggling to break through the clouds in his eyes.

'Dad, this is Abby,' Daniel said, looking up at him. 'She's my best friend. Abby, this is my dad.' He announced it with so much pride he might have burst with it.

'Hey, Abby,' Patrick said, shaking Abby's hand. 'It's good to meet you. Daniel's written me a lot about you.'

Abby's eyes slanted playfully at Daniel. 'It better have been good,' she warned.

Patrick's tone was sardonic as he said, 'Oh I don't think you need to worry on that score.'

Leanne gestured towards the sky. 'It's a lovely day,' she commented.

He looked up and put a hand on Daniel's head as he took in the brilliant blue, seeming to absorb the good omen right through to his soul.

Moved by all that he must be feeling, Leanne went to open the car door. 'So who's going to sit where?' she asked.

'Me and Abby in the back, Dad in the front,' Daniel answered, so quickly that he'd clearly already thought about it.

Obeying instructions, they all got in, belted up and as they set off towards Kesterly, Daniel said, 'Wilkie's making a shepherd's pie for lunch, Dad. I told her it's your favourite. She's a really great cook. She's made it before and it's nearly as good as Mum's.'

Hearing Patrick swallow, Leanne felt his grief and probable longing for his wife and wished she could reach out to squeeze his hand.

'You're going to really like the bakery,' Daniel chatted on. 'It's so cool. It's next to the stables where Klaudia lives with Mia and Adam. Remember, I told you about them? Adam is dead cute. He's only six, but he's my other best friend. I expect he'd like to come fishing with us if we go. Can we go fishing, Dad?'

Taking a moment to realise a question had been asked, Patrick said, hoarsely, 'We can do anything you like, son.'

Suspecting he was starting to feel overwhelmed, Leanne said, 'Daniel, why don't you ring Wilkie to let her know we're on our way?'

'Oh yes, we promised to do that,' he responded, and taking out his phone he rapidly made the call. When he'd finished, he passed the phone to Patrick. 'Do you want to see some of the photos we've taken while I've been at Ash Morley?'

As Patrick started to scroll through Daniel broke into a grin.

'It's so cool,' he declared, 'because now there are going to be photos of you there too.'

Patrick glanced at Leanne, and she sensed right away how awkward he was feeling. She wanted to tell him not to worry, that he was going to fit in just fine, but how could she be sure that was what he wanted to hear? He might already have other plans for him and Daniel, plans that would take them a long way from Ash Morley, and as soon as he became Daniel's legal guardian again they could be on their way.

Chapter Twenty-one

Having Patrick in their midst and Daniel no longer at the barn felt strange at first; however, it didn't take long to get used to it. The children were always rushing from one place to another, sharing homework time, playing games, chilling out in front of someone's TV or computer as though they'd lived like this for ever.

Fortunately Daniel didn't seem to notice that his father was still traumatised by the terrible things that had happened to him, both before and while he was in prison. Patrick was careful to hide it from him, and he never spoke to anyone at Ash Morley about it either. However, the haunted, hunted look that sometimes crept into his eyes told its own story. Thankfully he hadn't refused counselling, but it was too soon to tell how effective it was proving.

Just as hard to cope with in the early days was the media encampment that sprang up just beyond the gates of Ash Morley once the news of Patrick's whereabouts was discovered. The children found it quite exciting, and Wilkie was forever in and out with refreshments. (This was her ploy to make sure no one wrote anything bad about Patrick, though that never seemed to be anyone's intention. Patrick himself didn't engage with them; he had nothing to say and no lucrative offers of exclusives tempted him either. Eventually they went away, having captured endless shots of him and Daniel kicking a ball about the field, or crossing the courtyard, or driving through their midst in the car Patrick had been loaned by Yousseff at the garage. Though Patrick didn't have much money to call his own, Helen Hall and her team had made sure the local authority recognised the uniqueness of his case, so didn't try to palm him off with the usual discharge grant and risible welfare package. He'd been given enough to get by for at least a month and this was to be repeated the following month: a restorative for his pride, Leanne could tell. He'd obviously been dreading imposing on them any more than he had already been compelled to do.

As for compensation, Helen Hall was determined to make the Dean Valley force pay handsomely for their shoddy police work and all the damage it had done to both Patrick and Daniel. She'd already discovered that the bank had sold his home for the sum of the outstanding mortgage, providing her with further grounds for ensuring that the restitution figure was large enough to make a real difference to his life. Were it left up to Patrick, Leanne suspected he'd have been tempted to let the whole thing slide in order to move quietly on with his life, but that clearly wasn't an option when he had Daniel's as well as his own future to consider. What thoughts he was having about that he hadn't yet shared, but being the conscientious and principled man he was showing himself to be, Leanne felt sure he was having plenty.

A surprise came in the post just after Kylie's remains were buried. They'd watched the funeral on the news, each of them feeling so terrible for the little girl's parents that Wilkie, in her usual way, had been moved to write to them. She'd explained how Daniel had come to be fostered into her family, and that Patrick was now with them trying to recover from his ordeal. They'd written back to thank Wilkie for her kindness and to ask her to pass on their good wishes to Patrick for his and Daniel's future. After that Patrick wrote to them himself, but he hadn't shown anyone the letter he received in return, so only he knew what it said.

The day his legal guardianship of Daniel was restored was celebrated with an impromptu party at Ash Morley with everyone invited, including Andee, who'd visited several times since Patrick's release. Her announcement that evening that she was flying back to Stockholm in a couple of days was overshadowed minutes later by Bel going into labour and having to be rushed to hospital. She and Harry were now the proud parents of a four-kilo baby girl, Sofia, whose birth was celebrated at the party Wilkie threw two weeks later to say farewell to Richard and Jan York, who'd decided to move to Holland.

The following day Wilkie received an email from Eileen that both surprised and intrigued her, but she decided not to mention it to anyone until she'd actually spoken to Eileen and found out if she was reading the message correctly.

*　　*　　*

364

'Life is just too much fun here,' Patrick commented one evening after a boisterous badminton tournament involving all residents of Ash Morley in the back field, 'but I'm afraid we're outstaying our welcome.'

'No you're not,' Abby cried quickly. 'We love having you here, don't we?' She was looking at Leanne.

'Absolutely,' Leanne agreed.

'Stay as long as you like,' Wilkie insisted.

'I'm not sure we can manage without you now,' Klaudia told him earnestly. Since they'd discovered that he was a qualified accountant with a business diploma, she'd readily accepted his help with the extra bookkeeping she'd taken on after refusing to accept any more wages from Glory Days until their fortunes changed. So she really did value him being there.

They all did, and when Bill Simmons, the owner of a local landscaping company, popped in to offer Patrick a job at his offices, there really didn't seem any reason for him and Daniel to go.

'It would make sense to be here at least until the end of this school year,' Leanne reminded him, 'and by then you might have constructed a workable business plan for my and Klaudia's fashion shows and vintage teas. Not that I'm being selfish about this, you understand.'

Amused, he said, 'If you're sure, then I'll take the job so I can properly pay my way, and of course I'll help with your business plan.' He glanced at Klaudia and winked, giving Leanne the impression that they might already be on the case.

So Patrick started his new job administering the

landscaping company as well as working the land from time to time. He helped Wilkie with Ash Morley's garden beds, mowed Klaudia's lawn and installed colourful window boxes outside the shop. Though Leanne and Wilkie agreed that his friendship with Klaudia appeared to be deepening into something more meaningful, they said nothing to either, understanding that it needed to go at its own pace and required no help from them.

Soon the lighter nights were with them and Wilkie began spending more time on the project she and Rowzee Cayne had become passionate about, saving Kesterly's theatre. Their idea was to bring together all the different communities – or nationalities – in town to stage plays or musicals or pageants to showcase their various cultures. This, they believed, would help everyone to gain a better understanding and tolerance of one another. Currently Wilkie was tapping up local businesses to help with funding and so far, to her great delight, she'd met with some very generous responses. Getting funds out of the council, however, was proving a little trickier. Richie soon came to the rescue over that by publicising the scheme in the paper, which prompted – *shamed*, Wilkie insisted – the authority into providing some support.

Though Richie was a frequent visitor to Ash Morley he almost never spoke of his father, and Leanne managed to prevent herself from asking. There was nothing to be gained from quizzing Richie in the hope that his answers might provide some sort of romantic sustenance – or delusion, more like. She'd only appear sad, in a pathetic sense, and would definitely feel it if Richie were to tell her that his father had become involved with someone else. No, that was history; time, life, had moved on and so had she.

However, the day she drove into town and saw that Villa Tramonto was clad in scaffolding, she couldn't help mentioning it to Richie when he popped into the shop later to drop off some leaflets for Wilkie.

'Oh yes,' he said, going to help Klaudia climb out of the window display with an armful of lace dresses and feather boas. 'Apparently they're repairing the roof before the other work starts.'

'So has your father decided what he's going to do with the place?' Leanne asked.

'No idea, and it's no good asking Graeme Ogilvy, who's overseeing it all, because all he knows is that it's not going to remain a single family residence, as he puts it. So, luxury flats, nursing home, boutique hotel, spa, take your pick, or it could turn out to be something else altogether.'

Puzzled, Klaudia said, 'But how is Graeme going to know what to do if a decision hasn't been made?'

Richie shrugged. 'I guess it will be, soon enough. Personally I'd like it to be apartments so I could have one, but the old man's not swayed by that. He's convinced I'll be off to London the minute I get offered a job.'

'How's that going?' Leanne asked.

'I've done some interviews lately, but the competition's really tough, and maybe I don't try hard enough given how much I like it here. But this is coasting, really. Good experience, obviously, but the seriously gritty stuff . . .' He broke off as his phone rang. 'Sorry, I need to take this,' he said, 'cat stuck up a tree,' and giving them a cheery wave he clicked on and left the shop.

Leanne's heart leapt to her throat as Mia and Adam came racing into the barn trembling and shouting for help.

'It's Mummy!' Mia sobbed. 'Please make her stop.'

'Mummy!' Adam gasped. 'Stop.'

Quickly pushing the children into Abby's arms, Leanne ran across the courtyard, her heart thudding with dread as she heard the howls of rage and terrible crashing coming from inside the stables. *Who the hell was in there with her? What was happening?*

As Patrick came dashing over from the bakery he sped past her and went in first. They found Klaudia in the middle of her kitchen screaming in a frenzy of frustration as she hurled dishes, chairs, and books about the room. 'I can't stand any more,' she wailed, as Patrick quickly took a pot plant from her. 'I just can't.'

Grabbing her, Patrick held her tightly, keeping her arms pinned to her sides as he urged her to calm down and gestured for Leanne to take the plant away. 'It's OK, it's OK,' he murmured, folding Klaudia into a deeper embrace.

'No!' she wailed desperately. 'No it isn't.'

'Yes it is. You're fine. We're going to make this all right.'

Leanne watched, dumbfounded, as Klaudia sank against him, sobbing and gasping so hard that she could barely breathe.

'There, there,' Patrick soothed gently, as though she were a child. He turned to Leanne. 'It's OK,' he said, 'I've got this. Go see to the kids.'

Klaudia was calmer now, though still shaking in the aftermath of her outburst and trying to catch her breath. 'I'm sorry,' she murmured, as Patrick put a mug of tea into her hands. 'I don't know . . .'

'Ssh,' he cut in. 'It's OK. It got the better of you, I understand.'

Looking into his worried eyes, she said, 'I frightened my children. I've broken all these things . . .'

'Things can be fixed, and the children are safe with Leanne.'

'I should go to them.'

'You will when you've drunk that and got yourself together.'

She took a sip of the tea and looked around at the mess. 'I don't know what happened,' she said raggedly, 'one minute I was standing there and the next . . .' She took a breath and looked at him again, her eyes still heavy with tears and her face deathly pale. 'It's the pressure of not knowing,' she sighed. 'I keep telling myself it'll be all right, that I'll get my residency, but day after day goes by . . . Other people who applied after I did have already heard, and some of them have been told to make arrangements to leave. They didn't have the health insurance that no one knew anything about and nor do I, so I know it's going to happen to me . . .' She started to break down again. 'I know it's stupid to get into such a state, but I don't know where we'll go. The children don't even speak Polish, and we're so happy here.'

Smoothing the hair back from her face, he said, 'It's beyond my power to give you the reassurance you need, but there is something I can tell you.'

Her eyes went down as if she doubted his words, or maybe she didn't hear them.

Tilting her face up again, he said, 'I haven't told the others yet, I was waiting for the right time, but I've been offered a job in Ireland.'

She frowned, not quite understanding.

'An old college friend of mine got in touch a couple of weeks ago. He has a successful printing company in Cork and he's asked me to go and run it for him.'

Her eyes widened slightly.

'Apparently there's a great school nearby for Daniel,' he continued, 'and the job comes with a salary that should make a mortgage affordable. This could give us the fresh start we need, far away from anyone who knows us, but in a place where we can still speak the language.'

She was searching his face, taking in every last detail of it as she said, 'But you'll be an expat, an immigrant, like I am here, and if things don't work out you'll have to come back.'

'It's a chance I'm prepared to take. Daniel and I can't stay here . . .' As she started to protest he put a finger to her lips. 'We need to put the past behind us.

Everyone's been so kind, but outside of Ash Morley I'm always going to be that man. Someone will always remember, and the doubt will be there for some, and that's not what I want for Daniel.'

'But you've done nothing . . .'

'I know, but . . .'

'. . . and England's your home, it's where you belong.'

'It was where we belonged before Gracie died and before I went to prison. Now, like I just said, Daniel and I need a fresh start, and I wouldn't be doing the right thing as a father if I didn't take this opportunity.'

Wishing there was a way to keep him here, while understanding how he felt, she said, 'When will you go?'

'Not until after the end of term.'

She looked away as her eyes filled with tears. Adam was going to miss Daniel so much, but she couldn't use that, or her own feelings, as a way to persuade him to stay.

'I'm telling you this,' he said, taking her hand in his, 'because I want you to know that if things don't work out with your residency you will have somewhere to go.'

Leanne felt quietly devastated when Patrick broke his news. She didn't want to lose Daniel any more than Abby did, and reminding herself that a new start with his father would be the best for him didn't really help. She was going to miss them both so much, the place wouldn't feel the same without them, and the fear that

Klaudia might go too was making it all increasingly hard to bear. However, she was doing her best to feel pleased for them, trying to force herself to accept that things didn't stay the same for ever.

'There's going to come a time,' Wilkie said one night when they were talking it over, 'when none of us will be here either. Ash Morley will belong to another family . . .'

'Oh, stop, Mum, please,' Leanne complained. 'You're just making things worse. What we need is something to cheer us up.'

'It'll happen,' Wilkie assured her. 'And meantime, Patrick and Daniel aren't leaving until the middle of July, and Klaudia hasn't made up her mind yet.'

The reminder that many weeks had yet to elapse before Ash Morley began a new phase of its existence did nothing to improve Leanne's spirits. However, a phone call from Kate the following day did the trick. Well, for a few minutes, at least.

'Mum, it's me. I'm coming to see you. I'm at O'Hare airport now. Can someone pick me up from Heathrow?'

'Of course,' Leanne assured her. 'This is a surprise. What time do you get in?'

'I don't know exactly. I'll text you,' and before Leanne could ask any more she rang off.

Almost immediately Martin rang. 'Did Kate just call?' he asked, sounding worried.

'Yes, what's going on?'

'She's broken up with her boyfriend. It just happened, a couple of days ago. He's paired off with someone else apparently and she doesn't want to hang around, because the other girl is in her sorority and she can't bear to see either of them, especially not together.'

While understanding that, Leanne was torn between feeling pleased to be wanted and sorry for Kate's heartbreak. 'How can she leave her course just like that?' she demanded.

'She's about done for this semester, so she's decided to come and spend some extra time with you guys before she goes on to Africa.'

Naturally thrilled by the first part, Leanne said darkly, 'So Africa's still on the agenda?'

'I don't think she'll back out of it. Edinburgh's off now, but as far as I know she's still committed to Argentina.'

'Are you at the airport with her?'

'Yeah, she's gone to the bathroom, but her flight's just been called. You can meet her when she gets there?'

'Of course. Just let me know what time the plane lands.'

'Brace yourself. Eight o'clock, so you'll be leaving home about five in the morning.'

What fun it is having children, Leanne commented to herself as she rang off, and pouring herself a nice glass of wine she went to break the news to Abby, who, since their talk before Patrick's release, had become her new best friend. They'd even had the idea of visiting Kate in Africa, provided Kate wanted them there. Leanne guessed she'd find that out soon enough, and if Kate was up for it there was a good chance she'd persuade Wilkie to join them.

Chapter Twenty-two

Though to anyone else Kate might have appeared her usual beautiful and graceful self as she came through to Arrivals, Leanne saw right away that her natural radiance and *joie de vivre* had lost some of its lustre. Nevertheless, several young men's heads turned as they tried to get another glimpse of the girl with bubbly blonde hair, tired but exquisite blue eyes and legs so long they made her admirers sigh.

Leanne opened her arms and as Kate, weeping, ran into them she found that she was crying too, though in her case the tears were mostly of joy at holding her precious firstborn in her arms again.

'Oh Mum, it's so awful,' Kate sobbed as soon as they were in the car. 'I never knew anything could feel this bad. I don't think I'll ever get over it.'

Knowing that to tell her she would wouldn't be helpful, Leanne said, 'You did right to get away. There's no point having your face rubbed in it.'

Kate groaned and sobbed even harder. 'I really love him, Mum. I just don't know how he could have done it. Or *her*. She was supposed to be my best friend, I trusted her. She knows how I feel about him.' She dabbed her eyes, blew her nose and started crying again. 'I know this is terrible,' she choked, 'but I snuck into her room and cut up her favourite dress before I left.'

Leanne was impressed. Kate, always so sweet-natured, wouldn't normally have harmed a fly, so this was interesting. 'Doesn't sound terrible to me,' she retorted.

Kate shot her a glance. 'No?'

Leanne shook her head.

Kate gave it some thought. 'I guess I am Wilkie's granddaughter,' she said tentatively.

'She'll be proud of you.'

Kate started to laugh, but it lasted no more than a few seconds before she was off again, and she barely stopped the entire way home. 'I'm sorry, I'm sorry,' she kept saying, 'I shouldn't be laying all this on you,' and she was still saying it as they walked in the door. 'It just keeps coming over me,' she wept. 'I can't stop thinking about them together . . . Oh God, Mum, oh God, oh God.'

As Leanne folded her back into her arms, feeling terrible for her, Wilkie came through the door, full of grandmotherly concern and whacky advice.

'All you have to do,' she told Kate, taking over the hug, 'is listen to love songs and read romantic poems and howl and howl until it's all out of your system. There's nothing like a good purge.'

Leanne looked at her mother askance, but Wilkie was undaunted.

'I cut up her favourite dress,' Kate confessed again.

Wilkie lit up. 'That's my girl. I hope you flushed away all her favourite perfume at the same time, and cancelled the contract on her phone.'

'I would have if I'd thought of it,' Kate promised, seeming to warm to the theme. 'Oh, it's so wonderful to see you, Grandma,' she wailed. 'I've missed you so much, and you, Mum,' she added, bundling them into a group hug. 'I can't believe how long it's been since I was here.'

In spite of how miserable she was and how difficult she found it to focus on anything else for long, it truly was wonderful to have her with them. Leanne kept looking at her and feeling a great rush of pride. Was this stunning, tragic, exotic creature really hers? In some ways she felt almost in awe of her, while in others she kept willing her to change the subject for a while.

By the time Abby came home from school jet lag had got the better of Kate; however, Abby was having none of it. She wanted to see her sister and she was going to see her now.

They didn't emerge from Kate's room (still decorated for Daniel's use) until it was time to join the welcome-home dinner Wilkie had prepared at the farmhouse. Ordinarily Wilkie would have seized this excuse for another party; however, given the circumstances, she'd decided it should be a little more low key and involve only family. Family naturally included Patrick, Klaudia and the three children.

It was plain to see that the strong bond between Kate and Abby had already reasserted itself by the time they ventured downstairs, and Leanne had to hide a smile to see how important Abby was feeling. Clearly Kate had been confiding in her younger sister, and Abby in her generous, inexperienced and loving way had been offering all her younger-sisterly advice and support.

To Leanne's relief Kate managed to hold back the tears as she greeted everyone at Wilkie's, though only just, for she definitely welled up when Klaudia wrapped her in a tender embrace. She came close again as she was introduced to Patrick and Daniel. (Actually, anything was going to set her off, Leanne quickly realised.)

However, throughout dinner she was mostly able to be her usual charming self, and paid particular atten-tion to Patrick and Daniel, clearly wanting them to know that she was as ready to consider them a part of her family as the others did. There were only a few moments when her lovely eyes filled with tears, but she managed to recover herself before anyone, apart from Leanne, noticed.

That night, unable to bear the torment of lying alone in her bed, Kate came to snuggle in with her mother, and Leanne soon realised, to her dismay given how early she'd had to get up that morning, that her broken-hearted daughter was wide awake and intending to stay the night.

In the end Leanne fell asleep anyway, and when she awoke Kate had gone. She found her in Abby's room, dead to the world as Abby tiptoed around her getting ready for school.

'She's really upset,' Abby declared solemnly, as she

and Leanne sat down for breakfast. 'He's such a b. I told her he's not worth it. She can do much better than someone who treats her like that.'

'Quite right,' Leanne agreed.

'She sent him a text in the night, we wrote it together, but I don't think she's heard back yet.'

Wondering what the text had said, Leanne helped herself to more coffee and simply smiled. 'You're being a wonderful support to her,' she said fondly.

Clearly thrilled by the recognition, Abby said, 'I told her she can tell me anything. I mean, I'm her sister, so I'll always be there for her, and I know what she's going through. It happened to me with Josh, remember? He found someone else and it was terrible.'

Not daring to point out that Kate's situation was a little different, Leanne said, 'I'm sure it's helping her no end to know that you understand her situation.'

Abby nodded. 'I think it is,' she agreed, apparently surprised that her mother understood. 'It's a pity I have to go to school because she really needs me right now. Still, she always has you.'

'A poor second best,' Leanne admitted, almost giving in to the temptation to let Abby stay home for the day.

Kate finally woke at eleven and was immediately reunited with her heartbreak. And when she discovered there was no response to the text she'd sent in the night, she insisted on sitting Leanne down to go through all the things he might have thought on reading the text, his reasons for not texting back, and wondering if he'd even received it so maybe she should send it again.

In the end, gently suggesting she might feel better after a shower, Leanne slumped down in a chair and asked herself how she was going to get through the next few weeks if they carried on like this. Surely she'd never been so repetitive and boring when her relationships had broken up at that age?

'Oh you were,' Wilkie assured her cheerfully when she asked. 'Drove me completely nuts.'

'Are you serious?'

'Of course. Glory and I used to draw straws on who should deal with you next . . .'

'Hang on, I'd already had Kate by then . . .'

'. . . so think yourself lucky that you've got me *and* Abby to help you.'

Thankfully, over the next few days, Kate began to emerge from the absorption of her misery and engage more with what was going on around her. Rather like an invalid at first she ventured into town with Wilkie, spent an afternoon at the shop with Klaudia, and treated herself and Abby to the restorative pampering of a twilight spa. At the weekend she and Abby joined Patrick and Daniel on one of their rambles over the moor, and when they got back the four of them took Mia and Adam to the cinema.

By the end of her second week, though clearly still fractured inside, Kate began showing even more signs of recovery as she entered into some lively chats with Patrick about African politics or American football or the works of Kurt Vonnegut, who Patrick hadn't read, but was interested to know more about. After one of her afternoons with Klaudia she developed a fleeting but intense fascination for all things Polish, and was quite disappointed when she discovered that Klaudia had no relatives there as, for some reason, she'd come up with an idea to go and visit them. Her concern about Klaudia's residency status was expressed loudly and often, and with the kind of indignation that made her grandmother proud and Leanne wince.

This wasn't to say that she'd stopped having long heart-to-hearts with her mother and Abby about Cray (the boyfriend) because they were still happening, sometimes long into the night, and Leanne had no idea how many emails and texts she'd helped compose to the young man that were never sent. However, thankfully, Kate's natural love of life, and interest in everything going on around her, kept breaking free of her despair in reassuring bursts of revival.

The only cloud on Leanne's horizon, apart from the worry of where Kate was flying on to next, was the growing suspicion that Klaudia was going to follow Patrick and Daniel to Ireland. She could see that it made perfect sense for them to go; Klaudia and Patrick were close, and Daniel was so good for Adam that everyone was dreading how hard it might be for the dear little soul after his friend had gone. Leanne didn't talk about how hard it was going to be for her to lose her best friend. She wouldn't have dreamt of making things even more difficult for Klaudia. However, there was no getting away from the fact that staging fashion shows, vintage teas, or anything at all without Klaudia no longer had the same appeal as the projects had when she'd thought Klaudia was going to drive them with her.

Nevertheless, when Klaudia announced one morning that she had some news so could they all meet up later, Leanne, certain of what was coming, promised herself right away to be nothing but thrilled for her.

It was a balmy early-summer evening filled with the sounds of chirping birds and distant bleating sheep as Abby and Kate came to join Leanne at the circular table on the barn's spacious veranda. The three sets of French windows were wide open behind them, seeming to bring the inside out into the air, and mingling with the mouth-watering aroma of Wilkie's hors d'oeuvres in the kitchen were the heady perfumes of freshly mown grass and honeysuckle. Halfway down the field a clutch of mallards had landed on the pond beneath the weeping willow, and a squirrel was perched on the old love seat, munching the nuts he'd stolen from the feeders.

'Klaudia's just rung to say she'll be over in a few minutes,' Leanne told the girls, as Juno came to slump down beside them. 'Apparently she got held up at Dotty's.'

'I think it's so sweet that she still goes to see her old people,' Kate remarked, twisting her hair into a band and glancing idly at the magazine Leanne had been reading.

'She's amazing,' Abby agreed.

Deciding that she and her mother must take over the visits when Klaudia had gone, Leanne swallowed her sadness and said, 'It's just us girls this evening. Patrick's taken the younger ones to the circus on Barnwell Common.' Was that something he and Klaudia had organised between them, so she could have Leanne and the others to herself to break her news?

Stretching out her long legs to catch some sun, Kate said, 'So what's it all about? Do you know?'

Copying her sister with her shorter, chubbier legs, Abby said, 'She's being really secretive, but Mum thinks she's going to Ireland with Patrick and Daniel.'

Kate turned to Leanne. 'Would you mind?' she asked. Her eyes showed real concern. 'Yes, of course you would. You'll miss her like crazy.'

'You can't stop change,' Wilkie said from the kitchen.

'Don't get her started,' Leanne murmured, 'or she'll start going on about how we'll all be gone one day and this place will belong to somebody else.'

'I heard that,' Wilkie told her, 'and it's true.'

'Depressing,' Kate stated, picking up her phone in case a message had arrived without her noticing.

'You'll miss her too, Grandma,' Abby piped up.

'Of course I will. She's like a second daughter to me.'

As they sat with those words, their faces held up to the sun, Leanne looked at her girls in the soft golden glow and felt a surge of prideful love. A moment later she was reflecting on what a sorry trio they were, all of them having been rejected in the last few months. The same had happened to Klaudia with Antoni, but happily things were about to change for her, and there was no doubt in Leanne's mind that they would for Kate and Abby too.

'Hi, sorry to be late,' Klaudia sighed, sinking down in a vacant chair and dropping her phone on the table. 'Where's Wilkie?'

'In here,' Wilkie called back, and a moment later she appeared with a tray of bacon-wrapped halloumi, mini cheese soufflés and an assortment of Mediterranean slices. 'Haven't you opened any wine yet?' she scolded Leanne.

'Sorry, I forgot,' Leanne replied, grabbing a soufflé. 'I'll go and get it.'

As she started to get up, Klaudia said, 'Hang on, can I break my news first?'

Wishing there was a way to hold it back, Leanne smiled as she said, 'Of course. It's what this evening's all about, so we're dying to hear it.'

Klaudia appeared suddenly awkward, and as her eyes went down Leanne noticed how tightly she'd bunched her hands.

Sensing this wasn't going to be good, Kate and Abby stopped eating.

'Well,' Klaudia said gravely, 'I want to tell you . . .' she looked up, eyes suddenly sparkling with laughter, 'that I've been given my permanent residency.'

As Leanne tried to take it in the others cheered and leapt up to embrace her.

'Aren't you pleased, Leanne?' Klaudia teased.

Quickly catching up, Leanne yanked her into a bruising hug. 'I'm completely thrilled,' she told her. 'It's absolutely what we wanted to hear.'

'It's such a relief,' Klaudia laughed. 'I swear I nearly collapsed when I got the email.'

'Forget the wine,' Wilkie declared. 'This calls for champagne.'

'I've hidden some just around the corner,' Klaudia told her.

As Wilkie took off to retrieve it and Kate went inside for glasses, Abby said, 'So does this make you a British citizen?'

'No, but it means I can stay here indefinitely.' Klaudia threw out her arms and turned her face to the sun. 'Thank you, God, thank you, thank you,' she cried passionately.

Leanne said, 'So what about Ireland?' What an irony it was going to be if she'd been awarded her residency as she was on the point of leaving.

Klaudia's eyes came to hers. 'It was really lovely of Patrick to make the offer,' she replied, 'and it's wonderful to know that I have that option if things get any worse here . . .'

'Why would they get worse?' Kate asked, setting out the glasses. 'You've got your papers now.'

Wilkie said, 'There are a lot of people out there who don't want anyone in the country unless they were born here, but let's not worry about them, they'll get over it.'

'So you're not going to Ireland?' Abby asked.

Klaudia shook her head. 'We will see Patrick and Daniel all the time,' she insisted. 'We can go there, they will come here, but this is my home, you are my family.'

As Leanne's heart soared Wilkie exclaimed, 'Let's drink to that,' and quickly popping a cork she filled the glasses. 'To Klaudia,' she toasted, 'your home is with us for as long as you want it to be, and I hope that will be for a very long time.'

'Hear, hear,' Leanne cheered.

'To Klaudia,' Kate and Abby chorused. 'And to Mia and Adam,' Abby added.

'Have you told Patrick?' Leanne asked.

'No, I wanted to tell you first, but he knows that I will choose to stay here if I'm given the chance.'

'He'll be gutted,' Abby declared.

'Oh, poor Patrick,' Kate wailed. 'I know how he feels.'

Klaudia twinkled. 'I think he might be relieved,' she assured them. 'He has a lot of rebuilding to do, and he really doesn't need to be burdening himself with a new relationship and two more children at this time.'

Leanne was watching her carefully, but she genuinely didn't seem anything other than thrilled and relieved that the awful fear of being deported had been removed.

Raising her glass, Klaudia cried, 'To us. The ladies of Ash Morley.'

Loving the sound of that, they instantly echoed, 'The ladies of Ash Morley.'

'Do we need men?' Wilkie demanded.

'No!' they chorused.

They looked at one another, eyes sparkling the challenge to disagree. 'Yes,' they suddenly shouted, and burst into gales of laughter.

'No, no, we don't,' Leanne insisted, putting her glass down. 'They just upset the natural order of things.'

'True,' Kate agreed. 'They definitely do.'

Juno lifted his head and Abby wrinkled her nose at the sound of a car crossing the cattle grid. 'Who's that?' she asked. 'Are we expecting anyone?'

'I don't think so,' Leanne replied, looking at her mother.

Wilkie was grimacing awkwardly. 'It's probably Eileen,' she confessed.

Leanne's jaw dropped as Abby cried, 'You mean *Grandma* Eileen! Oh my God! What's she doing here?'

Wilkie was attempting to look innocent.

'Mum, what have you done?' Leanne scolded.

Facing them down, Wilkie said, 'She's rented a little holiday cottage over on Westleigh Bay. I found it for her when she called to say she wanted to come. Stop looking at me like that,' she instructed Leanne. 'I promise you, she's a changed woman. She wants to be a part of our family, and as she already is I think the least we can do is make her feel welcome.'

'But you know what she's like,' Leanne protested.

'I just said, she's changed. She's very keen to get involved in the theatre project with us, and believe it or not she's had some great ideas on how to set up the outreach . . .'

'Mum,' Abby murmured quietly.

Concerned by the tone, Leanne turned to her curiously.

Abby nodded for her to look up.

Leanne did so, and when she saw who was standing there her heart turned inside out.

'Tom!' Wilkie cried ecstatically. 'What a wonderful surprise. Please, come and join us. We're celebrating some very good news. Klaudia has been granted her permanent residency.'

'That is indeed excellent news,' he said warmly, coming to congratulate Klaudia, and laughing as Juno treated him to a welcoming howl.

Leanne was in such turmoil she hardly knew what to do or say – or even if she should believe that this was really happening.

'Tom, this is my sister, Kate,' Abby was telling him. 'Kate, this is Mum's . . .'

'. . . friend,' Leanne leapt in quickly, before Abby could embarrass her with some witty little epithet.

'Will you have some champagne?' Wilkie invited, pulling up another chair for him to sit down.

'That's very kind,' he replied, 'but I was hoping to have a word with Leanne.'

'Oh, of course,' Wilkie responded cheerily. 'Why don't you go inside? Or you could take . . .'

'Mum, we're quite capable of sorting things out,' Leanne interrupted, and ignoring her daughters' knowing grins she gestured for Tom to join her in a stroll across the lawn to the field.

'Well, this is a surprise,' she said, once they were out of earshot. 'I thought you were in Beijing.'

'The assignment came to an end earlier than we expected,' he explained. 'I got back yesterday and drove to Kesterly this morning.'

So he'd come straight here – presumably to see the villa. 'How are things going with the building work?' she asked.

'Slowly, which is mostly my fault for not making a decision, but before we get on to that tell me about Glory Days. I trust all is well there?'

Coming to a stop at the edge of the pond, she accidentally brushed against him and quickly apologised as she stepped aside. He was no longer too close, but his proximity was as present as the sun and making her feel just as warm. 'Well, since you ask,' she said, 'things are improving. We had a little flurry of orders only last week that helped us no end. We have your mother's wonderful dresses to thank for it, and a society wedding in Gloucestershire that's following a twenties theme.'

He looked impressed. 'She'd be very pleased to know that they've gone to good homes.'

Her smile turned into a grimace of apology. 'I hope you don't mind, but I've kept the Mariano Fortuny. It's too valuable and beautiful to go to strangers . . .'

'It's yours,' he reminded her, 'to do with as you please, but I'm glad you've kept it. I'm sure she'd have liked that too.'

She glanced down at the murky water and spotted the flicker of a fish in the sunlight. She still felt overwhelmed by his presence, afraid even to think of what it might mean . . .

'Kate's very like you,' he commented.

She said wryly, 'The younger, leggier version.'

'Richie's got a crush, did you know?'

'No, I didn't and I don't think she does either. She's on the rebound, I'm afraid, and she'll be off to Africa for an internship in a couple of weeks, so I wouldn't want him to get his hopes up.'

'I think he's OK. Where in Africa is she going?'

'Uganda first, then Rwanda.' She flicked him a quick look. 'I've decided not to worry about it,' she declared bravely. 'I'm just focusing on the gorilla safari that's on the agenda for when it's over.'

'What a great idea,' he commented. 'Some mother–daughter bonding in the jungle?'

She spluttered on a laugh. 'Something like that.'

A moment or two passed quietly, just the tuneful twittering of birds and delicate rustle of grass as frogs and crickets moved through it.

In the end, he said, 'You asked about the villa.'

Immediately interested, she turned back to him.

'I've given it a lot of thought over the past couple of months,' he continued, 'and I've decided to convert it into a small hotel.'

She felt surprised, though wasn't sure why.

He appeared sardonic. 'I have no experience in that field, of course, but I've taken a liking to the idea, so I'll have to learn from the experts.'

Not quite sure she was following him, she said, 'Do you mean you'll be running it?'

'Kind of. There'll be a management company involved, and grounds staff . . . Actually, I haven't really thought that far ahead. Still early days.' He glanced over at the next field, where the bleating had crescendoed as a sheepdog rounded up the flock.

'It's a great idea,' she told him.

His eyes remained on the activity as he said, 'I've come to the conclusion in recent weeks that I've had enough of flying about the world trying to do deals that don't want to be done, and negotiating terms that take months if not years to agree on.'

Her heartbeat was slowing and quickening as she tried not to read anything into his words. 'So you'll be living here, in Kesterly?' she ventured.

He nodded. 'Graeme's working with the architect to create an apartment on the top floor.'

She wasn't sure what to say to that. 'You'll have fabulous views,' she remarked, as if he didn't already know that. Feeling absurd, she added, 'Richie'll be pleased.'

He arched an eyebrow. 'You're right, he is, but as I told him, I'm not doing it for him. I'm doing it for me, and . . .' He broke off and dashed a hand through his hair. 'Do you know what I'm going to say?' he asked, seeming to think that she did.

She shook her head. Her thoughts were on hold, she didn't dare to let them loose.

He took a breath. 'OK, we know from experience that I'm not very good at this, but here goes. Being with you, spending time in Kesterly and here at Ash Morley . . . Well, after I left I couldn't stop thinking about you and I got to realising just how empty my life has become, and how important it is to . . . to connect and feel; to be with . . .' He took another breath. 'When you know someone is special, and that things don't seem to matter too much without them, it makes no sense to turn away from them.' He stopped and grimaced. 'How am I doing so far?'

Her smile was wry, slightly shaky. 'Pretty good,' she told him.

Tilting her face to his, he gazed far into her eyes as he said, 'I don't want to be presumptuous, or take anything for granted, but I'm hoping that if I'm around all the time we can get to know one another better, and maybe . . . Well, maybe one of these days, I might persuade you to accept that moonstone.'

As her heart swelled with feeling she watched his mouth and his eyes, so intense and so close . . .

'I really did miss you,' he murmured, and as his lips came to hers he pulled her so tightly to him that she swirled straight from the shadows of doubt and misgiving into a wonderful chaos of sunlight and promise.

Back on the veranda, the others were watching in a daze of romantic bliss.

'Well,' Wilkie sighed nostalgically, 'there went the natural order of things,' and reaching for the champagne she refilled their glasses, and raised hers to what looked very much like the beginning of a new chapter at Ash Morley.

391

Acknowledgements

My love and thanks go to Lucy Battersby, the inspiration for Leanne's daughter, Kate, and the generous provider of information for the course at Indiana University. Lucy's intrepid spirit is also behind Kate's adventures in Africa and Argentina.

More love and thanks go to the wonderfully glamorous Lady She – Shelia Lloyd-Graham – for giving life and colour to the vintage emporium, *Glory Days.*

A very special thank you goes to Alex Raikes MBE – Director of Stand Against Racial Inequality. Regrettably, I was unable to pursue the storyline I started out, which meant that so much of the vital and moving information I was so generously given went unused. The same thank you goes to Ruth Soandro-Jones. I am hopeful that this storyline will make its way into a future book.

I would also like to thank the team at Cornerstone Publishing, Susan Sandon, Viola Hayden, Sonny Marr, Aslan Byrne, Rebecca Ikin, Sarah Ridley, Natalia Cacciatore.

Last, but in many ways the most important thank you of all goes to my agent Luigi Buonomi.

Susan Lewis

Believe
In Me

Bonus Material

Susan Lewis

on
Believe In Me

Dear Reader,

I hope you've enjoyed the time you spent with this book as much as I enjoyed my time writing it. It's not often that a story flows so easily, and I couldn't be sure at the start that this one would, but to my surprise it soon took on a life of its own. I became very engaged with the family, loving their passions and tolerance of others, also Wilkie's quirkiness and the closeness she shared with her daughter. I was so drawn to Ash Morley that I didn't want to 'move out' when the story was over.

There are many reasons why a book does or doesn't work, and it's so difficult to predict how a reader will respond to the characters and story. It's always my aim to provide an environment that feels welcoming, even if it is fraught with troubles or frightening. Sometimes I'll hit on an issue you might identify with strongly either because you've experienced it yourself, or because it's happened to someone you know. Other times I might tackle an issue that hasn't affected your world, but hopefully it helps to bring about compassion and understanding for those who are trying to overcome certain challenges. I like to think Leanne and her family have given a gentle voice to the importance of tolerance, and a realisation of how even a small kindness can go a very long way.

Having read the reviews for the hardback, I am incredibly touched by how well *Believe In Me* has resonated with so many readers. I sincerely hope that it's been the same for you.

If you would like to be in touch, please know that I would love to hear from you. If you go to www.susanlewis.com and click on the Contact Susan link, your message will come straight through to me.

With warm wishes,

Susan

Coming August 2018

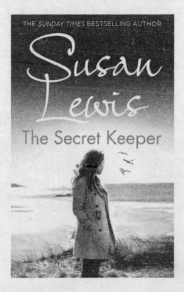

You never forget your first love. Eighteen years ago,
Olivia learned to live without Sean Kenyon.

She moved on, building a life with her husband
Richmond and their two children in the
picturesque town Kesterly-on-Sea.

But when Sean unexpectedly appears on Olivia's
doorstep, her world is turned upside down once more.

As old feelings resurface, and new truths come to light,
Olivia finds herself questioning everything.

Is her husband really the person she thought he was?

The past and present collide, and Olivia must
uncover the truth before it's too late.

But if everyone is keeping secrets,
how will she know who to trust?

Read and revisit
the Detective Andee Lawrence
collection

Available in paperback and ebook

About
Susan

I was born in 1956 to a happy, normal family living in a brand new council house on the outskirts of Bristol. My mother, at the age of twenty, and one of thirteen children, persuaded my father to spend his bonus on a ring rather than a motorbike and they never looked back. She was an ambitious woman determined to see her children on the right path: I was signed up for ballet, elocution and piano lessons and my little brother was to succeed in all he set his mind to.

Tragically, at the age of thirty-three, my mother lost the battle against cancer and died. I was nine, my brother was five.

My father was left with two children to bring up on his own. Sending me to boarding school was thought to be 'for the best' but I disagreed. No one listened to my pleas for freedom, so after a while I took it upon myself to get expelled. By the time I was thirteen, I was back in our little council house with my father and brother. The teenage years passed and before I knew it I was eighteen ... an adult.

I got a job at HTV in Bristol for a few years before moving to London at the age of twenty-two to work for Thames. I moved up the ranks, from secretary in news and current affairs, to a production assistant in light entertainment and drama. My mother's ambition and a love of drama gave me the courage to knock on the Controller's door to ask what it takes to be a success. I received the reply of 'Oh, go away and write something'. So I did!

Three years into my writing career I left TV and moved to France. At first it was bliss. I was living the dream and even found myself involved in a love affair with one of the FBI's most wanted! Reality soon dawned, however, and I realised that a full-time life in France was very different to a two-week holiday frolicking around on the sunny Riviera.

So I made the move to California with my beloved dogs Casanova and Floozie. With the rich and famous as my neighbours I was enthralled and inspired by Tinsel Town. The reality, however, was an obstacle course of cowboy agents, big-talking producers and wannabe directors. Hollywood was not waiting for me, but it was a great place to have fun! Romances flourished and faded, dreams were crushed but others came true.

After seven happy years of taking the best of Hollywood and avoiding the rest, I decided it was time for a change. My dogs and I spent a short while in Wiltshire before then settling once again in France, perched high above the Riviera with glorious views of the sea. It was wonderful to be back amongst old friends, and to make so many new ones. Casanova and Floozie both passed away during our first few years there, but Coco and Lulabelle are doing a valiant job of taking over their places – and my life!

Everything changed again three months after my fiftieth birthday when I met James, my partner, who lived and worked in Bristol. For a couple of years we had a very romantic and enjoyable time of flying back and forth to see one another at the weekends, but at the end of 2010 I finally sold my house on the Riviera and am now living in Gloucestershire in a delightful old barn with Coco and

Lulabelle. My writing is flourishing and over thirty books down the line I couldn't be happier. James continued to live in Bristol, with his boys, Michael and Luke – a great musician and a champion footballer! – for a while until we decided to get married in 2013.

It's been exhilarating and educational having two teenage boys in my life! Needless to say they know everything, which is very useful (saves me looking things up) and they're incredibly inspiring in ways they probably have no idea about.

Should you be interested to know a little more about my early life, why not try *Just One More Day*, a memoir about me and my mother, and then the story continues in *One Day at a Time*, a memoir about me and my father and how we coped with my mother's loss.

Memoirs by

Susan Lewis

Read the true story of Susan Lewis and her family and how they coped when tragedy struck. *Just One More Day* and its follow-up *One Day at a Time* are two memoirs that will hopefully make you laugh as well as cry as you follow Susan on her journey to love again.

Available in paperback and ebook

5 minutes with

Susan

Where does the inspiration for your books come from?

I often write about difficult issues, as you well know.
I don't necessarily write from experience in these cases but
I rely on listening and seeking the experience of others
who might have witnessed or been through challenging
situations. It's important as a writer to imagine how you'd
feel if it happened to you. I enjoy doing it but sometimes it
can be quite distressing – sometimes I cry, which tells me it's
working. This is how I really bring my characters to life.

Do you have any peculiar writing rituals or habits?

Nothing too peculiar! I'm very strict about the hours I write,
starting at 10 in the morning and going through until 5pm
or 6pm, usually six days a week. Then, I love to have a glass
of wine at the end of the day as I read back over what has
happened in 'my fictional world' over the last seven or eight
hours, socialising with the characters and often wanting
to gossip about them with someone else.

What advice would you offer to aspiring writers?

Remember to listen: listen to the way people speak,
to the rhythm of the words you are writing (you're most
likely to do this in your head), and always give your characters
room to be themselves. They'll have plenty to say if you
just let them chatter on to one another, often giving
you ideas you hadn't even thought of!

What is the last book you bought someone as a gift?

A variety of children's books for the recipients of the
Special Recognition Award that I'm sponsoring for the local
secondary school. They've chosen the titles themselves and what
a fascinating selection they've made – from *Diary of a
Wimpy Kid* to *The Curious Incident of the Dog in the Night-Time*
(one of my own favourites).

What's the best piece of advice you've ever been given?

If you want to be a producer you'd better write. I was
working in TV drama and this was what I was told to get
me out of the Controller's office! I took him at his word
and the rest, as they say, is history.

If you had a superpower, what would it be?

If I had a superpower I'd rescue all the children
and animals being subjected to cruelty.

What literary character is most like you?

Definitely Emma from Jane Austen's wonderful novel.

**If you were stranded on a desert island what song would
you choose to listen to, which book would you take and
what luxury item would you pack?**

That's a hard one. Song choice would have to be 'Just My
Imagination' by the Temptations. Book choice . . . *How to Survive
on a Desert Island* by anyone who's been thoughtful enough to
write such a useful guide. Luxury item: a double-ended stick
with a toothbrush at one end and a knife at the other . . .
I could give Bear Grylls a sure run for his money!

Have you read them all?

For a full list of books please visit
www.susanlewis.com

Connect with

Susan Lewis

online

Sign up to Susan's newsletter for
exclusive content, competitions and
all the latest news from Susan.

Want to know more? Visit

www.susanlewis.com

Connect with other fans and join in the
conversation at

f/SusanLewisBooks

Follow Susan on

🐦 @susandlewis